Cambridge School Shakespeare

中文详注剑桥莎士比亚

U0554458

第十二夜

原版创始主编：[英] 瑞克斯·吉布森（Rex Gibson）

原版主编：[英] 瑞查德·安褚斯（Richard Andrews）

[英] 维姬·维南德（Vicki Wienand）

原版编注：[英] 安东尼·帕廷顿（Anthony Partington）

[英] 瑞查德·斯班塞（Richard Spencer）

总主编：陈国华

分册主编：胡玫　孙冠群

北京语言大学出版社
BEIJING LANGUAGE AND CULTURE
UNIVERSITY PRESS

CAMBRIDGE
UNIVERSITY PRESS

社图号 21131

北京市版权局著作权合同登记图字：01-2020-4092 号

图书在版编目（CIP）数据

中文详注剑桥莎士比亚精选. 第十二夜 ／陈国华总主编 ；胡玫，孙冠群分册主编. -- 北京 ： 北京语言大学出版社，2021.10
书名原文：Cambridge School Shakespeare：Twelfth Night
ISBN 978-7-5619-5957-2

Ⅰ. ①中… Ⅱ. ①陈… ②胡… ③孙… Ⅲ. ①喜剧－剧本－英国－中世纪 Ⅳ. ① I561.33

中国版本图书馆 CIP 数据核字（2021）第 175024 号

中文详注剑桥莎士比亚精选：第十二夜
ZHONGWEN XIANG ZHU JIANQIAO SHASHIBIYA JINGXUAN: DI-SHI'ER YE

项目策划：李 亮		责任编辑：李 亮	
封面设计：乔 剑		排版制作：北京创艺涵文化发展有限公司	
责任印制：周 燚			

出版发行：北京语言大学出版社
社　　址：北京市海淀区学院路 15 号，100083
网　　址：www.blcup.com
电子信箱：service@blcup.com
电　　话：编 辑 部　8610-82301019/0178
　　　　　发 行 部　8610-82303650/3591/3648
　　　　　北语书店　8610-82303653
　　　　　网购咨询　8610-82303908
印　　刷：北京博海升彩色印刷有限公司

版　次：2021 年 10 月第 1 版		印　次：2021 年 10 月第 1 次印刷	
开　本：787 毫米 × 1092 毫米　1/16		印　张：12.75	
字　数：326 千字			
定　价：79.00 元			

PRINTED IN CHINA

序

由于观察角度不同，评判标准不同，关于哪个国家哪位诗人或小说家的成就最大，世人可能难以达成一致；可是说到剧作家，大家的共识是，莎士比亚不仅是英语国家有史以来最伟大的剧作家，也是全世界最伟大的剧作家，在知名度、影响力和传世作品的数量上，没有任何一位剧作家可以与之比肩。正是由于其公认的文学成就和人文精神，在过去400多年里，莎士比亚戏剧的演出在英语国家和许多非英语国家经久不衰，莎剧的阅读和鉴赏已成为这些国家英文教学的必选内容。

莎剧进入中国，已经有100多年历史，莎士比亚全集已经有了四个中文译本。不懂英文的人可以通过译本来欣赏莎士比亚剧作。然而文学作品的语言，尤其是诗歌的语言，具有相当程度的不可译性，而几乎所有莎剧的大部分台词都是素体诗（blank verse）。例如《哈慕雷》（*Hamlet*）里主人公的名言"To be, or not to be, that is the question"，不论怎样译，都难以完全再现原文的深刻内涵和形式特点。要想真正欣赏莎士比亚的语言和戏剧艺术，还得阅读其英文原作。最早由剑桥大学出版社出版的这套莎剧精选，收录了最受读者和观众喜爱的14部剧目，涵盖莎剧的各个类别，以其独具匠心的设计和编排，成为所有英文原版莎剧中最适合英语学习者阅读、最适合戏剧爱好者排演的莎剧选集。

本选集的创始主编瑞克斯·吉布森（Rex Gibson）在本书引言（Introduction）里指出："不论做什么，都要记住，莎士比亚写下他的剧本是为了演出、观看和享受的。"秉承这一宗旨，这一新版莎剧选集有四个鲜明的区别性特点：

一、书的开本和页面的宽高比例特别适合学校的老师和学生以及剧团的导演和演员在排练莎剧时把书打开，拿在手里，随时参阅，而且左边页面上有许多有关排演活动的建议。

二、书中配有大量世界各国莎剧演出的彩色剧照，为莎剧爱好者和剧团排演莎剧提供了灵感。

三、书的正文部分打开后，右页是未经删减、原汁原味的剧本原文，左页是多种不同栏目，包括导演技巧（Stagecraft）、剧中语言（Language in the play）、人物分析（Characters）、主题分析（Themes）、写作练习（Write about it）及词语注释等。每幕之间（本幕回顾）和最后一幕后（本剧回顾）有与剧情相关的各种思考题。

四、在剧本之后有各种针对全剧的专题论述，以《哈慕雷》为例，包括视角与主题（Perspectives and themes）、人物分析（Characters）、《哈慕雷》的语言（The language of *Hamlet*）、《哈慕雷》的演出（*Hamlet* in performance）、笔论莎士比亚（Writing about Shakespeare）、笔论《哈慕雷》（Writing about *Hamlet*），还有一份莎翁年表（William Shakespeare 1564–1616）。

左页上的栏目对于解读和排演莎剧特别有帮助，剧本后面的专题论述对于撰写有关莎士比亚的文章特别有帮助，而参加莎剧排演，背诵台词，撰写论文，又是提高英语水平的极好途径。

为了方便更多的中国读者阅读、欣赏、排演莎士比亚原作，北京语言大学出版社携手剑桥大学出版社，将这套莎剧精选引入中国。我有幸应邀担任这套书的中文版总主编，组织起一个团队，对原版进行一定程度的改编和汉化，以适应中国读者的需求。我们不仅将原版提供的关键注释基本译成了中文，而且针对中国英语学习者和莎剧爱好者阅读理解上的难点，主要做了以下四件事：

一、参考 *The Oxford Dictionary of Original Shakespearean Pronunciation* (David Crystal 2016)、*Oxford Dictionary of Pronunciation for Current English* (Clive Upton 2003) 和 *Shakespeare's Names: A Pronouncing Dictionary* (Helge Kökeritz 1950)，给每个剧本前面人物表里的人名加上了国际音标。为了便于读者识别，我们将第一本发音词典里一般中国读者不认识的个别音标替换成了大家熟悉的近似音标。

二、为左页顶端的剧情简介添加中文译文。

三、左页中以及剧本后面论文部分里有一些具有挑战性的词和术语（如tableau），我们为其中的大部分添加了相应的中文释义。

四、适当增加了原版里没有的词语注释。

给剧中人物的名字加了国际音标之后，我们发现，现有莎剧中文译本里一些人名的中文译名与原文的读音差别较大且互不相同。根据定名不咎、译音循本、音义兼顾、音系对应的原则，我们给出了新译名。根据前两个原则，我们将剧本 *Julius Caesar* /ˈdʒuːlɪəs ˈsiːzə(r)/ 译成《儒略·恺撒》，而没有采用《尤利/力乌斯·恺撒》《裘利/力斯·凯撒》《居里厄斯·恺撒》等现成译名中的任何一个，因为从公元前1世纪到公元16世纪西方使用的儒略历（Julian calendar）就是以这位 Julius Caesar（拉丁文读音是 /ˈjuːlɪʊs ˈkae̯sar/）命名的。根据音义兼顾的原则，我们将剧本 *Hamlet* /ˈ(h)amlət/ 译成《哈慕雷》而不是《哈姆莱特》或《哈姆雷特》，因为"慕雷"比"姆莱"或"姆雷"更适合用来给男子起名，结尾的辅音 /t/ 在实际说话中往往不发音。根据音系对应的原则，我们借鉴了曹禺的译法，将剧本 *Romeo and Juliet* 译成《柔密欧与茱丽叶》，没有将 Romeo 译成更常见的"罗密欧"，因为"柔 /rou/"比"罗 /luo/"更接近原名 Romeo /ˈroːmɪoː/ 的读音；同时我们将 Juliet /ˈdʒuːlɪət/ 译成"茱丽叶"而不是"朱丽叶"，因为这样做不容易让人误以为这个女孩姓"朱"。

这套经过改编并且带中文注释的《中文详注剑桥莎士比亚精选》不仅可以用作中国高中和大学的英文教材，而且适合中国所有具有较高英语能力的莎剧爱好者阅读和欣赏，将戏剧从书中提升到自己心中，将剧本从课堂搬演到戏台。

相信《中文详注剑桥莎士比亚精选》会带给中国广大英语爱好者一个惊喜。

陈国华

2020年5月于英国剑桥家中

Contents 目录

Cambridge School
Shakespeare

Introduction 引言

This *Twelfth Night* is part of the **Cambridge School Shakespeare** series. Like every other play in the series, it has been specially prepared to help all students in schools and colleges.

The **Cambridge School Shakespeare** *Twelfth Night* aims to be different. It invites you to lift the words from the page and to bring the play to life in your classroom, hall or drama studio. Through enjoyable and focused activities, you will increase your understanding of the play. Actors have created their different interpretations of the play over the centuries. Similarly, you are invited to make up your own mind about *Twelfth Night*, rather than having someone else's interpretation handed down to you.

Cambridge School Shakespeare does not offer you a cut-down or simplified version of the play. This is Shakespeare's language, filled with imaginative possibilities. You will find on every left-hand page: a summary of the action, an explanation of unfamiliar words, and a choice of activities on Shakespeare's stagecraft, characters, themes and language.

Between each act and in the pages at the end of the play, you will find notes, illustrations and activities. These will help to encourage reflection after every act, and give you insights into the background and context of the play as a whole.

This edition will be of value to you whether you are studying for an examination, reading for pleasure or thinking of putting on the play to entertain others. You can work on the activities on your own or in groups. Many of the activities suggest a particular group size, but don't be afraid to make up larger or smaller groups to suit your own purposes. Please don't think you have to do every activity: choose those that will help you most.

Although you are invited to treat *Twelfth Night* as a play, you don't need special dramatic or theatrical skills to do the activities. By choosing your activities, and by exploring and experimenting, you can make your own interpretations of Shakespeare's language, characters and stories.

Whatever you do, remember that Shakespeare wrote his plays to be acted, watched and enjoyed.

Rex Gibson
Founding editor

This new edition contains more photographs, more diversity and more supporting material than previous editions, whilst remaining true to Rex's original vision. Specifically, it contains more activities and commentary on stagecraft and writing about Shakespeare, to reflect contemporary interest. The glossary has been enlarged too. Finally, this edition aims to reflect the best teaching and learning possible, and to represent not only Shakespeare through the ages, but also the relevance and excitement of Shakespeare today.

Richard Andrews and Vicki Wienand
Series editors

This edition of *Twelfth Night* uses the text of the play established by Elizabeth Story Donno in **The New Cambridge Shakespeare**.

Viola (right) and Sebastian are shipwrecked off the coast of Illyria. Each thinks that the other is drowned. Viola decides to dress as a man and try her luck at the court of Duke Orsino to aid her search for her lost brother. Her disguise leads to comic mistaken identity and complex love tangles.

Orsino thinks that he is in love with the Countess Olivia, but he may simply be infatuated (迷恋). Viola, disguised as a man and calling herself Cesario, becomes Orsino's favourite courtier. He sends her to convince Olivia of his love, but Viola herself has fallen in love with Orsino.

Olivia has fallen head over heels (神
魂颠倒) in love with the disguised
Viola, believing that she is a man.
Viola hopes that the problem will
resolve itself with time.

After being told off by Olivia's steward (管家), the serious, puritanical (极拘谨，古板) Malvolio, Sir Toby and Maria devise a plan to humiliate him. They forge a letter from Olivia in which she professes her love for Malvolio. Malvolio finds the letter as planned, reads it and believes that Olivia loves him. The tricksters, Fabian, Sir Toby and Sir Andrew, hiding behind the hedge, are delighted that their plan has worked.

Malvolio follows the instructions in the letter, wearing yellow stockings and constantly smiling in an attempt to please Olivia. But Olivia, who knows nothing of the letter, is perplexed by his changed appearance and behaviour, and thinks it 'midsummer madness'. She orders that Sir Toby take care of Malvolio.

Sir Toby's further mischief – and more mistaken identity – leads to a duel between a terrified Sir Andrew (pictured here) and a reluctant and disguised Viola/Cesario, whom Sir Andrew is led to believe is a rival for the affections of Olivia.

▲ Sir Toby treats Malvolio as a madman and locks him in a dark room to further humiliate him. Others, including the 'fool', Feste, visit Malvolio to torment him.

◄ A moment of wonder as the twins are reunited, and Sebastian and Viola discover that they have both survived the shipwreck.

▶ Orsino (centre) switches his love to Viola (left), as the newly married Sebastian and Olivia look on.

▼ All misunderstandings seem resolved, but Malvolio (wearing yellow), newly released from imprisonment, feels he has been wronged and swears revenge 'on the whole pack'.

List of characters 人物表

Illyria 伊利瑞亚

The Duke's court 公爵的宫廷

ORSINO /ɔː(r)ˈsiːnoː/ (奥悉诺)
Duke of Illyria
VALENTINE /ˈvaləntəɪn/ (瓦伦廷)
a courtier
CURIO /ˈkjuːrɪoː/ (裴瑞欧) a courtier
Musicians
Lords
Officers

A PRIEST (祭司)
A SEA CAPTAIN (船长)

The Countess's household 女伯爵府中的人

OLIVIA /əˈlɪvɪə/ (娥丽维娅) a countess
SIR TOBY BELCH /ˈtoːbi belʧ/ (托比·贝尔奇) her uncle
MALVOLIO /malˈvoːlɪoː/ (马尔沃琉)
her steward
FESTE /ˈfestə/ (费斯特) her fool
MARIA /məˈrəɪə/ (玛蕊娅) her gentlewoman
FABIAN /ˈfeɪbɪən/ (费边) a servant

The visitors 来访者

VIOLA /ˈvəɪələ/ (薇娥菈) later called Cesario /sɪˈzarɪoː/ (席扎瑞欧)
SEBASTIAN /səˈbastɪən/ (塞巴斯田) her twin brother
SIR ANDREW AGUECHEEK /ˈandruː ˈeɪgjuːˌʧiːk/ (安褚·艾玖奇) suitor to Olivia
ANTONIO /anˈtoːnɪoː/ (安托纽) a friend to Sebastian
Sailors

The action of the play takes place in Illyria.

* TWELFTH NIGHT《第十二夜》：耶稣基督的生日被基督教会定为12月25日，传说12天后（即1月6日），东方来的三位贤士 (the Magi) 见到了出生后不久的耶稣，后来天主教会将这一天定为主显日 (Epiphany，又译作"显现日")，当天夜晚即主显夜 (Epiphany Eve)，俗称"第十二夜"；英格兰教会 (Church of England) 则将主显日的前夜，即1月5日夜，视为第十二夜。基督徒们在主显日举行各种狂欢庆祝活动，仆人常装扮成主人，男人常装扮成女人，做一些平时不允许做的事。

莎士比亚所在的剧团名为宫务大臣伶人剧团 (Lord Chamberlain's Men)，这部以"第十二夜"命名的喜剧应当是莎士比亚受其赞助人宫务大臣乔治·凯瑞 (George Carey) 委托创作的。1601年1月6日，该剧在王室的白厅宫 (Whitehall Palace) 首演，作为女王伊丽莎白为意大利大使奥悉诺公爵 (Duke of Orsino，与剧中公爵同名) 期满离任举行庆祝活动的一部分。Twelfth Night这一剧名向观众预告，剧情与人们这天晚上的狂欢有关。

Orsino calls for music to feed his hunger for love. He reflects that love is like the sea, absorbing and devaluing every other experience. He claims to be completely obsessed by his love for Olivia.

剧情简介： 奥悉诺命人演奏音乐以满足其对爱情的渴望。他深深体会到爱情就像大海，吞没并贬低了其他任何一种情感，声称自己已沉溺于对娥丽维娅的爱而无法自拔。

Themes 主题分析

Love – or infatuation? (in fours)

The opening lines of the play suggest that it will be about love. But they also introduce questions that the play will revisit as it progresses. What sort of love? What *is* love? Orsino appears to be the most 'in love' of all the characters, but many people believe that he is not truly interested in Olivia – he just enjoys wallowing (沉湎) in his emotions. Is Orsino in love, or just infatuated?

a Prepare four versions of lines 1–15 (for example, spoken thoughtfully, sadly, pompously and comically), with one person working on each. Think about which lines you will stress, where you will pause and what actions you will add.

b Perform your versions to each other, then talk together about which is the most effective. Do you think Orsino's language is that of a true lover, or of someone who is in love with being in love?

1 Play on!

In the production shown in the image above, subtle lighting and music were used to draw the audience into the world of Illyria. Orsino directly addressed the audience and demanded that they listen.

a How would you present this scene on stage? What type of music would you use? Would you play up the comedy at the point when Orsino changes his mind ('That strain again', then 'Enough; no more')?

b Make notes on the set, the costumes and the general impression you would wish to create of Orsino and his court. These should form the first part of a Director's Journal, in which you can record your ideas about staging the play as you read on.

1 **or What You Will** 或什么都行（在莎剧的第一对开本 [也是本剧的最早版本] 里，这部剧的名称是 "Twelfth Night, or what you will"。可见当时人们并不把 what you will 视为一个可替代 Twelfth Night 的剧名，如今各版本都将副标题首字母大写，并不妥当。莎士比亚之所以在 Twelfth Night 之后补上这样一个在其所有剧本中独一无二的副标题，很可能与教宗格瑞高略十三世 [Gregorius XIII] 于1582年举行的历法改革有关。改革前各国通行的是儒略历 [Julian calendar]，改革后历法沿用至今，称为格瑞高历 [Gregorian calendar，又译作"格里历"]，中文称之为公历或阳历。本剧首演之日，1601年的1月6日，在儒略历里是前一年的12月27日，这一天是圣诞节期 [Christmastide] 里的圣约翰盛宴日 [Feast of St John]。由此我们可以推断，what you will 既可表示人们在这一狂欢节里做什么都行，也可表示观众管这部剧叫什么都行。）

2 **surfeiting** 吃撑

3 **That strain again** 那段曲子再来一遍

4 **dying fall** 凄惨的渐弱

5 **sound** 音响（也可能是 south [= south wind] 的讹变）

6 **quick and fresh** 生猛有食欲

7 **Nought** = Nothing

8 **validity** 价值

9 **pitch** 高度；优异

10 **falls … price** 陷入低潮和低价

11 **fancy** 爱

12 **high fantastical** 极具想象力

13 **hart** 雄鹿（被奥悉诺理解成 heart）

14 **Methought** = It seemed to me

15 **purged** 净化

16 **pestilence** 瘟疫

17 **fell** 凶猛

18 **E'er** = Ever

19 **How now** = How is it going

Twelfth Night

or What You Will[1]

Act 1 Scene 1

Orsino's palace

Music. Enter ORSINO, *Duke of Illyria*, CURIO, *and other Lords*

ORSINO	If music be the food of love, play on;
	Give me excess of it, that surfeiting[2]
	The appetite may sicken and so die.
	That strain again[3], it had a dying fall[4];
	O it came o'er my ear like the sweet sound[5]
	That breathes upon a bank of violets,
	Stealing and giving odour. Enough; no more.
	'Tis not so sweet now as it was before.
	O spirit of love, how quick and fresh[6] art thou,
	That, notwithstanding thy capacity,
	Receiveth as the sea. Nought[7] enters there,
	Of what validity[8] and pitch[9] soe'er,
	But falls into abatement and low price[10]
	Even in a minute. So full of shapes is fancy[11],
	That it alone is high fantastical[12].
CURIO	Will you go hunt, my lord?
ORSINO	What, Curio?
CURIO	The hart[13].
ORSINO	Why so I do, the noblest that I have.
	O when mine eyes did see Olivia first,
	Methought[14] she purged[15] the air of pestilence[16];
	That instant was I turned into a hart,
	And my desires like fell[17] and cruel hounds
	E'er[18] since pursue me.

Enter VALENTINE

How now[19], what news from her?

Valentine tells of Olivia's vow to mourn her dead brother for seven years. Orsino says that this reveals how she will love him totally. Viola, landed safely after shipwreck, fears for her brother's life.

 剧情简介：瓦伦廷讲述了娥丽维娅的誓言，即要为亡兄哀悼七年。奥悉诺说这显示她将怎样全身心地爱他。海难后安全登陆的薇娥菈担心其兄已经丧命。

1 Olivia – first impressions (in pairs)

Valentine returns with bad news – Olivia has vowed to become a nun for seven years, not even seeing the sky, to mourn for her brother.

- Discuss what her decision and Orsino's response tell us about these two characters.

Stagecraft 导演技巧

Shipwrecked

It is clear from the first few lines of Act 1 Scene 2 that Viola and the Captain have been shipwrecked on the coast of Illyria. However, Shakespeare provides no stage directions and it is therefore up to the director to decide whether the shipwreck is seen or not. In some productions of the play, each scene flows swiftly into the next without delay for scene shifting. The shipwreck scene can provide an opportunity to use special effects and transport the audience from Orsino's palace to the coast.

- Write a list of reasons why you might 'stage' or 'not stage' the shipwreck. Share and discuss your ideas with a partner or a small group.

This production showed the shipwreck with flashing lights, crashing waves sounds and real water on the stage. Write a description of what theatrical effects you would use to heighten the dramatic impact of the shipwreck.

1	**element**	空气，天空
2	**seven years' heat**	七个酷暑
3	**behold … view**	饱览她的容颜
4	**cloistress**	修女（与世隔绝）
5	**eye-offending brine**	蜇眼睛的盐卤（苦楚的眼泪）
6	**season**	保存，保鲜
7	**fine frame**	精致的构造
8	**rich golden shaft**	珍贵的金箭杆（指丘比特射出的爱情之箭）
9	**all affections else**	所有其他爱意（除了对奥悉诺的爱）
10	**sovereign thrones**	人主之位（旧时人们认为肝主激情，脑主思考，心主情感）
11	**supplied**	占据
12	**perfections**	完美品质
13	**one selfsame king**	同一位王者（指奥悉诺自己）
14	**canopied with bowers**	有树冠作为华盖
15	*Exeunt*	（两个以上演员）退场，下场
16	**Illyria**	伊利瑞亚（欧洲的一个古国，位于巴尔干半岛西部，濒临亚德里亚海，公元前2世纪被罗马征服，成为罗马帝国的一个行省）
17	**Elysium**	天堂（又称为 Elysian Fields）
18	**Perchance**	也许
19	**perchance**	运气
20	**perchance**	或许有运气（薇娥菈现在用的是这个词的两个意思）

VALENTINE	So please my lord, I might not be admitted,
	But from her handmaid do return this answer: 25
	The element[1] itself, till seven years' heat[2],
	Shall not behold her face at ample view[3];
	But like a cloistress[4] she will veilèd walk,
	And water once a day her chamber round
	With eye-offending brine[5]; all this to season[6] 30
	A brother's dead love, which she would keep fresh
	And lasting, in her sad remembrance.
ORSINO	O she that hath a heart of that fine frame[7]
	To pay this debt of love but to a brother,
	How will she love, when the rich golden shaft[8] 35
	Hath killed the flock of all affections else[9]
	That live in her; when liver, brain, and heart,
	These sovereign thrones[10], are all supplied[11] and filled
	Her sweet perfections[12] with one selfsame king[13]!
	Away before me to sweet beds of flowers: 40
	Love-thoughts lie rich when canopied with bowers[14].

Exeunt[15]

Act 1 Scene 2
The sea-coast of Illyria[16]

Enter VIOLA, *a* CAPTAIN, *and Sailors*

VIOLA	What country, friends, is this?
CAPTAIN	This is Illyria, lady.
VIOLA	And what should I do in Illyria?
	My brother, he is in Elysium[17].
	Perchance[18] he is not drowned: what think you, sailors? 5
CAPTAIN	It is perchance[19] that you yourself were saved.
VIOLA	O my poor brother! And so perchance[20] may he be.

The Captain reassures Viola that her brother may also have survived the shipwreck. He tells of Orsino's love for Olivia, and says that Olivia's grief for her brother's death has made her a recluse.

剧情简介：船长安慰薇娥菈说她哥哥可能也在船难中幸存下来了。他讲述了奥悉诺对娥丽维娅的爱，并说娥丽维娅因伤感她哥哥的死而使自己成为一名隐士。

1 'Arion on the dolphin's back' (in threes)

The Captain uses **imagery** (see pp. 164–5) from classical mythology to describe Sebastian's escape from the shipwreck. He compares it with that of Arion, a legendary Greek musician. Arion leapt overboard to escape sailors who wished to murder him. A dolphin, enchanted by Arion's music, carried him safely to shore. The Captain's story gives Viola hope, and it also echoes the power of music suggested in Scene 1. Some stage productions show Sebastian's struggle to survive. Others leave it to the audience's imagination.

a Imagine you are directing the play, and want the audience to see what happens to Sebastian. Prepare a performance of lines 11–17. Use pictures, projections, action to one side or at the back of the stage or even tableaux (定格；活人画) (freeze-frames) to show Sebastian's 'acquaintance with the waves'.

b Perform your scene to another group. Afterwards, discuss the success of your staging, and consider different effects that you could create to maximise the scene's dramatic impact.

2 Reports are coming in (in pairs)

You are a television or radio crew in Illyria. Reports are coming in that a ship has crashed on the coast, but none of the passengers has been found (remember that no Illyrian has discovered Viola or Sebastian).

a One of you should be the news presenter in the studio and another the reporter on the scene. Prepare a dialogue in which the presenter interviews the on-scene reporter, and known details of the events of the shipwreck are revealed. You should also speculate about what might have happened, and about the possible identities of the missing passengers.

b With another pair, extend the news segment by having the reporter interview witnesses at the scene or having the presenter speak to shipwreck experts in the studio. Think about all the possible sources of news details – for example, the Captain who saved Viola might be able to pass on some details to you. You need to be quick, though, as your interview will be transmitted live after only a few minutes of preparation!

1 driving 漂泊
2 provident 足智多谋
3 lived 漂浮
4 Arion 阿里翁（古希腊诗人和乐师。据传说，他在西西里岛的音乐比赛上赢得头奖，回国途中遭遇海盗，海盗想杀死他，抢走他的奖品。危急时刻他求海盗让他先唱一首歌再死。他的歌声和他弹奏的吉塔拉琴声引得一群海豚随船而行。唱完后，他抱琴跳进大海。一头海豚见状游了过来，让阿里翁骑在自己身上，把他送到了陆地。）
5 hold acquaintance with 与……打交道
6 gold 金币
7 unfoldeth to 激起，燃起
8 Whereto ... authority 你的话证实
9 The like of him 他也获救了
10 very late 最近
11 murmur 传言
12 prattle 闲扯
13 abjured 拒绝，放弃
14 Till ... is 直到时机成熟再亮出我的真实身份
15 compass 实现
16 suit 追求，求爱

CAPTAIN	True, madam, and to comfort you with chance,
	Assure yourself, after our ship did split,
	When you, and those poor number saved with you,
	Hung on our driving[1] boat, I saw your brother
	Most provident[2] in peril, bind himself
	(Courage and hope both teaching him the practice)
	To a strong mast that lived[3] upon the sea;
	Where like Arion[4] on the dolphin's back
	I saw him hold acquaintance with[5] the waves
	So long as I could see.
VIOLA	For saying so, there's gold[6].
	Mine own escape unfoldeth to[7] my hope,
	Whereto thy speech serves for authority[8],
	The like of him[9]. Know'st thou this country?
CAPTAIN	Ay, madam, well, for I was bred and born
	Not three hours' travel from this very place.
VIOLA	Who governs here?
CAPTAIN	A noble duke in nature as in name.
VIOLA	What is his name?
CAPTAIN	Orsino.
VIOLA	Orsino! I have heard my father name him.
	He was a bachelor then.
CAPTAIN	And so is now, or was so very late[10];
	For but a month ago I went from hence,
	And then 'twas fresh in murmur[11] (as you know
	What great ones do, the less will prattle[12] of)
	That he did seek the love of fair Olivia.
VIOLA	What's she?
CAPTAIN	A virtuous maid, the daughter of a count
	That died some twelvemonth since, then leaving her
	In the protection of his son, her brother,
	Who shortly also died; for whose dear love
	(They say) she hath abjured[13] the sight
	And company of men.
VIOLA	O that I served that lady,
	And might not be delivered to the world
	Till I had made mine own occasion mellow
	What my estate is[14]!
CAPTAIN	That were hard to compass[15],
	Because she will admit no kind of suit[16],
	No, not the duke's.

Line numbers in right margin: 10, 15, 20, 25, 30, 35, 40, 45

Viola says that she trusts the Captain. She plans to disguise herself as a man and become an attendant to Orsino. In Scene 3, Sir Toby Belch complains that Olivia's mourning prevents all enjoyment.

剧情简介：薇娥菈说她信任船长。她打算把自己化装成男人，充当奥悉诺的侍从。在第三场中，托比·贝尔奇爵士抱怨娥丽维娅哀思过度，所有享乐一概拒绝。

Themes 主题分析

Appearance versus reality (in pairs)

In lines 48–9, Viola states one of Shakespeare's favourite themes: you can't judge by appearances. A beautiful appearance may conceal corruption ('nature with a beauteous wall / Doth oft close in pollution'). Much of *Twelfth Night* is about the difference between appearance and reality.

a   Work out a tableau to illustrate Viola's comment. Show this to another pair, holding the tableau for thirty seconds. Discuss the similarities and differences between your tableaux and respective interpretations of Viola's line.

b   Within moments of Viola's wise words about appearance, she is seeking to disguise her own 'outward character' to meet the 'form of [her] intent'. What is her purpose here? Discuss this with your partner, and try to refer to the play script to support your ideas.

c   Discuss what you think Viola is hoping to achieve in her disguise. Is she trying to hide something other than her femininity? Why does she, as a noble woman, disguise herself even when she is told a noble duke rules this country? Would he not help her return home?

Shakespeare provides very little direction about the casting (选角) of characters, but the choice of actor can have a big impact on the 'physical' comedy of the play. The Maria and Sir Toby in this image are not 'funny to look at' and yet their actions are comical. In pairs, discuss the ways in which actors playing Maria and Sir Toby might add actions to their comic lines to make the audience laugh more.

1   fair behaviour   举止庄重
2   oft = often
3   prithee   请，求你 (pray thee的变体)
4   bounteously   慷慨，大方
5   Conceal me what I am   隐瞒我的真实身份
6   haply = perhaps
7   become   适合
8   The form of my intent   我的计划
9   eunuch   阉人 (旧时欧洲有些男童被阉割后说话保持童声高音，能够成为高音男歌手)
10 It may be worth thy pains   你的辛苦会得到报偿
11 allow   证明
12 hap = happen
13 Only ... wit   照我说的去做，不要告诉任何人
14 mute   哑巴仆人
15 What a plague = What the devil ("这死……"，诅咒语；plague：瘟疫)
16 By my troth   我老实说
17 cousin   亲戚 (cousin一词在伊丽莎白时期意义较宽泛)
18 exceptions   反对
19 confine   约束 (也指"穿戴讲究"，后文托比爵士用此义反驳对方)
20 modest   适度
21 and = if

VIOLA	There is a fair behaviour[1] in thee, captain,
	And though that nature with a beauteous wall
	Doth oft[2] close in pollution, yet of thee
	I well believe thou hast a mind that suits 50
	With this thy fair and outward character.
	I prithee[3] (and I'll pay thee bounteously[4])
	Conceal me what I am[5], and be my aid
	For such disguise as haply[6] shall become[7]
	The form of my intent[8]. I'll serve this duke. 55
	Thou shalt present me as an eunuch[9] to him –
	It may be worth thy pains[10] – for I can sing,
	And speak to him in many sorts of music
	That will allow[11] me very worth his service.
	What else may hap[12], to time I will commit, 60
	Only shape thou thy silence to my wit[13].
CAPTAIN	Be you his eunuch, and your mute[14] I'll be;
	When my tongue blabs, then let mine eyes not see.
VIOLA	I thank thee. Lead me on.

Exeunt

Act 1 Scene 3
A room in Olivia's house

Enter SIR TOBY BELCH *and* MARIA

SIR TOBY	What a plague[15] means my niece to take the death of her brother thus? I am sure care's an enemy to life.
MARIA	By my troth[16], Sir Toby, you must come in earlier o'nights. Your cousin[17], my lady, takes great exceptions[18] to your ill hours.
SIR TOBY	Why, let her except, before excepted. 5
MARIA	Ay, but you must confine[19] yourself within the modest[20] limits of order.
SIR TOBY	Confine? I'll confine myself no finer than I am: these clothes are good enough to drink in, and so be these boots too; and[21] they be not, let them hang themselves in their own straps. 10

Maria warns Sir Toby that his drunkenness will be his downfall. She is scornful of Sir Andrew Aguecheek (a wooer of Olivia), thinking him stupid. Sir Andrew enters and immediately displays his foolishness.

✎ **剧情简介**：玛蕊娅警告托比爵士醉酒会毁了他。她鄙视安褚·艾玖奇爵士（娥丽维娅的一名追求者），认为他愚蠢。安褚爵士一上场就显出其愚蠢。

Language in the play 剧中语言
Word juggler (玩文字游戏的人) (in threes)

Sir Toby is a great juggler with words, even when drunk. His description of Sir Andrew is full of mockery – he says one thing but means another. Sir Toby calls Sir Andrew 'tall', meaning courageous, when he probably thinks him cowardly. Sir Andrew is cast in many productions as tall but slight and weak to accentuate this. Other descriptions also had double meanings for Elizabethan audiences:

'viol-de-gamboys' a sexual joke: a musical instrument held between the knees, like the cello

'without book' implies Andrew learnt by heart without understanding

'nature' picked up by Maria and turned into 'natural' (meaning 'idiot')

'Castiliano vulgo' 'Look solemn' (like a Castilian from Spain), or 'Think of all Sir Andrew's money' or 'Talk of the devil' or 'More Spanish wine!'

For a modern audience, wordplay can often be lost without such explanations, and this lessens the impact of the comedy.

- Prepare a performance of lines 1–50. Using the descriptions above, try to provide the audience with a visual or physical clue about the joke that is being made. Show your performance to another group and see whether your actions have the desired results.

1 A 'foolish knight'?

Sir Andrew Aguecheek's entrance provides the opportunity for great comedy, as we have heard so much about him (not much of it flattering) before he appears on stage.

a Read through lines 11–35, and complete a table like the one below to explore what Maria and Sir Toby mean in these lines.

What Maria says about Sir Andrew	What she means	What Sir Toby says about Sir Andrew	What he means

b Draw one picture of Sir Andrew based upon what Maria says, and another based on what Sir Toby says. Label the features shown in the picture with quotations from lines 11–35. Consider how the pictures are different, and why.

1. quaffing 酗酒
2. tall 勇敢
3. ducats 大公币（一种曾在欧洲通用的金币或银币）
4. have but a year 仅够他花一年
5. prodigal 败家子
6. Fie 呸
7. viol-de-gamboys 维奥尔琴（与大提琴近似，演奏时也是立在演奏者双腿之间）
8. gust 嗜好，喜好
9. the prudent 明智者
10. gift of a grave 坟墓作为礼物（前一个gift的意思是"天赋"）
11. scoundrels 恶棍
12. substractors = subtractors（减号）= detractors（减号；诋毁者，诽谤者）（substractors是subtractors的误读）
13. add 做加法（对应前面的substractors/subtractors的动词形式subtract［做减法］）
14. healths to 向……祝酒或敬酒
15. coistrill 无赖，混混
16. brains turn o'th'toe （由于醉酒）脑子变成了脚趾头；头重脚轻
17. like a parish top 像教区鞭陀（当时教区为信众提供一种用鞭子抽打、在地上不停旋转的陀螺，供大家游戏消遣）
18. *Castiliano vulgo* 说小鬼（小鬼到）
19. Agueface = Aguecheek（戏称）
20. shrew 鼩鼱（喻指"犀利女、悍妇"）
21. Accost 打招呼
22. front ... assail her 正对她，登上她，追她，攻打她（托比爵士此处对Accost的解释为海军术语，同时带有性暗示）

MARIA	That quaffing[1] and drinking will undo you: I heard my lady talk of it yesterday and of a foolish knight that you brought in one night here to be her wooer.
SIR TOBY	Who, Sir Andrew Aguecheek?
MARIA	Ay, he.
SIR TOBY	He's as tall[2] a man as any's in Illyria.
MARIA	What's that to th'purpose?
SIR TOBY	Why, he has three thousand ducats[3] a year.
MARIA	Ay, but he'll have but a year[4] in all these ducats. He's a very fool and a prodigal[5].
SIR TOBY	Fie[6], that you'll say so! He plays o'th'viol-de-gamboys[7], and speaks three or four languages word for word without book, and hath all the good gifts of nature.
MARIA	He hath indeed all, most natural: for besides that he's a fool, he's a great quarreller; and but that he hath the gift of a coward to allay the gust[8] he hath in quarrelling, 'tis thought among the prudent[9] he would quickly have the gift of a grave[10].
SIR TOBY	By this hand, they are scoundrels[11] and substractors[12] that say so of him. Who are they?
MARIA	They that add[13], moreover, he's drunk nightly in your company.
SIR TOBY	With drinking healths to[14] my niece! I'll drink to her as long as there is a passage in my throat and drink in Illyria; he's a coward and a coistrill[15] that will not drink to my niece till his brains turn o'th'toe[16] like a parish top[17]. What, wench! *Castiliano vulgo*[18]: for here comes Sir Andrew Agueface[19].

Enter SIR ANDREW [AGUECHEEK]

SIR ANDREW	Sir Toby Belch! How now, Sir Toby Belch?
SIR TOBY	Sweet Sir Andrew!
SIR ANDREW	Bless you, fair shrew[20].
MARIA	And you too, sir.
SIR TOBY	Accost[21], Sir Andrew, accost.
SIR ANDREW	What's that?
SIR TOBY	My niece's chambermaid.
SIR ANDREW	Good Mistress Accost, I desire better acquaintance.
MARIA	My name is Mary, sir.
SIR ANDREW	Good Mistress Mary Accost –
SIR TOBY	You mistake, knight. 'Accost' is front her, board her, woo her, assail her[22].
SIR ANDREW	By my troth, I would not undertake her in this company. Is that the meaning of 'accost'?

15

20

25

30

35

40

45

Maria mocks Sir Andrew, then leaves. Sir Toby jokes crudely about Sir Andrew's hair, and Andrew repeats that he intends to go home tomorrow because he is making no progress at all with his wooing of Olivia.

剧情简介：玛蕊娅嘲弄安褚爵士，然后离开。托比爵士粗鲁地拿安褚爵士的头发开玩笑，而安褚反复说自己打算明天回家，因为他对娥丽维娅的追求毫无进展。

Stagecraft 导演技巧
Stage business (戏台调度)

The actions, movements and pieces of physical theatre that actors use in comedy are often referred to as **business**. Popular actors in Shakespeare's time improvised (即兴发挥) by changing the words in the script and adding their own, to make the scene funnier and to put their own interpretation on the character. Actors nowadays tend to confine their additions to physical appearance (the way they stand, walk, enter, exit and so on), gestures and tics (习惯动作) (habitual short, sharp movements or sounds).

This additional physical theatre can be useful to help the audience understand complex and intricate language. In some cases – such as in lines 55–60, where the meaning is not at all clear even to the most informed modern reader – the actor will often add a bit of additional business to make the audience laugh and to make the meaning of the language clearer.

In one production, Maria took Sir Andrew's hand and placed it on the buttery-bar (a ledge for beer tankards). In another, to Sir Andrew's great embarrassment, she held his hand to her breast.

- Look at clips from two movie versions of this scene and compare the business that the actors use to heighten its comedy and playfulness.

▼ This is how one production presented Sir Andrew, Maria and Sir Toby. Look at the image and identify lines from the script that the actors, directors and designers have represented in the appearance of these characters. For example, Sir Andrew's hair 'hangs like flax on a distaff'.

1 **And thou let part so** = If you let her depart in this way（如果你让她就这么走了）
2 **would ... again** 愿你再也无法拔剑（"剑"有性暗示）
3 **have fools in hand** 把玩傻瓜
4 **have ... th'hand** 没有握您的手
5 **Marry** = (By the Virgin) Mary（向圣母马利亚发誓）
6 **thought is free** 出主意不要钱（成语）
7 **buttery-bar** 酒房或食品房柜台
8 **It's dry** 它是干的
9 **A dry jest** 一个干瘪玩笑（此处dry指"无能为力"）
10 **I am barren** 我就光了（即没有玩笑了；barren同时指女性无生育能力）
11 **canary** 加那利（一种甜白葡萄酒）
12 **Methinks** = It seems to me
13 **a ... man** 普通男人
14 **great eater of beef** 很能吃牛肉的人（当时有人认为吃牛肉会让人变笨；见第170页）
15 *Pourquoi* = Why（法语）
16 **I would ... tongues** 我要是把花在……上的时间花在外语上就好了（tongues与tongs [发夹] 同音）
17 **bear-baiting** 斗熊
18 **had I but** = if only I had
19 **Then hadst thou had** = Then you would have had
20 **mended** = improved
21 **flax on a distaff** 捆扎在纺线棒（一种纺线工具）上的一团乱麻（注意"纺线"英文是spin，与下面的spin it off [纺光] 呼应）
22 **huswife** = housewife/hussy（婆姨，妓女，伊丽莎白时代的人认为花柳病会造成脱发）
23 **it's four to one** 十有八九
24 （本条注释见第15页）
25 **hard by** 附近

MARIA   Fare you well, gentlemen. [*Leaving*]   50

SIR TOBY   And thou let part so[1], Sir Andrew, would thou mightst never draw sword again[2].

SIR ANDREW   And you part so, mistress, I would I might never draw sword again. Fair lady, do you think you have fools in hand[3]?

MARIA   Sir, I have not you by th'hand[4].   55

SIR ANDREW   Marry[5], but you shall have, and here's my hand.

MARIA   Now, sir, thought is free[6]. I pray you bring your hand to th'buttery-bar[7] and let it drink.

SIR ANDREW   Wherefore, sweetheart? What's your metaphor?

MARIA   It's dry[8], sir.   60

SIR ANDREW   Why, I think so: I am not such an ass but I can keep my hand dry. But what's your jest?

MARIA   A dry jest[9], sir.

SIR ANDREW   Are you full of them?

MARIA   Ay, sir, I have them at my fingers' ends; marry, now I let go   65
your hand, I am barren[10].   *Exit*

SIR TOBY   O knight, thou lack'st a cup of canary[11]. [*Hands him a cup*] When did I see thee so put down?

SIR ANDREW   Never in your life, I think, unless you see canary put me down. Methinks[12] sometimes I have no more wit than a Christian   70
or an ordinary man[13] has, but I am a great eater of beef[14], and I believe that does harm to my wit.

SIR TOBY   No question.

SIR ANDREW   And I thought that, I'd forswear it. I'll ride home tomorrow, Sir Toby.   75

SIR TOBY   *Pourquoi*[15], my dear knight?

SIR ANDREW   What is '*pourquoi*'? Do, or not do? I would I had bestowed that time in the tongues[16] that I have in fencing, dancing, and bear-baiting[17]. O had I but[18] followed the arts!

SIR TOBY   Then hadst thou had[19] an excellent head of hair.   80

SIR ANDREW   Why, would that have mended[20] my hair?

SIR TOBY   Past question, for thou seest it will not curl by nature.

SIR ANDREW   But it becomes me well enough, does't not?

SIR TOBY   Excellent; it hangs like flax on a distaff[21]; and I hope to see a huswife[22] take thee between her legs and spin it off.   85

SIR ANDREW   Faith, I'll home tomorrow, Sir Toby; your niece will not be seen, or if she be, it's four to one[23], she'll none of me. The count[24] himself here hard by[25] woos her.

Sir Toby quickly persuades Sir Andrew to stay, assuring him that Orsino will not marry Olivia. Sir Andrew boasts about his dancing skills, and Sir Toby encourages him to perform – but he capers to Toby's tune.

 剧情简介：托比爵士很快说服安褚爵士留下来，向他保证奥悉诺不会与娥丽维娅结婚。安褚爵士吹嘘自己的舞技，托比爵士鼓励他表演一下——而他随着托比爵士哼的曲子蹦蹦跳跳起来。

1 The Lord (or Lady) of Misrule (暴政) (in pairs)

In Shakespeare's time, celebrations for Twelfth Night, the final day of the Christmas season, included the appointment of a 'Lord of Misrule', usually one of the servants in a big household (see pp. 172–3). This tradition led to all sorts of fun, jokes and pranks (恶作剧). Sir Toby is often linked to this type of mischief-making (捣蛋), but after all his 'quaffing and drinking' is he really in charge and able to get the upper hand?

- One of you takes the character of Sir Toby and one of you becomes Maria. As you read through the whole scene again (lines 1–114), identify moments where your character seems to gain the upper hand or beat either your partner's character or Sir Andrew in a verbal contest. Write down each success on a small card. So, for example, the person representing Maria might produce a card like the one below.

> **Maria beats Sir Andrew**
>
> SIR ANDREW ... Fair lady, do you think you
>   have fools in hand?
> MARIA   Sir, I have not you by th'hand.

When you have both made cards for each example of your character's superior wit in these lines, you can use them to play a game. You can play this in two different ways:

1. One of you plays a card – choose your strongest – and the other tries to trump (赢), or better, this example with a more effective put-down or joke from the scene. On each turn, decide who has won between you. The winner collects the cards from that turn and places them in a separate pile. The player who collects the most cards wins the game.

2. Take turns to play a card and arrange them in order of effectiveness. You may arrange them in a vertical line with the funniest at the top, or perhaps a pyramid, acknowledging that some are just as funny as others. The winner is the person whose card makes it to the top position.

---

1 **match** 婚配

2 **degree** 地位；阶级

3 **estate** 财富

4 **Tut** （表示反对、厌烦或同情的啧啧声）

5 **there's life in't** 这事儿还有希望（来自谚语"While there's life there's hope."）

6 **masques and revels** （宫廷）化装舞会和狂欢作乐

7 **kickshawses** 玩意儿，把戏

8 **galliard** 嘎列舞（一种活泼的五步〔四步一跳〕舞）

9 **cut a caper** 跳跃（亦有"炮制调味料"的意思）

10 **mutton** 羊肉（亦有"妓女"的意思）

11 **back-trick** （舞蹈中的）后跳

12 **coranto** 库让特舞（一种欢快的三步舞，也叫 running〔跑步舞〕）

13 **jig** 吉格舞（一种起源于英格兰北方和苏格兰的民间舞，节奏欢快，今天的爱尔兰舞继承了这种舞蹈的特点）

14 **not ... sink-a-pace** 只愿意在小便舞池里撒尿（make water 即"撒尿"；sink-a-pace 既等于sink-apace〔附近的便池〕，又是法文cinque-pace〔五步舞〕的英文转写）

15 **dun-coloured stock** 灰褐色袜子

16 **Taurus** 金牛座（根据西方占星学的说法，金牛座支配人的颈和喉，并非这二人说的胸背和心或小腿和大腿）

SIR TOBY   She'll none o'th'count; she'll not match[1] above her degree[2], neither in estate[3], years, nor wit. I have heard her swear't. Tut[4], there's life in't[5], man.   90

SIR ANDREW   I'll stay a month longer. I am a fellow o'th'strangest mind i'th'world: I delight in masques and revels[6] sometimes altogether.

SIR TOBY   Art thou good at these kickshawses[7], knight?

SIR ANDREW   As any man in Illyria, whatsoever he be, under the degree   95
of my betters, and yet I will not compare with an old man.

SIR TOBY   What is thy excellence in a galliard[8], knight?

SIR ANDREW   Faith, I can cut a caper[9].

SIR TOBY   And I can cut the mutton[10] to't.

SIR ANDREW   And I think I have the back-trick[11] simply as strong as any   100
man in Illyria.

SIR TOBY   Wherefore are these things hid? Wherefore have these gifts a curtain before 'em? Are they like to take dust, like Mistress Mall's picture? Why dost thou not go to church in a galliard and come home in a coranto[12]? My very walk should be a jig[13]; I would not so   105
much as make water but in a sink-a-pace[14]. What dost thou mean? Is it a world to hide virtues in? I did think, by the excellent constitution of thy leg, it was formed under the star of a galliard.

SIR ANDREW   Ay, 'tis strong, and it does indifferent well in a dun-coloured stock[15]. Shall we set about some revels?   110

SIR TOBY   What shall we do else? Were we not born under Taurus[16]?

SIR ANDREW   Taurus? That's sides and heart.

SIR TOBY   No, sir, it is legs and thighs. Let me see thee caper. Ha, higher; ha, ha, excellent!

Exeunt

（第12页注释24）

24 **The count**   伯爵（这里的count显然指Duke of Orsino。在本剧中，Duke/duke共出现了8次，而指称Orsino的Count/count共出现16次。之所以出现 duke和count的混用，可能有两个原因：①在莎士比亚时代这两个词的意思没有什么实质区别；②这个剧本在排印之前没有经过仔细编校，保留了剧本初稿中的一些前后不一致之处。）

Viola, disguised as Cesario, a page, has won the favour of Orsino. He has told her all his secrets. Now Orsino instructs Viola/Cesario to visit Olivia on his behalf to tell her of the strength of his love.

剧情简介：薇娥拉装扮成一个名叫席扎瑞欧的侍童，已赢得奥悉诺的欢心。奥悉诺对她讲了自己的所有秘密。现在，奥悉诺吩咐薇娥拉/席扎瑞欧代表他去拜访娥丽维娅，向娥丽维娅转达他的深厚爱意。

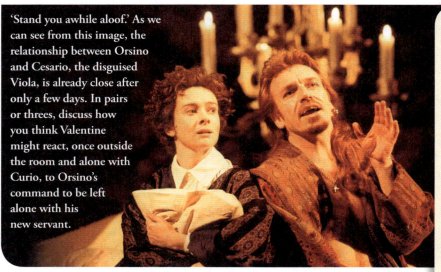

'Stand you awhile aloof.' As we can see from this image, the relationship between Orsino and Cesario, the disguised Viola, is already close after only a few days. In pairs or threes, discuss how you think Valentine might react, once outside the room and alone with Curio, to Orsino's command to be left alone with his new servant.

1	*attire* 装束
2	advanced 提拔
3	humour 性情；情绪
4	Stand you awhile aloof 你们去旁边站一会儿
5	address thy gait unto her 到她那里去（address thy gait = go，这里体现了奥悉诺说话矫揉造作的风格）
6	grow 扎根
7	abandoned 不加节制，沉溺于
8	leap all civil bounds 不理睬所有文明礼貌
9	make unprofited return 无功而返，空手而回
10	unfold 揭示
11	discourse 话语，故事
12	nuncio 信使
13	grave aspect 严肃表情

Write about it 写作练习

Why do you want this job?

Although it does not seem so, Viola, disguised as Cesario, has only been a page to Orsino for three days. Yet how did she (he!) get the job? How did she convince Orsino that she is who she says she is, and that she has the skills for the role?

a Imagine the missing scenes where the Captain prepares Viola for her presentation to Orsino. Think about how he might coach her to speak, to walk, to stand, what to say and when. Then move on to the interview between Orsino and Cesario (Viola), where he will want to learn about her (his) past and experience in this type of work.

b In the Director's Journal that you began on page 2, write up outlines of these scenes and add notes giving instructions to the actors about what to say and how to behave.

c To link with the theme of appearance and reality, remember to include details for the actors about concealing their identity and their true thoughts. What might they be really thinking about the situation or each other? Why do Orsino and Viola get on well so quickly?

d Write a script for these imagined scenes and direct a performance acted by others in your class. Afterwards, edit your script and actors' notes to improve the scenes and their onstage interpretation.

Act 1 Scene 4
Orsino's palace

Enter valentine, *and* viola *in man's attire*[1]

VALENTINE If the duke continue these favours towards you, Cesario, you are like to be much advanced[2]; he hath known you but three days, and already you are no stranger.

VIOLA You either fear his humour[3], or my negligence, that you call in question the continuance of his love. Is he inconstant, sir, in his   5
favours?

VALENTINE No, believe me.

VIOLA I thank you. Here comes the count.

Enter duke [orsino], curio, *and Attendants*

ORSINO Who saw Cesario, ho?

VIOLA On your attendance, my lord, here.   10

ORSINO [*To Curio and Attendants*] Stand you awhile aloof[4]. Cesario,
Thou know'st no less but all: I have unclasped
To thee the book even of my secret soul.
Therefore, good youth, address thy gait unto her[5],
Be not denied access; stand at her doors,   15
And tell them there thy fixèd foot shall grow[6]
Till thou have audience.

VIOLA   Sure, my noble lord,
If she be so abandoned[7] to her sorrow
As it is spoke, she never will admit me.

ORSINO Be clamorous, and leap all civil bounds[8],   20
Rather than make unprofited return[9].

VIOLA Say I do speak with her, my lord, what then?

ORSINO O then unfold[10] the passion of my love,
Surprise her with discourse[11] of my dear faith;
It shall become thee well to act my woes: 25
She will attend it better in thy youth
Than in a nuncio's[12] of more grave aspect[13].

Orsino praises the disguised Viola's feminine appearance. Viola reveals (in an aside) that she loves Orsino. In Scene 5, Feste won't take Maria seriously when she tells him he's in trouble.

 剧情简介： 奥悉诺夸奖乔装后的薇娥拉有女人风韵。薇娥拉（在旁白中）透露她爱奥悉诺。在第五场中，当玛蕊娅告诉费斯特他已身陷麻烦时，费斯特不拿她的话当真。

Stagecraft 导演技巧
Dramatic irony (戏剧反讽) (in pairs)

Scene 4 is rich in **dramatic irony** (where the audience knows something that a character on stage does not). Orsino has no idea that he is speaking to a female when he praises Cesario, saying how like a woman 'he' looks. For Shakespeare's audience, there was a double irony here, because at that time only males were allowed to act. So Viola/Cesario was a boy, playing a girl, playing a boy!

- How do you think Viola/Cesario should react to lines 28–33? Discuss with your partner.
- Take turns in trying out various reactions while your partner reads the lines. Decide which reactions are the most convincing, and why.

1 'myself would be his wife' (in pairs)

This scene ends with a shock for the audience. Three days after meeting him, and whilst disguised as a male servant, Viola decides that she would like to be Orsino's wife (line 41)! Love at first sight and high-speed romances are not unusual in Shakespeare. Neither, though, are infatuations, when characters convince themselves that they are in love without any real foundation.

Viola is already behaving oddly by dressing up as a man and working as a servant even though she is a noble lady. After she was shipwrecked on the island, she seemed just as interested in the marital status of Duke Orsino as she was in her own safety and that of her brother (Act 1 Scene 2, line 29). Viola has some explaining to do!

- One of you steps into role as Viola while the other asks her questions about her interest in Orsino. Then swap roles so the other partner gets a turn as Viola in the hot-seat*. Below are some ideas around which you might frame your questions:

  Intentions Why does she want to stay in Illyria? Why hasn't she decided to leave and return home?

  Depth of love How sure is Viola that she loves Orsino? What does she know of him?

  Marriage Other than love, what reasons might she have for wanting to marry? (Remember that noble women were once married into families for wealth and power rather than purely for love.)

1 belie 歪曲
2 Diana 荻阿娜（月神和贞洁守护神）
3 rubious 红宝石似的
4 small pipe 小细嗓
5 maiden's organ, shrill and sound 少女的嗓音，尖细而圆润
6 is semblative 相似
7 woman's part 女性角色
8 constellation （受星座影响的）性情，性格
9 apt 合适
10 Aside 旁白
11 barful 障碍重重
12 fear no colours 不畏惧敌人（colours：军旗）
13 Make that good 证明这一点
14 A good lenten answer 好一个大斋期的 [没劲 / 无味] 回答（大斋期的饭食十分简单）
15 foolery 插科打诨
16 talents 天赋

* hot-seat 热座位，一种课堂游戏，玩法是请一位同学坐到讲台上的一把椅子上，其他同学轮番给他 / 她出难题，哪个问题他 / 她回答不出就算输。

VIOLA	I think not so, my lord.
ORSINO	Dear lad, believe it;

For they shall yet belie[1] thy happy years
That say thou art a man: Diana's[2] lip   30
Is not more smooth and rubious[3]; thy small pipe[4]
Is as the maiden's organ, shrill and sound[5],
And all is semblative[6] a woman's part[7].
I know thy constellation[8] is right apt[9]
For this affair. Some four or five attend him –   35
All if you will, for I myself am best
When least in company. Prosper well in this,
And thou shalt live as freely as thy lord
To call his fortunes thine.

VIOLA	I'll do my best

To woo your lady. [*Aside*[10]] Yet a barful[11] strife!   40
Whoe'er I woo, myself would be his wife.

Exeunt

Act 1 Scene 5
Olivia's house

Enter MARIA *and* FESTE

MARIA	Nay, either tell me where thou hast been, or I will not open my lips so wide as a bristle may enter in way of thy excuse. My lady will hang thee for thy absence.
FESTE	Let her hang me: he that is well hanged in this world needs to fear no colours[12]. 5
MARIA	Make that good[13].
FESTE	He shall see none to fear.
MARIA	A good lenten answer[14]. I can tell thee where that saying was born, of 'I fear no colours.'
FESTE	Where, good Mistress Mary? 10
MARIA	In the wars, and that may you be bold to say in your foolery[15].
FESTE	Well, God give them wisdom that have it; and those that are fools, let them use their talents[16].

Feste continues to joke with Maria. He hints that she is in a relationship with Sir Toby. Olivia orders Feste to leave, but he challenges her by offering to prove she is a fool.

剧情简介：费斯特继续与玛蕊娅开玩笑，暗示她与托比爵士有私情。娥丽维娅命令费斯特离开，但费斯特向她挑战，提出要证实她是个傻瓜。

Characters 人物分析

Feste – the unfoolish fool

The term 'fool' has altered in meaning since Shakespeare's time. Feste is not foolish; he is an entertainer who plays with words. Occasionally, he seems to talk nonsense – for instance, when he invents an imaginary philosopher, Quinapalus (line 29). Even at these moments, he is able to insult one of the other characters and make the audience laugh with a witty line.

There is truth in what Feste says, and he reminds Olivia that he has all his wits: 'I wear not motley in my brain'. His Latin quotation 'cucullus non facit monachum' (the hood does not make the monk) is a reminder of a major theme of the play: don't judge by appearance.

a Find quotations from this scene that exemplify Feste's role as the fool. What does his language and behaviour suggest about his function in the play?

b Arrange the quotations in a table like the one below, and add to the table as the play develops. You might use this as the basis for an essay about Feste.

What Feste says	What is revealed about the type of fool he is	What others say about Feste	What is revealed about the type of fool he is
'"Better a witty fool, than a foolish wit"' – God bless thee, lady.'	Clever use of language reveals his intelligence and ability to judge others.	OLIVIA: 'Go to, y'are a dry fool: I'll no more of you'	Feste can be an annoyance to others, if they are not as witty; he may be inappropriate with what he says.

1 'simple syllogism'

A syllogism is a logical argument that moves carefully from one point to the next. Feste mocks this philosophical method of reasoning in lines 35–43, but, as usual, there is some sense in what he says.

- Imagine the actor playing Feste says to you: 'I want to play the lines like a philosophy teacher proving an argument. How can I do it? What tone, gestures and props (道具) are needed?' Write notes in your Director's Journal to help him or her.

1 **turned away** 赶走；开除
2 **bear it out** 证明
3 **points** 事情；（裤袜或半截裤的）裤带
4 **gaskins** = galligaskins/gaskin breeches（宽松半截裤）
5 **in good faith** 确实
6 **a piece of Eve's flesh** 夏娃身上的一块肉（即一名女性）
7 **you were best** = you had better
8 **pass for** 被当作……蒙混过去
9 **Quinapalus**（费斯特造的一个字母异位词 [anagram]，由 Aquinas + Paul 组成，前者是欧洲中世纪经院派哲学家和神学家圣托马斯•阿奎那 [St Thomas Aquinas，约1225—1274] 的姓，后者是使徒圣保罗 [St Paul the Apostle] 的教名，这两人都有不少关于傻人傻事的名言）
10 **Go to** 算了
11 **madonna** = my lady（意大利文）
12 **botcher** 补衣工
13 **patched** 打补丁
14 **syllogism** 推理，三段论
15 **cuckold** 戴绿帽子的丈夫
16 **Misprision** = Mistaken（错误，误解）
17 **cucullus non facit monachum** 戴上兜帽未必就是僧人（拉丁文）
18 **motley** 彩格衣（丑角的服装，一般带有花格或花斑，类似中国的百衲衣）
19 **Dexteriously** 巧妙

MARIA	Yet you will be hanged for being so long absent – or to be turned away[1]: is not that as good as a hanging to you?	15
FESTE	Many a good hanging prevents a bad marriage; and for turning away, let summer bear it out[2].	
MARIA	You are resolute then?	
FESTE	Not so neither, but I am resolved on two points[3] –	
MARIA	That if one break, the other will hold, or if both break, your gaskins[4] fall.	20
FESTE	Apt, in good faith[5], very apt. Well, go thy way; if Sir Toby would leave drinking, thou wert as witty a piece of Eve's flesh[6] as any in Illyria.	
MARIA	Peace, you rogue, no more o'that; here comes my lady: make your excuse wisely, you were best[7]. [*Exit*]	25

Enter LADY OLIVIA [*attended*,] *with* MALVOLIO

FESTE	Wit, and't be thy will, put me into good fooling! Those wits that think they have thee do very oft prove fools, and I that am sure I lack thee may pass for[8] a wise man. For what says Quinapalus[9]? 'Better a witty fool than a foolish wit' – God bless thee, lady.	30
OLIVIA	Take the fool away.	
FESTE	Do you not hear, fellows? Take away the lady.	
OLIVIA	Go to[10], y'are a dry fool: I'll no more of you; besides, you grow dishonest.	
FESTE	Two faults, madonna[11], that drink and good counsel will amend: for give the dry fool drink, then is the fool not dry; bid the dishonest man mend himself; if he mend, he is no longer dishonest; if he cannot, let the botcher[12] mend him. Anything that's mended is but patched[13]: virtue that transgresses is but patched with sin, and sin that amends is but patched with virtue. If that this simple syllogism[14] will serve, so; if it will not, what remedy? As there is no true cuckold[15] but calamity, so beauty's a flower. The lady bade take away the fool; therefore I say again, take her away.	35 40
OLIVIA	Sir, I bade them take away you.	
FESTE	Misprision[16] in the highest degree! Lady, *cucullus non facit monachum*[17]: that's as much to say as I wear not motley[18] in my brain. Good madonna, give me leave to prove you a fool.	45
OLIVIA	Can you do it?	
FESTE	Dexteriously[19], good madonna.	
OLIVIA	Make your proof.	50

Feste 'proves' Olivia to be a fool, but is treated with contempt by Malvolio. Olivia criticises Malvolio's sour attitude, urging greater charity and generosity of spirit. Maria tells of a visitor.

 剧情简介：费斯特"证明"娥丽维娅是个傻瓜，但遭到马尔沃琉的蔑视。娥丽维娅批评马尔沃琉酸溜溜的态度，主张要更加宽厚大度。玛蕊娅说有一位客人来访。

Characters 人物分析

Contrasting spirits of Malvolio and Olivia (in pairs)

This scene provides the audience with our first introduction to Olivia's steward, Malvolio. Although he says very little, his few lines give us a strong impression of his character.

Malvolio lets his feelings about Feste be known, wishing death and sickness upon the fool (lines 61–2), and he patronises (对……居高临下，盛气凌人) Olivia at the same time. The first and last sentences of his speech in lines 67–72 are barbed criticisms of Olivia and her dead father. He hints that Olivia does not behave like someone who has vowed to shut herself away for seven years. Olivia seems amused by Feste's joking, and she urges Malvolio to show more generosity of spirit.

- Take parts and experiment with different ways of speaking lines 67–78. Try Malvolio as sneering (轻蔑) or pompous (自大) or deadly serious. Try Olivia as gentle or sharply critical or mildly reproving.

1 **catechise** 盘问（通常由牧师提出有关宗教和虔诚方面的问题）
2 **want of other idleness** 缺少其他消遣
3 **bide** 等着
4 **mend** 改善（但马尔沃琉理解为"越来越蠢"）
5 **infirmity** 年老体虚
6 **no fox** 不滑头
7 **crow** 哄然大笑
8 **zanies** 小丑的助手
9 **distempered** 不健康
10 **bird-bolts** 钝箭头
11 **slander** 言语冒犯
12 **allowed** 得到许可，可畅所欲言
13 **rail** 责骂，嘲笑
14 **Mercury** 墨丘利（罗马神话中众神的使者，欺骗之神）
15 **endue thee with leasing** 赋予你说谎的技能
16 **hold him in delay** 阻拦／滞留他

▼ Malvolio (right) looks on disapprovingly as Feste 'catechises' Olivia. What line do you think is being delivered here, and how might each character respond?

FESTE	I must catechise[1] you for it, madonna. Good my mouse of virtue, answer me.
OLIVIA	Well, sir, for want of other idleness[2], I'll bide[3] your proof.
FESTE	Good madonna, why mourn'st thou?
OLIVIA	Good fool, for my brother's death.	55
FESTE	I think his soul is in hell, madonna.
OLIVIA	I know his soul is in heaven, fool.
FESTE	The more fool, madonna, to mourn for your brother's soul being in heaven. Take away the fool, gentlemen.
OLIVIA	What think you of this fool, Malvolio? Doth he not mend[4]?	60
MALVOLIO	Yes, and shall do, till the pangs of death shake him; infirmity[5], that decays the wise, doth ever make the better fool.
FESTE	God send you, sir, a speedy infirmity, for the better increasing your folly! Sir Toby will be sworn that I am no fox[6], but he will not pass his word for twopence that you are no fool.	65
OLIVIA	How say you to that, Malvolio?
MALVOLIO	I marvel your ladyship takes delight in such a barren rascal. I saw him put down the other day with an ordinary fool that has no more brain than a stone. Look you now, he's out of his guard already. Unless you laugh and minister occasion to him, he is gagged. I protest I take these wise men that crow[7] so at these set kind of fools no better than the fools' zanies[8].	70
OLIVIA	O you are sick of self-love, Malvolio, and taste with a distempered[9] appetite. To be generous, guiltless, and of free disposition is to take those things for bird-bolts[10] that you deem cannon bullets. There is no slander[11] in an allowed[12] fool though he do nothing but rail[13]; nor no railing in a known discreet man though he do nothing but reprove.	75
FESTE	Now Mercury[14] endue thee with leasing[15], for thou speak'st well of fools!	80

Enter MARIA

MARIA	Madam, there is at the gate a young gentleman much desires to speak with you.
OLIVIA	From the Count Orsino, is it?
MARIA	I know not, madam; 'tis a fair young man and well attended.
OLIVIA	Who of my people hold him in delay[16]?	85
MARIA	Sir Toby, madam, your kinsman.

Olivia sends Malvolio to dismiss the visitor. Sir Toby, who is drunk, muddles his words – or makes a sexual pun. Malvolio returns to explain that the visitor insists on speaking to Olivia.

剧情简介：娥丽维娅让马尔沃琉打发来客。托比爵士喝醉了，话说含混不清——或许说了有关性的双关语。马尔沃琉回来解释说来客坚持要面见娥丽维娅。

1 Playing a drunk (in threes)

It's very difficult to play the part of a drunken person convincingly. Can you do it? Here are two tips for imitating a drunk:

- Imagine your left foot is nailed to the floor. Try to walk in all directions with the other.

- Drunks have problems with speaking and hearing. They misunderstand words, as when Sir Toby confuses 'lethargy' and 'lechery'. Struggle with your words, but remember you have to make them perfectly clear to the audience, even if you slur them. Take your time and search slowly for each word in your mind, as if you are having difficulty finding it.

a Take turns to play Sir Toby, Feste and Olivia. Act out lines 96–106, incorporating the tips above for playing drunkenness. How helpful are these suggestions?

b After acting out the scene, write notes for an actor playing the part of Sir Toby about the movements and gestures he should use. Link these to quotations and line references to make the instructions very clear for the actor.

c Swap your notes with another group and watch to see if they perform the scene as you intended.

2 'what you will'

Line 90 contains the subtitle of the play: 'what you will' (whatever you like). The saying was in common use in Shakespeare's time. When the title of a play is used within the play, it can sometimes signal an important or pivotal moment to the audience.

- Why might this moment be regarded as significant? What do you think is going to happen? You have now seen enough of the play and its characters to have some ideas about what might take place. On a piece of paper, write down and complete the following statements:

I think that the following will happen in the play…
My evidence for this is…
This is alluded to in line _____ / in _____'s actions.

Seal the predictions in an envelope. Return to them at the end of the play to see whether or not you were correct, and what happened differently than you expected.

---

1 **Fetch him off** 把他（托比爵士）带走

2 **Fie on him** 他这个人真讨厌

3 **old** 陈旧，过时

4 **Jove** 乔武（即Jupiter，罗马神话中的主神；见第165页）

5 *pia mater* 大脑（拉丁文）

6 **pickle herring** 腌鲱鱼（托比爵士在为自己的打嗝找借口）

7 **sot** 傻瓜，醉鬼

8 **lethargy** 酩酊大醉

9 **Lechery** 淫荡

10 **one draught above heat** 暖了身子后再多喝一口

11 **crowner** = coroner（验尸官）

12 **sit o'my coz** 对我这位亲戚进行勘验

13 **look to** 照料

14 **yond** 那个

15 **fortified against any denial** 坚决不接受拒绝

OLIVIA	Fetch him off[1], I pray you; he speaks nothing but madman. Fie on him[2].

[Exit Maria]

Go you, Malvolio. If it be a suit from the count, I am sick, or not at home – what you will to dismiss it.   90

Exit Malvolio

Now you see, sir, how your fooling grows old[3], and people dislike it.

FESTE	Thou hast spoke for us, madonna, as if thy eldest son should be a fool: whose skull Jove[4] cram with brains, for – here he comes –

Enter SIR TOBY *[staggering]*

one of thy kin has a most weak *pia mater*[5].   95

OLIVIA	By mine honour, half drunk! What is he at the gate, cousin?
SIR TOBY	A gentleman.
OLIVIA	A gentleman? What gentleman?
SIR TOBY	'Tis a gentleman here – *[Hiccuping]* a plague o'these pickle herring[6]! How now, sot[7]? 100
FESTE	Good Sir Toby –
OLIVIA	Cousin, cousin, how have you come so early by this lethargy[8]?
SIR TOBY	Lechery[9]! I defy lechery. There's one at the gate.
OLIVIA	Ay, marry, what is he?
SIR TOBY	Let him be the devil and he will, I care not: give me faith, 105 say I. Well, it's all one. *Exit*
OLIVIA	What's a drunken man like, fool?
FESTE	Like a drowned man, a fool, and a madman: one draught above heat[10] makes him a fool, the second mads him, and a third drowns him. 110
OLIVIA	Go thou and seek the crowner[11], and let him sit o'my coz[12], for he's in the third degree of drink: he's drowned. Go look after him.
FESTE	He is but mad yet, madonna, and the fool shall look to[13] the madman. *[Exit]*

Enter MALVOLIO

MALVOLIO	Madam, yond[14] young fellow swears he will speak with you. 115 I told him you were sick; he takes on him to understand so much and therefore comes to speak with you. I told him you were asleep; he seems to have a foreknowledge of that too, and therefore comes to speak with you. What is to be said to him, lady? He's fortified against any denial[15]. 120

Malvolio haughtily describes Viola's appearance as sexually ambiguous. Olivia commands Maria to veil her. Viola enters (disguised as Cesario) and seeks to discover which woman is Olivia.

 剧情简介： 马尔沃琉鄙夷地将薇娥菈的长相描述为雌雄难辨。娥丽维娅令玛蕊娅给她戴面纱。薇娥菈（装扮成席扎瑞欧）上，试图辨认出哪个女人是娥丽维娅。

1 Malvolio's tone (in pairs)

In Malvolio's disdainful description of Viola/Cesario (lines 130–4), he likens 'him' to an unripe apple ('codling'), and to the time when the tide turns ('in standing water').

a To achieve Malvolio's haughty tone, pinch your nose between forefinger and thumb, lean your head back, and speak the lines slowly, pausing after every punctuation mark. Listen to the note of superiority, condescension and disdain in your voice.

b Imagine that you are a puppet. Your partner will manipulate you, or 'pull your strings', so your actions and facial expressions match the haughty tone that you are using to deliver Malvolio's lines. If you are happy to be 'moulded', your partner may move your body and face into position. Otherwise, he or she should tell you exactly what to do with your body and face, confirming when you have adopted the correct position or suggesting further tweaks to match Malvolio's disdain.

Viola/Cesario begins 'his' address to Olivia in high style: 'Most radiant, exquisite, and unmatchable beauty'. But as we can see in this image, Olivia's veil prevents Viola/Cesario from knowing if it is really Olivia she is speaking to. Viola is disconcerted and never gets to finish the elaborate speech that Orsino may well have written for her. Write the next few lines of Viola/Cesario's (unfinished) prepared speech. To follow on seamlessly from the high-sounding opening words, you may wish to use blank verse (无韵诗；素体诗) (see p. 167).

(see p. 167)

1 **sheriff's post** 郡长桩（郡长公署门前矗立的有装饰的桩子，上面可张贴布告）

2 **supporter to a bench** 长凳子的腿

3 **manner** = kind, sort

4 **squash** 未成熟的豌豆荚

5 **peascod** = peapod（豌豆荚）

6 **codling** 不熟的苹果

7 **in standing water** 在潮汐涨落之间

8 **well-favoured** 英俊

9 **shrewishly** （嗓音）尖锐

10 **embassy** 消息，信息

11 **exquisite** 精致

12 **cast away** 浪费

13 **comptible** 敏感

14 **least sinister usage** 丝毫的失礼

15 **comedian** 演员（自莎士比亚时代以来意思发生了变化）

16 **usurp** 冒充

OLIVIA	Tell him he shall not speak with me.	
MALVOLIO	H'as been told so; and he says he'll stand at your door like a sheriff's post[1], and be the supporter to a bench[2], but he'll speak with you.	
OLIVIA	What kind o'man is he?	125
MALVOLIO	Why, of mankind.	
OLIVIA	What manner[3] of man?	
MALVOLIO	Of very ill manner: he'll speak with you, will you or no.	
OLIVIA	Of what personage and years is he?	
MALVOLIO	Not yet old enough for a man, nor young enough for a boy: as a squash[4] is before 'tis a peascod[5], or a codling[6] when 'tis almost an apple. 'Tis with him in standing water[7], between boy and man. He is very well-favoured[8] and he speaks very shrewishly[9]. One would think his mother's milk were scarce out of him.	130
OLIVIA	Let him approach. Call in my gentlewoman.	135
MALVOLIO	Gentlewoman, my lady calls. *Exit*	

Enter MARIA

OLIVIA	Give me my veil; come throw it o'er my face. We'll once more hear Orsino's embassy[10].	

Enter VIOLA

VIOLA	The honourable lady of the house, which is she?	
OLIVIA	Speak to me; I shall answer for her. Your will?	140
VIOLA	Most radiant, exquisite[11], and unmatchable beauty – I pray you tell me if this be the lady of the house, for I never saw her. I would be loath to cast away[12] my speech: for besides that it is excellently well penned, I have taken great pains to con it. Good beauties, let me sustain no scorn; I am very comptible[13], even to the least sinister usage[14].	145
OLIVIA	Whence came you, sir?	
VIOLA	I can say little more than I have studied, and that question's out of my part. Good gentle one, give me modest assurance if you be the lady of the house, that I may proceed in my speech.	150
OLIVIA	Are you a comedian[15]?	
VIOLA	No, my profound heart; and yet, by the very fangs of malice, I swear, I am not that I play. Are you the lady of the house?	
OLIVIA	If I do not usurp[16] myself, I am.	

After some verbal fencing, Viola says her message is for Olivia alone. Maria is dismissed. Olivia playfully questions Viola, who asks to see her face. Olivia unveils.

剧情简介： 一阵唇枪舌剑之后，薇娥菈说她带的口信只告诉娥丽维娅一个人。玛蕊娅被打发走。娥丽维娅开玩笑地询问薇娥菈，薇娥菈要求看她的脸，娥丽维娅揭开面纱。

Language in the play 剧中语言

Help the audience (in pairs)

Shakespeare may be, in the writer Ben Jonson's words, 'for all time', but some of his language is definitely 'of an age'. Certain expressions have not survived into modern usage and if directors choose to leave them in, the lines must be clarified by the actors with actions and gestures.

- **Lines 164–5** 'Tis not that time of moon with me to make one in so skipping a dialogue' (the moon was thought to bring on lunacy)
- **Line 173** 'taxation of homage' (a demand for submission and loyalty)
- **Line 180** 'What is your text?' (Olivia begins questioning Viola as though conducting a catechism (基督教的教义问答) – an examination by a series of questions)
- **Line 186** 'To answer by the method' (to make the reply in the appropriate style in this catechism you are putting me through)
- **Lines 191–2** 'such a one I was this present' (here's a portrait of me now).

Look at the expressions and explanations above, then discuss what an actor might do to make them understandable to the audience.

1 from my commission 不是我的任务
2 on = go on
3 feigned 虚情假意
4 saucy 粗鲁，直率
5 make one in 参与
6 skipping 轻率，轻浮
7 hoist sail 升帆；离去
8 swabber 甲板清洗工，船员
9 hull 停泊
10 mollification 安慰，安抚
11 Speak your office 说出您的口信
12 overture 宣告
13 the olive 橄榄枝（象征和平）
14 entertainment 接待
15 maidenhead 童贞；处女
16 profanation 亵渎神明
17 by the method 用我们说的方法
18 heresy 异端邪说

▼ Olivia has vowed to avoid men for seven years, but at line 191 she unveils her face. We see her thoughts and feelings are far from sad, and she is interested by Viola/Cesario's appearance and language. Write notes linked to lines and actions to advise an actor how to show Olivia's growing fascination. Add these notes to your Director's Journal.

VIOLA	Most certain, if you are she, you do usurp yourself: for what is your to bestow is not yours to reserve. But this is from my commission[1]. I will on[2] with my speech in your praise, and then show you the heart of my message.	155
OLIVIA	Come to what is important in't: I forgive you the praise.	
VIOLA	Alas, I took great pains to study it, and 'tis poetical.	160
OLIVIA	It is the more like to be feigned[3]; I pray you keep it in. I heard you were saucy[4] at my gates, and allowed your approach rather to wonder at you than to hear you. If you be not mad, be gone; if you have reason, be brief. 'Tis not that time of moon with me to make one in[5] so skipping[6] a dialogue.	165
MARIA	Will you hoist sail[7], sir? Here lies your way.	
VIOLA	No, good swabber[8], I am to hull[9] here a little longer. Some mollification[10] for your giant, sweet lady! Tell me your mind, I am a messenger.	
OLIVIA	Sure you have some hideous matter to deliver, when the courtesy of it is so fearful. Speak your office[11].	170
VIOLA	It alone concerns your ear. I bring no overture[12] of war, no taxation of homage; I hold the olive[13] in my hand; my words are as full of peace as matter.	
OLIVIA	Yet you began rudely. What are you? What would you?	175
VIOLA	The rudeness that hath appeared in me I learned from my entertainment[14]. What I am, and what I would, are as secret as maidenhead[15]: to your ears, divinity; to any other's, profanation[16].	
OLIVIA	Give us the place alone; we will hear this divinity.	

[Exeunt Maria and Attendants]

	Now, sir, what is your text?	180
VIOLA	Most sweet lady –	
OLIVIA	A comfortable doctrine, and much may be said of it. Where lies your text?	
VIOLA	In Orsino's bosom.	
OLIVIA	In his bosom? In what chapter of his bosom?	185
VIOLA	To answer by the method[17], in the first of his heart.	
OLIVIA	O I have read it. It is heresy[18]. Have you no more to say?	
VIOLA	Good madam, let me see your face.	
OLIVIA	Have you any commission from your lord to negotiate with my face? You are now out of your text, but we will draw the curtain and show you the picture. [*Unveiling*] Look you, sir, such a one I was this present. Is't not well done?	190

Viola accuses Olivia of keeping her beauty to herself by not having children. Olivia replies mockingly. Viola explains that if she were the one who loved Olivia, every action would express her love and move Olivia to pity her.

剧情简介：薇娥菈指责娥丽维娅不生儿育女，不让自己的美貌延续。娥丽维娅嘲弄地回答她。薇娥菈解释说，如果她是爱娥丽维娅的那个人，她的每个行动都会表达她的爱并让娥丽维娅怜悯她。

1 Lists (in pairs)

In lines 197–9, Viola appeals to Olivia to marry and have children ('copy'). In this way, Olivia can ensure that her beauty is handed on and kept alive after her death. Viola's plea echoes the theme of the first seventeen of Shakespeare's sonnets. But Olivia mocks Viola by taking 'copy' literally. She proposes to leave various lists ('divers schedules') itemising all the elements of her beauty. In lines 213–17, Olivia lists at least nine of Orsino's qualities.

a Discuss why Shakespeare uses lists in this way. What effect do they have on the audience? What might they say about the person using the list?

b Take parts and read lines 197–204. Play Viola as sincere and discouraged, and make Olivia's response mocking and teasing.

c Identify Orsino's various qualities from Olivia's list, then prepare a series of charades (actions without words) to show each quality – 'virtuous', 'noble' and so on. Present your version to the class. Can other pairs guess which of Orsino's qualities you are acting out?

2 'Make me a willow cabin at your gate' (in fours)

Lines 223–31 contain some of Shakespeare's best-known love poetry. Work out a group presentation of the lines that highlights their sentiment. You could use some of the following techniques to make the performance dramatically effective:

- speak in chorus (together) or echo particular words and phrases
- share out the lines between speakers and add in different voices
- add sound effects
- use accompanying mimes (哑剧手势) or actions
- sing the lines.

Bear in mind the following:

- the 'willow' was an emblem (象征) of sorrowful love
- 'cantons' are songs
- 'contemnèd' means 'rejected' or 'despised'
- 'Hallow' means 'shout'
- 'babbling gossip' means 'echo'.

Perform your finished piece to another group and together evaluate how effectively your performance drew out the meaning of Shakespeare's words.

1 **in grain** 天生；永驻
2 **blent = blended** (调配)
3 **cunning hand laid on** 妙手绘制
4 **divers schedules** 几份不同清单
5 **inventoried** 登记在册
6 **'praise = appraise** (鉴赏，评估)
7 **if = even if**
8 **such … beauty** 这种爱，哪怕给您戴上无与伦比的美女的王冠，也不过与之相称
9 **Of great estate** 家产巨大
10 **In voices well divulged** 众口一词，好评如潮
11 **flame** 激情
12 **willow cabin** 柳枝小屋（柳枝象征失恋）
13 **my soul** 我的心上人
14 **cantons** 歌曲
15 **contemnèd** 轻视
16 **Hallow … hills** 冲着能响起回声的山峦呼喊您的名字
17 **babbling gossip** 呜呜私语（指回音）
18 **rest** 得到宁静
19 **Between … earth** 天地间
20 **But** 除非

VIOLA	Excellently done, if God did all.	
OLIVIA	'Tis in grain[1], sir; 'twill endure wind and weather.	
VIOLA	'Tis beauty truly blent[2], whose red and white	195
	Nature's own sweet and cunning hand laid on[3].	
	Lady, you are the cruell'st she alive,	
	If you will lead these graces to the grave,	
	And leave the world no copy.	
OLIVIA	O sir, I will not be so hard-hearted: I will give out divers	200
	schedules[4] of my beauty. It shall be inventoried[5] and every particle	
	and utensil labelled to my will, as, *item*, two lips, indifferent red;	
	item, two grey eyes, with lids to them; *item*, one neck, one chin,	
	and so forth. Were you sent hither to 'praise[6] me?	
VIOLA	I see you what you are. You are too proud;	205
	But if[7] you were the devil, you are fair!	
	My lord and master loves you. O such love	
	Could be but recompensed, though you were crowned	
	The nonpareil of beauty[8].	
OLIVIA	How does he love me?	
VIOLA	With adorations, fertile tears,	210
	With groans that thunder love, with sighs of fire.	
OLIVIA	Your lord does know my mind. I cannot love him.	
	Yet I suppose him virtuous, know him noble,	
	Of great estate[9], of fresh and stainless youth;	
	In voices well divulged[10], free, learned, and valiant,	215
	And in dimension, and the shape of nature,	
	A gracious person. But yet I cannot love him.	
	He might have took his answer long ago.	
VIOLA	If I did love you in my master's flame[11],	
	With such a suff'ring, such a deadly life,	220
	In your denial I would find no sense;	
	I would not understand it.	
OLIVIA	Why, what would you?	
VIOLA	Make me a willow cabin[12] at your gate,	
	And call upon my soul[13] within the house;	
	Write loyal cantons[14] of contemnèd[15] love,	225
	And sing them loud even in the dead of night;	
	Hallow your name to the reverberate hills[16],	
	And make the babbling gossip[17] of the air	
	Cry out 'Olivia!' O you should not rest[18]	
	Between the elements of air and earth[19]	230
	But[20] you should pity me!	

31

Viola rejects payment. She leaves, wishing that Olivia, like Orsino, may suffer from rejected love. Olivia fears that she is falling in love with Viola/Cesario. She sends Malvolio on a false errand to ensure that Viola returns.

 剧情简介：薇娥菈拒绝了赏钱，转身离开，希望娥丽维娅会像奥悉诺一样经受爱意被拒绝的痛苦。娥丽维娅担心自己爱上了薇娥菈/席扎瑞欧。她派马尔沃琉去办一件虚假的差事，以确保薇娥菈会再来。

Stagecraft 导演技巧

Olivia's response – an anti-climax (反高潮；高潮突降)?

Viola/Cesario's 'willow cabin' speech has bewitched (迷住) Olivia. She is now well and truly in love with this attractive young man. Her initial response is just four words in line 231: 'You might do much.' But how does she speak those words?

- Write notes for an actor on how Olivia should react throughout the 'willow cabin' speech, and on how she says 'What is your parentage?' In your Director's Journal, copy out the relevant lines and then annotate them with your ideas about how to act them.

Themes 主题分析

Judging by appearance (in small groups)

Olivia judges Viola/Cesario to be a 'gentleman' by five qualities ('five-fold blazon', line 248): speech, looks, body, behaviour and spirit. However, at line 264, Olivia worries that she may have been deceived by appearances: 'Mine eye too great a flatterer for my mind'. Certainly, she has been deceived by Viola/Cesario's outward appearance.

a Discuss each of the five qualities (line 247) in turn, and produce a mind map (see the example below) listing the 'pluses' and 'pitfalls' of using these as a reliable guide to character.

b Where possible, add a quotation from the text where Olivia refers to each of the 'pluses' and 'pitfalls' that you note.

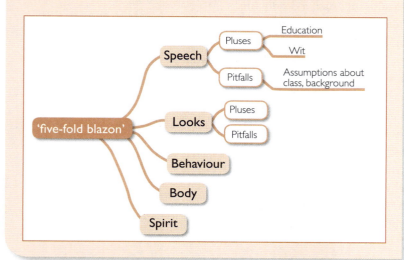

1	parentage	出身，家世
2	Above … well	比我现在的地位高，不过我现在的地位也不错
3	fee'd post	拿赏钱的信使
4	fervour	激情
5	five-fold blazon	五重的盾徽描述（盾徽是绅士的标志，这种盾徽描述说明盾徽的五个属性）
6	catch the plague	感染上爱情
7	stealth	悄无声息
8	To … eyes	通过眼睛钻进我的心
9	peevish	固执，执拗
10	county	伯爵（指奥悉诺）
11	Would I, or not	不管我是否愿意要
12	flatter with	鼓励
13	hold him up	让他产生幻觉
14	Hie thee	赶快
15	owe	拥有
16	decreed	命中注定

OLIVIA	You might do much.
	What is your parentage[1]?
VIOLA	Above my fortunes, yet my state is well[2]:
	I am a gentleman.
OLIVIA	Get you to your lord.
	I cannot love him. Let him send no more – 235
	Unless (perchance) you come to me again,
	To tell me how he takes it. Fare you well.
	I thank you for your pains. Spend this for me.
VIOLA	I am no fee'd post[3], lady; keep your purse;
	My master, not myself, lacks recompense. 240
	Love make his heart of flint that you shall love,
	And let your fervour[4] like my master's be
	Placed in contempt. Farewell, fair cruelty. *Exit*
OLIVIA	'What is your parentage?'
	'Above my fortunes, yet my state is well: 245
	I am a gentleman.' I'll be sworn thou art;
	Thy tongue, thy face, thy limbs, actions, and spirit
	Do give thee five-fold blazon[5]. Not too fast! Soft, soft!
	Unless the master were the man – How now?
	Even so quickly may one catch the plague[6]? 250
	Methinks I feel this youth's perfections
	With an invisible and subtle stealth[7]
	To creep in at mine eyes[8]. Well, let it be.
	What ho, Malvolio!

Enter MALVOLIO

MALVOLIO	Here, madam, at your service.
OLIVIA	Run after that same peevish[9] messenger, 255
	The county's[10] man. He left this ring behind him,
	Would I, or not[11]. Tell him, I'll none of it.
	Desire him not to flatter with[12] his lord,
	Nor hold him up[13] with hopes; I am not for him.
	If that the youth will come this way tomorrow, 260
	I'll give him reasons for't. Hie thee[14], Malvolio!
MALVOLIO	Madam, I will. *Exit*
OLIVIA	I do I know not what, and fear to find
	Mine eye too great a flatterer for my mind.
	Fate, show thy force; ourselves we do not owe[15]. 265
	What is decreed[16] must be; and be this so. [*Exit*]

Looking back at Act 1 第1幕回顾
Activities for groups or individuals

1 Appearance versus reality

Act 1 reveals key aspects of the major characters: Orsino's self-indulgence, Viola's resourcefulness, the drunken Sir Toby's mocking of the foolish Sir Andrew, Feste's edgy (尖刻) humour, Malvolio's arrogance and Olivia's readiness to abandon her mourning as she falls in love with Viola/Cesario. All characters share something in common: they are affected in some way by the difference between reality and appearance.

a Write down the name of each character on a sticky note and attach it to a wall or board. On other sticky notes, write one or two sentences describing how each character is affected by the difference between reality and appearance. Stick your note under or around the note with the character's name on it.

b Consider who is most affected by the appearance/reality theme at this moment in the play. Continue to add to the wall or board as you read on, and note how the position of characters changes as the play progresses.

2 'How does he love me?'

The other major theme introduced in Act 1 is love.

a Divide the scenes of the first act between groups. Each group tries to find as many quotations about love as possible in that scene.

b Sort the quotations into different types of love. If you write the quotations on cards, you can move them as you discuss.

c Each group presents their ideas about the categories of love to the class, in scene order. Examine what Shakespeare suggests to the audience about love. Is it consistent or changing? Suggest reasons for this.

d Write an essay in which each paragraph discusses a different type of love shown by Shakespeare in

Twelfth Night. Use the play script to support your ideas. You might attempt to answer this question: 'Do you think that Shakespeare is positive about love, or is he a sceptic?'

3 'What country, friends, is this?'

Historical Illyria lay along the Adriatic coast of present-day Albania and Croatia. But the Illyria of *Twelfth Night* is a never-never land of romantic comedy, where anything can happen. Shakespeare plays on the verbal similarity of Illyria to Elysium (heaven) and illusion, suggesting that the place is otherworldly and magical.

• Imagine you are about to stage a production of the play. How will you present Illyria? Will you give your production a Mediterranean atmosphere, a setting in Elizabethan England or will you imagine some other location (see pp. 169–71)? Sketch and describe your ideas for a set. Annotate your design and provide textual references in the form of quotations or explanations based on what you have read in the play.

4 Boy played by girl (played by boy)

In Shakespeare's time, the actor playing Viola was a boy (dressed as a girl for a short period of the play), so Viola playing Cesario was easy. Viola's disguise can cause problems in modern staging.

• Make notes in your Director's Journal about what Viola should wear and the other ways in which she could resemble a young man. Use the pictures opposite and elsewhere in the book for ideas. Consider whether you would completely hide Viola's feminine appearance, or whether you would make it possible to see that she is a woman. What might these decisions add to, or take away from, the audience's enjoyment of the scene?

When Viola first appears as Cesario, do you think the audience should be able to recognise her immediately? Discuss with a partner what costume, make-up and props you would use to create the transformation.

Antonio has rescued Sebastian from the shipwreck and wishes to be his servant. Sebastian rejects Antonio's offer and tells of his grief for his twin sister Viola, whom he believes drowned.

 剧情简介：安托纽已将塞巴斯田从海难中救起，希望做他的仆人。塞巴斯田拒绝了安托纽的提议，讲述自己对失去双胞胎妹妹薇娥菈的悲痛，他认为薇娥菈已经溺亡。

1 Parallel scenes, different directions (in pairs)

This scene has many echoes of, and similarities with, Act 1 Scene 2. The Captain and Antonio are both experienced seafarers who offer their eager support and assistance to Viola and Sebastian. Often, productions try to emphasise this parallel by staging the scenes in similar or near-identical ways, sometimes dressing Viola and Sebastian in the same colours or using the same styles of clothing and haircuts.

a Each taking one part, read through the whole scene. Then go back and read through Act 1 Scene 2 in the same way. Agree on three gestures or actions (for example, a reassuring hand on the shoulder or the use of a handkerchief) that both Sebastian and Viola, and then Antonio and the Captain, could use in both scenes to emphasise their parallel nature. Share your interpretation with another pair or the whole class, and challenge your audience to pick out the common actions and evaluate their effectiveness.

b Discuss how you think using similar staging techniques in this way could enrich the scenes and deepen our understanding of the characters. Why do you think this might be a powerful approach for a director to take? Is there any comic potential in such an interpretation?

▼ In this Royal Shakespeare Company production, the relationship between Antonio and Sebastian was portrayed as one of real physical affection, almost a romance. What evidence can you find for the strength of Antonio's feelings? Is there anything to suggest his devotion goes beyond simple duty or friendship towards more passionate feelings?

1 **Nor … you?** 也不想让我同您一起去吗？

2 **By your patience = By your leave**（请原谅，对不起）

3 **malignancy of my fate** 我的晦气／命运之背

4 **distemper** 感染

5 **crave of you your leave** 求您许可

6 **evils** 不幸

7 **were = would be**

8 **whither you are bound** 您打算前往何方

9 **sooth** 说实话

10 **determinate voyage** 决定的航行

11 **extravagancy** 流浪，漂泊

12 **a touch of modesty** 一种礼貌

13 **extort from me** 向我强求

14 **it charges me in manners** 礼节要求我

15 **Messaline** 摩萨林（莎士比亚虚构的一个城市）

16 **so ended = ended in an hour**（即既同生又共死）

17 **breach** 大涌，大浪

18 **could … that** 不可如此赞美太过笃信（因为我们是双胞胎的关系）

19 **publish** 宣布

20 **salt water** 眼泪

21 **bad entertainment** 招待不周

22 **your trouble = troubling you**

Act 2 Scene 1
The sea-coast of Illyria

Enter ANTONIO *and* SEBASTIAN

ANTONIO Will you stay no longer? Nor will you not that I go with you?[1]

SEBASTIAN By your patience[2], no. My stars shine darkly over me; the malignancy of my fate[3] might perhaps distemper[4] yours; therefore I shall crave of you your leave[5] that I may bear my evils[6] alone. It were[7] a bad recompense for your love to lay any of them on you.　5

ANTONIO Let me know of you whither you are bound[8].

SEBASTIAN No, sooth[9], sir. My determinate voyage[10] is mere extravagancy[11]. But I perceive in you so excellent a touch of modesty[12] that you will not extort from me[13] what I am willing to keep in. Therefore it charges me in manners[14] the rather to express myself. You must know　10 of me then, Antonio, my name is Sebastian (which I called Roderigo); my father was that Sebastian of Messaline[15] whom I know you have heard of. He left behind him myself and a sister, both born in an hour: if the heavens had been pleased, would we had so ended[16]! But you, sir, altered that, for some hour before you took　15 me from the breach[17] of the sea was my sister drowned.

ANTONIO Alas the day!

SEBASTIAN A lady, sir, though it was said she much resembled me, was yet of many accounted beautiful; but though I could not with such estimable wonder overfar believe that[18], yet thus far I will boldly　20 publish[19] her: she bore a mind that envy could not but call fair. She is drowned already, sir, with salt water[20], though I seem to drown her remembrance again with more.

ANTONIO Pardon me, sir, your bad entertainment[21].

SEBASTIAN O good Antonio, forgive me your trouble[22].　25

ANTONIO If you will not murder me for my love, let me be your servant.

Sebastian again rejects Antonio's offer of service, but Antonio determines to follow him in spite of all dangers. In Scene 2, Viola puzzles over Malvolio's message: has Olivia fallen in love with her?

剧情简介： 塞巴斯田再次拒绝了安托纽想要当他仆人的提议，但安托纽决意不管什么危险都要追随他。在第二场，薇娥菈对马尔沃琉带来的消息感到困惑：娥丽维娅爱上她了吗？

1 Antonio's feelings for Sebastian (in pairs)

At the end of Act 2 Scene 1, Antonio decides to follow Sebastian to Orsino's court, even though he has many enemies there. Some productions of *Twelfth Night* use this scene to show that Antonio has a passionate affection for Sebastian, but is unwilling to show it openly. He offers himself as Sebastian's servant, but Sebastian refuses.

• Perform the scene in two ways and discuss which works better.

Interpretation A Emphasise the intense, uncontrolled nature of Sebastian's grief, and show Antonio simply seeking to gently soothe and calm him. Avoid any sense of attraction or desire from Antonio; instead emphasise his pity and respectful admiration for Sebastian.

Interpretation B Use facial expressions and actions to suggest deeper warmth between Sebastian and Antonio. Try to show Antonio struggling to hide his true feelings through the scene, but then fervently revealing his adoration of Sebastian in lines 32–6.

2 Viola's lie (in pairs)

Viola tells a downright (彻头彻尾) lie to Malvolio in line 10 of Act 2 Scene 2. Why do you think she does this?

• Talk together about what this lie suggests to you about her character.

1	**recovered**	救起
2	**ye**	您（ye 在古代英文里是复数第二人称代词的名格 [即主格] 形式，you是其致使格 [即宾格] 形式。中代英文里ye开始和you一起用作对第二人称的敬称 [相当于您]。由于单数第二人称代词的主格和宾格分别是thou和thee，ye和you的格于是逐渐发生了相互转换。）
3	**manners of my mother**	女人的行为方式
4	**mine … me**	我的眼睛会（通过眼泪）暴露我的感情
5	**bound to**	前往（回答安托纽之前问他的问题）
6	**sport**	娱乐，消遣
7	**even now** = just now	
8	**on a moderate pace**	以不紧不慢的步伐
9	**saved me my pains**	省去我的麻烦
10	**desperate assurance**	彻底死心
11	**hardy**	斗胆
12	**peevishly**	气冲冲
13	**outside**	外观；相貌
14	**lost her tongue**	让她丧失了正常说话的能力
15	**in starts distractedly**	断断续续，语无伦次

SEBASTIAN   If you will not undo what you have done, that is, kill him
whom you have recovered[1], desire it not. Fare ye[2] well at once; my
bosom is full of kindness, and I am yet so near the manners of my
mother[3] that, upon the least occasion more, mine eyes will tell tales   30
of me[4]. I am bound to[5] the Count Orsino's court. Farewell.   *Exit*

ANTONIO   The gentleness of all the gods go with thee!
I have many enemies in Orsino's court,
Else would I very shortly see thee there.
But come what may, I do adore thee so   35
That danger shall seem sport[6], and I will go.   *Exit*

Act 2 Scene 2
A street near Olivia's house

Enter VIOLA *and* MALVOLIO

MALVOLIO   Were you not even now[7] with the Countess Olivia?

VIOLA   Even now, sir; on a moderate pace[8], I have since arrived but
hither.

MALVOLIO   She returns this ring to you. You might have saved me my
pains[9] to have taken it away yourself. She adds, moreover, that you   5
should put your lord into a desperate assurance[10]: she will none of
him. And one thing more, that you be never so hardy[11] to come again
in his affairs, unless it be to report your lord's taking of this. Receive
it so.

VIOLA   She took the ring of me. I'll none of it.   10

MALVOLIO   Come, sir, you peevishly[12] threw it to her; and her will is,
it should be so returned. If it be worth stooping for, there it lies,
in your eye; if not, be it his that finds it.   *Exit*

VIOLA   I left no ring with her: what means this lady?
Fortune forbid my outside[13] have not charmed her!   15
She made good view of me, indeed so much
That, methought, her eyes had lost her tongue[14],
For she did speak in starts distractedly[15].

Perplexed, Viola fears Olivia loves her, whilst she herself loves Orsino. She hopes that time will resolve the difficulties. Scene 3 reveals that Sir Toby and Sir Andrew have been drinking all night.

 剧情简介： 薇娥菈困惑不解，担心娥丽维娅爱上了自己，而她自己却爱上了奥悉诺。她希望时间会解决这些难题。第三场显示出托比爵士和安褚爵士喝了一夜的酒。

Characters 人物分析

Viola's soliloquy (独白) (in small groups)

Viola realises (lines 14–38) that her disguise as a man has caused Olivia to fall in love with her. Appearance has triumphed over reality!

a Two members of your group read aloud Viola's **soliloquy** (an extended speech by an individual who is usually alone on stage) in the two following ways:

- **Excited and amused** Some actors choose to portray an element of playful, energetic excitement in Viola as she realises Olivia has become infatuated.
- **Perplexed and nervous** Viola's feelings for Orsino, and her desire to please him, sometimes lead actors to interpret Viola's reaction as full of fear and anxiety at where the situation may lead.

Afterwards, discuss which approach you found more effective and realistic. Suggest any other emotions Viola could display in her soliloquy.

b This soliloquy is like a one-person conversation in which Viola asks herself questions and tries to answer them. In your group, speak or perform the soliloquy to highlight this. One person reads each question, and the other members of the group take turns in reading out the responses. This should give the impression of many Violas debating different aspects of her conflicted feelings.

c Prepare an audio recording of your preferred interpretation of the speech (you could use a single performer or have multiple voices representing Viola). When you are happy with the recording, prepare a sequence of images (these may be photographs, captions or sketches you have taken, made or researched) to overlay and accompany the recording as a presentation. The images should represent Viola's feelings and the 'knot' in which she finds herself.

1 Drunk again! (in pairs)

To establish a mood for Act 2 Scene 3, take parts and read lines 1–12 in the style of drunken men (see Activity 1 on p. 24). Deliver the lines very, very slowly, as if you are muddled but still trying to develop a logical argument.

---

1 **in this churlish messenger**
通过这个粗野的送信的

2 **pregnant enemy** 狡猾的魔鬼

3 **the proper-false** 英俊的伪君子

4 **waxen** 蜡一样（可塑）

5 **frailty** 脆弱；软弱

6 **fadge** 有结果

7 **dote on** = fond of

8 **thriftless** 徒劳，无益

9 **betimes** 一大早

10 *diluculo surgere* 黎明即起，有益身体（拉丁文成语）

11 **can** 酒杯，饮具

12 **four elements** 四种元素（指土、气、火、水）

40

She loves me sure; the cunning of her passion
Invites me in this churlish messenger[1].   20
None of my lord's ring? Why, he sent her none;
I am the man; if it be so, as 'tis,
Poor lady, she were better love a dream.
Disguise, I see thou art a wickedness,
Wherein the pregnant enemy[2] does much.   25
How easy is it for the proper-false[3]
In women's waxen[4] hearts to set their forms!
Alas, our frailty[5] is the cause, not we,
For such as we are made of, such we be.
How will this fadge[6]? My master loves her dearly,   30
And I (poor monster) fond as much on him
As she (mistaken) seems to dote on[7] me.
What will become of this? As I am man,
My state is desperate for my master's love;
As I am woman – now alas the day! –   35
What thriftless[8] sighs shall poor Olivia breathe?
O time, thou must untangle this, not I;
It is too hard a knot for me t'untie.   [*Exit*]

Act 2 Scene 3
A room in Olivia's house

Enter SIR TOBY *and* SIR ANDREW

SIR TOBY   Approach, Sir Andrew. Not to be abed after midnight is to
be up betimes[9], and *diluculo surgere*[10], thou know'st –

SIR ANDREW   Nay, by my troth, I know not; but I know to be up late
is to be up late.

SIR TOBY   A false conclusion: I hate it as an unfilled can[11]. To be up after   5
midnight and to go bed then is early; so that to go to bed after
midnight is to go to bed betimes. Does not our lives consist of the
four elements[12]?

SIR ANDREW   Faith, so they say, but I think it rather consists of eating
and drinking.   10

Feste mimics Sir Andrew's stupidity, and talks a good deal of nonsense. But Sir Andrew enjoys the joke and calls for a song. At Sir Toby's request, Feste sings a love song.

 剧情简介： 费斯特模仿安褚爵士的愚蠢言行，说了一大堆废话。安褚爵士却喜欢这些玩笑，并要求费斯特唱一首歌。在托比爵士的要求下，费斯特唱了一首情歌。

Language in the play 剧中语言

Feste makes a fool of Sir Andrew! (in pairs)

Feste has been mocking Sir Andrew without Sir Andrew realising it. Lines 19–25 include a sequence of made-up terms – 'Pigrogromitus', 'the Vapians' and 'the equinoctial of Queubus' are all Shakespeare's own nonsense language inventions. Feste has been spinning Sir Andrew line after line of intellectual-sounding nonsense, which Sir Andrew has taken to be sincere. Notice that earlier in the scene (line 11) Sir Toby scorns Sir Andrew's silliness, sarcastically calling him 'a scholar'.

a Make a list of every nonsense word or phrase that Feste uses. Improvise a scene in which Feste and Sir Andrew exchange some of these nonsense terms. You may wish to invent a few of your own to add to the list. Try to create the sense that Sir Andrew is impressed by Feste's skills with language, whereas Feste is scornful and mocking of Sir Andrew's gullibility (轻信).

b A few critics think that some sense can be made of lines 23–5, whereas others think it is sheer playful nonsense. Discuss this, and decide what you think 'impeticos thy gratility' could possibly mean.

Themes 主题分析

A bittersweet love song (in threes)

Feste's song begins in an upbeat way, depicting hopes of love. However, the second verse is more poignant (痛苦) and bittersweet, suggesting that one should seize the moments for fun and love when they come along, because youth ends all too quickly.

a Divide the lines of each verse equally between Sir Toby, Sir Andrew and Feste. Explore different ways of delivering the song (either speaking or singing). The first verse should convey hope and romantic sentiments; the second should be much more introspective (内省) and gentle, expressing fear of wasted opportunity, lost youth and possible loneliness.

b Do you think that the contrast between hopeful, joyful romance and lost opportunities in this song reflects the play as a whole? Discuss and share ideas about which characters and ideas in the play are reflected by the words of this song.

1 **Marian** （Maria 的昵称）

2 **stoup** （能装1升多酒的）酒罐

3 **i'faith** = in faith （真的，确实）

4 **'We Three'** （显示有两个傻瓜头像的著名酒馆标志，提示看此标志的人是第三个傻瓜）

5 **catch** 对歌，联唱（第45页52行、54行catch均为此义）

6 **breast** 嗓子

7 **leg** （跳舞的）腿

8 **Pigrogromitus** （这很可能是安褚对教宗格瑞高略 [Pont. Gregorius] 的误读，包括随后的Vapians和 Queubus在内，这种误读的结果实际上形成了考验读者和观众知识和智力的字母异位词）

9 **Vapians** 维帕亚人（费斯特或莎士比亚以为意大利帕维亚大学 [University of Pavia] 的学者参与了这场历法改革，安褚显然记错了Pavians的读音）

10 **equinoctial** = equatorial rule （关于赤道的规定，更准确地说是关于赤道年 [tropical year] 或阳历年 [solar year] 的规定。新历法将一年的平均长度由儒略历的365.25天缩短为365.2425天，还规定以后一般每四年一闰。为了让春分 [vernal equinox] 回到325年基督教第一次尼西亚公会议 [The First Council of Nicaea] 时的基准点，格瑞高略决定将当年10月4日后的10天删去，日历直接跳到10月15日，这样原先的12月27日在新历中就成了下一年的1月6日，即主显日。）

11 **Queubus** （恺撒瑞的尤色博 [Eusebius Caesariensis，约260—339年] 出席并记录下第一次尼西亚公会议，被视为基督教史之父。安褚没有听明白费斯特说的是谁，将其稀里糊涂地说成Queubus。）

（后续注释见第50页）

SIR TOBY   Th'art a scholar; let us therefore eat and drink. Marian[1], I
        say, a stoup[2] of wine!

Enter CLOWN [FESTE]

SIR ANDREW   Here comes the fool, i'faith[3].

FESTE   How now, my hearts? Did you never see the picture of 'We
        Three'[4]?   15

SIR TOBY   Welcome, ass. Now let's have a catch[5].

SIR ANDREW   By my troth, the fool has an excellent breast[6]. I had rather
        than forty shillings I had such a leg[7], and so sweet a breath to sing,
        as the fool has. In sooth, thou wast in very gracious fooling last
        night, when thou spok'st of Pigrogromitus[8], of the Vapians[9] passing   20
        the equinoctial[10] of Queubus[11]. 'Twas very good, i'faith: I sent thee
        sixpence for thy leman[12]; hadst it?

FESTE   I did impeticos thy gratillity[13]: for Malvolio's nose is no whipstock[14];
        my lady has a white hand[15], and the Myrmidons[16] are no bottle-ale
        houses[17].   25

SIR ANDREW   Excellent! Why this is the best fooling, when all is done.
        Now a song.

SIR TOBY   Come on, there is sixpence for you. Let's have a song.

SIR ANDREW   There's a testril[18] of me, too; if one knight give a –

FESTE   Would you have a love song or a song of good life?   30

SIR TOBY   A love song, a love song.

SIR ANDREW   Ay, ay. I care not for good life.

(*Clown [Feste] sings*)

    O mistress mine, where are you roaming?
    O stay and hear, your true love's coming,
        That can sing both high and low[19].   35
    Trip[20] no further, pretty sweeting;
    Journeys end in lovers meeting,
        Every wise man's son[21] doth know.

SIR ANDREW   Excellent good, i'faith.

SIR TOBY   Good, good.   40

FESTE   [*Sings*] What is love? 'Tis not hereafter;
    Present mirth hath present laughter;
        What's to come is still[22] unsure.
    In delay there lies no plenty[23],
    Then come kiss me, sweet and twenty[24];   45
        Youth's a stuff will not endure.

The three men sing together. Maria pleads with them to be quiet, but they carry on regardless. Malvolio enters and rebukes the revellers.

剧情简介：三人一起唱起来。玛蕊娅请他们安静些，但他们继续唱，不加理会。马尔沃琉上场，责备这些狂欢者。

▲ 'Sneck up!' Sir Toby shows absolute disdain and disgust when Malvolio attempts to break up their party and tell them off. Can you suggest a couple of different ways of delivering this line?

Stagecraft 导演技巧

Malvolio the party pooper (派对杀手；扫兴的人)

Staging Malvolio's entrance invites every director and actor to surprise and amuse the audience. Often he is carrying a lamp or a candle, and sometimes he throws on the lights dramatically or shines torches in the faces of the revellers. One Malvolio was portrayed with curlers in his hair!

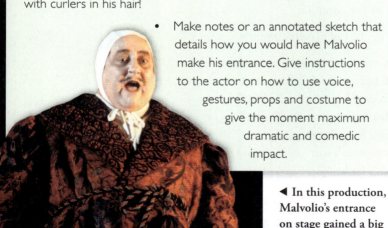

- Make notes or an annotated sketch that details how you would have Malvolio make his entrance. Give instructions to the actor on how to use voice, gestures, props and costume to give the moment maximum dramatic and comedic impact.

◄ In this production, Malvolio's entrance on stage gained a big laugh from the audience due to his ridiculous nightcap and dressing gown. He also entered from a raised balcony, allowing him to literally 'look down' on the revellers.

1 mellifluous 甜美
2 contagious 有传染性（暗示费斯特有口臭）
3 dulcet 动听
4 welkin 天空
5 draw … weaver 让一名织工焕发出三个人精（当时织工有擅于唱圣歌的名声）
6 And = If
7 dog 擅长
8 By'r lady = By Our Lady（向圣母发誓）
9 catch 对歌
10 Thou knave 你这奴才（对歌时的对骂语）
11 constrain'd 迫不得已（因对歌要求）
12 caterwauling 猫叫，难听的号叫
13 Cataian 契丹人（此处指骗子）
14 Peg-a-Ramsey 像个醋坛子婆娘（一首古老歌谣的名字）
15 consanguineous 同宗，血亲
16 Tilly vally 瞎扯，胡扯
17 Beshrew me 活见鬼
18 gabble 咕哝
19 tinkers 补锅匠
20 alehouse 酒馆
21 coziers 鞋匠
22 mitigation or remorse 停下来或放低声音
23 time 节拍
24 Sneck up! 滚开！去死吧！

SIR ANDREW   A mellifluous[1] voice, as I am true knight.

SIR TOBY   A contagious[2] breath.

SIR ANDREW   Very sweet, and contagious, i'faith.

SIR TOBY   To hear by the nose, it is dulcet[3] in contagion. But shall we   50
make the welkin[4] dance indeed? Shall we rouse the night owl in a
catch that will draw three souls out of one weaver[5]? Shall we do
that?

SIR ANDREW   And[6] you love me, let's do't: I am dog[7] at a catch.

FESTE   By'r lady[8], sir, and some dogs will catch[9] well.   55

SIR ANDREW   Most certain. Let our catch be, 'Thou knave'[10].

FESTE   'Hold thy peace, thou knave', knight? I shall be constrain'd[11] in't
to call thee knave, knight.

SIR ANDREW   'Tis not the first time I have constrained one to call me
knave. Begin, fool. It begins, 'Hold thy peace.'   60

FESTE   I shall never begin if I hold my peace.

SIR ANDREW   Good, i'faith. Come, begin.

(*Catch sung*)

Enter MARIA

MARIA   What a caterwauling[12] do you keep here! If my lady have not
called up her steward Malvolio and bid him turn you out of doors,
never trust me.   65

SIR TOBY   My lady's a Cataian[13], we are politicians, Malvolio's a
Peg-a-Ramsey[14], and [*Sings*] 'Three merry men be we.' Am not I
consanguineous[15]? Am I not of her blood? Tilly vally[16]! 'Lady!'
[*Sings*] 'There dwelt a man in Babylon, lady, lady.'

FESTE   Beshrew me[17], the knight's in admirable fooling.   70

SIR ANDREW   Ay, he does well enough if he be disposed, and so do I,
too; he does it with a better grace, but I do it more natural.

SIR TOBY   [*Sings*] O'the twelfth day of December –

MARIA   For the love o'God, peace!

Enter MALVOLIO

MALVOLIO   My masters, are you mad? Or what are you? Have you no   75
wit, manners, nor honesty but to gabble[18] like tinkers[19] at this time
of night? Do ye make an alehouse[20] of my lady's house, that ye squeak
out your coziers'[21] catches without any mitigation or remorse[22] of
voice? Is there no respect of place, persons, nor time in you?

SIR TOBY   We did keep time[23], sir, in our catches. Sneck up![24]   80

Malvolio tells Sir Toby that Olivia wishes him to reform or leave her house. Sir Toby mocks Malvolio, who leaves, threatening Maria. She advises Sir Toby to behave, and begins to lay a plan to trick Malvolio.

 剧情简介：马尔沃琉告诉托比爵士娥丽维娅希望他改过自新，不然就离开她家。托比爵士嘲笑马尔沃琉。马尔沃琉离去，走之前还威胁了玛蕊娅。玛蕊娅劝托比爵士要守规矩，并开始谋划捉弄马尔沃琉。

1 Mocking Malvolio (in fours)

Sir Toby and Feste sing an old song to annoy Malvolio, refusing to take him seriously. Sir Toby forcefully reminds Malvolio of his inferior social status: 'Go, sir, rub your chain with crumbs' (as Olivia's steward, Malvolio wears a chain of office – Sir Toby is suggesting Malvolio polishes it).

- Take parts and act out the episode in lines 75–105. Malvolio must try to remain dignified throughout, but Sir Toby (with support from Feste) should be as irritating and obstinate as possible. Maria has to decide to what extent she will join in.

Write about it 写作练习

'cakes and ale' – competing visions of 'virtue'

In Shakespeare's time, many Puritans (strictly disciplined English Protestants) hated the celebrations surrounding Christmas and Easter, thinking they were just an excuse to over-eat and get drunk. Malvolio can be viewed as a representation of such puritan values. 'Cakes and ale' is Sir Toby's **metaphor** (隐喻) for enjoyment and celebration (see p. 164). Equally offensive to Puritans would have been Feste's mention of the Catholic figure St Anne, mother of the Virgin Mary (line 100).

Decide whether you think Malvolio is being fairly treated. Is he just a puritan killjoy or does he have good cause to criticise Sir Toby? Write a paragraph exploring your views on the balance of blame and virtue in this scene. You could use the prompts below to get you started, or devise your own.

- Sir Toby is right to insult and ignore Malvolio because …
- For example, he says …
- On the other hand, Malvolio is justified in his criticism because …
- The audience can see this when he says … (insert evidence/ quotation)
- I think the most virtuous character in this scene is _____ because …

Malvolio's report to Olivia (in pairs)

- In character as Malvolio and Olivia, improvise Malvolio reporting to Olivia on what has happened. What questions will Olivia ask? Will Malvolio exaggerate or report accurately?
- One of you writes an exaggerated report of the incident from Malvolio to Olivia, and the other writes Olivia's response.

1 be round　直言
2 bade　指示，吩咐
3 harbours　收留
4 nothing allied to your disorders
　完全不能容忍您的胡言乱语
5 misdemeanours　不端行为
6 and it would please you = if it would be so kind of you
7 by St Anne　向圣安妮发誓
　（圣安妮为伪经中圣母马利亚之母）
8 ginger　姜（用来给啤酒调味）
9 give … rule　为这些不守规矩的行为提供办法（指酒）
10 the field　决斗
11 indignation　愤怒
12 gull him into an ayword　把他哄成个大笑料
13 a common recreation　常见的消遣对象
14 Possess us　告诉我们

46

MALVOLIO   Sir Toby, I must be round[1] with you. My lady bade[2] me tell you that, though she harbours[3] you as her kinsman, she's nothing allied to your disorders[4]. If you can separate yourself and your misdemeanours[5], you are welcome to the house; if not, and it would please you[6] to take leave of her, she is very willing to bid you farewell.   85

SIR TOBY   [*Sings*] Farewell, dear heart, since I must needs be gone.

MARIA   Nay, good Sir Toby.

FESTE   [*Sings*] His eyes do show his days are almost done.

MALVOLIO   Is't even so?

SIR TOBY   [*Sings*] But I will never die.   90

FESTE   [*Sings*] Sir Toby, there you lie.

MALVOLIO   This is much credit to you.

SIR TOBY   [*Sings*] Shall I bid him go?

FESTE   [*Sings*] What and if you do?

SIR TOBY   [*Sings*] Shall I bid him go, and spare not?   95

FESTE   [*Sings*] O no, no, no, no, you dare not.

SIR TOBY   Out o'time, sir? Ye lie! Art any more than a steward? Dost thou think because thou art virtuous there shall be no more cakes and ale?

FESTE   Yes, by St Anne[7], and ginger[8] shall be hot i'th'mouth too.   100

[*Exit*]

SIR TOBY   Th'art i'th'right. Go, sir, rub your chain with crumbs. A stoup of wine, Maria!

MALVOLIO   Mistress Mary, if you prized my lady's favour at anything more than contempt, you would not give means for this uncivil rule[9]; she shall know of it, by this hand.   *Exit*   105

MARIA   Go shake your ears.

SIR ANDREW   'Twere as good a deed as to drink when a man's a-hungry, to challenge him the field[10], and then to break promise with him, and make a fool of him.

SIR TOBY   Do't, knight. I'll write thee a challenge, or I'll deliver thy indignation[11] to him by word of mouth.   110

MARIA   Sweet Sir Toby, be patient for tonight. Since the youth of the count's was today with my lady, she is much out of quiet. For Monsieur Malvolio, let me alone with him. If I do not gull him into an ayword[12], and make him a common recreation[13], do not think I have wit enough to lie straight in my bed. I know I can do it.   115

SIR TOBY   Possess us[14], possess us, tell us something of him.

MARIA   Marry, sir, sometimes he is a kind of puritan.

SIR ANDREW   O if I thought that, I'd beat him like a dog!   120

Maria criticises Malvolio's self-importance and reveals her plan. She will write him a love letter, supposedly from Olivia. Malvolio's vanity will make a fool of him. Sir Toby again attempts to get more of Sir Andrew's money.

剧情简介：玛蕊娅批评马尔沃琉的妄自尊大并说出了她的计划。她会给马尔沃琉写一封情书，假装是娥丽维娅写给他的。马尔沃琉的虚荣会使他成为一个傻瓜。托比爵士又一次试图从安褚爵士那里捞到更多的钱。

Themes 主题分析

Debating the right to party (in large groups)

Act 2 Scene 3 explores the conflict between an enjoyment of excess (Sir Toby and Sir Andrew) and the need for restraint and self-control (Malvolio).

- Divide into two groups, the 'pleasure-seekers' and the 'Puritans', to debate the following motion: 'We believe that Sir Toby and his friends are innocent pleasure-seekers.' Both sides have ten minutes to prepare their arguments, which should be supported by quotations from the play (from the script opposite and elsewhere). Decide who will speak on which points. Everyone in the group should make at least one point.

- The 'pleasure-seekers' propose the motion and speak first. They should defend Sir Toby and his friends. The 'Puritans' oppose and speak second. They should defend Malvolio's point of view. Alternate your speakers between the proposition and the opposition.

1 Planning to trick Malvolio (in threes)

Take parts as Maria, Sir Toby and Sir Andrew. Put your heads close together. Whisper lines 124–48 to each other, like conspirators plotting Malvolio's downfall. Afterwards, discuss how the lines could be delivered on stage to increase the audience's enjoyment.

Characters 人物分析

Views on Malvolio (in pairs)

In lines 124–9, Maria describes in detail how she sees Malvolio:

'a time-pleaser' he's a time-server (趋炎附势者) or sycophant (马屁精) (creep)

'an affectioned ass' and an affected fool

'that cons state ... swarths' who learns high-sounding jargon (行话) by heart and quotes it endlessly

'The best persuaded of himself' he thinks he's wonderful

'so crammed ... excellencies' and has every desirable quality

'that it is ... love him' he believes everyone loves him.

- Mime each of these descriptions twice: once from Maria's point of view, and then again to reflect Malvolio's own view of himself.

1. exquisite 绝妙
2. cons ... swarths 熟记名言名句，再大段大段背出来
3. The best persuaded of himself 自认为天下第一
4. vice 弱点
5. epistles 书信
6. gait 步态
7. complexion 肤色，面色
8. personated 描述，描写
9. device 计谋，圈套
10. a horse of that colour 这样一件事
11. physic 药
12. construction 理解，解释
13. Penthesilea 潘瑟悉莉娅（又译作"彭忒西勒亚"，希腊神话中的亚马孙女王，身材矮小，在特洛伊战争中率军增援特洛伊，先大败希腊联军，后单挑阿喀琉斯，被对手所杀）
14. Before me 以我的灵魂起誓（Before God 的仿句）
15. beagle 比格犬（一种小猎犬，暗指玛蕊娅个头小）
16. recover 赢得（娶）
17. a foul way out 差得太远
18. cut 被剪短尾巴的马或骟马
19. burn some sack 温一些雪莉酒

48

SIR TOBY   What, for being a puritan? Thy exquisite[1] reason, dear knight?

SIR ANDREW   I have no exquisite reason for't, but I have reason good enough.

MARIA   The devil a puritan that he is, or anything constantly but a time-pleaser, an affectioned ass, that cons state without book and utters it by great swarths[2]. The best persuaded of himself[3]: so crammed (as he thinks) with excellencies, that it is his grounds of faith that all that look on him love him; and on that vice[4] in him will my revenge find notable cause to work.   125

SIR TOBY   What wilt thou do?   130

MARIA   I will drop in his way some obscure epistles[5] of love, wherein by the colour of his beard, the shape of his leg, the manner of his gait[6], the expressure of his eye, forehead, and complexion[7], he shall find himself most feelingly personated[8]. I can write very like my lady your niece; on a forgotten matter we can hardly make distinction of our hands.   135

SIR TOBY   Excellent, I smell a device[9].

SIR ANDREW   I have't in my nose, too.

SIR TOBY   He shall think by the letters that thou wilt drop that they come from my niece, and that she's in love with him.   140

MARIA   My purpose is indeed a horse of that colour[10].

SIR ANDREW   And your horse now would make him an ass.

MARIA   Ass, I doubt not.

SIR ANDREW   O 'twill be admirable!

MARIA   Sport royal, I warrant you: I know my physic[11] will work with him. I will plant you two, and let the fool make a third, where he shall find the letter. Observe his construction[12] of it. For this night, to bed, and dream on the event. Farewell.   *Exit*   145

SIR TOBY   Good night, Penthesilea[13].

SIR ANDREW   Before me[14], she's a good wench.   150

SIR TOBY   She's a beagle[15], true bred, and one that adores me. What o'that?

SIR ANDREW   I was adored once, too.

SIR TOBY   Let's to bed, knight. Thou hadst need send for more money.

SIR ANDREW   If I cannot recover[16] your niece, I am a foul way out[17].   155

SIR TOBY   Send for money, knight; if thou hast her not i'th'end, call me 'cut[18]'.

SIR ANDREW   If I do not, never trust me; take it how you will.

SIR TOBY   Come, come, I'll go burn some sack[19]; 'tis too late to go to bed now. Come, knight, come, knight.   160

Exeunt

Orsino calls for music to cheer him up, and sends for Feste. Orsino then claims that he is the model of all true lovers, because Olivia is constantly in his thoughts.

剧情简介：奥悉诺吩咐奏乐以使自己振奋，并派人去请费斯特。奥悉诺后又声称他是所有真心恋人的典范，因为他一直想着娥丽维娅。

Stagecraft 导演技巧

Every picture tells a story

Theatre is a very powerful medium of communication, because spoken words are accompanied by physical action and images. Even actors who do not speak can convey a rich variety of meanings through the way they stand, move and relate to others on stage. Viola does not speak until line 19. What is she doing up to then? What is her 'business' (see p. 12) on stage?

- In your Director's Journal, write a set of instructions to an actor playing Viola, to help describe how she (or he) should physically express Viola's thoughts and feelings as Orsino speaks. Describe where Viola should stand or sit (or lie) in relation to Orsino.

Characters 人物分析

Orsino: the example of 'all true lovers'? (in small groups)

As usual, Orsino is self-indulgently casting himself in the role of the 'true lover': melancholy, changeable, obsessed with thoughts of his beloved. Has Orsino got it right, or is he just deceiving himself?

a Talk together about whether you agree that 'true lovers' always have a 'constant image' of their beloved in mind.

b What 'constant image' do you think Orsino really has in mind? Olivia? Himself? Some abstract notion of 'love'? Or something else?

c Write a list of the things you think define a 'true lover', and a parallel list of the things you think Orsino might look for in one. Are they similar or very different?

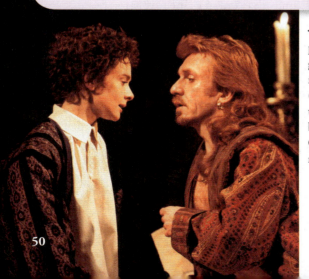

◀ Lines 13–20 are very poetic, and Shakespeare gives them a background musical accompaniment (伴奏). In many productions, there is clear sexual tension between Orsino and Viola/Cesario during this seemingly romantic moment.

1 good morrow = good morning
2 but = only
3 antique 古香古色
4 light airs 轻松的曲子
5 recollected terms 精美的歌词
6 brisk and giddy-pacèd 轻佻又节拍飞快
7 pangs 极度的痛苦
8 Unstaid and skittish 毫无节制，反复无常
9 all motions else 所有其他情感（motion = emotion）
10 Save ... beloved 只有对那位可爱生灵的朝思暮想例外
11 gives a very echo to 与……共鸣
12 seat 宝座（指心）
13 throned 即位

（上接第42页）

12 leman 情人，心上人
13 impeticos ... gratillity 收下……赏钱 / 小费（这是费斯特生造的两个词）
14 whipstock 鞭子把
15 has a white hand 手很白净（出身高贵）
16 Myrmidons 莫弥敦人（特洛伊战争时阿喀琉斯的追随者；这里用作高档宾馆的名称，因为伦敦当时有一家豪华宾馆名叫Mermaid Inn）
17 bottle-ale houses 酒栈（这里指低档酒店）
18 testril 泰斯特（一种面值六便士的硬币，大致相当于我们今天说的"五毛钱"）
19 both high and low 声音既可高又可低
20 Trip = Go
21 wise man's son 智者之子（在这句成语里实指"傻子"）
22 still = always
23 plenty = profit（好处）
24 sweet and twenty = sweet twenty-year-old或twenty sweethearts

Act 2 Scene 4
Orsino's palace

Enter DUKE ORSINO, VIOLA, CURIO, *and Lords and Musicians*

ORSINO   Give me some music –
         [*Musicians step forward*]
                 Now good morrow[1], friends;
   Now, good Cesario – but[2] that piece of song,
   That old and antique[3] song we heard last night;
   Methought it did relieve my passion much,
   More than light airs[4] and recollected terms[5]   5
   Of these most brisk and giddy-pacèd[6] times.
   Come, but one verse.

CURIO   He is not here, so please your lordship, that should sing it.

ORSINO   Who was it?

CURIO   Feste, the jester, my lord, a fool that the Lady Olivia's father   10
took much delight in. He is about the house.

ORSINO   Seek him out, and play the tune the while.

                                     [*Exit Curio*]

         (*Music plays*)
   Come hither, boy; if ever thou shalt love,
   In the sweet pangs[7] of it, remember me:
   For such as I am, all true lovers are,   15
   Unstaid and skittish[8] in all motions else[9],
   Save in the constant image of the creature
   That is beloved[10]. How dost thou like this tune?

VIOLA   It gives a very echo to[11] the seat[12]
   Where love is throned[13].

Orsino advises Viola that women should marry men older than themselves, because men are fickle, and women soon lose their looks. He asks Feste to sing an old song of love.

 剧情简介：奥悉诺向薇娥拉提议说女人应该嫁给比自己年长一些的男人，因为男人三心二意，而女人的美貌会很快消失。他让费斯特唱一首老情歌。

Write about it 写作练习

Shakespeare's own experience? Your views?

It is possible that Shakespeare was thinking of his own marriage when he wrote lines 27–39. In 1582, aged just eighteen, he married Anne Hathaway, who was eight years older than him. Orsino advises Viola that a woman should marry a man older than herself. She will thus be better able to keep her husband's affection, because men's emotions are more unstable than women's, and women's beauty quickly fades.

- Using quotations and examples from the play to support your ideas, write a paragraph exploring, explaining and justifying your own opinion of one of the following statements:

  'Orsino's advice is good.'

  'Shakespeare is allowing Orsino to give Viola/Cesario sexist advice.'

  'Men are more fickle than women.'

1 More personal experience? (in pairs)

Orsino calls for a song. He uses an image that Shakespeare may have seen and heard in Stratford-upon-Avon: women outside their cottages spinning flax or wool, and young girls lace-making with bone bobbins (线轴), all singing at their work. Or perhaps Shakespeare remembered what he saw as he walked from his lodgings in the City of London to the Globe Theatre on Bankside: the Huguenots (胡格诺派教徒，指16—17世纪法国基督教新教徒), refugees from France, who became lace-makers and cloth-workers.

a Read lines 41–6 aloud three or four times. Then close your eyes. Imagine the picture the lines evoke. Describe to your partner what you 'see' in your head.

b 'Lines 41–6 are simply the dreamy fantasies of a self-indulgent, rich man, in love with the idea of being in love, and quite out of touch with reality.' Discuss the extent to which you agree with this statement. Is it too harsh? Is Orsino more sincere than this?

c There is comic potential in the romantic sentimentality and yearning Orsino displays next to Viola's obvious and growing infatuation. Perform lines 34–46 with an emphasis on showing Orsino's hunger for love and Viola's barely concealed hunger for Orsino!

1 masterly   像大师一样
2 stayed upon some favour   盯在某个脸蛋上 (favour = face)
3 by your favour   您可以说
4 Of your complexion   像您这相貌的
5 still = always
6 wears (to)   合身；适合
7 So sways she level   这样她才能保持势均力敌
8 fancies   爱情
9 giddy and unfirm   轻佻，不稳
10 worn   遗忘
11 hold the bent   （像拉开的弓一样）保持满弓状态
12 displayed   绽放
13 spinsters and the knitters   纺线工和针织工
14 free … bones   无忧无虑地用拐骨线轴织花边的少女
15 chant   唱
16 silly sooth   大实话
17 dallies   玩弄

ORSINO	Thou dost speak masterly[1]. 20
	My life upon't, young though thou art, thine eye
	Hath stayed upon some favour[2] that it loves;
	Hath it not, boy?
VIOLA	A little, by your favour[3].
ORSINO	What kind of woman is't?
VIOLA	Of your complexion[4].
ORSINO	She is not worth thee then. What years, i'faith? 25
VIOLA	About your years, my lord.
ORSINO	Too old, by heaven! Let still[5] the woman take
	An elder than herself; so wears[6] she to him;
	So sways she level[7] in her husband's heart;
	For, boy, however we do praise ourselves, 30
	Our fancies[8] are more giddy and unfirm[9],
	More longing, wavering, sooner lost and worn[10],
	Than women's are.
VIOLA	I think it well, my lord.
ORSINO	Then let thy love be younger than thyself,
	Or thy affection cannot hold the bent[11]: 35
	For women are as roses, whose fair flower,
	Being once displayed[12], doth fall that very hour.
VIOLA	And so they are. Alas, that they are so:
	To die, even when they to perfection grow!

Enter CURIO *and* CLOWN [FESTE]

ORSINO	O fellow, come, the song we had last night. 40
	Mark it, Cesario, it is old and plain;
	The spinsters and the knitters[13] in the sun,
	And the free maids that weave their thread with bones[14],
	Do use to chant[15] it; it is silly sooth[16],
	And dallies[17] with the innocence of love 45
	Like the old age.
FESTE	Are you ready, sir?
ORSINO	Ay, prithee sing.

Feste sings a sad song about a true lover who died for love. He leaves, commenting on Orsino's changeable moods. Orsino instructs Viola to tell Olivia that he loves not her wealth, but her beauty.

剧情简介： 费斯特唱了一首歌颂殉情恋人的悲歌。他离开时对奥悉诺变化无常的情绪进行了一番评论。奥悉诺吩咐薇娥拉去告诉娥丽维娅，他爱的不是她的财富而是她的美貌。

Stagecraft 导演技巧

Feste's mournful song

Feste's song is about a melancholy lover who dies for love and wants to be forgotten. Cypress and yew trees (红豆杉) were traditionally associated with death. They were – and still are – found in many churchyards. Coffins were often made of cypress wood ('sad cypress'). In the production above, the director emphasised the sombre (阴郁) nature of the song by having dark costumes and candles on stage, and by placing the actress playing Olivia behind a large frame.

a Why you think the director decided to have Olivia on stage during Feste's song? What do you think this adds to the scene?

b Sketch or write a set of notes in your Director's Journal to describe how you would stage this scene. Make reference to costume, lighting and the actions and positions of characters on stage. Try to come up with something original.

1 I love you, not your money (in pairs)

That's the message (lines 75–82) that Orsino orders Viola to carry to Olivia, 'yond same sovereign cruelty'. To bring out Orsino's concern about choosing what he thinks are the right words to express his feelings, try the following activities.

a One person reads the lines aloud. The other echoes every elaborate or grand phrase (e.g. 'sovereign cruelty', 'more noble than the world').

b Write down the advice you would offer an actor playing Orsino. Suggest how, in speech and action, he or she could express Orsino's character through these eight lines.

1 **Come away** 快过来
2 **sad cypress** 柏木棺材
3 **Fie away** 飞走
4 **stuck all with yew** 上面布满红豆杉枝
5 **My part ... it** = The part I have played as a dying lover is so true that no one has shared it
6 **strown** 撒，散
7 **melancholy god** 忧郁之神（即土星 [Saturn]，主管忧郁）
8 **taffeta** 塔夫绸（从不同角度看颜色会变化）
9 **opal** 澳宝石（又因其常见的蛋白色而译作"蛋白石"，类似变石或猫眼石之类的金绿宝石，在不同光线下显出不同颜色）
10 **give place** 退下
11 **yond same sovereign cruelty** 那个狠心女王
12 **Prizes** 看重
13 **parts** 遗产，财富
14 **pranks** 装扮，打扮

54

(*Music*)
The Song

Come away[1], come away, death,
And in sad cypress[2] let me be laid.   50
Fie away[3], fie away, breath,
I am slain by a fair cruel maid;
   My shroud of white, stuck all with yew[4],
     O prepare it.
   My part of death no one so true   55
     Did share it[5].
Not a flower, not a flower sweet,
On my black coffin let there be strown[6];
Not a friend, not a friend greet
My poor corpse, where my bones shall be thrown: 60
   A thousand thousand sighs to save,
     Lay me, O where
   Sad true lover never find my grave,
     To weep there.

ORSINO   There's for thy pains. [*Gives money*]   65

FESTE   No pains, sir, I take pleasure in singing, sir.

ORSINO   I'll pay thy pleasure then.

FESTE   Truly, sir, and pleasure will be paid, one time or another.

ORSINO   Give me now leave to leave thee.

FESTE   Now the melancholy god[7] protect thee, and the tailor make thy   70
doublet of changeable taffeta[8], for thy mind is a very opal[9]. I would
have men of such constancy put to sea, that their business might
be everything and their intent everywhere, for that's it that always
makes a good voyage of nothing. Farewell.   *Exit*

ORSINO   Let all the rest give place[10].

[*Curio and attendants retire*]

        Once more, Cesario,   75
Get thee to yond same sovereign cruelty[11].
Tell her my love, more noble than the world,
Prizes[12] not quantity of dirty lands;
The parts[13] that fortune hath bestowed upon her
Tell her I hold as giddily as fortune;   80
But 'tis that miracle and queen of gems
That nature pranks[14] her in attracts my soul.

VIOLA   But if she cannot love you, sir?

ORSINO   I cannot be so answered.

Orsino claims that his capacity for love is greater than that of any woman. Viola, hinting at her love for Orsino, says that women love as deeply as men, and that men boast about being in love.

 剧情简介：奥悉诺声称他对爱情的投入比任何女人都多。薇娥拉暗示自己爱奥悉诺，说女人可以像男人一样爱得深沉，她还说男人会炫耀自己坠入爱河。

Themes 主题分析

'My father had a daughter loved a man' (in pairs)

Much of the comedy in the play is generated by the gender confusion and sexual tension between characters who appear to be something that they are not. This is perhaps most evident in lines 100–20. Remember that when the play was originally performed, Viola would have been played by a young male actor pretending to be a young woman who is pretending to be a young man.

Viola's hints of her love for Orsino present every actor playing the duke with a problem: how should he respond? Does he simply not notice, or does he begin to suspect that his servant Cesario is not quite what he seems? Is Orsino unsettled by Viola's words, or is he charmed?

a Discuss how you would advise Orsino to respond to Viola's words in lines 101–18. Perform two versions: one where Orsino seems oblivious to the obvious hints from Viola, and one where he gradually becomes aware. Decide which interpretation works most effectively.

b Either devise a tableau to represent lines 110–11, or write or draw what 'Patience on a monument, / Smiling at grief' suggests to you.

c Line 117 often marks an abrupt shift in tone, as Viola realises she has almost given herself away and quickly corrects herself ('And all the brothers, too –'). Rehearse a reading or performance of lines 115–18 that makes the most of this moment for comic effect.

1 **pang of heart** 痛彻心扉
2 **sides** 前胸后背
3 **bide** 承受，经受
4 **motion of the liver** 发自肺腑的情感（当时人们认为激情生自肝脏）
5 **palate** 味觉；胃口
6 **suffers surfeit, cloyment, and revolt** 感到厌食、腹胀和恶心
7 **owe** 对……怀有
8 **blank** 空白
9 **worm i'th'bud** 花蕾里的虫
10 **damask** 粉红（原产于大马士革的一种粉红蔷薇）
11 **pined** 煎熬
12 **Patience on a monument** 墓碑上的苦人
13 **Our ... will** 我们表露出来的总是比实际感受的多
14 **that's the theme** 说的正是这事
15 **can give no place** 不会放弃
16 **denay** = denial（拒绝）

▼ In some productions, there is a lot of physical contact between Orsino and Viola in this scene to emphasise the growing (and unspoken) attraction between the pair. How far would you go with this to create maximum tension and/or maximum humour?

VIOLA	Sooth, but you must.
	Say that some lady, as perhaps there is, 85
	Hath for your love as great a pang of heart[1]
	As you have for Olivia. You cannot love her.
	You tell her so. Must she not then be answered?
ORSINO	There is no woman's sides[2]
	Can bide[3] the beating of so strong a passion 90
	As love doth give my heart; no woman's heart
	So big, to hold so much. They lack retention.
	Alas, their love may be called appetite,
	No motion of the liver[4], but the palate[5],
	That suffers surfeit, cloyment, and revolt[6], 95
	But mine is all as hungry as the sea,
	And can digest as much. Make no compare
	Between that love a woman can bear me,
	And that I owe[7] Olivia.
VIOLA	Ay, but I know –
ORSINO	What dost thou know? 100
VIOLA	Too well what love women to men may owe.
	In faith, they are as true of heart as we.
	My father had a daughter loved a man
	As it might be perhaps, were I a woman,
	I should your lordship.
ORSINO	And what's her history? 105
VIOLA	A blank[8], my lord. She never told her love,
	But let concealment like a worm i'th'bud[9]
	Feed on her damask[10] cheek. She pined[11] in thought,
	And with a green and yellow melancholy
	She sat like Patience on a monument[12], 110
	Smiling at grief. Was not this love indeed?
	We men may say more, swear more, but indeed
	Our shows are more than will[13]: for still we prove
	Much in our vows, but little in our love.
ORSINO	But died thy sister of her love, my boy? 115
VIOLA	I am all the daughters of my father's house,
	And all the brothers, too – and yet I know not.
	Sir, shall I to this lady?
ORSINO	Ay, that's the theme[14].
	To her in haste; give her this jewel; say
	My love can give no place[15], bide no denay[16]. 120
	Exeunt

Sir Toby and Fabian look forward to tricking Malvolio. Fabian has a personal grudge against Malvolio. Maria orders the men to hide and sets the trap for Malvolio: the forged letter.

剧情简介：托比爵士和费边期待着戏弄马尔沃琉。费边与马尔沃琉有个人恩怨。玛蕊娅让他们藏起来，并为马尔沃琉下了套：一封伪造的信。

1 **Come thy ways** 你过来
2 **a scruple** 一丁点儿
3 **niggardly** 小气
4 **rascally** 卑鄙
5 **sheep-biter** 咬羊的狗；嫖客
6 **exult** 非常高兴
7 **metal of India** 印度金，纯金；宝贝儿
8 **box-tree** 黄杨树（一种常青灌木或小乔木，常用于园林绿化）
9 **walk** （花园）小路
10 **contemplative** 想入非非
11 **Close** 藏好
12 **trout** 鳟鱼

Characters 人物分析

Fabian

Malvolio has reported Fabian to Olivia for bear-baiting (a cruel 'sport', not considered gentlemanly, in which a bear, chained to a post, was attacked by dogs). So Fabian is in disgrace. But just who is he? We know that he is a servant, but that's about all we've been told.

- Write a few paragraphs of an invented biography of Fabian, exploring who he is and imagining how Malvolio caught him bear-baiting. What sort of man would do that? Include details of what Fabian looks like, how he's dressed and any mannerisms (言谈举止) he may display.

Language in the play 剧中语言

Imagery (in pairs)

Lines 1–19 contain vivid imagery. Explain the meaning and effect of each of the following in just fifty words:

- **Lines 2–3** 'boiled to death with melancholy'
- **Line 5** 'sheep-biter' (insult, meaning 'woman-chaser')
- **Lines 8–9** 'fool him black and blue'
- **Line 12** 'metal of India' (Sir Toby uses other fantastic terms to describe Maria – what does this suggest about their relationship?)
- **Lines 18–19** 'the trout that must be caught by tickling' (flattery – trout can be caught by gently stroking them on their underside).

Act 2 Scene 5
Olivia's garden

Enter SIR TOBY, SIR ANDREW *and* FABIAN

SIR TOBY   Come thy ways[1], Signior Fabian.

FABIAN   Nay, I'll come. If I lose a scruple[2] of this sport, let me be boiled to death with melancholy.

SIR TOBY   Wouldst thou not be glad to have the niggardly[3] rascally[4] sheep-biter[5] come by some notable shame?   5

FABIAN   I would exult[6], man. You know he brought me out o'favour with my lady about a bear-baiting here.

SIR TOBY   To anger him, we'll have the bear again; and we will fool him black and blue, shall we not, Sir Andrew?

SIR ANDREW   And we do not, it is pity of our lives.   10

SIR TOBY   Here comes the little villain.

Enter MARIA

How now, my metal of India[7]?

MARIA   Get ye all three into the box-tree[8]. Malvolio's coming down this walk[9]. He has been yonder i'the sun practising behaviour to his own shadow this half hour. Observe him, for the love of mockery, for   15
I know this letter will make a contemplative[10] idiot of him. Close[11], in the name of jesting!

[*The men hide*]

Lie thou there [*Drops a letter*]; for here comes the trout[12] that must be caught with tickling.   *Exit*

Malvolio reveals his private fantasies. He daydreams aloud, persuading himself that Olivia loves him, and imagining that they are married. Sir Toby and Sir Andrew are enraged.

 剧情简介：马尔沃琉流露出内心的幻想，大声做着白日梦，让自己相信娥丽维娅爱上他了，并想象他们结了婚。托比爵士和安褚爵士被激怒。

Stagecraft 导演技巧

Overhearing: how do they hide? (in small groups)

Every director of the play seizes the challenge of 'the box-tree' (literally, an evergreen shrub), and aims to make this overhearing scene as hilarious as possible. There's a huge amount of potential for laughter in how Sir Toby and his friends hide. They are always on the brink of being seen by Malvolio, but just manage to avoid discovery.

In different productions, these characters have hidden behind benches, trees, hedges, statues, walls and windows. You can see some different examples on pages 58 and 62 of this book.

a Look at the photographs, then discuss which method of hiding seems the most potentially comical to you.

b Clearly the context (historical or geographical setting) that a director chooses for the play can influence how this scene is staged. Come up with an interesting context of your own, and a corresponding way of staging the 'box-tree' scene. Share your ideas with other groups.

1 Malvolio's daydreaming: a fantasy of power and revenge (in pairs)

Malvolio fantasises about becoming a count and enjoying a physical relationship with Olivia. He relishes the thought of disdainfully condescending to Sir Toby, and he daydreams haughtily about how he will treat the people under him once he has married Olivia and is all powerful. But he almost slips at lines 50–1...

a What might Malvolio have been thinking of playing with before he changed his thought to 'some rich jewel'? Try to outdo each other with the most amusing delivery of this line!

b Try imitating two of Malvolio's ways of looking superior. One of you should speak the line while the other models the 'look' he describes:

- **Lines 44–5** 'demure travel of regard' (a cool look at the servants)
- **Line 55** 'austere regard of control' (a cold and superior stare).

1 **fortune** 运气
2 **affect** 爱慕
3 **uses** 对待
4 **exalted** 高
5 **overweening** 妄自尊大
6 **Contemplation** 痴心妄想
7 **rare turkey-cock** 难得一见的公火鸡（自以为老子天下第一的家伙）
8 **jets** 趾高气扬；神气活现
9 **advanced plumes** 竖起的羽毛
10 **'Slight = by God's light** （以上帝之光发誓）
11 **Pistol him** 毙了他
12 **the Lady of the Strachy** 斯特拉奇的贵妇人（据说嫁给了自己的一个仆人）
13 **yeoman of the wardrobe** 衣柜侍从（贵族家里负责打理衣物的仆人）
14 **Jezebel** 耶洗别（《圣经》里记载的古以色列王亚哈的妻子。她信奉异教，荒淫无耻，心狠手辣，最后死于叛乱，尸体被野狗分食。）
15 **blows him** 使他自我膨胀
16 **stone-bow** 弹弓
17 **branched** 绣有花枝的
18 **humour of state** 有权有势的样子
19 **demure travel of regard** 用严肃的目光扫过
20 **Bolts and shackles!** 给他上镣铐！
21 **with an obedient start** 顺从地一个激灵
22 **make out for** 去找
23 **curtsies** 鞠躬
24 **by th'ears** （其他版本多作 with the cars）用车刑（将受审者的双手和双脚分别绑在两辆车上，将车向相反方向驱赶，以逼迫受审者招供）
25 **austere regard of control** 掌权者的严厉凝视

Enter MALVOLIO

MALVOLIO   'Tis but fortune[1]; all is fortune. Maria once told me she did   20
affect[2] me, and I have heard herself come thus near, that should she
fancy, it should be one of my complexion. Besides, she uses[3] me with
a more exalted[4] respect than any one else that follows her. What
should I think on't?

SIR TOBY   Here's an overweening[5] rogue!   25

FABIAN   O peace! Contemplation[6] makes a rare turkey-cock[7] of him; how
he jets[8] under his advanced plumes[9]!

SIR ANDREW   'Slight[10], I could so beat the rogue!

FABIAN   Peace, I say!

MALVOLIO   To be Count Malvolio!   30

SIR TOBY   Ah, rogue!

SIR ANDREW   Pistol him[11], pistol him!

FABIAN   Peace, peace!

MALVOLIO   There is example for't: the Lady of the Strachy[12] married
the yeoman of the wardrobe[13] –   35

SIR ANDREW   Fie on him, Jezebel[14]!

FABIAN   O peace! Now he's deeply in. Look how imagination blows him[15].

MALVOLIO   Having been three months married to her, sitting in my state –

SIR TOBY   O for a stone-bow[16] to hit him in the eye!

MALVOLIO   Calling my officers about me, in my branched[17] velvet gown,   40
having come from a day-bed, where I have left Olivia sleeping –

SIR TOBY   Fire and brimstone!

FABIAN   O peace, peace!

MALVOLIO   And then to have the humour of state[18]; and after a demure
travel of regard[19] – telling them I know my place, as I would they   45
should do theirs – to ask for my kinsman Toby –

SIR TOBY   Bolts and shackles![20]

FABIAN   O peace, peace, peace! Now, now.

MALVOLIO   Seven of my people, with an obedient start[21], make out for[22]
him. I frown the while, and perchance wind up my watch, or play   50
with my – some rich jewel. Toby approaches; curtsies[23] there to me –

SIR TOBY   Shall this fellow live?

FABIAN   Though our silence be drawn from us by th'ears[24], yet peace!

MALVOLIO   I extend my hand to him thus, quenching my familiar smile
with an austere regard of control[25] –   55

SIR TOBY   And does not 'Toby' take you a blow o'the lips then?

Fabian tries to prevent Sir Toby's enraged comments being overheard. Malvolio discovers the letter and thinks that he recognises the handwriting as Olivia's. He tries to figure out the contents.

✒ 剧情简介：费边尽量不让托比爵士的愤怒评论被人偷听到。马尔沃琉发现那封信，并自以为认出了娥丽维娅的笔迹，接下来试图弄懂信的内容。

In one 2007 production, Sir Toby and friends hid behind a giant Chinese parasol (遮阳伞). Another production, from 1988, used a Christmas tree in reference to the title *Twelfth Night* (see pp. 172–3).

1 prerogative　特权
2 amend　改掉
3 scab　无赖，泼皮
4 break the sinews　打断……的筋骨；破坏，毁掉
5 treasure of your time　您的宝贵时间
6 employment　事情，情况
7 woodcock near the gin　捕鸟器附近的丘鹬（谚语里的笨鸟）
8 spirit ... him　愿举止之神提示他朗读出来
9 thus ... P's = thus she makes her great P's（之前的三个字母c、u、t组成cut，意思是"切口"或"水道"，俚语里cut指"女阴"；"尿"或"撒尿"俗称pee，简称P）
10 in contempt of question　毫无疑问
11 wax　蜂蜡（古时用来给信件封口）
12 Soft　且慢
13 impressure her Lucrece　印的是她的鲁克瑞霞章（鲁克瑞霞 [Lucretia，英文转写成Lucrece] 是古罗马的一位女贵族，公元前510年遭国王塞克图·塔昆涅 [Sextus Tarquinius] 强暴后自杀，由此激发民变，导致罗马王朝的覆灭和共和国的诞生。鲁克瑞霞遂成为贞洁的象征。这里指刻有其头像的印章指环 [seal ring]。莎士比亚1594年做了一首长篇叙事诗 The Rape of Lucrece。）
14 numbers　韵律
15 brock　獾；臭东西
16 gore　刺穿
17 sway　决定；操控
18 fustian　故弄玄虚

Language in the play 剧中语言

Crude fun at Malvolio's expense! (in fours)

Shakespeare uses a crude joke in lines 72–5. Elizabethans knew that 'cut' was slang for the female genitals, and they would hear 'P's' as 'pees'. They would probably find it very funny that Sir Andrew fails to see the dirty joke. In modern productions, directors have to decide what to do with the lines and the extent to which the wordplay should be emphasised. Try performing lines 70–5 in the following ways. Decide as a group which you think is most effective, giving reasons.

- None of the three watchers, or Malvolio, are aware of the rudeness of what is being said.
- Malvolio is unaware of the rudeness of his words, while the other three can barely contain their laughter.
- Malvolio is well aware of the crudeness of his words and seems to enjoy being rude.

1 'What employment have we here?' (in small groups)

Malvolio's discovery of the letter can be creatively and comically staged (in one production, it stuck to his shoe).

- How would you stage the 'discovery'? Try it two or three different ways and share your favourite version with the class.

MALVOLIO   Saying, 'Cousin Toby, my fortunes having cast me on your niece, give me this prerogative[1] of speech – '

SIR TOBY   What, what?

MALVOLIO   'You must amend[2] your drunkenness.'   60

SIR TOBY   Out, scab[3]!

FABIAN   Nay, patience, or we break the sinews[4] of our plot.

MALVOLIO   'Besides, you waste the treasure of your time[5] with a foolish knight – '

SIR ANDREW   That's me, I warrant you.   65

MALVOLIO   'One Sir Andrew – '

SIR ANDREW   I knew 'twas I, for many do call me fool.

MALVOLIO   [Taking up the letter] What employment[6] have we here?

SIR TOBY   Now is the woodcock near the gin[7].

FABIAN   O peace, and the spirit of humours intimate reading aloud to him[8]!   70

MALVOLIO   By my life, this is my lady's hand: these be her very c's, her u's, and her t's, and thus makes she her great P's[9]. It is, in contempt of question[10], her hand.

SIR ANDREW   Her c's, her u's, and her t's: why that?   75

MALVOLIO   [Reads] 'To the unknown beloved, this, and my good wishes' – her very phrases! By your leave, wax[11]. Soft[12]! And the impressure her Lucrece[13], with which she uses to seal: 'tis my lady. To whom should this be? [Opens the letter]

FABIAN   This wins him, liver and all.   80

MALVOLIO   [Reads]   Jove knows I love,
                    But who?
                Lips, do not move:
                    No man must know.

'No man must know.' What follows? The numbers[14] altered! 'No man must know'! If this should be thee, Malvolio!   85

SIR TOBY   Marry, hang thee, brock[15]!

MALVOLIO   [Reads]   I may command where I adore,
                    But silence, like a Lucrece knife,
                With bloodless stroke my heart doth gore[16];   90
                    M.O.A.I. doth sway[17] my life.

FABIAN   A fustian[18] riddle!

SIR TOBY   Excellent wench, say I.

MALVOLIO   'M.O.A.I. doth sway my life.' Nay, but first let me see, let me see, let me see.   95

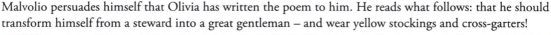Malvolio persuades himself that Olivia has written the poem to him. He reads what follows: that he should transform himself from a steward into a great gentleman – and wear yellow stockings and cross-garters!

剧情简介：马尔沃琉使自己相信这首诗是娥丽维娅写给他的。他往下读，信中说：他应该把自己从小管家变成大绅士，而且要穿黄色长袜，把袜带交叉着系！

1 Reading the letter (in small groups)

Lines 118–32 give every actor playing Malvolio a great chance to entertain the audience. Most read the letter slowly, sentence by sentence. They leave long pauses in which they can insert stage business (see p. 12), milking (榨取) the speech for laughs. For example, at 'revolve' (line 119), one Malvolio slowly turned round and round with increasing glee, as if he had made a great discovery.

a Take turns to read the letter aloud, a sentence at a time. For each sentence or phrase, create 'business' that you think will be entertaining.

b What do the overhearers do as Malvolio reads? They'll certainly be finding it hard to stop laughing. But imagine that they put on a little show for each other to illustrate each sentence of the letter, and mock Malvolio at the same time. Perform their parody*, which takes place behind Malvolio's back.

1 dressed 调制，准备
2 wing 飞行的动作或方式
3 staniel 红隼
4 checks at it （鹰）转身飞向它
5 to any formal capacity 对任何一般智力的人
6 position portend 意味
7 at a cold scent 嗅不到踪迹
8 Sowter 搜特狗
9 though ... fox 就像那气味跟狐狸的一样臭
10 The ... faults 那狗东西擅长嗅出断掉的踪迹
11 no ... probation 后面的拼写顺序对不上号
12 cudgel him 给他一棒子
13 detraction 坏话
14 simulation 谜语
15 crush this a little 在它上面加把劲
16 bow to 臣服于
17 revolve 细想
18 inure 使习惯于
19 cast thy humble slough 蜕掉你那卑微的外皮
20 tang arguments of state 当当作响地谈论政治话题
21 the trick of singularity 独特的行为习惯
22 ever cross-gartered 总是把袜带交叉着系
23 thou ... so 只要心想就会事成
24 fellow 同僚
25 alter services 变换位置

* parody 戏仿，指对一部作品进行借用，以达到调侃、嘲讽甚至致敬的目的，例如周星驰的《大话西游》。

FABIAN   What dish o'poison has she dressed[1] him!

SIR TOBY   And with what wing[2] the staniel[3] checks at it[4]!

MALVOLIO   'I may command where I adore.' Why, she may command me: I serve her; she is my lady. Why, this is evident to any formal capacity[5]. There is no obstruction in this, and the end – what should that alphabetical position portend[6]? If I could make that resemble something in me – Softly! 'M.O.A.I.' –   100

SIR TOBY   O ay, make up that! He is now at a cold scent[7].

FABIAN   Sowter[8] will cry upon't for all this, though it be as rank as a fox[9].   105

MALVOLIO   'M' – Malvolio. 'M' – why, that begins my name!

FABIAN   Did not I say he would work it out? The cur is excellent at faults[10].

MALVOLIO   'M' – but then there is no consonancy in the sequel that suffers under probation[11]. 'A' should follow, but 'O' does.   110

FABIAN   And O shall end, I hope.

SIR TOBY   Ay, or I'll cudgel him[12] and make him cry 'O'!

MALVOLIO   And then 'I' comes behind.

FABIAN   Ay, and you had any eye behind you, you might see more detraction[13] at your heels than fortunes before you.   115

MALVOLIO   'M.O.A.I.' This simulation[14] is not as the former, and yet, to crush this a little[15], it would bow to[16] me, for every one of these letters are in my name. Soft, here follows prose. [*Reads*] 'If this fall into thy hand, revolve[17]. In my stars I am above thee, but be not afraid of greatness. Some are born great, some achieve greatness,   120 and some have greatness thrust upon 'em. Thy fates open their hands; let thy blood and spirit embrace them, and, to inure[18] thyself to what thou art like to be, cast thy humble slough[19] and appear fresh. Be opposite with a kinsman, surly with servants; let thy tongue tang arguments of state[20]; put thyself into the trick of singularity[21]. She thus   125 advises thee that sighs for thee. Remember who commended thy yellow stockings and wished to see thee ever cross-gartered[22]: I say, remember. Go to, thou art made if thou desir'st to be so[23]; if not, let me see thee a steward still, the fellow[24] of servants, and not worthy to touch Fortune's fingers. Farewell. She that would alter services[25]   130 with thee,

The Fortunate-Unhappy.'

Malvolio is overjoyed. He is supremely confident that Olivia loves him. He will follow the instructions in every detail – even smiling! The conspirators are ecstatic about the success of their plot.

 剧情简介： 马尔沃琉心花怒放，信心满满地认为娥丽维娅爱上他了。他愿意逐字逐句遵照指令行事——甚至如何微笑！阴谋家们为他们的阴谋得逞而狂喜。

1 Malvolio is caught! Show his delight (in pairs)

Malvolio's joy knows no bounds. The trick has worked, and Malvolio is caught in the net of his own self-importance. Explore ways of speaking lines 133–47 to find the most entertaining presentation. Here are some suggestions to help you work out a final version:

- One person reads, and the other echoes every 'I', 'me', 'my'.
- Echo and emphasise every verb: 'discovers', 'is', 'will' and so on.
- Create a gesture or action for every sentence or phrase.
- Read the postscript (信末附言) (lines 143–6) in different ways (for example, very fast, with increasing delight, or with puzzlement).
- Turn the lines into a conversation, in which each partner reads alternate sentences or phrases. Try to outdo each other in joyfulness!
- One partner reads each sentence (or phrase) as a question. The other repeats it immediately as an emphatic statement. At 'I will smile', use all sorts of ways of showing Malvolio's difficulty in producing a smile!
- 'Exit': how does Malvolio leave the stage? Practise different ways in which he might go off. Decide the style you most prefer to give the audience maximum enjoyment.

Themes 主题分析

'when the image of it leaves him, he must run mad'
(in small groups)

After Malvolio exits at line 147, Sir Toby and friends are bubbling with excitement and delight at the trap they have set for him. Although it is certainly a great 'jest', have they gone too far? Do you think the audience will have some sympathy for Malvolio? Although he is doubtless pompous and humourless, do you think Malvolio deserves to be made to 'run mad'?

- Split your group in two. One half takes roles as 'Puritans' and the other half as 'revellers'. Each half should come up with at least three points in defence of their side – either Malvolio (the Puritans) or the tricksters (the revellers). Stand at opposite ends of the room and, in turn, argue as passionately as you can for your point of view by 'throwing' alternative viewpoints across the room at each other like a tennis ball across a court. Have a heated argument!

1 champain   旷野
2 politic authors   政论作家
3 baffle   羞辱
4 point-device   在每一点
5 jade   欺骗
6 commend   表扬，称赞
7 manifests herself to   表明自己是
8 injunction   命令
9 habits   衣着
10 strange, stout   高冷，自豪
11 entertain'st   接受
12 sophy   索菲（古波斯国王 [Shah]，见第100页）
13 gull-catcher   专骗傻瓜的人
14 tray-trip   走三点（一种掷骰游戏，以掷得三点为胜）
15 bondslave   契约奴隶
16 acqua-vitae   生命之水（白兰地类的酒）
17 disposition   脾气，秉性
18 a notable contempt   声名远扬的笑料
19 gates of Tartar   鞑靼之门；地狱

Daylight and champain[1] discovers not more! This is open. I will be proud, I will read politic authors[2], I will baffle[3] Sir Toby, I will wash off gross acquaintance, I will be point-device[4], the very man. I do 135 not now fool myself to let imagination jade[5] me; for every reason excites to this, that my lady loves me. She did commend[6] my yellow stockings of late, she did praise my leg being cross-gartered; and in this she manifests herself to[7] my love, and with a kind of injunction[8] drives me to these habits[9] of her liking. I thank my stars, 140 I am happy. I will be strange, stout[10], in yellow stockings and cross-gartered, even with the swiftness of putting on. Jove and my stars be praised! Here is yet a postscript. [*Reads*] 'Thou canst not choose but know who I am. If thou entertain'st[11] my love, let it appear in thy smiling; thy smiles become thee well. Therefore in my 145 presence still smile, dear my sweet, I prithee.' Jove, I thank thee. I will smile; I will do every thing that thou wilt have me. *Exit*

FABIAN   I will not give my part of this sport for a pension of thousands to be paid from the sophy[12].

SIR TOBY   I could marry this wench for this device – 150

SIR ANDREW   So could I, too.

SIR TOBY   And ask no other dowry with her but such another jest.

SIR ANDREW   Nor I neither.

FABIAN   Here comes my noble gull-catcher[13].

Enter MARIA

SIR TOBY   Wilt thou set thy foot o'my neck? 155

SIR ANDREW   Or o'mine either?

SIR TOBY   Shall I play my freedom at tray-trip[14] and become thy bondslave[15]?

SIR ANDREW   I'faith, or I either?

SIR TOBY   Why, thou hast put him in such a dream that when the image 160 of it leaves him, he must run mad.

MARIA   Nay, but say true, does it work upon him?

SIR TOBY   Like acqua-vitae[16] with a midwife.

MARIA   If you will then see the fruits of the sport, mark his first approach before my lady. He will come to her in yellow stockings, and 'tis 165 a colour she abhors, and cross-gartered, a fashion she detests; and he will smile upon her, which will now be so unsuitable to her disposition[17], being addicted to a melancholy as she is, that it cannot but turn him into a notable contempt[18]. If you will see it, follow me.

SIR TOBY   To the gates of Tartar[19], thou most excellent devil of wit! 170

SIR ANDREW   I'll make one, too. *Exeunt*

Looking back at Act 2　第2幕回顾
Activities for groups or individuals

1 Five locations, common themes

The locations may change, but each scene contains elements of common themes: love; appearance versus reality; madness and melancholy; fun and excess.

a　Complete a table like the one below, giving as many examples as possible of how and where you think each of the themes listed above appears in Act 2. Support each example with a relevant quotation from the play script.

Love	Appearance versus reality	Madness and melancholy	Fun and excess
Antonio 'loves' Sebastian (Act 2 Scene 1)	Viola tries desperately to hide the reality of her love for Orsino (Act 2 Scene 4)		
'I do adore thee so' (line 35)	'As it might be perhaps, were I a woman' (line 104)		

b　Use this table as the basis for an extended piece of writing (several paragraphs) exploring the following question: How do the ideas and themes expressed in Act 2 help to create a sense of comedy and drama?

2 Casting Act 2

Casting the right actors is essential to any play. Discuss and consider who could play each of the roles in Act 2 (perhaps people you have seen in movies or on television or stage, or maybe your friends!). Prepare a 'cast sheet', including references to the play script to explain how specific elements of each character would suit that particular actor or person.

3 Staging challenges

The five scenes of Act 2 are set on the coast of the sea, in a street outside Olivia's house, inside Olivia's house, at Duke Orsino's house and in Olivia's garden.

- Design a set to show how you would ensure that the action on stage flows smoothly from scene to scene, without interruption or long delays for scenery shifting. Include your ideas on how you would use colour, lighting and sound to reflect the mood and events of the act. Study the images in this book for inspiration.

4 Prominent and striking imagery

Every scene includes striking **imagery**. Find a creative way of presenting the following images. This could be through a sequence of tableaux, drawings, image collages (拼贴画) , music or any other practical method that you think would have a strong visual impact.

- **Scene 1** 'My stars shine darkly over me' (line 2)
- **Scene 2** 'Disguise, I see thou art a wickedness' (line 24)
- **Scene 3** 'cakes and ale' (lines 98–9)
- **Scene 4** 'Now the melancholy god protect thee' (line 70)
- **Scene 5** 'here comes the trout that must be caught with tickling' (lines 18–19)

▲ Fabian, Sir Toby and Sir Andrew watch Malvolio swallow the bait. In this production, the mournful atmosphere of the house is emphasised by the presence of Olivia in the background throughout this moment of high comedy. In some productions, the tricksters crawl frantically around the stage to avoid discovery as Malvolio strolls about, totally self-obsessed. In one production, Sir Andrew became a garden bench and Malvolio sat on him!

▼ In Act 2 Scene 3, Feste's song ends with a reminder that 'Youth's a stuff will not endure'. In Scene 4, his melancholy song tells of the lover who dies because he is rejected by 'a fair cruel maid'. Experiment with ways of presenting both songs, singing or speaking them.

Feste juggles with words, declining to give Viola a straight answer. He comments sceptically on the slipperiness of language, on Viola herself, and on the foolishness of husbands.

剧情简介： 费斯特耍嘴皮子，不直接回答薇娥菈的问题。他带着怀疑态度评论语言的不明确性，评论薇娥菈本人和丈夫们的愚蠢。

Language in the play 剧中语言

'corrupter of words' (in pairs)

Feste's joking and punning arises from his slippery (油滑) use of language: 'words are very rascals (真正的赖皮)' (line 17) and 'words are grown so false' (lines 20–1). Feste enjoys playing with different meanings of the same word (for example 'live' = 'earn money' or 'have a house'). He accuses Viola of doing just the same – twisting words to give different meanings ('A sentence is but a cheveril glove to a good wit').

When Feste says that words have become unreliable 'since bonds [promises] disgraced them', he is pointing again to the way in which a word can change its meaning. Promises are made of words, which can be interpreted differently, so it's difficult to keep them.

a To gain a sense of how Feste keeps twisting Viola's questions and statements, take parts and speak lines 1–49. Make a list of the words and phrases that are twisted. It will be quite long!

b Identify three words or phrases that you do not understand. Use the information on this page and on page 72 to help you work out their meanings. Share your definitions with another pair, and invite them to offer other meanings or interpretations.

c Write the phrases at the centre of a large sheet of paper, and annotate them with your collected meanings and interpretations to create a poster that can be displayed in the classroom.

Write about it 写作练习

Foolish musician

Feste is a 'fool', an entertainer, but many find his presence sinister (凶险). Is he comic, relieving worries, or melancholic, reminding the characters and audience of their problems? At the start of this scene, Olivia tells Feste to stop playing a tabor (a drum). There are no stage directions about the style, tone and delivery of his songs in the play.

- On sticky notes or cards, write down ways that this complex character might be played. Organise your notes into 'desirable' and 'possible' groups. Add quotations to support your ideas, and imagine the effects on the audience that your decisions will have. Write your preferred interpretations as directions for an actor in your Director's Journal.

1 *tabor* 泰伯鼓（一种小腰鼓）
2 Save thee （上帝）保佑你
3 You have said 随您怎么说
4 cheveril 小羊皮（又薄又软）
5 wrong … outward 把里子翻到外面（即意思被曲解）
6 dally nicely 玩得巧妙
7 wanton 水性杨花
8 bonds 契约，约定
9 yield 透露，揭示
10 loath … them 不愿用它们来证明理由
11 fool 俳优
12 fool 傻瓜
13 as pilchards are to herrings 就像沙丁鱼跟鲱鱼（半斤八两）

Act 3 Scene 1
In Olivia's orchard

Enter VIOLA *and* FESTE, *playing on a pipe and tabor*[1]

VIOLA	Save thee[2], friend, and thy music! Dost thou live by thy tabor?
FESTE	No, sir, I live by the church.
VIOLA	Art thou a churchman?
FESTE	No such matter, sir. I do live by the church; for I do live at my house, and my house doth stand by the church.
VIOLA	So thou mayst say the king lies by a beggar, if a beggar dwell near him; or the church stands by thy tabor if thy tabor stand by the church.
FESTE	You have said[3], sir. To see this age! A sentence is but a cheveril[4] glove to a good wit – how quickly the wrong side may be turned outward[5]!
VIOLA	Nay, that's certain: they that dally nicely[6] with words may quickly make them wanton[7].
FESTE	I would therefore my sister had had no name, sir.
VIOLA	Why, man?
FESTE	Why, sir, her name's a word, and to dally with that word might make my sister wanton; but, indeed, words are very rascals, since bonds[8] disgraced them.
VIOLA	Thy reason, man?
FESTE	Truth, sir, I can yield[9] you none without words, and words are grown so false, I am loath to prove reason with them[10].
VIOLA	I warrant thou art a merry fellow and car'st for nothing.
FESTE	Not so, sir, I do care for something; but in my conscience, sir, I do not care for you: if that be to care for nothing, I would it would make you invisible.
VIOLA	Art not thou the Lady Olivia's fool[11]?
FESTE	No, indeed, sir. The Lady Olivia has no folly. She will keep no fool[12], sir, till she be married, and fools are as like husbands as pilchards are to herrings[13] – the husband's the bigger. I am indeed not her fool but her corrupter of words.

5

10

15

20

25

30

Feste, still juggling with words, talks Viola into giving him money. She reflects on the need for fools to be clever. Sir Toby invites Viola to visit Olivia.

 剧情简介：费斯特仍在耍嘴皮子，说服薇娥菈给他钱。薇娥菈深思能做俳优者必定聪明。托比爵士邀请薇娥菈去拜访娥丽维娅。

1 A man of his times (in pairs)

Shakespeare's plays often contain references to the theatre and to other matters familiar to the audiences of the times.

- **Pandarus, Cressida, Troilus (lines 43–4)** Shakespeare's *Troilus and Cressida* is a play about two young lovers, set during the siege of Troy by the Greeks. Pandarus was the Trojan lord who acted as go-between for the ill-starred young lovers.
- **'I might say "element"' (line 49)** Shakespeare may be defending (or mocking) a fellow playwright, Ben Jonson, who was attacked for his fondness for using the word 'element'.
- **A tribute to an actor? (lines 50–8)** These lines may be Shakespeare's tribute to Robert Armin, the actor who first played Feste. The good joker ('wise fool') suits his humour to the particular audience and occasion, rather than cracking jokes about everything.
- **Speaking French (lines 61–2)** These two French phrases mean 'God save you, sir' / 'And you also; your servant'. French was considered a language of sophistication and its use was a sign of nobility.
- **Dramatic irony (line 40)** Viola's aside at this point is a great opportunity to make the audience laugh or smile. Dramatic irony is a powerful technique that Shakespeare often used.

Consider how Shakespeare's use of these features might be received by a modern audience. Make three lists giving reasons whether such features should be 'kept', 'cut' or 'updated'. Compare with another pair or with your whole class.

Characters 人物分析

Feste: 'wise enough to play the fool' (in small groups)

Shakespeare's plays often contain fools and madmen who appear to speak more sense than those who are supposed to be wise. In this play, those in charge – Olivia and Orsino – seem more concerned with their emotions than with running their households or the country.

- Divide your group in two. One half should propose, and then the other half oppose, the idea that 'It is folly to be wise and wise to be foolish'. Rehearse your arguments and then listen carefully to the ideas being presented. Try to use examples from the play, other Shakespeare plays or even real life to support your ideas.

1 late 最近
2 orb 地球
3 your wisdom 您大驾（模仿称呼your worship）
4 and thou pass upon me 如果你开我的玩笑（pass upon是击剑术语，意思是"剑指"）
5 Hold 拿着
6 expenses 零花钱
7 commodity 供应
8 Would … bred 这玩意儿要是一对的话可以生崽了吗
9 put to use 生利息（use 有"高利贷"［usury］的意思）
10 play Lord Pandarus of Phrygia 扮演弗瑞吉亚潘德若勋爵的角色（希腊神话里的潘德若是特洛伊阵营的一位神射手。在中世纪文学里，他被塑造成一个口吐莲花的皮条客。他安排表亲克莱希达和特洛伊勒在自己的花园里见面，将二人撮合在一起。弗瑞吉亚是古代特洛伊附近的一个国家，位于今天土耳其西部。）
11 bring … Troilus 给这位特洛伊勒带来一位克莱希达（克莱希达是希腊预言家凯尔柯［Calchas］的女儿，凯尔柯预见到特洛伊的灭亡，只身投奔到希腊阵营。经亲戚潘德若撮合，被遗弃的克莱希达与特洛伊国王子特洛伊勒成为恋人，可是与父亲在希腊阵营团聚后，又与联军勇士狄俄墨德［Diomedes］偷情，被视为用情不专的典型。）
12 matter 钱数
13 conster 解释
14 welkin 天职（本义是"天"，这里指职权范围）
15 element 天地（本义也是"天"，这里相当于"一亩三分地"）
16 craves 需要
17 haggard, check at every feather 野鹰，截击每一只鸟
18 fit 合适，切题
19 folly-fall'n 变得愚蠢
20 *Dieu vous garde, monsieur.* 上帝保佑您，我的先生。（法文）
21 *Et vous aussi; votre serviteur.* 您也一样；（我是）您的奴仆。（法文）
22 encounter 走向
23 your trade be to her 您的公干是找她
24 list 目标，终点

VIOLA	I saw thee late[1] at the Count Orsino's.
FESTE	Foolery, sir, does walk about the orb[2] like the sun; it shines everywhere. I would be sorry, sir, but the fool should be as oft with your master as with my mistress: I think I saw your wisdom[3] there.
VIOLA	Nay, and thou pass upon me[4], I'll no more with thee. Hold[5], there's expenses[6] for thee. [*Gives a coin*]
FESTE	Now Jove, in his next commodity[7] of hair, send thee a beard!
VIOLA	By my troth, I'll tell thee, I am almost sick for one – [*Aside*] though I would not have it grow on my chin. Is thy lady within?
FESTE	Would not a pair of these have bred[8], sir?
VIOLA	Yes, being kept together and put to use[9].
FESTE	I would play Lord Pandarus of Phrygia[10], sir, to bring a Cressida to this Troilus[11].
VIOLA	I understand you sir; 'tis well begged. [*Gives another coin*]
FESTE	The matter[12], I hope, is not great, sir – begging but a beggar: Cressida was a beggar. My lady is within, sir. I will conster[13] to them whence you come. Who you are, and what you would are out of my welkin[14] – I might say 'element[15]', but the word is overworn.

Exit

VIOLA	This fellow is wise enough to play the fool,
	And to do that well craves[16] a kind of wit;
	He must observe their mood on whom he jests,
	The quality of persons, and the time;
	Not, like the haggard, check at every feather[17]
	That comes before his eye. This is a practice,
	As full of labour as a wise man's art:
	For folly that he wisely shows is fit[18];
	But wise men, folly-fall'n[19], quite taint their wit.

Enter SIR TOBY *and* [SIR] ANDREW

SIR TOBY	Save you, gentleman.
VIOLA	And you, sir.
SIR ANDREW	*Dieu vous garde, monsieur.*[20]
VIOLA	*Et vous aussi; votre serviteur.*[21]
SIR ANDREW	I hope, sir, you are, and I am yours.
SIR TOBY	Will you encounter[22] the house? My niece is desirous you should enter, if your trade be to her[23].
VIOLA	I am bound to your niece, sir; I mean, she is the list[24] of my voyage.

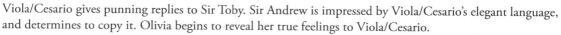

Viola/Cesario gives punning replies to Sir Toby. Sir Andrew is impressed by Viola/Cesario's elegant language, and determines to copy it. Olivia begins to reveal her true feelings to Viola/Cesario.

剧情简介：薇娥菈/席扎瑞欧一语双关地回答了托比爵士。安褚爵士对薇娥菈/席扎瑞欧优雅的谈吐印象深刻，决意模仿她。娥丽维娅开始吐露自己对薇娥菈/席扎瑞欧的真实感受。

Stagecraft 导演技巧

Sir Andrew's responses

Viola addresses Olivia in highly elaborate, courteous speech. Her compliments greatly impress Sir Andrew.

a Write notes for the actor playing Sir Andrew, advising him how he should speak, move, gesture (with hands and face) and even think at each of the moments listed below. Try to convey the correct degree of awe or annoyance at Viola, whom he regards as a more skilful lover than himself.

- As he says 'well' (line 73), is he impressed? Contemptuous?
- 'I'll get 'em all three' (lines 76–7): is he memorising the words, or writing them down in a notebook? Or something else?
- When Olivia says 'leave me' (line 78), how does Sir Andrew exit with Maria and Sir Toby? Willingly? With great reluctance? In some other way? (Remember that he's only visiting Sir Toby in order to woo Olivia, and he's probably not had a chance even to talk with her.)

b Try presenting your notes as annotations around written-out quotations, or as extended prose under these quotations and divided into sections on voice, movement, gesture, thoughts. Add these notes to your Director's Journal.

1 'music from the spheres'

Many Elizabethans believed that the planets were contained in concentric crystal spheres (同心的水晶球). The spheres rotated, creating wonderfully harmonious music that could not be heard by humans. Should Olivia and Viola/Cesario chime (一致) at this point, or should there be discord to their exchanges?

- In pairs, read lines 80 to the end of the scene. Experiment with ways to show the harmony, or lack of it, in the respective thoughts of Olivia and Viola/Cesario.

1	Taste 尝试
2	understand me = stand under me
3	taste my legs 尝我的腿
4	gait 步伐（与 gate 读音相同）
5	prevented 先行一步
6	accomplished 完美
7	rain odours on you 往您身上洒香水
8	courtier 朝臣；追求者
9	My … ear 我的公干只能冲着您本人那极为包容而又耐心的耳朵发声
10	get … ready 把这三个词都记在心里
11	'Twas never merry world 欢乐世界就没有了
12	lowly feigning 伴装的谦卑
13	Would = I wish
14	whet 磨砺，激励
15	solicit 请求
16	spheres 星空；天堂
17	beseech 恳请，恳求
18	the last enchantment you did 您上一次释放的魅力 / 魔力
19	I fear me = I am afraid

SIR TOBY	Taste[1] your legs, sir; put them to motion.
VIOLA	My legs do better understand me[2], sir, than I understand what you mean by bidding me taste my legs[3].
SIR TOBY	I mean, to go, sir, to enter. 70
VIOLA	I will answer you with gait[4] and entrance – but we are prevented[5].

Enter OLIVIA *and* GENTLEWOMAN [MARIA]

Most excellent accomplished[6] lady, the heavens rain odours on you[7]!

SIR ANDREW   That youth's a rare courtier[8] – 'rain odours' – well.

VIOLA   My matter hath no voice, lady, but to your own most pregnant and vouchsafed ear[9].   75

SIR ANDREW   'Odours', 'pregnant', and 'vouchsafed': I'll get 'em all three all ready[10].

OLIVIA   Let the garden door be shut, and leave me to my hearing.

[*Exeunt Sir Toby, Sir Andrew, and Maria*]

Give me your hand, sir.

VIOLA   My duty, madam, and most humble service.   80

OLIVIA   What is your name?

VIOLA   Cesario is your servant's name, fair princess.

OLIVIA   My servant, sir? 'Twas never merry world[11]
Since lowly feigning[12] was called compliment.
Y'are servant to the Count Orsino, youth.   85

VIOLA   And he is yours, and his must needs be yours:
Your servant's servant is your servant, madam.

OLIVIA   For him, I think not on him; for his thoughts,
Would[13] they were blanks, rather than filled with me!

VIOLA   Madam, I come to whet[14] your gentle thoughts   90
On his behalf.

OLIVIA   O by your leave, I pray you!
I bade you never speak again of him;
But would you undertake another suit
I had rather hear you to solicit[15] that,
Than music from the spheres[16].

VIOLA   Dear lady –   95

OLIVIA   Give me leave, beseech[17] you. I did send,
After the last enchantment you did[18] here,
A ring in chase of you. So did I abuse
Myself, my servant, and, I fear me[19], you.

Olivia hints at the agonies of love she feels. She says her feelings are clearly visible. After seeming to dismiss Viola/Cesario, Olivia calls her back. Viola/Cesario declares that she is not what she seems.

剧情简介： 娥丽维娅暗示她因爱而感到痛苦，说其感情显而易见。在表面上让薇娥菈/席扎瑞欧离开后，娥丽维娅又把她叫回来。薇娥菈/席扎瑞欧声称她并不像她看上去的那样。

Language in the play 剧中语言

Cruel love (in pairs)

Olivia tries some reverse psychology, saying the opposite to what she means, to win over Viola/Cesario. She wants to make him jealous or eager to prove her words wrong. Examine the examples below and discuss why you think Shakespeare has included these fierce animal comparisons.

- **Bear-baiting (lines 103–5)** Olivia uses the image of bear-baiting ('stake', 'baited' and 'unmuzzled') to describe how her secret love for Viola/Cesario tears at her. Theatregoers in Shakespeare's time might have been able to see such events as part of the day's entertainment.
- **Lions and wolves (line 114)** Who does Olivia have in mind in line 114? Does she think of Viola/Cesario or Orsino as the lion (proud creature) or the wolf (cruel predator)?

Themes 主题分析

'I am not what I am'

In Shakespeare's time, line 126 would have been spoken by a boy playing a girl playing a boy, making the words rich in dramatic irony and emphasising the theme of appearance and reality. Today, Viola is more often played by a woman, but the line is still full of dramatic irony, because the audience knows what Olivia does not – the 'man' she is wooing is actually a woman. In the production pictured below, however, the director returned to the original practice of a man playing Viola (and Olivia).

- List the different perspectives that a man's performance in the role of Viola might present to an audience. Consider whether you feel casting a male or female Viola is more effective.

1	hard construction	严厉的判断
2	a shameful cunning	可耻的花招儿（这不是娥丽维娅惯常的做法）
3	unmuzzled	不戴笼头；不受限制
4	receiving	理解
5	cypress	塞浦路斯布（原产于塞浦路斯的一种昂贵布料，有的织有金线，有的透明如蝉翼）
6	a degree	（上行或下行的）一步
7	a grise	（更常见的拼写是grize或grece，指楼梯或台阶的一阶）
8	vulgar proof	寻常的体验
9	apt	倾向于
10	upbraids	责备
11	westward ho!	西边去喽！（旧时伦敦船夫招揽乘客去迅速发展的西区时发出的吆喝，反方向则喊eastward ho!）

	Under your hard construction[1] must I sit,	100
	To force that on you in a shameful cunning[2]	
	Which you knew none of yours. What might you think?	
	Have you not set mine honour at the stake,	
	And baited it with all th'unmuzzled[3] thoughts	
	That tyrannous heart can think? To one of your receiving[4]	105
	Enough is shown; a cypress[5], not a bosom,	
	Hides my heart: so, let me hear you speak.	
VIOLA	I pity you.	
OLIVIA	That's a degree[6] to love.	
VIOLA	No, not a grise[7]; for 'tis a vulgar proof[8]	
	That very oft we pity enemies.	110
OLIVIA	Why then, methinks 'tis time to smile again.	
	O world, how apt[9] the poor are to be proud!	
	If one should be a prey, how much the better	
	To fall before the lion than the wolf!	
	(Clock strikes)	
	The clock upbraids[10] me with the waste of time.	115
	Be not afraid, good youth; I will not have you –	
	And yet when with and youth is come to harvest,	
	Your wife is like to reap a proper man.	
	There lies your way, due west.	
VIOLA	Then westward ho![11]	
	Grace and good disposition attend your ladyship!	120
	You'll nothing, madam, to my lord by me?	
OLIVIA	Stay!	
	I prithee tell me what thou think'st of me.	
VIOLA	That you do think you are not what you are.	
OLIVIA	If I think so, I think the same of you.	125
VIOLA	Then think you right: I am not what I am.	
OLIVIA	I would you were as I would have you be.	
VIOLA	Would it be better, madam, than I am?	
	I wish it might, for now I am your fool.	

Olivia, admiring Viola's beauty and convinced that her own feelings are obvious, declares her love for Viola/Cesario. Viola swears that no woman has her heart except she herself.

剧情简介：娥丽维娅爱慕薇娥菈的俊美，并确信自己的情感显而易见，向薇娥菈/席扎瑞欧表白了爱意。薇娥菈发誓除了自己，她心里没有任何女人。

Characters 人物分析

Olivia in love (in pairs)

Olivia's transformation from being in mourning for her brother to being in love with Viola/Cesario seems rapid. But is it? Is she really in mourning when we first meet her in Act 1 Scene 5, or is it a convenient excuse to dismiss the unwanted attention from Orsino? She soon abandons her veil for Viola/Cesario and sends her servant after him with a ring. We might see her declaration of love in lines 130–49 as either deeply moving or very funny.

- The subtleties of Shakespeare's characters can be difficult to pick up on when you read *Twelfth Night* for the first time. Review the character of Olivia in the play so far by creating a Venn diagram (文氏图，用以表示集合或类) of her subtleties and ambiguities (things that are not clear). Draw four circles on a large sheet of paper, and into each circle place evidence to support whether Olivia is *in mourning*, *in love*, *serious* or *comic*.

Where the circles overlap, record evidence that supports more than one idea.

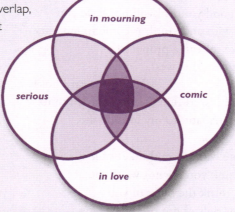

1 what a deal of 这么多的
2 Love's night is noon 爱情在夜间也会像在正午一样（即大放光芒，遮挡不住）
3 maugre 尽管
4 extort ... clause 从这句话中索求你想要的理由
5 For ... cause 因为虽然我表白了，你不一定因此就接受
6 reason thus with reason fetter 用理性来这样给理性戴镣铐（即管住刨根问底的意念）
7 that no woman has = that has no woman
8 nor never none （三重否定用以强化效果，且此处运用了头韵）
9 Shall mistress be of it = Shall be its mistress
10 deplore 哀诉

◄ Does this image portray the closing of the scene accurately? How might the actors deliver the rhyming couplets (押韵二行连句; 对偶句) of lines 132–49 to fit with the tone suggested in the image?

78

OLIVIA   [*Aside*] O what a deal of[1] scorn looks beautiful   130
In the contempt and anger of his lip!
A murd'rous guilt shows not itself more soon,
Than love that would seem hid. Love's night is noon[2].
Cesario, by the roses of the spring,
By maidhood, honour, truth, and everything,   135
I love thee so that, maugre[3] all thy pride,
Nor wit nor reason can my passion hide.
Do not extort thy reasons from this clause[4],
For that I woo, thou therefore hast no cause[5];
But rather reason thus with reason fetter[6]:   140
Love sought is good, but giv'n unsought is better.

VIOLA   By innocence I swear, and by my youth,
I have one heart, one bosom, and one truth,
And that no woman has[7]; nor never none[8]
Shall mistress be of it[9], save I alone.   145
And so, adieu, good madam; never more
Will I my master's tears to you deplore[10].

OLIVIA   Yet come again: for thou perhaps mayst move
That heart which now abhors to like his love.

                                             Exeunt

79

Sir Andrew determines to leave because Olivia is paying more attention to Viola/Cesario. Fabian and Sir Toby persuade him to stay. He must challenge Viola/Cesario to a duel and so win Olivia's affection by his bravery.

剧情简介：安褚爵士决心离开，因为娥丽维娅把更多注意力放在了薇娥菈/席扎瑞欧身上。费边和托比爵士劝他留下来。他必须向薇娥菈/席扎瑞欧发起决斗，才能以自己的勇敢赢得娥丽维娅的芳心。

Stagecraft 导演技巧

Casting

Shakespeare staged his performances using a company of players, so he wrote parts for the same actors in different plays. Many of his plays feature one thin and one fat comic character, and a lot of his comedy relies on physical actions as well as clever language.

a Look at the image below of Sir Toby and Sir Andrew. Bearing in mind what you have learnt about these characters so far, do you think these actors are well suited to the parts?

b Consider who you might cast in these roles. Would you maintain the tradition of casting one thin and one fat actor (or at least one with a lot of padding)? Or would you consider casting 'against type'? If so, what effect might this have on the physical comedy in the scene?

c Collect images of current actors and comedians who you would cast in these roles, and create a collage. Annotate the collage with your reasons. Share your display with others and discuss your respective ideas.

1 Echoes of Elizabethan England (in pairs)

Shakespeare's audiences would have picked up references to recent events in the script opposite (detailed in the glossary).

• Discuss what 'comic business' or other visual means you might use to make these references relevant to a modern audience. Try to act one out for another pair.

Act 3 Scene 2
A room in Olivia's house

Enter SIR TOBY, SIR ANDREW *and* FABIAN

SIR ANDREW   No, faith, I'll not stay a jot[1] longer!

SIR TOBY   Thy reason, dear venom[2], give thy reason.

FABIAN   You must needs yield your reason, Sir Andrew.

SIR ANDREW   Marry, I saw your niece do more favours[3] to the count's
servingman than ever she bestowed upon me. I saw't i'th'orchard.   5

SIR TOBY   Did she see thee the while, old boy? Tell me that.

SIR ANDREW   As plain as I see you now.

FABIAN   This was a great argument[4] of love in her toward you.

SIR ANDREW   'Slight! Will you make an ass o'me?

FABIAN   I will prove it legitimate[5], sir, upon the oaths of judgement and   10
reason.

SIR TOBY   And they have been grand-jurymen since before Noah was
a sailor[6].

FABIAN   She did show favour to the youth in your sight only to
exasperate you, to awake your dormouse[7] valour, to put fire in your   15
heart, and brimstone[8] in your liver. You should then have accosted
her, and with some excellent jests, fire-new from the mint[9], you
should have banged the youth into dumbness. This was looked for
at your hand, and this was balked[10]. The double gilt[11] of this
opportunity you let time wash off, and you are now sailed into the   20
north of my lady's opinion, where you will hang like an icicle on
a Dutchman's beard[12] unless you do redeem it by some laudable
attempt, either of valour or policy[13].

SIR ANDREW   And't be any way, it must be with valour, for policy I
hate. I had as lief be a Brownist as a politician[14].   25

SIR TOBY   Why then, build me thy fortunes upon the basis of valour.
Challenge me the count's youth to fight with him, hurt him in eleven
places – my niece shall take note of it – and assure thyself, there
is no love-broker in the world can more prevail[15] in man's commen-
dation with woman than report of valour.   30

Sir Toby instructs Sir Andrew how to write the challenge in fierce, military language, but tells Fabian that Sir Andrew is a coward. Maria brings news that Malvolio has been transformed!

剧情简介： 托比爵士指导安褚爵士如何用凶狠的军事语言写挑战信，却告诉费边安褚爵士是个胆小鬼。玛蕊娅带来消息说马尔沃琉已经变换了一个人。

Language in the play 剧中语言
'Thou' and 'you' (in threes)

To Elizabethans, words like 'thou', 'thy' and 'thee' were very significant. 'Thou' was used for a close friend, but was also used insultingly to someone you saw as an inferior (as Sir Toby advises in line 35). 'You' was a more formal way of speaking to someone.

- Make a table to explore how Sir Toby and Fabian address Sir Andrew in this scene (as 'thou' or 'you'). How do you explain the difference? What is the effect or intention behind the use?

Character	You/thou quotation	Line reference	Effect/intention
Fabian	'toward you'	8	Polite address to social superior
Sir Toby			

1 Sir Toby: truth or trick? (in pairs)

Sir Toby is a mischief-maker. Although he pretends to be Sir Andrew's friend, he continually mocks and tricks him. But sometimes Sir Toby reveals his true thoughts – for instance, 'I have been dear to him' in line 43 means 'I've spent his money'.

- One person reads aloud everything Sir Toby says in this scene, one sentence at a time, pausing at the end of each sentence. The other person says either 'trick' or 'truth' in each pause. When you have finished, discuss whether there is more 'trick' or 'truth', and what this reveals about the friendship.

2 More Elizabethan England echoes (in pairs)

The 'bed of Ware' (line 37) was a huge bed that could sleep a dozen people. It is now in the Victoria and Albert Museum, London. The 'new map' (line 62) was a map of India and the Far East, published in 1600, which had lines that radiated out from different points like wrinkles around the eyes.

- Research one of these Elizabethan echoes, or one of those listed in the glossary on page 80. Present your findings and comment on what you think such references add to the play. In a modern performance, should they be left in, updated or cut?

1 **bear … him** 替我向他送挑战书
2 **curst** 恶毒
3 **so it be** = so long as it be
4 **invention** 想象；创新说法
5 **Tout … ink** 用墨水随心所欲地讥讽他
6 **'thou'st' him some thrice** 对他用大约三次"你"字（以示不敬）
7 **bed of Ware** 韦尔大床（指伊丽莎白一世时期英国赫特福德郡韦尔镇生产的四柱橡木雕花超大床）
8 **goose-pen** 羽翎笔
9 **cubiculo** 卧室（拉丁文）
10 **dear manikin** 珍贵的玩偶
11 **some two thousand strong** 每年花销大约两千金币
12 **wainropes** 马车绳
13 **hale** 拖，拉，拽
14 **clog** 黏住
15 **anatomy** 身体，骨架
16 **presage** 迹象，预兆
17 **wren** 鹪鹩
18 **spleen** 一阵大笑
19 **heathen** 异教徒
20 **renegado** 叛教者（主要指背叛基督教）
21 **passages of grossness** 胡言乱语
22 **pedant** 教书先生
23 **the new … Indies** 扩大版的东印度群岛地图（可能指爱德华·莱特 [Edward Wright] 1600年把新地岛 [Novaya Zemlya，又转写为 Nova Zembla] 纳入地图）

FABIAN   There is no way but this, Sir Andrew.

SIR ANDREW   Will either of you bear me a challenge to him[1]?

SIR TOBY   Go, write it in a martial hand, be curst[2] and brief; it is no matter how witty, so it be[3] eloquent, and full of invention[4]. Taunt him with the licence of ink[5]. If thou 'thou'st' him some thrice[6], it shall not be amiss, and as many lies as will lie in thy sheet of paper, although the sheet were big enough for the bed of Ware[7] in England, set 'em down. Go, about it! Let there be gall enough in thy ink; though thou write with a goose-pen[8], no matter. About it!   35

SIR ANDREW   Where shall I find you?   40

SIR TOBY   We'll call thee at the cubiculo[9]. Go!

Exit Sir Andrew

FABIAN   This is a dear manikin[10] to you, Sir Toby.

SIR TOBY   I have been dear to him, lad, some two thousand strong[11], or so.

FABIAN   We shall have a rare letter from him, but you'll not deliver't?   45

SIR TOBY   Never trust me then, and by all means stir on the youth to an answer. I think oxen and wainropes[12] cannot hale[13] them together. For Andrew, if he were opened and you find so much blood in his liver as will clog[14] the foot of a flea, I'll eat the rest of th'anatomy[15].

FABIAN   And his opposite, the youth, bears in his visage no great presage[16] of cruelty.   50

Enter MARIA

SIR TOBY   Look where the youngest wren[17] of mine comes –

MARIA   If you desire the spleen[18], and will laugh yourselves into stitches, follow me. Yond gull Malvolio is turned heathen[19], a very renegado[20]; for there is no Christian that means to be saved by believing rightly can ever believe such impossible passages of grossness[21]. He's in yellow stockings.   55

SIR TOBY   And cross-gartered?

MARIA   Most villainously. Like a pedant[22] that keeps a school i'th'church. I have dogged him like his murderer. He does obey every point of the letter that I dropped to betray him. He does smile his face into more lines than is in the new map with the augmentation of the Indies[23]; you have not seen such a thing as 'tis. I can hardly forbear hurling things at him; I know my lady will strike him. If she do, he'll smile and take't for a great favour.   60   65

SIR TOBY   Come bring us, bring us where he is.

Exeunt

Antonio has followed Sebastian out of friendship and to protect him. Sebastian invites Antonio to join him in sightseeing. Antonio declines, fearing capture – he was once Orsino's enemy.

 剧情简介：安托纽出于友情一直跟随塞巴斯田并保护他。塞巴斯田邀请安托纽与他一起观光游览。安托纽回绝了，因为他害怕被抓——他曾是奥悉诺的敌人。

Stagecraft 导演技巧

Changing the tone

In Act 3 Scene 3, Shakespeare shifts the attention away from the love plot and the practical jokes being played on Malvolio and Sir Andrew to focus on Sebastian and Antonio. These two characters will add yet more complications to the already tangled plots.

a Imagine the two actors in the image above have asked for your advice and sent the following requests:

- 'When we look at lines 1–18, Antonio seems to care for Sebastian more than Sebastian cares for him. How should we play the lines?'

- 'Antonio is a wanted man in Illyria, as we hear in lines 25–8. How does he show by his manner that he's taking a considerable risk? How does Sebastian react to that manner?'

Write notes in your Director's Journal advising the actors on each point. You should include directions on how to speak certain lines and what gestures and movements the actors should use to accompany them. Remember that the reactions of the person listening are just as important as the actions of the person speaking, so make sure that you advise the actors how they should react to the other's lines.

b When you have written your notes, give them to others in your class to try out. Consider whether your notes have been effective and conveyed your thoughts well.

1 **chide** 责备

2 **filèd steel** 磨利的钢刀（filè 的字面意思是"用锉子锉"）

3 **not … you** 并不全是要看到您的愿望

4 **so … one** 这愿望大到很可能激励一个人

5 **jealousy … travel** 担心您的旅途可能会出什么事

6 **skilless** 不熟悉

7 **The rather by** 更多是因为

8 **good … pay** 好人好事就用这种无法流通的酬金（指不能当钱使的感激话）打发了

9 **were … firm** 一旦我有了真金白银

10 **dealing** 回报

11 **relics** 古迹

12 **the count his galleys** 公爵的舰队（count his = count's）

13 **were I tane = If I were captured** （tane = taken）

14 **scarce be answered** 很难辩白开脱

84

Act 3 Scene 3
A street

Enter SEBASTIAN *and* ANTONIO

SEBASTIAN   I would not by my will have troubled you,
But since you make your pleasure of your pains,
I will no further chide[1] you.

ANTONIO   I could not stay behind you. My desire,
More sharp than filèd steel[2], did spur me forth;   5
And not all love to see you[3] (though so much
As might have drawn one[4] to a longer voyage),
But jealousy what might befall your travel[5],
Being skilless[6] in these parts which to a stranger,
Unguided, and unfriended, often prove   10
Rough and unhospitable. My willing love,
The rather by[7] these arguments of fear,
Set forth in your pursuit.

SEBASTIAN   My kind Antonio,
I can no other answer make but thanks,
And thanks, and ever thanks; and oft good turns   15
Are shuffled off with such uncurrent pay[8];
But were my worth, as is my conscience, firm[9],
You should find better dealing[10]. What's to do?
Shall we go see the relics[11] of this town?

ANTONIO   Tomorrow, sir; best first go see your lodging.   20

SEBASTIAN   I am not weary, and 'tis long to night.
I pray you, let us satisfy our eyes
With the memorials and the things of fame
That do renown this city.

ANTONIO   Would you'd pardon me.
I do not without danger walk these streets.   25
Once in a sea-fight 'gainst the count his galleys[12]
I did some service, of such note indeed
That were I tane[13] here, it would scarce be answered[14].

Antonio is a wanted man in Illyria because he has not repaid what he captured in a sea-fight. He lends Sebastian money. The two men promise to meet later at the Elephant.

 剧情简介: 安托纽在伊利瑞亚被通缉，因为他没有退还在一次海战中缴获该国的东西。他借给塞巴斯田一些钱。两人约定晚些时候在大象旅店碰头。

Write about it 写作练习

Antonio – the story so far

Writers and filmmakers sometimes create sequels (续集) and prequels (前传) to extend their stories. Prequels give the back-story of characters and explore how they ended up in the story in the first place. Often these prequels challenge assumptions and opinions of the character that we know from the original story.

Certain aspects of Antonio appear incongruous (不一致) – they do not fit with the overall impression given of his character in the play:

- Antonio appears to be a kind man and a faithful servant to Sebastian, yet he is a wanted man in Illyria.
- Antonio indicates that this is because of a sea-fight between the ships of his city and those of Duke Orsino.
- All Antonio's fellow citizens have made their peace by returning what they captured in the battle. Only Antonio has refused.
- Antonio's involvement, or what he took, must have been significant if he would still be remembered on the streets of Illyria.

Write the summary, or a couple of scenes, of a prequel to *Twelfth Night* that focuses on Antonio. You might include:

- a description of the sea-battle and how Antonio was involved
- details of what Antonio took and why he would not return it. Was he a thief, or is there more to it?
- how Antonio came to be in service to Sebastian's family, and the extent of their knowledge or involvement with Antonio's past.

Stagecraft 导演技巧

'I'll be your purse-bearer' (in pairs)

Shakespeare allows significant actions to pass without highlighting them. This develops complexity in the story and increases intrigue for the audience, who might recall and notice these details.

- Discuss what you think might happen later in the play as a result of Antonio's loan (line 47). Write down your ideas and seal them in an envelope. Open them when you reach the end of the play to see if you are right.

1 **Belike** 大概
2 **traffic** 贸易
3 **stood out** 不参与，不买账
4 **lapsèd** 被捕
5 **Do ... open** 那就不要太张扬
6 **It doth not fit me** 我的确不宜那样
7 **the Elephant** 大象旅店（莎士比亚时期伦敦环球剧院附近确实有这么一家旅店）
8 **bespeak our diet** 为我们订餐
9 **beguile** 打发，消磨
10 **have me** 找到我
11 **light upon** （目光）落在
12 **toy** 小玩意儿
13 **your store ... markets** 我觉得，您的钱不是用来在市场上乱花的

86

SEBASTIAN	Belike[1] you slew great number of his people?
ANTONIO	Th'offence is not of such a bloody nature, 30
	Albeit the quality of the time and quarrel
	Might well have given us bloody argument.
	It might have since been answered in repaying
	What we took from them, which for traffic's[2] sake
	Most of our city did. Only myself stood out[3], 35
	For which if I be lapsèd[4] in this place
	I shall pay dear.
SEBASTIAN	Do not then walk too open[5].
ANTONIO	It doth not fit me[6]. Hold, sir, here's my purse.
	In the south suburbs at the Elephant[7]
	Is best to lodge; I will bespeak our diet[8], 40
	Whiles you beguile[9] the time, and feed your knowledge
	With viewing of the town; there shall you have me[10].
SEBASTIAN	Why I your purse?
ANTONIO	Haply your eye shall light upon[11] some toy[12]
	You have desire to purchase; and your store, 45
	I think, is not for idle markets[13], sir.
SEBASTIAN	I'll be your purse-bearer and leave you for
	An hour.
ANTONIO	To th'Elephant.
SEBASTIAN	I do remember.

Exeunt

Olivia is looking forward to Viola/Cesario's return, and thinking about how she will entertain 'him'. She sends for Malvolio, expecting him to be formal and sad. He appears – transformed and speaking very strangely!

 剧情简介： 娥丽维娅期盼着薇娥拉/席扎瑞欧回来，一心想着要怎样款待"他"。她差人去请马尔沃琉，期待着他神色庄重而严肃的样子。马尔沃琉出现了——形象大变，而且说起话来非常奇怪！

1 Making an entrance (in sixes)

The first part of Scene 4 (lines 1–106) shows how the deluded Malvolio behaves towards Olivia, and what happens to him. For those who have never seen the play, the entrance of the 'gulled' Malvolio comes as a shock. For those that know the play, the comedy of his arrival seldom disappoints. Malvolio's appearance, cross-gartered and in yellow stockings, is one of the best-loved moments in Shakespeare's plays.

a How would you produce this great moment? Take parts as Olivia, Maria, Malvolio, the Servant, Sir Toby and Fabian and read through lines 1–106, adding actions, gestures and expressions.

b Remember, Malvolio is convinced that Olivia loves him. Olivia, knowing nothing of the forged letter, is astonished by his appearance and behaviour. The conspirators are beside themselves with glee, and are determined to add to the impression that Malvolio is mad. Try reading through lines 1–106 again, and get as much fun from the 'mistakings' as you can!

▶ 'cross-gartering, but what of that?' Costume designers go to great lengths to give Malvolio's entrance added impact by creating elaborate clothes. Produce your own drawing or design brief for Malvolio's new look.

1 feast 宴请
2 bestow of him 赠予他
3 sad and civil 严肃而清醒
4 fortunes 境况（娥丽维娅仍在哀悼亡兄）
5 possessed 着魔，魔怔
6 rave 胡言乱语
7 Your … you 小姐您身边最好有个护卫
8 tainted in's wits 他精神出了问题
9 obstruction in the blood 血液瘀阻
10 sonnet 小歌（一种十四行诗）
11 black in my mind 忧伤
12 executed 执行
13 Roman hand 罗马字体（一种斜体书写）

Act 3 Scene 4
Olivia's garden

Enter OLIVIA *followed by* MARIA

OLIVIA	[*Aside*] I have sent after him; he says he'll come –
	How shall I feast[1] him? What bestow of him[2]?
	For youth is bought more oft than begged or borrowed.
	I speak too loud –
	Where's Malvolio? He is sad and civil[3],
	And suits well for a servant with my fortunes[4].
	Where is Malvolio?
MARIA	He's coming, madam, but in very strange manner. He is sure possessed[5], madam.
OLIVIA	Why, what's the matter? Does he rave[6]?
MARIA	No, madam, he does nothing but smile. Your ladyship were best to have some guard about you[7], if he come, for sure the man is tainted in's wits[8].
OLIVIA	Go call him hither.

[*Exit Maria*]

I am as mad as he
If sad and merry madness equal be.

Enter [MARIA *with*] MALVOLIO

	How now, Malvolio?
MALVOLIO	Sweet lady, ho, ho!
OLIVIA	Smil'st thou? I sent for thee upon a sad occasion.
MALVOLIO	Sad, lady? I could be sad. This does make some obstruction in the blood[9], this cross-gartering, but what of that? If it please the eye of one, it is with me as the very true sonnet[10] is: 'Please one, and please all.'
OLIVIA	Why, how dost thou, man? What is the matter with thee?
MALVOLIO	Not black in my mind[11], though yellow in my legs. It did come to his hands, and commands shall be executed[12]. I think we do know the sweet Roman hand[13].

5

10

15

20

25

Olivia is amazed by Malvolio's behaviour and appearance as he quotes the forged letter to her. She thinks he is mad, and gives orders for Sir Toby and others to look after him.

 剧情简介： 马尔沃琉向娥丽维娅引述那封假信的内容时，他的行为和外貌让她很吃惊。她认为这个人疯了，令托比爵士和其他人照看他。

1 What does she make of it all? (in pairs)

What does the last sentence spoken by Olivia (Lines 56–7) suggest to you about her true feelings for Malvolio? How does it compare with her reaction in this image?

- Choose five moments in lines 1–57 and describe how the actor playing Olivia should respond. Consider her tone of voice, the delivery of her words, and her gestures and movements. Remember to comment on her reactions to others' actions, as this is where most of the comedy in this scene will be generated.

1	**To bed?**	上床？（同床共眠）
2	**kiss thy hand**	飞吻
3	**At your request!**	回您的话！（马尔沃琉在遵照信中的指示行事）
4	**daws**	寒鸦（叫声嘈杂，被视为一种呆鸟）
5	**restore**	治愈
6	**midsummer**	仲夏（据说人在这个季节容易因暑热发狂）
7	**I … back**	我简直没法劝他回来
8	**miscarry**	遭不幸

OLIVIA	Wilt thou go to bed, Malvolio?
MALVOLIO	To bed?[1] Ay, sweetheart, and I'll come to thee.
OLIVIA	God comfort thee! Why dost thou smile so and kiss thy hand[2] so oft?
MARIA	How do you, Malvolio?
MALVOLIO	At your request![3]
	Yes, nightingales answer daws[4]!
MARIA	Why appear you with this ridiculous boldness before my lady?
MALVOLIO	'Be not afraid of greatness': 'twas well writ.
OLIVIA	What mean'st thou by that, Malvolio?
MALVOLIO	'Some are born great – '
OLIVIA	Ha?
MALVOLIO	'Some achieve greatness – '
OLIVIA	What say'st thou?
MALVOLIO	'And some have greatness thrust upon them.'
OLIVIA	Heaven restore[5] thee!
MALVOLIO	'Remember who commended thy yellow stockings –'
OLIVIA	Thy yellow stockings?
MALVOLIO	'And wished to see thee cross-gartered.'
OLIVIA	Cross-gartered?
MALVOLIO	'Go to, thou art made, if thou desir'st to be so – '
OLIVIA	Am I made?
MALVOLIO	'If not, let me see thee a servant still.'
OLIVIA	Why, this is very midsummer[6] madness.

Enter SERVANT

SERVANT	Madam, the young gentleman of the Count Orsino's is returned; I could hardly entreat him back[7]. He attends your ladyship's pleasure.
OLIVIA	I'll come to him.

[*Exit Servant*]

Good Maria, let this fellow be looked to. Where's my cousin Toby? Let some of my people have a special care of him; I would not have him miscarry[8] for the half of my dowry.

[*Exeunt Olivia and Maria*]

Malvolio convinces himself that what Olivia has just said means that she loves him. Following the letter's instructions, he is rude to Sir Toby, who accuses him of being possessed by devils.

 剧情简介：马尔沃琉说服自己相信娥丽维娅刚才说的话意味着她爱他。按照信里的指示，当托比爵士说他被魔鬼附了身时，他对托比爵士很无理。

Stagecraft 导演技巧

Malvolio speaks ... to himself (in small groups)

Unusually for a Shakespearean character left alone on stage and talking, it seems that Malvolio is speaking to himself and not to the audience. Soliloquies (see p. 40) tend to reveal a character's innermost thoughts and feelings, and they can often explain details of the motivation for the character's actions. However, here Malvolio spends the time congratulating himself and rehearsing the conversations that he has wanted to have with Olivia and others for some time. He even appears to 'do' their voices.

- Read through lines 58–73 and identify the people involved in Malvolio's rehearsed conversations. Perform a 'radio' version (where you focus on the sound quality) and give a different voice to each person identified, or take turns to say a line. You might speak some parts in chorus to swell the sound and give emphasis to certain lines.

Themes 主题分析

'Legion': the many devils who cause suffering (in threes)

Sir Toby and Fabian are determined to treat Malvolio as if he is possessed by devils. 'Legion' (line 75) is mentioned in the Bible (St Mark's Gospel, Chapter 5), where Jesus casts out a legion (a very great number) of devils from a madman.

Some critics see the image as yet another way in which the play links suffering with love – Malvolio is accused of being mad because he believes that Olivia loves him even though the others have tricked him.

a Discuss whether you agree with the idea that some characters suffer for love in *Twelfth Night*. Think about which characters are in love and about the other types of love – such as that between brother and sister, and between friends – that may cause suffering.

b Produce a poster or presentation, entitled 'Suffering for Love', that you will share with your class. You might have sections or slides that deal with the different types of love and the characters for whom they cause suffering in the play.

1 **come near** 开始理解
2 **concurs directly with** 正好符合
3 **incites** 鼓励
4 **reverend carriage** 庄重的举止
5 **limed** 捉住（字面义：用胶粘鸟）
6 **Fellow** 伴侣（这是马尔沃琉的误解）
7 **adheres** 符合，一致
8 **dram** 丁点儿，丝毫
9 **sanctity** 神圣，圣洁
10 **Legion** 妖魔鬼怪（指所有地狱恶魔的集合；托比爵士误以为这是撒旦 [Satan] 的另一个名字）
11 **Lo = Look**
12 **Go to, go to** 行了，行了
13 **Let me alone** 让我一个人来
14 **La you** 看，瞧
15 **water** 尿液
16 **wise woman** 女郎中（据说能通过验尿诊断一人是否着魔）

MALVOLIO   O ho, do you come near[1] me now? No worse man than Sir
Toby to look to me! This concurs directly with[2] the letter: she sends
him on purpose that I may appear stubborn to him; for she incites[3]   60
me to that in the letter. 'Cast thy humble slough', says she; 'be
opposite with a kinsman, surly with servants, let thy tongue tang
with arguments of state, put thyself into the trick of singularity',
and consequently sets down the manner how: as a sad face, a
reverend carriage[4], a slow tongue, in the habit of some sir of note,   65
and so forth. I have limed[5] her, but it is Jove's doing, and Jove make
me thankful! And when she went away now, 'Let this fellow be
looked to' – 'Fellow[6]'! Not 'Malvolio', nor after my degree, but
'fellow'. Why, everything adheres[7] together, that no dram[8] of a
scruple, no scruple of a scruple, no obstacle, no incredulous or   70
unsafe circumstance – what can be said? Nothing that can be can
come between me and the full prospect of my hopes. Well, Jove,
not I, is the doer of this, and he is to be thanked!

Enter [SIR] TOBY, FABIAN, *and* MARIA

SIR TOBY   Which way is he, in the name of sanctity[9]? If all the devils
of hell be drawn in little, and Legion[10] himself possessed him, yet   75
I'll speak to him.

FABIAN   Here he is, here he is. How is't with you, sir?

SIR TOBY   How is't with you, man?

MALVOLIO   Go off, I discard you. Let me enjoy my private. Go off!

MARIA   Lo[11], how hollow the fiend speaks within him! Did not I tell you?   80
Sir Toby, my lady prays you to have a care of him.

MALVOLIO   Ah ha! Does she so?

SIR TOBY   Go to, go to[12]; peace, peace! We must deal gently with him.
Let me alone[13]. How do you, Malvolio? How is't with you? What,
man, defy the devil! Consider, he's an enemy to mankind.   85

MALVOLIO   Do you know what you say?

MARIA   La you[14], and you speak ill of the devil, how he takes it at heart!
Pray God he be not bewitched!

FABIAN   Carry his water[15] to th'wise woman[16].

MARIA   Marry, and it shall be done tomorrow morning if I live. My lady   90
would not lose him for more than I'll say.

MALVOLIO   How now, mistress?

MARIA   O Lord!

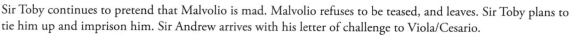

Sir Toby continues to pretend that Malvolio is mad. Malvolio refuses to be teased, and leaves. Sir Toby plans to tie him up and imprison him. Sir Andrew arrives with his letter of challenge to Viola/Cesario.

剧情简介：托比爵士继续假装马尔沃琉疯了。马尔沃琉拒绝被戏弄，走开了。托比爵士打算把他捆上再关押起来。安褚爵士拿着他写给薇娥菈/席扎瑞欧的挑战信来了。

1 Charting the changes

One of the ways in which Shakespeare successfully captures characters is by showing them undergoing subtle changes throughout the play. Characters develop between the beginning and the end of a play, and sometimes this change is noticeable between scenes. Malvolio's language in lines 79–106 shows that his feelings change by degrees as the others taunt him.

- Consider each of Malvolio's lines 79–106 in turn. For each, write down what Malvolio is feeling and thinking at that moment. Give instructions about how the actor playing the part might signal the emotion or feeling with a movement or gesture. Write your notes in a table like the one below.

Malvolio's line	Thought or feeling reflected	Accompanying gesture/ movement
'Go off, I discard you'	Superior to others. Letter instructions give him confidence.	Flick of the hand and turns away from the others in disdain.

Themes 主题分析

Fabian's reality check (in pairs)

Fabian's words (lines 108–9) remind the audience that they are in the theatre and that this is not reality. In Shakespeare's time, it was common for there to be more interaction between the audience and the performers than we expect today. Modern performances often try to give the appearance of reality, and avoid addressing the audience directly.

a Fabian's lines 108–9 often amuse the audience. Talk about what it is that makes the audience members laugh. Where might you still expect this connection between performer and audience? Consider other media, such as movies and television, as well as theatre.

b Experiment with ways of speaking the lines to create the funniest effect. It helps if you consider how, and to whom, Fabian speaks: to the characters on stage, to the whole audience or to a single person. Rehearse your preferred version and perform it to the class, within the context of the scene, to see whether it has the desired effect.

SIR TOBY	Prithee, hold thy peace; this is not the way. Do you not see you move him? Let me alone with him.

       95

SIR TOBY Prithee, hold thy peace; this is not the way. Do you not see you move him? Let me alone with him.   95

FABIAN No way but gentleness; gently, gently: the fiend is rough[1], and will not be roughly used.

SIR TOBY Why, how now, my bawcock[2]? How dost thou, chuck[3]?

MALVOLIO Sir!

SIR TOBY Ay, biddy[4], come with me. What, man, 'tis not for gravity to play at cherry-pit with Satan[5]. Hang him, foul collier[6]!   100

MARIA Get him to say his prayers, good Sir Toby, get him to pray.

MALVOLIO My prayers, minx[7]!

MARIA No, I warrant you, he will not hear of godliness.

MALVOLIO Go hang yourselves all! You are idle[8], shallow things; I am not of your element. You shall know more hereafter.   *Exit*   105

SIR TOBY Is't possible?

FABIAN If this were played upon a stage now, I could condemn it as an improbable fiction.

SIR TOBY His very genius[9] hath taken the infection of the device[10], man.   110

MARIA Nay, pursue him now, lest the device take air and taint[11].

FABIAN Why, we shall make him mad indeed.

MARIA The house will be the quieter.

SIR TOBY Come, we'll have him in a dark room and bound. My niece is already in the belief that he's mad. We may carry it thus for our pleasure, and his penance[12], till our very pastime, tired out of breath, prompt us to have mercy on him; at which time we will bring the device to the bar[13] and crown thee for a finder[14] of madmen. But see, but see!   115

Enter SIR ANDREW

FABIAN More matter for a May morning![15]   120

SIR ANDREW Here's the challenge; read it. I warrant there's vinegar and pepper in't.

FABIAN Is't so saucy[16]?

SIR ANDREW Ay, is't. I warrant him; do but read.

SIR TOBY Give me. [*Reads*] 'Youth, whatsoever thou art, thou art but a scurvy fellow[17].'   125

FABIAN Good, and valiant.

SIR TOBY [*Reads*] 'Wonder not, nor admire not in thy mind, why I do call thee so, for I will show thee no reason for't.'

FABIAN A good note! That keeps you from the blow of the law[18].   130

Sir Toby reads Sir Andrew's contorted letter and orders him to challenge Viola/Cesario forcefully in the orchard. Sir Andrew leaves, and Sir Toby reveals he plans to trick both duellists into mutual fright.

剧情简介：托比爵士读了安褚爵士写的歪曲事实的信，令他去与薇娥菈/席扎瑞欧在果园里竭力决斗。安褚爵士离开，托比爵士表示他要蒙骗决斗双方使他们彼此恐惧。

1 Tangled web of deceit (in threes)

Malvolio has just left the stage and Sir Toby is up to no good yet again. He wants to further humiliate his friend, Sir Andrew. He plans to trick both Sir Andrew and Viola-Cesario into believing that the other is a superb swordsman, so that they will be terrified of each other.

a Take turns to speak Sir Toby's plot in lines 154–63. Put as much malicious glee into your voices as possible.

b Chart the 'tricks' that are currently being played on characters in the play. Construct a diagram like the one below that connects characters involved in deceits. Write your explanations and evidence from the script along the lines (include line references, so that you can find them in the future!)

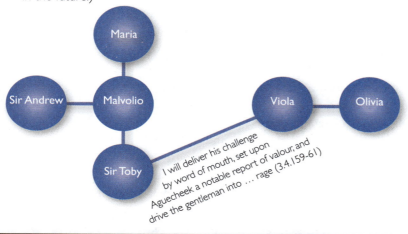

I will deliver his challenge by word of mouth, set upon Aguecheek a notable report of valour, and drive the gentleman into … rage (3.4.159–61)

1	**waylay** 埋伏，伏击
2	**o'th'windy … law** 没有法律风险
3	**move** 挑动
4	**commerce** 来往，交易
5	**scout me** 替我搜寻
6	**bumbaily** 鬼衙役（善于从背后拿人）
7	**swaggering** 不可一世
8	**twanged off** （鼻孔出气）哼了一声
9	**approbation** 认可，证明
10	**good capacity and breeding** 不错的能力和教养
11	**clodpole** 榆木棍子
12	**set upon** 把……说得
13	**his … it** 这年轻人没经验，会信以为真
14	**cockatrices** 鸡蛇（传说中鸡身蛇尾的妖怪，目光可置人于死地）
15	**presently after him** 马上找他（presently = immediately）
16	**meditate the while** 想一下
17	**horrid** 可怕，骇人听闻

Sir Toby encourages Sir Andrew to challenge Viola/Cesario. Discuss whether you think Sir Toby is a good friend who likes some fun, or whether he only cares about himself.

SIR TOBY [*Reads*] 'Thou com'st to the Lady Olivia, and in my sight she uses thee kindly. But thou liest in thy throat. That is not the matter I challenge thee for.'

FABIAN Very brief, and to exceeding good sense [*Aside*] – less.

SIR TOBY [*Reads*] 'I will waylay¹ thee going home, where if it be thy chance to kill me –' 135

FABIAN Good.

SIR TOBY [*Reads*] 'Thou kill'st me like a rogue and a villain.'

FABIAN Still you keep o'th'windy side of the law². Good.

SIR TOBY [*Reads*] 'Fare thee well, and God have mercy upon one of 140 our souls! He may have mercy upon mine, but my hope is better, and so look to thyself. Thy friend, as thou usest him, and thy sworn enemy,

Andrew Aguecheek.'

If this letter move³ him not, his legs cannot. I'll give't him. 145

MARIA You may have very fit occasion for't; he is now in some commerce⁴ with my lady and will by and by depart.

SIR TOBY Go, Sir Andrew, scout me⁵ for him at the corner of the orchard like a bumbaily⁶. So soon as ever thou seest him, draw, and as thou draw'st, swear horrible; for it comes to pass oft that a terrible oath, 150 with a swaggering⁷ accent sharply twanged off⁸, gives manhood more approbation⁹ than ever proof itself would have earned him. Away!

SIR ANDREW Nay, let me alone for swearing. *Exit*

SIR TOBY Now will not I deliver his letter; for the behaviour of the young gentleman gives him out to be of good capacity and breeding¹⁰; 155 his employment between his lord and my niece confirms no less. Therefore this letter, being so excellently ignorant, will breed no terror in the youth; he will find it comes from a clodpole¹¹. But, sir, I will deliver his challenge by word of mouth, set upon¹² Aguecheek a notable report of valour, and drive the gentleman (as I know his 160 youth will aptly receive it¹³) into a most hideous opinion of his rage, skill, fury, and impetuosity. This will so fright them both that they will kill one another by the look, like cockatrices¹⁴.

FABIAN Here he comes with your niece; give them way till he take leave and presently after him¹⁵. 165

Enter OLIVIA *and* VIOLA

SIR TOBY I will meditate the while¹⁶ upon some horrid¹⁷ message for a challenge.

[*Exeunt Sir Toby, Fabian, and Maria*]

Olivia reveals her passionate love to Viola/Cesario, and gives 'him' a jewel. Viola/Cesario tells her to love Orsino instead. Sir Toby tells Viola/Cesario to draw 'his' sword and face Sir Andrew's rage and supreme swordsmanship.

 剧情简介：娥丽维娅向薇娥菈/席扎瑞欧吐露了自己的痴情，并送给"他"一件珠宝。薇娥菈/席扎瑞欧却告诉她应该爱奥悉诺。托比爵士让薇娥菈/席扎瑞欧拔出"他"的剑，直面安褚爵士的愤怒和高超的剑术。

Stagecraft 导演技巧

A brief 'love' episode (in pairs)

The brief episode in which Olivia and Viola talk together is a reminder of the absurdity of Olivia's love. It is also a type of 'dramatic bridge' to continue the comic plot, ensuring that Viola will be drawn into Sir Toby's malicious scheme.

a Read lines 168–84. Earlier, Olivia was impatiently awaiting the arrival of Viola/Cesario. Now she enters with 'I have said too much unto a heart of stone' (line 168), and says that she has spoken without caution ('unchary') of her love for 'him'.

b Improvise the offstage conversation in which Olivia again reveals her love, but Viola/Cesario rejects it. Decide on a dramatically effective way for Olivia to leave at line 184.

1 Mistaken identity? (in pairs)

Shakespeare's scripts were copied by hand and sometimes mistakes crept into the accepted version. Talk about whether Shakespeare might have written 'friend' instead of 'fiend' in line 184. Which do you prefer, and why?

2 The comedy continues (in pairs)

The next episode in Scene 4 presents the rather comic preparations for the 'duel' between Viola/Cesario and Sir Andrew (lines 185–263). First, Sir Toby paints a picture of a furious and formidable (令人生畏) Sir Andrew (lines 185–219). Viola is puzzled and probably frightened.

a List all the images that Sir Toby creates to intimidate Viola, and below them describe what the reality is. See the example below.

Claim

'thy intercepter, full of despite, bloody as the hunter'

Meaning

Your opponent, full of spite, bloody like a hunter

Reality

Sir Andrew is terrified about what will happen and has no combat skills.

b Take parts and read the lines. Change roles and read through again, with Viola trying to get away from Sir Toby while he constantly pursues her. Emphasise all the violent words that he includes to frighten Viola/Cesario.

1 unchary 轻率
2 With … griefs （指奥悉诺承受了同样的痛苦）
3 vex 使烦恼
4 acquit 使解脱
5 betake thee to't 你要准备好
6 intercepter 阻击你的人
7 despite 憎恶
8 Dismount thy tuck 把你的剑拔出来
9 yare 轻快，敏捷
10 opposite 对手，敌手
11 dubbed with unhatched rapier 用一把未劈砍过的剑封爵
12 on carpet consideration 在地毯上（指出于政治考虑而非因军功受封）
13 sepulchre 坟墓
14 Hob nob is his word 他的座右铭是：有没有拉到

OLIVIA	I have said too much unto a heart of stone,	
	And laid mine honour too unchary[1] on't;	
	There's something in me that reproves my fault,	170
	But such a headstrong potent fault it is,	
	That it but mocks reproof.	
VIOLA	With the same 'haviour that your passion bears	
	Goes on my master's griefs[2].	
OLIVIA	Here, wear this jewel for me; 'tis my picture.	175
	Refuse it not; it hath no tongue to vex[3] you.	
	And, I beseech you, come again tomorrow.	
	What shall you ask of me that I'll deny,	
	That honour, saved, may upon asking give?	
VIOLA	Nothing but this – your true love for my master.	180
OLIVIA	How with mine honour may I give him that	
	Which I have given to you?	
VIOLA	I will acquit[4] you.	
OLIVIA	Well, come again tomorrow. Fare thee well.	
	A fiend like thee might bear my soul to hell.	[*Exit*]

Enter SIR TOBY *and* FABIAN

SIR TOBY	Gentleman, God save thee.	185
VIOLA	And you, sir.	
SIR TOBY	That defence thou hast, betake thee to't[5]. Of what nature the wrongs are thou hast done him, I know not; but thy intercepter[6], full of despite[7], bloody as the hunter, attends thee at the orchard-end. Dismount thy tuck[8], be yare[9] in thy preparation, for thy assailant is quick, skilful, and deadly.	190
VIOLA	You mistake, sir. I am sure no man hath any quarrel to me. My remembrance is very free and clear from any image of offence done to any man.	
SIR TOBY	You'll find it otherwise, I assure you. Therefore, if you hold your life at any price, betake you to your guard; for your opposite[10] hath in him what youth, strength, skill, and wrath can furnish man withal.	195
VIOLA	I pray you, sir, what is he?	
SIR TOBY	He is knight, dubbed with unhatched rapier[11], and on carpet consideration[12], but he is a devil in private brawl. Souls and bodies hath he divorced three, and his incensement at this moment is so implacable that satisfaction can be none but by pangs of death and sepulchre[13]. Hob nob is his word[14]: give't or take't.	200

Viola tries to avoid the duel, but Sir Toby, then Fabian, prevent her and tell of Sir Andrew's anger and bravery. Sir Toby then similarly frightens Sir Andrew with report of Viola's sword-fencing skill.

 剧情简介: 薇娥菈试图避免决斗，但托比爵士以及后来费边都阻止她那样做，并告诉她安褚爵士很生气，也很英勇。托比爵士接着用同样的方法恐吓安诸爵士，谎称薇娥菈剑术高超。

Language in the play 剧中语言

'he has been a fencer to the sophy' (in pairs)

In 1600, Sir Anthony Sherley published an account of his adventures whilst serving as ambassador to the Shah of Persia ('the sophy'). Elizabethans were fascinated by the story and this may have been included to amuse the audience. Sir Anthony's brother, Robert, was still serving in the Shah's army when the play was written.

• One of you reads the lines in which Sir Toby 'describes' Viola (lines 232–6), while the other in your pair plays the part of Sir Andrew reacting to the information through facial expressions, movements and sounds. After each line, 'Sir Andrew' should thought-track his response, speaking out loud the words that he is thinking but which he cannot say to the other characters.

1	conduct	护卫，守护
2	quirk	特性
3	competent	充分
4	injury	冒犯
5	meddle	战斗
6	iron	剑
7	courteous office	礼貌行为
8	incensed against	对……恼怒
9	mortal arbitrement	决一死战
10	read him by his form	通过他的外表判断
11	be ... for't	为此而对您感激不尽
12	mettle	性情，脾气
13	firago	健妇（如亚马孙女武士）
14	stuck-in	刺，戳（击剑用语）
15	Pox on't	该死的

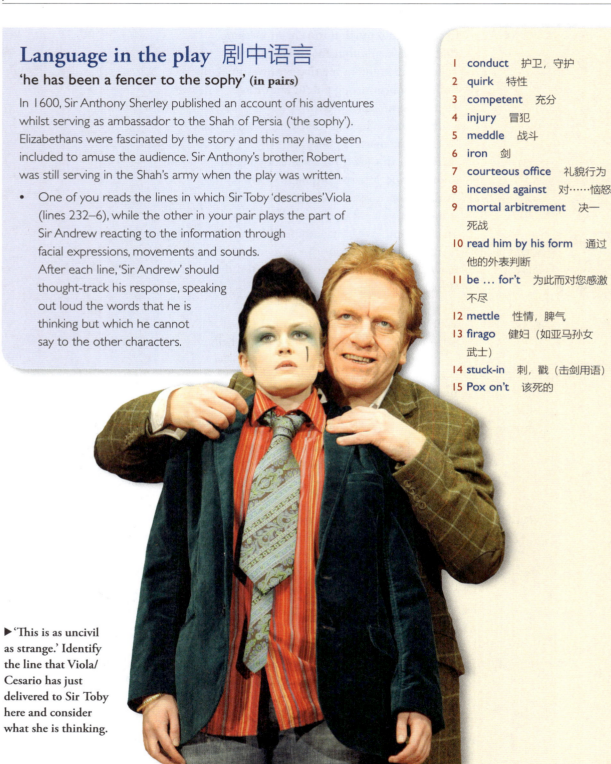

▶ 'This is as uncivil as strange.' Identify the line that Viola/ Cesario has just delivered to Sir Toby here and consider what she is thinking.

VIOLA   I will return again into the house and desire some conduct[1] of   205
the lady. I am no fighter. I have heard of some kind of men that
put quarrels purposely on others to taste their valour; belike this
is a man of that quirk[2].

SIR TOBY   Sir, no. His indignation derives itself out of a very competent[3]
injury[4]; therefore get you on and give him his desire. Back you shall   210
not to the house, unless you undertake that with me which with
as much safety you might answer him; therefore on, or strip your
sword stark naked; for meddle[5] you must, that's certain, or forswear
to wear iron[6] about you.

VIOLA   This is as uncivil as strange. I beseech you, do me this courteous   215
office[7] as to know of the knight what my offence to him is. It is
something of my negligence, nothing of my purpose.

SIR TOBY   I will do so. Signior Fabian, stay you by this gentleman till
my return.   *Exit [Sir] Toby*

VIOLA   Pray you, sir, do you know of this matter?   220

FABIAN   I know the knight is incensed against[8] you, even to a mortal
arbitrement[9], but nothing of the circumstance more.

VIOLA   I beseech you, what manner of man is he?

FABIAN   Nothing of that wonderful promise, to read him by his form[10],
as you are like to find him in the proof of his valour. He is indeed,   225
sir, the most skilful, bloody, and fatal opposite that you could
possibly have found in any part of Illyria. Will you walk towards
him? I will make your peace with him if I can.

VIOLA   I shall be much bound to you for't[11]. I am one that had rather
go with sir priest than sir knight. I care not who knows so much   230
of my mettle[12].

Exeunt

Enter [SIR] TOBY *and* [SIR] ANDREW

SIR TOBY   Why, man, he's a very devil. I have not seen such a firago[13].
I had a pass with him, rapier, scabbard, and all, and he gives me
the stuck-in[14] with such a mortal motion that it is inevitable; and on
the answer, he pays you as surely as your feet hits the ground they   235
step on. They say he has been fencer to the sophy.

SIR ANDREW   Pox on't[15]. I'll not meddle with him.

SIR TOBY   Ay, but he will not now be pacified. Fabian can scarce hold
him yonder.

Andrew promises to give Sir Toby his horse if he can persuade Viola/Cesario to call off the duel. Viola is equally terrified. Sir Toby forces them to draw swords, but Antonio enters and intervenes on Viola's behalf.

剧情简介：安褚承诺，如果托比爵士能说服薇娥菈/席扎瑞欧取消决斗，就把自己的马送给托比爵士。薇娥菈同样吓坏了。托比爵士逼迫他们拔剑，但安托纽上台，挺身为薇娥菈出面干预。

1. in fence　在击剑方面
2. ere = before
3. Capilet　卡皮雷马（一种矮马）
4. motion　提议
5. perdition of souls　失去生命
6. horribly conceited　满是可怕的印象
7. for's oath sake　他已经发誓
8. supportance of his vow　维护他的誓言
9. A little ... man　一样小东西就会迫使我告诉他们我多么没有男人样
10. Give ground　让步
11. bout　回合
12. duello　决斗的规则
13. undertaker　打抱不平的人

1 Tension versus comedy (in fours)

Lines 220–63 make wonderfully funny theatre. Viola and Sir Andrew are terrified of each other, and Fabian and Sir Toby do all they can to heighten their fear. Sometimes the mock fight lasts for several minutes as the petrified opponents, spurred on by Sir Toby and Fabian, ludicrously (可笑) fence with each other. In some productions, they cover their eyes and jump back fearfully at any touch of swords. In addition, Viola speaks an aside (lines 255–6) that, with its irony and sexual humour, usually causes great audience amusement.

* Take parts and work out how to stage lines 220–63 to create maximum dramatic tension. Then try this again but with the aim of creating maximum comic effect. Safety warning: don't use real swords or sharp objects – rubber swords would be even funnier when creating a comic scene!

SIR ANDREW Plague on't, and I thought he had been valiant, and so   240
cunning in fence[1], I'd have seen him damned ere[2] I'd have challenged
him. Let him let the matter slip, and I'll give him my horse, Grey
Capilet[3].

SIR TOBY I'll make the motion[4]. Stand here, make a good show on't.
This shall end without the perdition of souls[5]. [Aside] Marry, I'll   245
ride your horse as well as I ride you.

Enter FABIAN *and* VIOLA

[*To Fabian*] I have his horse to take up the quarrel. I have
persuaded him the youth's a devil.

FABIAN He is as horribly conceited[6] of him and pants and looks pale,
as if a bear were at his heels.   250

SIR TOBY [*To Viola*] There's no remedy, sir. He will fight with you
for's oath sake[7]. Marry, he hath better bethought him of his quarrel,
and he finds that now scarce to be worth talking of. Therefore, draw
for the supportance of his vow[8]. He protests he will not hurt you.

VIOLA [*Aside*] Pray God defend me! A little thing would make me tell   255
them how much I lack of a man[9].

FABIAN Give ground[10] if you see him furious.

SIR TOBY Come, Sir Andrew, there's no remedy: the gentleman will
for his honour's sake have one bout[11] with you; he cannot by the
duello[12] avoid it, but he has promised me, as he is a gentleman and   260
a soldier, he will not hurt you. Come on, to't.

SIR ANDREW Pray God he keep his oath!

VIOLA I do assure you, 'tis against my will.

[*They draw*]

Enter ANTONIO

ANTONIO [*Drawing*] Put up your sword! If this young gentleman
Have done offence, I take the fault on me;   265
If you offend him, I for him defy you.

SIR TOBY You, sir? Why, what are you?

ANTONIO One, sir, that for his love dares yet do more
Than you have heard him brag to you he will.

SIR TOBY Nay, if you be an undertaker[13], I am for you. [*Draws*]   270

Enter OFFICERS

FABIAN O good Sir Toby, hold! Here comes the officers.

Viola/Cesario and Sir Andrew make peace. The officers arrest Antonio. He asks Viola/Cesario for his money, mistaking 'him' for Sebastian, and is disappointed at 'his' apparent ingratitude.

剧情简介： 薇娥菈/席扎瑞欧和安褚爵士和解。官差逮捕了安托纽。安托纽错把薇娥菈/席扎瑞欧当成了塞巴斯田，向"他"要自己的钱，并对"他"显而易见的忘恩负义感到失望。

1 'You stand amazed'

Shakespeare often builds stage directions into characters' language. Here, Antonio's line 'You stand amazed' sums up exactly Viola's position. It's no wonder that Viola is bewildered. First she finds herself participating in a duel for reasons that she does not fully understand. Then Sir Andrew says something very odd to her, promising her a horse (lines 274–5) she knows nothing about. Now her rescuer, a man she has never seen before, is arrested and asks her to return his money! (Remember you made a prediction about this earlier – see p. 86.)

- Read through lines 274–90 (in which Viola does not speak). Write suggestions as to how Viola could react to each line or track her thoughts.

2 'I hate ingratitude' (in pairs)

Shakespeare seems to have hated ingratitude. He refers to it very critically in several plays:

Ingratitude! Thou marble-hearted fiend,
More hideous when thou show'st thee in a child
Than the sea-monster.

King Lear, Act 1 Scene 4

Those scraps are good deeds past, which are devoured
As fast as they are made, forgot as soon
As done.

Troilus and Cressida, Act 3 Scene 3

Now Antonio, mistaking Viola/Cesario for Sebastian, harshly accuses her of ingratitude.

a Do you share Viola's judgement (lines 305–8) that ingratitude is more hateful than any other vice? Begin by discussing the other three vices – 'lying, vainness, babbling drunkenness' – that Viola mentions. Consider whether they are worse vices than ingratitude. You might rank them and compare your conclusions with other pairs.

b Antonio is incredulous at his friend's apparent ingratitude in Scene 4. Take parts as Viola and Antonio and speak lines 282–323 (leave out the Officers' lines). Try to convincingly express Antonio's disappointment and increasing anger, and Viola's bewilderment.

1	anon	马上
2	reins well	容易驾驭
3	office	职责
4	at the suit	根据起诉
5	favour	长相，面容
6	amazed	困惑，迷茫
7	entreat of	向……恳求
8	part	一部分
9	My having	我所拥有的
10	my present	我现有的钱
11	coffer	钱柜
12	deserts	值得报答的行为或品质
13	tempt	激起，引发
14	unsound	不道德
15	vainness	虚荣

SIR TOBY [*To Antonio*] I'll be with you anon[1].

VIOLA [*To Sir Andrew*] Pray, sir, put your sword up, if you please.

SIR ANDREW Marry, will I, sir; and for that I promised you, I'll be
as good as my word. He will bear you easily and reins well[2].   275

1 OFFICER This is the man; do thy office[3].

2 OFFICER Antonio, I arrest thee at the suit[4]
Of Count Orsino.

ANTONIO   You do mistake me, sir.

1 OFFICER No, sir, no jot. I know your favour[5] well,
Though now you have no sea-cap on your head.   280
Take him away; he knows I know him well.

ANTONIO I must obey. [*To Viola*] This comes with seeking you.
But there's no remedy; I shall answer it.
What will you do, now my necessity
Makes me to ask you for my purse? It grieves me   285
Much more for what I cannot do for you
Than what befalls myself. You stand amazed[6],
But be of comfort.

2 OFFICER Come, sir, away.

ANTONIO I must entreat of[7] you some of that money.   290

VIOLA What money, sir?
For the fair kindness you have showed me here,
And part[8] being prompted by your present trouble,
Out of my lean and low ability
I'll lend you something. My having[9] is not much;   295
I'll make division of my present[10] with you.
Hold, there's half my coffer[11].

ANTONIO Will you deny me now?
Is't possible that my deserts[12] to you
Can lack persuasion? Do not tempt[13] my misery,   300
Lest that it make me so unsound[14] a man
As to upbraid you with those kindnesses
That I have done for you.

VIOLA   I know of none,
Nor know I you by voice or any feature.
I hate ingratitude more in a man   305
Than lying, vainness[15], babbling drunkenness,
Or any taint of vice whose strong corruption
Inhabits our frail blood.

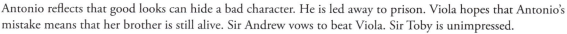

Antonio reflects that good looks can hide a bad character. He is led away to prison. Viola hopes that Antonio's mistake means that her brother is still alive. Sir Andrew vows to beat Viola. Sir Toby is unimpressed.

剧情简介：安托纽表示好看的长相可以遮掩糟糕的人品。他被押往监狱。薇娥菈希望安托纽认错人这件事意味着她哥哥仍活着。安褚爵士发誓要打败薇娥菈。托比爵士不以为然。

1 Putting Sebastian on a pedestal (in small groups)

Antonio has clearly put Sebastian on a pedestal, worshipping him like a god ('sanctity', 'image', 'venerable', 'devotion', 'idol', 'god').

- Talk together about how Antonio's 'religious' language adds to your impression of his friendship with Sebastian. What does it suggest about the authority and power in their relationship? Is this an equal relationship? Is one friend going to be let down by the other? Make a note of your ideas, using quotations from the script as evidence to support your ideas. Review your predictions later to see if you are correct.

Themes 主题分析

'beauteous-evil'

Antonio's lines (318–21) are another reference to the theme of appearance versus reality. He reflects that only an unkind nature can be called 'deformed'. Wickedness can hide behind good looks ('beauteous-evil').

- Turn back to Act 1 Scene 2, lines 48–51, where Viola says something similar. Do you agree with Antonio? Make a list of arguments for and against the idea that wickedness can hide behind good looks. Give examples of contemporary or historical figures that exemplify this idea.

Write about it 写作练习

The Officers' report (in pairs)

Orsino's Officers have very little to say in this scene. Imagine that they are expected to write their report for the duke on all they saw and heard in lines 271–323. Set out the report in a formal style and ensure that you write in the third person to reflect the purpose, audience and effect of an official document. Use the example to the right as a starting point if you like.

1	**Relieved** 解救
2	**venerable worth** 值得人崇敬
3	**vile** 卑鄙
4	**idol** 偶像
5	**done good feature shame** 辱没了你英俊的外表
6	**blemish** 瑕疵，污点
7	**trunks** 大木箱；躯壳
8	**o'er-flourished** 装饰
9	**sage saws** 睿智的箴言
10	**Yet living in my glass** 还活着，跟我一模一样（就像我的镜像）
11	**prove** 证明是真的
12	**salt waves fresh** 海浪就是淡水
13	**paltry** 可鄙
14	**'Slid** = By God's eyelid（以上帝的眼皮起誓）
15	**cuff him soundly** 好好暴打他一顿
16	**lay any money** 赌多少钱都可以

ROYAL COURT OF ILLYRIA
Report of Arrest

Suspect: Antonio
Nationality: ???
Occupation: Mercenary（雇佣兵）

Officers apprehended Antonio in the evening at the Elephant Inn. He was found to be in …

ANTONIO	O heavens themselves!	
2 OFFICER	Come, sir, I pray you go.	
ANTONIO	Let me speak a little. This youth that you see here,	310
	I snatched one-half out of the jaws of death,	
	Relieved[1] him with such sanctity of love;	
	And to his image, which methought did promise	
	Most venerable worth[2], did I devotion.	
1 OFFICER	What's that to us? The time goes by. Away!	315
ANTONIO	But O how vile[3] an idol[4] proves this god!	
	Thou hast, Sebastian, done good feature shame[5].	
	In nature there's no blemish[6] but the mind:	
	None can be called deformed but the unkind.	
	Virtue is beauty, but the beauteous-evil	320
	Are empty trunks[7], o'er-flourished[8] by the devil.	
1 OFFICER	The man grows mad. Away with him! Come, come, sir.	
ANTONIO	Lead me on.	

Exit [with Officers]

VIOLA	Methinks his words do from such passion fly	
	That he believes himself; so do not I.	325
	Prove true, imagination, O prove true,	
	That I, dear brother, be now tane for you!	
SIR TOBY	Come hither, knight, come hither, Fabian. We'll whisper o'er a couplet or two of most sage saws[9].	
VIOLA	He named Sebastian. I my brother know	330
	Yet living in my glass[10]; even such and so	
	In favour was my brother, and he went	
	Still in this fashion, colour, ornament,	
	For him I imitate. O if it prove[11],	
	Tempests are kind, and salt waves fresh[12] in love. *[Exit]*	335
SIR TOBY	A very dishonest paltry[13] boy, and more a coward than a hare; his dishonesty appears in leaving his friend here in necessity, and denying him; and for his cowardship, ask Fabian.	
FABIAN	A coward, a most devout coward, religious in it.	
SIR ANDREW	'Slid[14], I'll after him again and beat him.	340
SIR TOBY	Do, cuff him soundly[15], but never draw thy sword.	
SIR ANDREW	And I do not – *[Exit]*	
FABIAN	Come, let's see the event.	
SIR TOBY	I dare lay any money[16], 'twill be nothing yet.	

Exeunt

Looking back at Act 3 第3幕回顾
Activities for groups or individuals

1 Appearance versus reality revisited

At the end of Act 1 (see p. 34), you considered how individual characters were affected in some way by the difference between reality and appearance. Charting how themes develop is a significant step in understanding how Shakespeare structures his plays to create tension and comedy.

a Look again at the board where you recorded on sticky notes the name of each character and how they were affected by appearance and reality. Add any new developments since Act 1 for each character by adding, removing or amending the sticky notes.

b Act 3 is marked by people making mistakes, especially mistaking identity. Alongside each name, write who or what they have mistaken.

c Consider who is now most affected by the differences between appearance and reality. Has this changed and developed? Why? What is the effect of any such changes on the audience?

d Use the sticky notes to write a paragraph on each character in turn. Examine the effect of appearance and reality upon them. Conclude with a paragraph that explores who you think is the most affected, your reasons for this decision and the effect on the audience of the character being thus affected.

e Write an essay that explores how appearance and reality develops in the play. Carefully examine how Shakespeare uses the play's language, structure and links between characters to develop the theme.

2 Realism in the theatre

Actors and audience in the open-air theatres of Elizabethan England or the temporary performance spaces in great houses, halls and inns were all too aware of where they were. Distractions and limitations, such as the weather, lack of lighting and restricted special effects, meant the play had to rely on the audience's imagination. Like Fabian (Act 3 Scene 4, line 108), Shakespeare's characters often make reference to the theatre or playing a part.

With advances in theatre settings, actors in the nineteenth century sought more realistic performances. Twentieth-century 'method' actors used techniques to create lifelike performances by imagining their character's internal thoughts and emotions. These actors were seeking to affect the audience members in a more profound way and to immerse them more completely in the play.

a In groups, discuss whether you think that Shakespeare wanted the audience to be immersed in the drama and the characters' lives, forgetting the world outside for the duration of the play. Did he perhaps want the audience to remain objective and aware of the 'pretence', so that they could judge the characters? Should characters who have soliloquies and asides or who display dramatic irony, such as Malvolio (Act 3 Scene 4, lines 58–73) and Viola (Act 3 Scene 4, lines 255–6), speak to the audience and involve them?

b Act out lines 58–73 and 255–6 to an audience. Ignore the audience members at first and allow them to be immersed. Then replay the lines, involving them. Discuss and decide which is the most effective.

3 Event after event after event

The pictures opposite show some of the events in Act 3 Scene 4; it is pretty action packed!

• In pairs, compile a detailed list of the events that take place in this scene. In fours, discuss why Shakespeare has decided to set all of these in one scene and one place (Olivia's garden). Compose an explanation of why he has chosen for there to be no breaks in the action, considering the intended effect on the audience as well as practical and staging reasons.

▲ In this production, the sword duel between Viola and Sir Andrew became a boxing match. Discuss how you might stage this scene.

► Discuss what you think about Olivia's rapidly changing persona. Is it realistic? Is there a dramatic purpose to the change?

This Malvolio displays the yellow that Olivia 'requested', but his cross-garters have been altered to reflect another culture and style of dress. Discuss the amendments that you might make to reflect your culture.

Feste has mistaken Sebastian for Viola. Sebastian tries to get rid of him with money and a threat. Sir Andrew makes the same mistake, strikes Sebastian – and is hit in return!

剧情简介：费斯特错把塞巴斯田当成薇娥菈。塞巴斯田试图用金钱和威胁把他打发走。安褚爵士犯了同样错误，还打了塞巴斯田，结果遭到还击！

Themes 主题分析

'Nothing that is so is so' (in fives)

Scene 1 opens with yet another example of mistaken identity: Feste thinks Sebastian is Viola/Cesario. Feste's words could be the motto of the play. They express the theme of appearance versus reality: appearances are deceptive. As the scene develops, Sir Andrew, Sir Toby and Olivia will also mistake Sebastian for Viola/Cesario. For their mistakes:

- Feste receives money and the threat of a beating
- Sir Andrew gets a beating
- Sir Toby almost fights a duel
- Olivia seems about to get the man of her dreams.

Take parts as Feste, Sebastian, Sir Andrew, Sir Toby and Olivia and read the whole scene. As you speak lines 1–20, try to bring out Sebastian's increasing irritation, and Feste's conviction that he is speaking to Cesario.

1 Sir Andrew receives 'worse payment' (in fives)

In many productions, the entrance of Sir Toby, Sir Andrew and Fabian is a very funny moment as the audience realises that the characters have mistaken Sebastian for Viola/Cesario and anticipate what will happen next. Often, the characters enter full of exaggerated swagger and machismo (大男子主义行为). Much of the humour in lines 20–4 depends on the reactions the actors give to the beating they are either witnessing, giving out or receiving.

- Each person should take a part and stand in a line. Be careful at this point – there is no need for physical contact in the classroom or studio! While facing the front, act out in mime different ways Sir Andrew might 'strike' Sebastian and different ways Sebastian might 'beat' him in return. Those playing Feste, Fabian and Sir Toby should use exaggerated winces (挤眉弄眼), facial expressions and body language to express their shock, horror or amusement with every blow. You should have fun showing the reactions as well as depicting the clear mismatch in strength and fighting ability on display!

1 **held out** 坚持，继续
2 **vent thy folly** 卖你的傻
3 **great lubber** 大呆子，大笨蛋
4 **cockney** 娘炮
5 **ungird thy strangeness** 别再假装陌生人
6 **Greek** 希腊人；小丑
7 **If … payment** 要是再待下去，我就赏你个苦头吃吃
8 **open hand** 出手大方
9 **report** 名声
10 **after fourteen years' purchase** 付了14年的高价之后（伊丽莎白时期英国地块的售价相当于其12年地租的收益，以14年地租的价格买地即花了高价）
11 **Hold** 站住
12 **dagger** 短剑

Act 4 Scene 1
The street outside Olivia's house

Enter SEBASTIAN *and* FESTE

FESTE   Will you make me believe that I am not sent for you?

SEBASTIAN   Go to, go to, thou art a foolish fellow.
Let me be clear of thee.

FESTE   Well held out[1], i'faith! No, I do not know you, nor I am not sent
to you by my lady to bid you come speak with her; nor your name   5
is not Master Cesario; nor this is not my nose neither. Nothing that
is so is so.

SEBASTIAN   I prithee, vent thy folly[2] somewhere else.
Thou know'st not me.

FESTE   Vent my folly! He has heard that word of some great man and   10
now applies it to a fool. Vent my folly! I am afraid this great lubber[3]
the world will prove a cockney[4]. I prithee now, ungird thy
strangeness[5] and tell me what I shall vent to my lady. Shall I vent
to her that thou art coming?

SEBASTIAN   I prithee, foolish Greek[6], depart from me.   15
There's money for thee. If you tarry longer,
I shall give worse payment[7].

FESTE   By my troth, thou hast an open hand[8]. These wise men that give
fools money get themselves a good report[9] – after fourteen years'
purchase[10].   20

Enter [SIR] ANDREW, [SIR] TOBY, *and* FABIAN

SIR ANDREW   Now, sir, have I met you again? There's for you!
[*Strikes Sebastian*]

SEBASTIAN   Why, there's for thee, and there, and there!
[*Beats Sir Andrew*]
Are all the people mad?

SIR TOBY   Hold[11], sir, or I'll throw your dagger[12] o'er the house.

Sir Toby challenges Sebastian to a fight, but Olivia intervenes and orders Sir Toby and his friends to leave. She invites Sebastian to go with her. He willingly agrees, wondering if it is all a dream.

剧情简介：托比爵士向塞巴斯田挑战，但娥丽维娅出面干预，并命令托比爵士和他的朋友们离开。她邀请塞巴斯田跟她走，他欣然同意，寻思着这一切是不是一场梦。

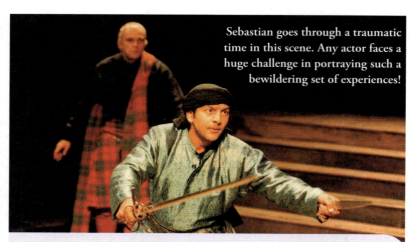

Sebastian goes through a traumatic time in this scene. Any actor faces a huge challenge in portraying such a bewildering set of experiences!

Characters 人物分析

Sebastian

Consider the scene from Sebastian's point of view. First, he meets a fool who calls him 'Cesario' and talks incomprehensibly about an invitation from a lady. Then he is assaulted by one man and threatened by another. Finally, a beautiful woman invites him lovingly into her house. No wonder he thinks he's either mad or dreaming – and wants to continue dreaming! ('Let fancy still my sense in Lethe steep' means 'Let my imagination always drown my reason with forgetfulness'.)

a Record an imagined voicemail message from Sebastian to Antonio, explaining (as best he can!) what has just happened to him.

b Draw a rough sketch of a brain. Divide the brain into five, and label each section with one emotion you think Sebastian experiences in this scene. Fill the rest of each section with at least one quotation to illustrate the relevant emotion. You should have a visual representation of the confusion Sebastian is experiencing.

Stagecraft 导演技巧

Olivia (in pairs)

Olivia's lines 38–44 give every actor a tremendous opportunity to play the grand lady. Some productions give her a stately entrance, but in one production she charged (冲) on carrying an enormous spear!

• Experiment in turn with saying the lines to each other in the most powerful way you can. Add appropriate gestures. Remember, at this moment Olivia must totally command the stage.

1 in some of your coats 穿你们的外套；跟你们交换位置
2 go another way 另想办法
3 have an action of battery 提起人身侵犯诉讼
4 put up your iron 收起您的剑来
5 well fleshed 手痒痒，想打架
6 malapert 张狂
7 Ungracious wretch 混账东西
8 Rudesby 痞子
9 uncivil and unjust extent 不文明且无道理的行为
10 fruitless pranks 无聊的恶作剧
11 ruffian 恶棍
12 botched up 拼凑起来
13 shalt not choose but go 怎么都行，就是别走
14 Beshrew 诅咒
15 started 惊动了
16 relish 好事
17 fancy 想象
18 Lethe 遗忘河（希腊神话里冥界的五条河之一，死者进入冥界后会被要求喝这条河里的水，以忘却尘世）

112

FESTE   This will I tell my lady straight; I would not be in some of your   25

coats[1] for twopence.   [*Exit*]

SIR TOBY   Come on, sir, hold!

SIR ANDREW   Nay, let him alone. I'll go another way[2] to work with him;

I'll have an action of battery[3] against him, if there be any law in

Illyria. Though I struck him first, yet it's no matter for that.   30

SEBASTIAN   Let go thy hand!

SIR TOBY   Come, sir, I will not let you go. Come, my young soldier,

put up your iron[4]. You are well fleshed[5]. Come on!

SEBASTIAN   I will be free from thee. [*Draws his sword*] What wouldst

thou now?

If thou dar'st tempt me further, draw thy sword.   35

SIR TOBY   What, what! Nay, then, I must have an ounce or two of this

malapert[6] blood from you. [*Draws*]

Enter OLIVIA

OLIVIA   Hold, Toby! On thy life I charge thee hold!

SIR TOBY   Madam –

OLIVIA   Will it be ever thus? Ungracious wretch[7],   40

Fit for the mountains and the barbarous caves,

Where manners ne'er were preached! Out of my sight!

Be not offended, dear Cesario.

Rudesby[8], be gone!

[*Exeunt Sir Toby, Sir Andrew, and Fabian*]

I prithee, gentle friend,

Let thy fair wisdom, not thy passion, sway   45

In this uncivil and unjust extent[9]

Against thy peace. Go with me to my house

And hear thou there how many fruitless pranks[10]

This ruffian[11] hath botched up[12], that thou thereby

Mayst smile at this. Thou shalt not choose but go[13].   50

Do not deny. Beshrew[14] his soul for me,

He started[15] one poor heart of mine, in thee.

SEBASTIAN   What relish[16] is in this? How runs the stream?

Or I am mad, or else this is a dream.

Let fancy[17] still my sense in Lethe[18] steep;   55

If it be thus to dream, still let me sleep!

OLIVIA   Nay, come, I prithee; would thou'dst be ruled by me!

SEBASTIAN   Madam, I will.

OLIVIA   O say so, and so be!

Exeunt

Maria encourages Feste to disguise himself as Sir Topas, the curate. He jokes with Sir Toby, and then begins to torment the imprisoned Malvolio, treating Malvolio as if he were mad.

剧情简介：玛蕊娅怂恿费斯特假扮成助理祭司托珀神父。他与托比爵士开玩笑，然后开始折磨被关了禁闭的马尔沃琉，像对待疯子那样对待他。

Stagecraft 导演技巧

Creating Malvolio's 'dark room'

Modern theatres allow for many technical methods of staging Malvolio's imprisonment (see the examples on this page and on pages 118 and 125). It is worth remembering that although most Elizabethan theatres were open air and performed in daylight, many scholars believe that the first production of *Twelfth Night* was probably staged indoors by candlelight. Modern productions often use trapdoors (活板门), constructed cages, lighting effects or even projected images to create an interesting and impactful dark 'house'.

- Design a set for Act 4 Scene 2 using sketches and annotations. Include a dark room as Malvolio's prison. How will you present the darkness? How will you make sure that the audience can see Feste fooling him as Sir Topas?

Themes 主题分析

Appearance and reality: priests (in small groups)

In Elizabethan times, priests like Sir Topas were regarded as great scholars. But they also became the subject of many jokes. Feste parodies the academic style of churchmen, using pretentious language and mock logic. He invents fictitious experts ('the old hermit of Prague') and imitates philosophical talk ('That that is, is'). In the previous scene, Feste said 'Nothing that is so is so'. So now he says just the opposite. It's all part of the topsy-turvy (上下颠倒) world of Illyria, where appearances and truth are rarely the same thing!

a Take turns to speak lines 11–14 as if you were an old, learned professor, talking of very important truths.

b Play a short game in which one person mimes a character from the play. When guessing who it is, say 'That that is, is…'

1	curate　助理祭司
2	dissemble myself　给自己换个模样
3	tall　高大（这里可能指"敦实"，与后文的lean形成对比）
4	become the function　适合履行这一职责
5	student　学者
6	competitors　同谋，同伙
7	Parson　教区牧师
8	*Bonos dies* = Good day（蹩脚的拉丁文）
9	Gorboduc　高勃达（传说中李尔王之后的一位不列颠国王，命运与李尔王类似）
10	The knave counterfeits well　这个奴才扮演得不错
11	hyperbolical fiend　自夸自大的恶鬼
12	vexest thou　你折磨

◀ All types of sets have been used to show Malvolio's imprisonment in this scene. He has been chained like a bear to a stake, and caged like a lion. Here you can see the director placed poor Malvolio in a dog kennel!

Act 4 Scene 2
A room in Olivia's house

Enter MARIA *and* FESTE

MARIA Nay, I prithee put on this gown and this beard; make him believe thou art Sir Topas the curate[1]. Do it quickly. I'll call Sir Toby the whilst.   [*Exit*]

FESTE Well, I'll put it on, and I will dissemble myself[2] in't, and I would I were the first that ever dissembled in such a gown. I am not tall[3]   5
enough to become the function[4] well, nor lean enough to be thought a good student[5]; but to be said an honest man and a good housekeeper goes as fairly as to say a careful man and a great scholar. The competitors[6] enter.

Enter [SIR] TOBY [*and* MARIA]

SIR TOBY Jove bless thee, Master Parson[7].   10

FESTE *Bonos dies*[8], Sir Toby. For as the old hermit of Prague, that never saw pen and ink, very wittily said to a niece of King Gorboduc[9], 'That that is, is', so I, being Master Parson, am Master Parson; for what is 'that' but 'that' and 'is' but 'is'?

SIR TOBY To him, Sir Topas.   15

FESTE What ho, I say! Peace in this prison!

SIR TOBY The knave counterfeits well[10]. A good knave.

MALVOLIO (*Within*) Who calls there?

FESTE Sir Topas the curate, who comes to visit Malvolio the lunatic.

MALVOLIO Sir Topas, Sir Topas, good Sir Topas, go to my lady.   20

FESTE Out, hyperbolical fiend[11]! How vexest thou[12] this man! Talk'st thou nothing but of ladies?

SIR TOBY Well said, Master Parson.

MALVOLIO Sir Topas, never was man thus wronged. Good Sir Topas, do not think I am mad. They have laid me here in hideous darkness.   25

FESTE Fie, thou dishonest Satan! I call thee by the most modest terms, for I am one of those gentle ones that will use the devil himself with courtesy. Say'st thou that the house is dark?

MALVOLIO As hell, Sir Topas.

Malvolio protests that he is not mad, and that his prison is too dark. Feste (as Sir Topas) refuses to believe him and continues to torment him. Sir Toby wishes the whole business was over.

 剧情简介：马尔沃琉坚称自己没有疯，而且关他的禁闭室太黑了。费斯特（装扮成托珀神父）不相信，继续折磨他。托比爵士希望整个事件到此为止。

1 Tormenting Malvolio (in pairs)

Whatever Malvolio says, he is in a 'Catch 22' situation: he cannot win. Feste treats all his remarks as if they were made by a madman. Feste's strategy is clear: he will torment Malvolio by turning logic on its head to increase the steward's confusion and frustration. For example, he says that 'barricadoes' are 'transparent' and 'ebony' (black wood) is 'lustrous'.

a Take parts as Feste and Malvolio. Read lines 20–48. Feste should sound as rational as possible. Swap roles and read again.

b After your readings, talk together about whether you feel sympathy for Malvolio. Do you think Feste's humour is genuinely funny, or is it bitter and vicious?

Language in the play 剧中语言
Contrasts and comparisons

Lines 26–50 feature a number of **similes** (明喻) (see p. 164) and contrasting ideas. Malvolio's 'house' is as dark 'as hell', and the mention of a 'wildfowl' (bird) contrasts with his lack of freedom.

a Make a list of as many similes or contrasting ideas as you can find in lines 26–50.

b Write a short paragraph analysing how the language used here makes the audience feel about Malvolio's situation.

Characters 人物分析
Sir Toby: remorse or self-preservation? (in pairs)

Some actors deliver line 53 in such a way as to suggest that Sir Toby feels a little remorse and concern that he may have gone too far. He is certainly aware of the 'offence' (trouble) he is in with Olivia and seems to doubt he can get away with tormenting Malvolio further.

a Decide together which motive you think is strongest in Sir Toby, remorse or self preservation. Try performing lines 53–7 in contrasting ways, with one of you emphasising each interpretation.

b Improvise a scene in which Sir Toby visits Malvolio in the 'dark room' and tells him exactly what he thinks of him. Malvolio might also have some strong words for Sir Toby! Explore the very opposite nature of their characters.

1 **bay windows** 外凸窗

2 **barricadoes** 拒马（一种木制的可以移动的障碍物）

3 **clerestories toward the south-north** 南北高窗

4 **as lustrous as ebony** 锃亮如乌木

5 **obstruction** 没有光线（被挡住了）

6 **errest** 弄错了

7 **Egyptians in their fog** 雾中的埃及人（在《旧约·出埃及记》中，为了让法老允许以色列人摆脱奴役，以色列人的上帝给埃及带来十场灾难，其中第九场是，让摩西朝天空一伸手，就让埃及笼罩在连续三天使人伸手不见五指的黑雾之中）

8 **Make … question** 用符合逻辑的问答来测验一下

9 **Pythagoras** 毕达哥拉斯（古希腊哲学家和数学家，相信人的灵魂会转世投胎）

10 **grandam** 祖母

11 **haply inhabit a bird** 或许会投胎到一只鸟身上

12 **allow of thy wits** 承认你神智正常

13 **I am for all waters** 要我干啥都行

14 **knavery** 恶作剧

15 **conveniently delivered** 稳妥地放了

16 **upshot** 结束

17 **perdy = by God**（向上帝发誓；法文是 *par Dieu*）

FESTE   Why, it hath bay windows[1] transparent as barricadoes[2], and the   30
             clerestories toward the south-north[3] are as lustrous as ebony[4]; and
             yet complain'st thou of obstruction[5]?

MALVOLIO   I am not mad, Sir Topas; I say to you this house is dark.

FESTE   Madman, thou errest[6]. I say there is no darkness but ignorance,
             in which thou art more puzzled than the Egyptians in their fog[7].   35

MALVOLIO   I say this house is as dark as ignorance, though ignorance
             were as dark as hell; and I say there was never man thus abused.
             I am no more mad than you are. Make the trial of it in any constant
             question[8].

FESTE   What is the opinion of Pythagoras[9] concerning wildfowl?   40

MALVOLIO   That the soul of our grandam[10] might haply inhabit a bird[11].

FESTE   What think'st thou of his opinion?

MALVOLIO   I think nobly of the soul, and no way approve his opinion.

FESTE   Fare thee well. Remain thou still in darkness. Thou shalt hold
             th'opinion of Pythagoras ere I will allow of thy wits[12], and fear to   45
             kill a woodcock lest thou dispossess the soul of thy grandam. Fare
             thee well.

MALVOLIO   Sir Topas, Sir Topas!

SIR TOBY   My most exquisite Sir Topas!

FESTE   Nay, I am for all waters[13].   50

MARIA   Thou mightst have done this without thy beard and gown; he
             sees thee not.

SIR TOBY   To him in thine own voice, and bring me word how thou
             find'st him. I would we were well rid of this knavery[14]. If he may
             be conveniently delivered[15], I would he were, for I am now so far   55
             in offence with my niece that I cannot pursue with any safety this
             sport to the upshot[16]. [*To Maria*] Come by and by to my chamber.

                                    Exit [*with Maria*]

FESTE   [*Sings*] Hey Robin, jolly Robin,
                       Tell me how thy lady does.

MALVOLIO   Fool!   60

FESTE   [*Sings*] My lady is unkind, perdy[17].

MALVOLIO   Fool!

FESTE   [*Sings*] Alas, why is she so?

MALVOLIO   Fool, I say!

FESTE   [*Sings*] She loves another –   65
             Who calls, ha?

Malvolio begs Feste for pen and paper to write a letter to Olivia. Feste continues to torment him by pretending to have a conversation with Sir Topas. Feste agrees to help the 'mad' Malvolio.

 剧情简介： 马尔沃琉要给娥丽维娅写信，向费斯特讨要纸和笔。费斯特假装与托珀神父交谈以继续折磨马尔沃琉。费斯特同意帮助这个 "疯了" 的马尔沃琉。

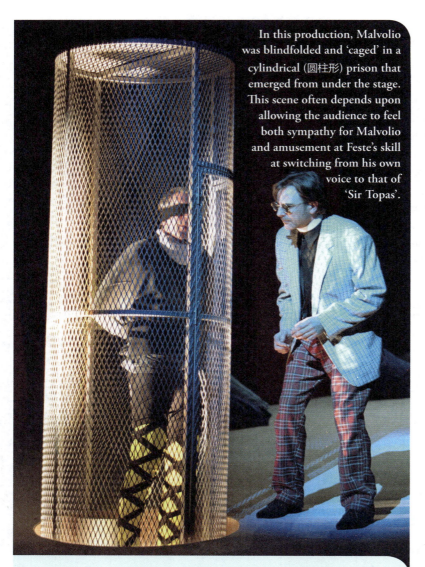

In this production, Malvolio was blindfolded and 'caged' in a cylindrical (圆柱形) prison that emerged from under the stage. This scene often depends upon allowing the audience to feel both sympathy for Malvolio and amusement at Feste's skill at switching from his own voice to that of 'Sir Topas'.

1 deserve well 得到好报
2 how ... wits 您您怎么把五智丢了（莎士比亚时代人们的观念是，人既有视、听、嗅、味、触这五种外在感官 [senses]，又有常识、想象、幻想、直觉、记忆 [common sense, imagination, fantasy, instinct, memory] 这五种内在心智）
3 notoriously 异乎寻常
4 propertied me 拿我当一个物件对待
5 face ... wits 把我欺负得简直要疯掉
6 Advise 小心
7 bibble babble 胡扯
8 Maintain no words 别说话
9 God b'w'you = God be with you = Goodbye
10 shent 遭责骂
11 advantage thee 让你得到好处

Write about it 写作练习

How to 'convey what I will set down to my lady'

The contents of Malvolio's letter to Olivia are eventually revealed in Act 5. At this point, what do you imagine Malvolio would want to say to Olivia about the way he has been treated?

- Write two contrasting short drafts of Malvolio's letter to Olivia. The first should be full of anger and bitterness at his treatment; the second should be more honestly reflective and remorseful, perhaps suggesting that he can see why some of his past behaviour has been unreasonable or pompous.

MALVOLIO   Good fool, as ever thou wilt deserve well[1] at my hand, help
me to a candle and pen, ink, and paper. As I am a gentleman, I
will live to be thankful to thee for't.

FESTE   Master Malvolio?   70

MALVOLIO   Ay, good fool.

FESTE   Alas, sir, how fell you besides your five wits[2]?

MALVOLIO   Fool, there was never man so notoriously[3] abused. I am as
well in my wits, fool, as thou art.

FESTE   But as well? Then you are mad indeed, if you be no better in   75
your wits than a fool.

MALVOLIO   They have here propertied me[4]: keep me in darkness, send
ministers to me, asses, and do all they can to face me out of my
wits[5].

FESTE   Advise[6] you what you say. The minister is here. [*As Sir Topas*]   80
Malvolio, Malvolio, thy wits the heavens restore. Endeavour thyself
to sleep and leave thy vain bibble babble[7].

MALVOLIO   Sir Topas!

FESTE   [*As Sir Topas*] Maintain no words[8] with him, good fellow. [*As
himself*] Who, I, sir? Not I, sir. God b'w'you[9], good Sir Topas.   85
[*As Sir Topas*] Marry, amen. [*As himself*] I will, sir, I will.

MALVOLIO   Fool, fool, fool, I say!

FESTE   Alas, sir, be patient. What say you, sir? I am shent[10] for speaking
to you.

MALVOLIO   Good fool, help me to some light and some paper; I tell   90
thee, I am as well in my wits as any man in Illyria.

FESTE   Well-a-day, that you were, sir!

MALVOLIO   By this hand, I am! Good fool, some ink, paper and light,
and convey what I will set down to my lady. It shall advantage thee[11]
more than ever the bearing of letter did.   95

FESTE   I will help you to't. But tell me true, are you not mad indeed
or do you but counterfeit?

MALVOLIO   Believe me, I am not. I tell thee true.

FESTE   Nay, I'll ne'er believe a madman till I see his brains. I will fetch
you light and paper and ink.   100

Malvolio promises to reward Feste who, with a song, leaves to fetch pen and paper. In Scene 3, Sebastian reflects on his good fortune. He wonders what has happened to Antonio, whose advice he needs.

 剧情简介： 马尔沃琉许诺会酬谢费斯特，费斯特哼着歌离开去取笔和纸。在第三场，塞巴斯田思索自己的好运气。他想知道安托纽怎么样了，他需要安托纽的建议。

1 Feste's song – more ridiculing of Malvolio?
(in pairs)

The song may be more mockery at Malvolio's expense. As a Puritan, Malvolio would be offended to think he was being helped by 'the old Vice' (see glossary) and the devil.

a Compose an appropriate tune for Feste's song.

b Add actions to each line as you sing or speak the song.

c Write down in your own words (or use images to illustrate) what you think this song means.

1 requite 报答
2 trice 片刻
3 old Vice 老罪恶（中世纪道德剧中的一个常见角色，用木头匕首割魔鬼的指甲）
4 Your need to sustain 满足您的需求
5 of lath 木制
6 Pare 剪
7 Adieu 再见（法文）
8 goodman 好人（通常加在卑贱职业前面构成对这人的称谓）
9 feel't and see't = feel it and see it
10 enwraps 包围
11 there he was 他去过那里
12 credit 消息，传闻
13 range 转来转去

Stagecraft 导演技巧
A change of scene and a soliloquy

From the darkness of Malvolio's prison, the scene changes to the sunlight of Olivia's garden. Scene 3 presents Sebastian's wonder at what has happened: Olivia's gift to him and Antonio's mysterious disappearance. Just like Malvolio, Sebastian is convinced that he is not mad, even though bewildering and strange things have happened to him! The mood, however, is very different in this scene, something most directors seek to emphasise through the use of staging, light and sound or music.

- Design (sketch and label or use a computer package) a transition from Scene 2 to Scene 3 so that the action flows swiftly but the mood and tone changes. How will you use lights to show the 'glorious sun'? Come up with some imaginative ways of staging Sebastian's entrance and removing Malvolio and his 'prison' from the stage. How could the 'pearl' referred to in line 2 be emphasised or represented through the staging?

Characters 人物分析
Sebastian

In Scene 3, Sebastian is satisfied that neither he nor Olivia are mad and willingly accepts when Olivia proposes marriage (a very unusual thing for a woman in Elizabethan times to do!).

- Decide whether you think Sebastian should speak lines 1–21 to himself, or speak some or all of them directly to the audience. Try out different interpretations to see which is the most effective.

MALVOLIO   Fool, I'll requite[1] it in the highest degree. I prithee be gone.

FESTE   [*Sings*] I am gone, sir,

        And anon, sir,

          I'll be with you again,

        In a trice[2]   105

        Like to the old Vice[3],

          Your need to sustain[4];

        Who, with dagger of lath[5],

        In his rage and his wrath,

          Cries, 'Ah ha' to the devil,   110

        Like a mad lad,

        'Pare[6] thy nails, dad?'

          Adieu[7], goodman[8] devil.   *Exit*

Act 4 Scene 3
In Olivia's garden

Enter SEBASTIAN

SEBASTIAN   This is the air, that is the glorious sun,

        This pearl she gave me, I do feel't and see't[9],

        And though 'tis wonder that enwraps[10] me thus,

        Yet 'tis not madness. Where's Antonio then?

        I could not find him at the Elephant,   5

        Yet there he was[11], and there I found this credit[12],

        That he did range[13] the town to seek me out.

        His counsel now might do me golden service,

Sebastian decides that Olivia cannot be mad, because she rules her household with total competence. Olivia arrives with a priest and proposes instant marriage. Sebastian accepts.

✒ **剧情简介**：塞巴斯田确认娥丽维娅不可能疯了，因为她把自己的家管理得井井有条。娥丽维娅同一位祭司一起到来，她提议立即结婚。塞巴斯田接受了。

What does the body language in this picture suggest about who is in control in this scene?

1	disputes well with　与……好好讨论了一番
2	instance　先例
3	discourse　推理
4	wrangle　争辩
5	trust　观点，信念
6	sway　操持，管理
7	dispatch　处理
8	bearing　举止
9	deceivable　让人迷惑
10	the chantry by　附近的小教堂
11	consecrated　神圣
12	Plight me　给我发誓
13	conceal it　保守秘密
14	Whiles　直到
15	come to note　公布
16	What time　到那时
17	According to my birth　符合我的身份
18	fairly note　看好

1 A secret marriage (in small groups)

Olivia proposes an instant marriage, but promises it will be kept secret until Sebastian is willing to make it public. Discuss the following questions that arise from this scene in small groups. Assign roles within the group, such as chair, scribe (抄写员), questioner and challenger, to ensure that everyone contributes and a range of perspectives are explored.

- Why does Olivia want a secret marriage?
- What do you think the grand ceremony ('celebration'), suitable for her high social status ('birth') will look like?
- What's happened to her vow to mourn her brother for seven years?
- It was very unusual for a proposal to come from the woman in Elizabethan times. Why do you think Shakespeare decided to have Olivia make the first move?

Write about it 写作练习

Give the priest a voice

What must the silent priest make of it all? In many productions, his facial expressions provide a lot of humour.

- Step into role as the priest and write his account of what happened (perhaps in the form of a sermon he will later deliver). Explore his reaction to events and decide what he might think is the moral of the story.

For though my soul disputes well with[1] my sense

That this may be some error, but no madness,   10

Yet doth this accident and flood of fortune

So far exceed all instance[2], all discourse[3],

That I am ready to distrust mine eyes,

And wrangle[4] with my reason that persuades me

To any other trust[5] but that I am mad,   15

Or else the lady's mad; yet if 'twere so,

She could not sway[6] her house, command her followers,

Take and give back affairs and them dispatch[7],

With such a smooth, discreet, and stable bearing[8]

As I perceive she does. There's something in't   20

That is deceivable[9]. But here the lady comes.

Enter OLIVIA *and* PRIEST

OLIVIA	Blame not this haste of mine. If you mean well,

Now go with me, and with this holy man

Into the chantry by[10]; there before him,

And underneath that consecrated[11] roof,   25

Plight me[12] the full assurance of your faith,

That my most jealous and too doubtful soul

May live at peace. He shall conceal it[13]

Whiles[14] you are willing it shall come to note[15];

What time[16] we will our celebration keep   30

According to my birth[17]. What do you say?

SEBASTIAN   I'll follow this good man, and go with you,

And having sworn truth, ever will be true.

OLIVIA   Then lead the way, good father, and heavens so shine,

That they may fairly note[18] this act of mine!   35

Exeunt

Looking back at Act 4 第4幕回顾
Activities for groups or individuals

1 Appearance and reality: mistaken identity

In all three scenes of Act 4, characters mistake other characters' identities.

- Write down who mistakes whom, and the consequence of that, in each scene. Use a table like the one below to record your findings.

'Mistaking'	Consequence
Scene 1: Sir Andrew mistakes Sebastian for Viola/Cesario.	A beating!

2 Madness and melancholy: tormenting Malvolio

Scene 2 presents problems for a modern audience: how should they respond to the sight of Malvolio being humiliated? It seems that Elizabethans gave little thought to that question. It was an age when people were fascinated by what they called 'madness'. They visited asylums (精神病院) where mentally disturbed people were kept, and gained enjoyment from watching the 'mad' people. It seems likely that Shakespeare's audiences enjoyed the sight of Malvolio being treated as a madman.

Today, people with mental problems are treated much more compassionately, and the response of a modern audience is more complicated. Many feel uncomfortable about the baiting of Malvolio (pictured opposite, chained like a bear).

- Write a short opinion-led piece entitled 'The case for and against Malvolio'. Describe your own views of the way Malvolio is treated, suggesting both the arguments in favour of such humiliation (the Elizabethan approach) and explaining the reasons why modern audiences may find his treatment cruel and unusual. Try to include quotations from this act to support the points you make.

3 Frozen moments of madness (with music)

In groups of five or six, prepare a cut-down, silent tableau presentation of Act 4 in seven key moments. The transition from one tableau to the next should be accompanied by music and movement that reflects the tone or mood of the scene or moment you are depicting. You may have commercial songs in mind that you think would work well, or, you may want to compose your own music. For example, you might choose to begin with a tableau showing Sir Andrew striking Sebastian set to a 'thumping' drum beat or rock song, before transitioning to a softer piece of string music or love song for Sebastian's first meeting with Olivia!

4 Interpreting imagery

Act 4 is full of rich imagery and metaphors.

a Locate the following images in the script, and try to explain what each means or makes you think of.

Scene 1 'I'll throw your dagger o'er the house'
Scene 2 'Out, hyperbolical fiend!'
Scene 3 'this accident and flood of fortune'

b Identify other strong 'images' or metaphors used in Act 4, and interpret or explain their effect or meaning.

5 True lover?

Has Sebastian fallen in love with Olivia? Or is he just taking advantage of her money and status?

- Think about your view of Sebastian's character and prepare a short monologue (独白) or write a blog or diary entry exploring his inner thoughts at the end of this act.

Throughout this book there are a number of images depicting different interpretations of Malvolio and of how his captivity and humiliation are staged. Decide which you think are most intriguing or appropriate, and discuss why you think they might have been effective approaches to the character in performance.

Feste will not let Fabian see Malvolio's letter. He entertains Orsino with his word-juggling, and encourages him to hand over more money.

剧情简介：费斯特不让费边看马尔沃琉的信。他玩文字把戏取悦奥悉诺，并促使公爵给他更多的钱。

---

1 Straight man/funny man (in threes)

'Explaining' a joke is a sure way to kill the humour. But two things Feste says would have been particularly funny to Shakespeare's audiences because they were familiar jokes. Line 5 refers to a story about Queen Elizabeth I begging to be gifted the dog of one of her courtiers. She promised to grant any request in return and he replied 'Give me my dog again'! Lines 16 and 17 refer to an Elizabethan joke about men desperately trying to interpret a girl who repeatedly answers 'no' when she means 'yes'.

Feste treats both Fabian and Orsino as the 'stooge' or 'straight man', the partner who feeds lines to a comedian so that the comedian can make a witty point.

a Practise reading lines 1–38 with Feste as a kind of music-hall or double-act comedian, scoring points off his partner.

b Orsino is the most powerful person in Illyria, but Feste is almost rude to him. Try reading lines 6–38 so that Feste mocks Orsino, coming extremely close to being disrespectful to him. How does Orsino speak his lines if Feste is almost openly cheeky? Experiment with ways of showing that Orsino half-suspects that he is being mocked, and becomes increasingly irritated about it.

c Experiment with other styles of speaking – perhaps trying different accents or having Feste and Fabian attempt to mimic other characters. Which do you think is the most appropriate tone for Feste to use?

1 **grant me another request** 问我要另一样东西吧

2 **give … again** 给人一只狗，又想把这狗作为回报要回来（据最早 [1602年] 提到《第十二夜》这出戏的一份日记记载，伊丽莎白女王向一位贵族索要他珍爱的一只狗，说他要什么作为回报都行；贵族说，那就把狗还给他）

3 **trappings** 饰件，摆件

4 **foes** 敌人

5 **profit** 获益

6 **four … affirmatives** 四个否定等于两个肯定（按照"负负得正"来推，当女人对想吻她的人说"不，不"时，她等于在说"好"）

7 **But = Except**

8 **double-dealing** 当面一套，背后一套（这句话的逻辑是：既然公爵刚才说不会让我吃亏，那么负负得正，就该再给我一枚金币）

9 **ill counsel** 坏建议

10 **Put … pocket** 把您的恩德放到您口袋里（作为金币，**your grace** 同时也是对公爵的正式称呼）

11 **let … it** 让您的血肉之体（**flesh and blood** 指"天性"）听命于它（即"我的建议"）

126

Act 5 Scene 1
In Olivia's garden

Enter FESTE *and* FABIAN

FABIAN	Now, as thou lov'st me, let me see his letter.
FESTE	Good Master Fabian, grant me another request[1].
FABIAN	Anything.
FESTE	Do not desire to see this letter.
FABIAN	This is to give a dog and in recompense desire my dog again[2].

Enter DUKE [ORSINO], VIOLA, CURIO, *and Lords*

ORSINO	Belong you to the Lady Olivia, friends?
FESTE	Ay, sir, we are some of her trappings[3].
ORSINO	I know thee well. How dost thou, my good fellow?
FESTE	Truly, sir, the better for my foes[4], and the worse for my friends.
ORSINO	Just the contrary: the better for thy friends.
FESTE	No, sir, the worse.
ORSINO	How can that be?
FESTE	Marry, sir, they praise me, and make an ass of me. Now my foes tell me plainly I am an ass, so that by my foes, sir, I profit[5] in the knowledge of myself, and by my friends I am abused; so that, conclusions to be as kisses, if your four negatives make your two affirmatives[6], why then, the worse for my friends and the better for my foes.
ORSINO	Why, this is excellent.
FESTE	By my troth, sir, no, though it please you to be one of my friends.
ORSINO	Thou shalt not be the worse for me; there's gold.
FESTE	But[7] that it would be double-dealing[8], sir, I would you could make it another.
ORSINO	O you give me ill counsel[9].
FESTE	Put your grace in your pocket[10], sir, for this once, and let your flesh and blood obey it[11].

5

10

15

20

25

127

Feste tries to persuade Orsino to give him more money, but is sent to fetch Olivia. The officers bring Antonio. He is recognised by Orsino as a past enemy, and by Viola as the one who rescued her in the duel.

 剧情简介： 费斯特试图说服奥悉诺给他更多钱，却被派去请娥丽维娅。官差带来了安托纽。奥悉诺认出安托纽是昔日的一个敌人，薇娥菈也认出安托纽是她决斗时救了她的人。

Characters 人物分析

Orsino the leader (in small groups)

Orsino is the military commander as well as the ruler of Illyria. All his previous appearances have been concerned with love, but in this scene we see him take on his official duties and speak as a leader. However, we also see his generosity and good humour in the way he deals with Feste.

Feste tries to beg a third coin from Orsino by counting in Latin and referring to triple time in dance music ('measure' = dance) and the three bells of St Bennet's (a London church). Feste says he's not greedy for money, but clearly hopes that bringing Olivia will result in a further reward from Orsino. Notice how he seizes on Orsino's word 'awake' to develop an extended pun on sleeping.

- Devise some actions Feste might use when delivering lines 29–38. Are there opportunities to use the garden setting? What should Orsino's response be? Would he laugh at Feste's cheek or take offence at his impertinence?

Write about it 写作练习

Report the sea battle

Antonio obviously did great deeds in a destructive fight against Orsino's fleet. His own ship was tiny and hardly worth capturing, but he outfought Orsino's best ship and captured another with all its cargo from Crete ('the Phoenix and her fraught [载货] from Candy'). Antonio's bravery made his Illyrian enemies admire him, even though he inflicted (使遭受) terrible losses on them.

- Write the report of the sea battle (based on lines 40–52) from the viewpoint of one or more of the following: Antonio, Titus, Orsino, the captain of the *Phoenix* or the *Tiger*, or an ordinary seaman.

1. *Primo, secundo, tertio* 一、二、三（拉丁文）
2. triplex 三拍
3. tripping measure 舞步
4. St Bennet 圣本笃教堂（Bennet是Benedict的简称，伦敦市内的一座老教堂，周日上午11点和下午3点举行礼拜）
5. at this throw 这一次（掷骰子）
6. bounty 赏钱
7. covetousness 贪婪（天主教教义中列举的七种原罪之一）
8. besmeared 蓬头垢面
9. Vulcan 伏尔坎（罗马神话中的火与锻冶之神，见第165页）
10. baubling 微不足道
11. For shallow draught and bulk 因为吃水和船体浅
12. unprizable 不值钱
13. scathful grapple 恶战
14. most noble bottom 最好的船
15. the Phoenix and her fraught "凤凰号" 船及其所载（后面的 the Tiger也是船名）
16. Candy = Candia = Crete（克里特岛，今希腊第一大岛，位于地中海北部，是希腊乃至欧洲最早文明 [Minoan civilization，前2700—1420年] 的发祥地）
17. desp'rate of shame and state 不顾羞耻和（危险）处境
18. brabble 斗殴
19. apprehend 拘捕
20. but distraction 除了精神错乱
21. Notable 臭名昭著
22. in ... dear 通过给他们造成如此血腥和惨重的损失

ORSINO	Well, I will be so much a sinner to be a double-dealer; there's another.	
FESTE	*Primo, secundo, tertio*[1] is a good play, and the old saying is 'The third pays for all'; the triplex[2], sir, is a good tripping measure[3]; or the bells of St Bennet[4], sir, may put you in mind – one, two, three.	30
ORSINO	You can fool no more money out of me at this throw[5]. If you will let your lady know I am here to speak with her, and bring her along with you, it may awake my bounty[6] further.	
FESTE	Marry, sir, lullaby to your bounty till I come again. I go, sir, but I would not have you to think that my desire of having is the sin of covetousness[7]; but, as you say, sir, let your bounty take a nap. I will awake it anon. *Exit*	35

Enter ANTONIO *and* OFFICERS

VIOLA	Here comes the man, sir, that did rescue me.	
ORSINO	That face of his I do remember well;	40
	Yet when I saw it last, it was besmeared[8]	
	As black as Vulcan[9], in the smoke of war.	
	A baubling[10] vessel was he captain of,	
	For shallow draught and bulk[11] unprizable[12],	
	With which, such scathful grapple[13] did he make	45
	With the most noble bottom[14] of our fleet,	
	That very envy, and the tongue of loss,	
	Cried fame and honour on him. What's the matter?	
1 OFFICER	Orsino, this is that Antonio	
	That took the Phoenix and her fraught[15] from Candy[16],	50
	And this is he that did the Tiger board,	
	When your young nephew Titus lost his leg.	
	Here in the streets, desp'rate of shame and state[17],	
	In private brabble[18] did we apprehend[19] him.	
VIOLA	He did me kindness, sir, drew on my side,	55
	But in conclusion put strange speech upon me,	
	I know not what 'twas, but distraction[20].	
ORSINO	Notable[21] pirate! Thou salt-water thief!	
	What foolish boldness brought thee to their mercies,	
	Whom thou, in terms so bloody and so dear[22],	60
	Hast made thine enemies?	

Antonio tells the story of how he rescued Sebastian, protected him and lent him money. Orsino dismisses the explanation as madness. Olivia arrives and, mistaking Viola for Sebastian, reproves and questions 'him'.

 剧情简介：安托纽讲述了他如何救起塞巴斯田，保护了他并借给他钱。奥悉诺不理会这个解释，认为他精神错乱。娥丽维娅到来，错把薇娥菈当成塞巴斯田，责备并盘问"他"。

Characters 人物分析

Antonio: act out his story (in small groups)

Lines 66–81 tell the story of Antonio and Sebastian, and the 'mistaking' of Viola.

a As one person speaks the lines slowly, the others mime what is described. You'll find it good fun (and helpful to your understanding) if you play a speeded-up version after your first acting-out.

b Antonio's line 78 is a vivid and bitter image of rejection and betrayal. Prepare two tableaux of the image: 'before' and 'after'. The first tableau shows warm friendship, the second shows what happens after twenty years' separation.

c Sebastian would no doubt be devastated if he knew what poor Antonio was experiencing. As one person speaks Antonio's lines slowly, another steps into role as Sebastian, invisible to all around him but desperate to be able to tell Antonio and the others the truth. Allow the actor playing Sebastian to freeze the action at any point by tapping Antonio on the shoulder. He can then speak his thoughts and try to explain what has gone wrong.

Stagecraft 导演技巧

Olivia's garden as a dramatic setting (in small groups)

All of the action in Act 5 takes place in the setting of Olivia's garden. Directors and stage designers have taken advantage of the dramatic potential of such a setting in a variety of ways. For example, the space could be open and light, or enclosed and claustrophobic (引起幽闭恐惧的). Outdoor furniture, plants, hedges, furniture or walls can be used to create different levels or opportunities for concealment.

This is the first time that Orsino and Olivia meet in the play. It can often be a very funny moment as a confused Olivia sees Viola by Orsino's side.

a Sketch or describe how you would stage: 'Enter OLIVIA and Attendants' in order to maximise the power of Olivia and the humour of this dramatic moment. If possible, act it out.

b What is your vision of how the garden could appear? Sketch and annotate a design in your Director's Journal. Explain how the set will enhance and contribute to the action of the play's climax.

1 base and ground 根据和理由
2 redeem 拯救
3 wrack 遭难者
4 retention 保留
5 All his in dedication 都奉献给了他
6 adverse 敌对
7 beset 受围攻
8 partake 分担
9 face ... acquaintance 厚颜无耻地否认他认识我
10 grew a twenty-years' removèd thing 让他成了一个20年没有见过的东西
11 While one would wink 一眨眼工夫
12 No ... vacancy 无时无刻，哪怕一分钟空闲都没有
13 for = as for
14 tended upon 侍奉
15 What ... have 大人想要什么，除了他不能得到的（即我的爱情）
16 serviceable 愿意效劳

ANTONIO	Orsino, noble sir,

Be pleased that I shake off these names you give me.
Antonio never yet was thief or pirate,
Though I confess, on base and ground[1] enough,
Orsino's enemy. A witchcraft drew me hither.   65
That most ungrateful boy there by your side,
From the rude sea's enraged and foamy mouth
Did I redeem[2]; a wrack[3] past hope he was.
His life I gave him, and did thereto add
My love without retention[4], or restraint,   70
All his in dedication[5]. For his sake,
Did I expose myself, pure for his love,
Into the danger of this adverse[6] town,
Drew to defend him when he was beset[7];
Where being apprehended, his false cunning   75
(Not meaning to partake[8] with me in danger)
Taught him to face me out of his acquaintance[9],
And grew a twenty-years' removèd thing[10]
While one would wink[11]; denied me mine own purse,
Which I had recommended to his use   80
Not half an hour before.

VIOLA	How can this be?
ORSINO	When came he to this town?
ANTONIO	Today, my lord, and for three months before,

No int'rim, not a minute's vacancy[12],
Both day and night did we keep company.   85

Enter OLIVIA *and Attendants*

ORSINO   Here comes the countess; now heaven walks on earth.
But for[13] thee, fellow – Fellow, thy words are madness.
Three months this youth hath tended upon[14] me,
But more of that anon. Take him aside.

OLIVIA   What would my lord, but that he may not have[15],   90
Wherein Olivia may seem serviceable[16]?
Cesario, you do not keep promise with me.

VIOLA	Madam!
ORSINO	Gracious Olivia –
OLIVIA	What do you say, Cesario? Good my lord – 95

131

Olivia rejects Orsino's love. He threatens to kill her, then threatens to kill Viola/Cesario, suspecting Olivia loves 'him'. Viola willingly agrees to go with Orsino. Olivia feels deceived, and sends for the Priest.

剧情简介： 娥丽维娅拒绝了奥悉诺的求爱。奥悉诺先是威胁要杀死娥丽维娅，又威胁要杀死薇娥菈/席扎瑞欧，因为他怀疑娥丽维娅爱上了"他"。薇娥菈心甘情愿地同意跟奥悉诺走。娥丽维娅感到被骗了，派人去请祭司来。

In this production, Orsino grabbed Olivia's arm while Viola/Cesario and Fabian struggled to tear him away from her.

1 **aught to the old tune** 任何老调重弹
2 **fat and fulsome** 让人厌恶、恶心
3 **perverseness** 顽固，倔强
4 **ingrate** 不领情，忘恩负义
5 **unauspicious** 不吉利
6 **tendered** 提供，奉献
7 **become him** 适合他做
8 **savours nobly** 有高贵的嗜好
9 **non-regardance** 漠视
10 **screws me from** 把我从……挤走
11 **marble-breasted** 铁石心肠
12 **minion** 宠爱的人
13 **tender** 善待，珍视
14 **spite** 羞辱
15 **jocund** 高兴
16 **apt** 欣然
17 **do you rest** 让您心安
18 **feign** 说谎
19 **witnesses above** 天上的见证人；天上的神
20 **Punish … love!** 如果我败坏了自己的爱情，让我不得好死！
21 **detested** 被抛弃
22 **beguiled** 蒙骗
23 **holy father** 神圣的牧师

Themes 主题分析

A strange lover: he threatens to kill! (in small groups)

Within moments of meeting Olivia, Orsino is criticising her. Even worse, he threatens to kill her! His criticism is full of religious language ('altars', 'soul', 'faithfull'st', 'devotion'). He threatens her by comparing himself to Thyamus, a legendary Egyptian thief, who, surrounded by his enemies, attempted to kill the woman he loved so that she would not fall into their hands.

a Everyone should have a go at delivering Orsino's criticism of Olivia in lines 101–4. Does he snap (厉声说出) the lines? Or try to win her sympathy? How does he speak the four words 'What shall I do?' Decide which interpretation works best and discuss how these lines reflect an obsessive type of love.

b Similarly, each of you should give a delivery of Olivia's line 105. How does she reply: off-handedly (不假思索), challengingly, sharply, coldly, dismissively or sympathetically?

c Look at the image above. Orsino suddenly turns cruel, threatening first Olivia, then Viola/Cesario (to spite Olivia). Speak lines 106–20 as dangerous threats, then as hopeless pleas. Do you think he really intends to kill either woman?

d Is there any possible excuse for the way Orsino behaves? Divide your group in two; one half should come up with points in defence of Orsino, while the other half prepares points of prosecution.

VIOLA	My lord would speak; my duty hushes me.
OLIVIA	If it be aught to the old tune[1], my lord,
	It is as fat and fulsome[2] to mine ear
	As howling after music.
ORSINO	Still so cruel?
OLIVIA	Still so constant, lord. 100
ORSINO	What, to perverseness[3]? You uncivil lady,
	To whose ingrate[4] and unauspicious[5] altars
	My soul the faithfull'st off'rings have breathed out
	That e'er devotion tendered[6]! What shall I do?
OLIVIA	Even what it please my lord that shall become him[7]. 105
ORSINO	Why should I not – had I the heart to do it –
	Like to th'Egyptian thief at point of death
	Kill what I love – a savage jealousy
	That sometimes savours nobly[8]? But hear me this.
	Since you to non-regardance[9] cast my faith, 110
	And that I partly know the instrument
	That screws me from[10] my true place in your favour,
	Live you the marble-breasted[11] tyrant still.
	But this your minion[12], whom I know you love,
	And whom, by heaven I swear, I tender[13] dearly, 115
	Him will I tear out of that cruel eye
	Where he sits crownèd in his master's spite[14].
	Come, boy, with me; my thoughts are ripe in mischief.
	I'll sacrifice the lamb that I do love,
	To spite a raven's heart within a dove. [*Leaving*] 120
VIOLA	And I most jocund[15], apt[16], and willingly,
	To do you rest[17], a thousand deaths would die. [*Following*]
OLIVIA	Where goes Cesario?
VIOLA	After him I love
	More than I love these eyes, more than my life,
	More, by all mores, than e'er I shall love wife. 125
	If I do feign[18], you witnesses above[19]
	Punish my life for tainting of my love![20]
OLIVIA	Ay me, detested[21]! How am I beguiled[22]!
VIOLA	Who does beguile you? Who does do you wrong?
OLIVIA	Hast thou forgot thyself? Is it so long? 130
	Call forth the holy father[23].

[Exit an Attendant]

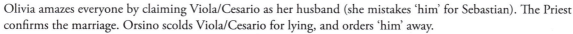

Olivia amazes everyone by claiming Viola/Cesario as her husband (she mistakes 'him' for Sebastian). The Priest confirms the marriage. Orsino scolds Viola/Cesario for lying, and orders 'him' away.

剧情简介：娥丽维娅声称薇娥菈/席扎瑞欧是她的丈夫（她将"他"错认为塞巴斯田），这让所有人大吃一惊。祭司证实了这桩婚姻。奥悉诺责骂薇娥菈/席扎瑞欧撒谎，命令"他"走开。

1 'Cesario, husband, stay!'

(in small groups)

Olivia's command 'Cesario, husband, stay!' shocks and astonishes everyone on stage (and the audience into delight at that astonishment). Orsino's bewildered 'Husband?' increases the audience's enjoyment. It is a moment that every production wants to make as funny as possible.

- Two members of your group take parts as Olivia and Orsino, and each remaining member of the group directs them in his/her own preferred way of speaking those four words. Have great fun with this moment. Distribute other parts from the play to the rest of the group, and have these characters repeat the word 'Husband?' in a style you think would reflect their reaction at this point in the play if they were on stage.

Write about it 写作练习

The truth will out!

At line 138, Olivia challenges the play's theme of false identity: 'Be that thou know'st thou art' (admit what you truly are, namely my husband). But her appeal is full of unconscious irony. It actually reinforces the notion that things in Illyria are never what they seem.

- Explore what you understand the 'truth' in this scene to be by writing a short (100-word) explanation. You might be very literal, exploring what the audience knows but some characters are unaware of (dramatic irony), or you might be more conceptual and analyse why Shakespeare is playing with appearance and reality. Begin with the following line, and see where your ideas and knowledge take you: 'It seems to me that the truth in this scene is ...'

Language in the play 剧中语言

Powerful actions, powerful words (in fours)

Lines 145–60 are filled with powerful language relating to the Priest's solemn actions in marrying Olivia and Sebastian and his instructions to poor Viola. The way an actor delivers the verbs in this section of the play is very important.

- Highlight or list all the verbs you can find in lines 145–60. Read the lines, placing particular emphasis upon these words. Discuss and explore the way Shakespeare uses verbs here.

1 sirrah 小子（旧时对下人的称呼语）
2 baseness 卑鄙
3 strangle thy propriety 掐死你（作为丈夫）的身份
4 take thy fortunes up 接受你的好运
5 reverence 尊贵身份
6 'tis ripe 时机成熟
7 newly passed 最近发生
8 mutual joinder 双方紧握
9 Attested 证明，作证
10 interchangement 交换
11 compact 婚约
12 Sealed in my function 以我（祭司）的职权批准
13 dissembling cub 骗人的狐狸崽子
14 sowed 播种
15 a grizzle 一丝灰色
16 case 身体，皮囊
17 trip 绊子
18 henceforth 从今以后
19 Hold little faith 留点儿信誉吧

ORSINO	Come, away!
OLIVIA	Whither, my lord? Cesario, husband, stay!
ORSINO	Husband?
OLIVIA	Ay, husband. Can he that deny?
ORSINO	Her husband, sirrah[1]?
VIOLA	No, my lord, not I.
OLIVIA	Alas, it is the baseness[2] of thy fear 135

135

OLIVIA Alas, it is the baseness[2] of thy fear
That makes thee strangle thy propriety[3].
Fear not, Cesario, take thy fortunes up[4];
Be that thou know'st thou art, and then thou art
As great as that thou fear'st.

Enter PRIEST

          O welcome, father!
Father, I charge thee by thy reverence[5]   140
Here to unfold – though lately we intended
To keep in darkness what occasion now
Reveals before 'tis ripe[6] – what thou dost know
Hath newly passed[7] between this youth and me.

PRIEST A contract of eternal bond of love,   145
Confirmed by mutual joinder[8] of your hands,
Attested[9] by the holy close of lips,
Strengthened by th'interchangement[10] of your rings,
And all the ceremony of this compact[11]
Sealed in my function[12], by my testimony;   150
Since when, my watch hath told me, toward my grave
I have travelled but two hours.

ORSINO [*To Viola*] O thou dissembling cub[13]! What wilt thou be
When time hath sowed[14] a grizzle[15] on thy case[16]?
Or will not else thy craft so quickly grow   155
That thine own trip[17] shall be thine overthrow?
Farewell, and take her, but direct thy feet
Where thou and I henceforth[18] may never meet.

VIOLA My lord, I do protest –
OLIVIA   O do not swear!
Hold little faith[19], though thou hast too much fear.   160

Sir Andrew complains that Viola/Cesario has wounded him. Viola/Cesario denies it. Sir Toby enters – he has also been attacked. He scornfully dismisses Sir Andrew's offer of help.

✒ **剧情简介：** 安褚爵士抱怨说薇娥菈/席扎瑞欧把他打伤了。薇娥菈/席扎瑞欧否认此事。托比爵士上台，说他也遭到攻击。托比爵士轻蔑地拒绝了安褚爵士要提供的帮助。

▲ Sir Toby and Sir Andrew nurse their 'bloody coxcombs'. This 2008 production had a young cast (全体演员), and actors played multiple roles to create a fast-paced, cut-down version of the play.

1 Comedy, bewilderment and pathos (悲悯) (in sixes)

After the amazement of the 'husband' episode, and Orsino's vehement rejection of Viola/Cesario, Shakespeare dramatises another bittersweet comic incident. Sir Andrew, beaten by Sebastian, usually performs a fearful and incredulous double-take (愣一下才恍然大悟) as he catches sight of Viola and exclaims, "Od's lifelings, here he is!' Sir Toby's contemptuous spurning (拒绝) of Sir Andrew's friendship often evokes audience sympathy for the foolish knight.

a Take parts as Sir Andrew, Olivia, Orsino, Viola, Sir Toby and Feste and act out this episode. Consider the points listed below as you rehearse your performance:

- Make Sir Andrew pitiable, and his 'double-take' at Viola as comic as possible.
- Ensure that Olivia, Orsino and Viola are mystified (不解) by what they see and hear. But bring out Olivia's compassion for Sir Toby as she says 'let his hurt be looked to'.
- Sir Toby rejects Sir Andrew's offer to help him, and shows what he really thinks of Sir Andrew in lines 190–1. Make Sir Toby's scornful dismissal as cruel as you can.
- This is the final appearance of Sir Andrew and Sir Toby. Try different ways of presenting the stage direction *Exeunt Feste, Fabian, Sir Toby, and Sir Andrew* to show each man's personality. Think about how you might expect the audience to respond to Sir Toby and Sir Andrew. (In some productions the two men exit scuffling (扭打) or pushing one another!)

b **Pathos** is a feeling of sympathy or pity. Discuss which line you feel evokes the strongest moment of pathos on this page.

1 **bloody coxcomb** = bleeding cockscomb （头破血流；coxcomb可以是鸡冠、鸡冠帽或戴鸡冠帽的小丑）

2 **incardinate** 转世；化身（正确的说法是incarnate）

3 **'Od's lifelings** = By God's little lives （天哪）

4 **bespake you fair** 对您说话客气

5 **halting** 一瘸一拐

6 **in drink** 喝醉了

7 **tickled** 吊打，教训

8 **othergates** = otherwise （另外一种样子）

9 **That's all one** 都一样

10 **didst ... sot** 你看见棒槌医生了吗，呆子（Dick是"阴茎"的俗称）

11 **his eyes were set** 他两眼定住了（醉酒导致）

12 **passy-measures pavin** （意大利文，指一种缓慢庄严的舞步，这里指醉酒后的缓慢行动）

13 **havoc** 浩劫

14 **dressed** 包扎（伤口）

15 **ass-head** 笨蛋

16 **looked to** 得到处理

Enter SIR ANDREW [*his head bleeding*]

SIR ANDREW	For the love of God, a surgeon! Send one presently to Sir Toby.
OLIVIA	What's the matter?
SIR ANDREW	H'as broke my head across, and has given Sir Toby a bloody coxcomb[1], too. For the love of God, your help! I had rather than forty pound I were at home.
OLIVIA	Who has done this, Sir Andrew?
SIR ANDREW	The count's gentleman, one Cesario. We took him for a coward, but he's the very devil incardinate[2].
ORSINO	My gentleman Cesario?
SIR ANDREW	'Od's lifelings[3], here he is! You broke my head for nothing, and that that I did, I was set on to do't by Sir Toby.
VIOLA	Why do you speak to me? I never hurt you. You drew your sword upon me without cause, But I bespake you fair[4], and hurt you not.

165

170

175

Enter [SIR] TOBY *and* CLOWN [FESTE]

SIR ANDREW	If a bloody coxcomb be a hurt, you have hurt me; I think you set nothing by a bloody coxcomb. Here comes Sir Toby halting[5] – you shall hear more; but if he had not been in drink[6], he would have tickled[7] you othergates[8] than he did.
ORSINO	How now, gentleman? How is't with you?
SIR TOBY	That's all one[9]. H'as hurt me, and there's th'end on't. Sot, didst see Dick Surgeon, sot[10]?
FESTE	O he's drunk, Sir Toby, an hour agone; his eyes were set[11] at eight i'th'morning.
SIR TOBY	Then he's a rogue, and a passy-measures pavin[12]. I hate a drunken rogue.
OLIVIA	Away with him! Who hath made this havoc[13] with them?
SIR ANDREW	I'll help you, Sir Toby, because we'll be dressed[14] together.
SIR TOBY	Will you help – an ass-head[15], and a coxcomb, and a knave, a thin-faced knave, a gull?
OLIVIA	Get him to bed, and let his hurt be looked to[16].

180

185

190

[*Exeunt Feste, Fabian, Sir Toby, and Sir Andrew*]

Sebastian's appearance amazes everyone. Antonio expresses everyone's thoughts on seeing a double vision. The twins question each other and begin to find out that they are indeed related.

剧情简介：塞巴斯田的出现使每个人都大吃一惊。安托纽说他以为看到了重影，道出了其他人的心里话。这对双胞胎相互询问，开始发现他们确实是一家人。

Write about it 写作练习

'Most wonderful!'

How can a person be in two places at once? Antonio voices what everyone is thinking: 'An apple cleft in two is not more twin'. No one believes the evidence of their own eyes. Orsino calls it 'A natural perspective' (a distorting mirror that makes one image into two). Olivia's exclamation as she sees she has two husbands causes audience laughter: 'Most wonderful!'

- Write a short **monologue** (a passage in which a single speaker voices internal thoughts) for either Olivia or Orsino, expressing bewilderment and amazement. You might want to integrate some of the lines or phrases used on this page into your original piece of writing.

1. kinsman 亲戚
2. strange regard 陌生的目光
3. but so late ago 不久之前
4. racked 使痛苦，折磨
5. made division of yourself 自我分身；让自己一分为二
6. deity 神性
7. Of charity 行行好（告诉我）
8. So went he suited 他就是穿着你这样的衣服去了
9. spirit 鬼；妖精
10. in ... participate 仍套着从娘胎里出来便有的躯壳
11. as the rest goes even 由于其他一切都对得上号
12. Thrice 三呼（表示加强）

1 Uncertainty – hope – joy! (in pairs)

The twins' reunion, as they move from hope to certainty that the other lives, is a moving episode.

a Take parts as Sebastian and Viola and speak lines 210–42. Try to express their initial puzzlement, then growing hope, as they exchange details of their father, and their final joy as they each realise they really have found their lost sibling.

b After your reading, discuss how each moment in the exchange could be played (tone of voice, body language, gestures, facial expressions), giving reasons for your choices. For example, explain how and why you think Viola forbids an embrace at line 235. Make notes in your Director's Journal.

Enter SEBASTIAN

SEBASTIAN	I am sorry, madam, I have hurt your kinsman[1].
	But had it been the brother of my blood,
	I must have done no less with wit and safety.
	You throw a strange regard[2] upon me, and by that
	I do perceive it hath offended you.
	Pardon me, sweet one, even for the vows
	We made each other but so late ago[3].
ORSINO	One face, one voice, one habit, and two persons –
	A natural perspective, that is and is not!
SEBASTIAN	Antonio! O my dear Antonio,
	How have the hours racked[4] and tortured me,
	Since I have lost thee!
ANTONIO	Sebastian are you?
SEBASTIAN	Fear'st thou that, Antonio?
ANTONIO	How have you made division of yourself[5]?
	An apple cleft in two is not more twin
	Than these two creatures. Which is Sebastian?
OLIVIA	Most wonderful!
SEBASTIAN	Do I stand there? I never had a brother;
	Nor can there be that deity[6] in my nature
	Of here and everywhere. I had a sister,
	Whom the blind waves and surges have devoured.
	Of charity[7], what kin are you to me?
	What countryman? What name? What parentage?
VIOLA	Of Messaline. Sebastian was my father;
	Such a Sebastian was my brother, too;
	So went he suited[8] to his wat'ry tomb.
	If spirits can assume both form and suit,
	You come to fright us.
SEBASTIAN	A spirit[9] I am indeed,
	But am in that dimension grossly clad
	Which from the womb I did participate[10].
	Were you a woman – as the rest goes even[11] –
	I should my tears let fall upon your cheek,
	And say, 'Thrice[12] welcome, drownèd Viola.'

Line numbers: 195, 200, 205, 210, 215, 220, 225

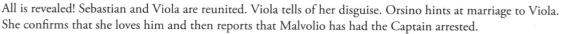

All is revealed! Sebastian and Viola are reunited. Viola tells of her disguise. Orsino hints at marriage to Viola. She confirms that she loves him and then reports that Malvolio has had the Captain arrested.

剧情简介：一切真相大白！塞巴斯田和薇娥菈重逢。薇娥菈讲述了她怎样女扮男装。奥悉诺示意要与薇娥菈结婚。薇娥菈确认她爱奥悉诺，然后禀告说马尔沃琉已经逮捕了船长。

Language in the play 剧中语言

Imagery: nature sorts things out!

In lines 200–56, Shakespeare uses a lot of interesting imagery to create a strong impression in the minds of audience members. For example, in line 244 Sebastian tells Olivia that she could have been engaged to Viola, 'But nature to her bias drew in that'. The image is from the game of bowls (草地滚球) . Because each bowl has a lead weight (a bias) inside, it does not run straight but instead runs towards its target along an indirect, curved route. So Sebastian suggests that eventually, if indirectly, nature sorts out muddles and mistakes as it follows its course.

a Make a list of up to four examples of imagery you can find in lines 200–56. Try to explain their meaning and effect in the same way as the bowling image is explained in the paragraph above.

b Suggest or demonstrate actions or gestures the actors might use to make these meanings clearer to the audience.

▶ What do the facial expressions of these two actors suggest to you about the 'mood' the twins' mutual recognition creates on stage?

1	mole	痣
2	record	记忆
3	mortal act	人生
4	lets	妨碍
5	masculine usurped attire	假装男性的行头
6	cohere and jump	一致，相符
7	maiden weeds	少女的衣服
8	occurrence of my fortune	我命运里发生的事
9	nature … that	那是心意照自己的偏好做出的选择（bias: 偏向）
10	maid and man	童贞男子
11	glass	镜子（这里是说，第201行的观点是真实的）
12	happy wreck	幸运的海难
13	like to me	像我一样
14	overswear	再次发誓
15	As … fire = As that orbèd continent keeps the fire（就像那天上的火球永葆火焰）
16	action	法律行动，诉讼
17	in durance	被羁押
18	suit	起诉

Write about it 写作练习

Orsino's love abruptly changes – is he a true lover?

a Orsino suddenly switches his love from Olivia to Viola (line 250) when he discovers that his handsome page is really a woman. As director of the play, would you want to make the audience laugh at this sudden switch of affection? What does it suggest about Orsino?

b Write the script of an interview with Orsino for the imaginary *Illyria Herald* newspaper, in which Orsino explains his sudden passion for Viola. Perhaps refer to some of the 'moments' they share, or to how he now feels about Olivia.

VIOLA	My father had a mole[1] upon his brow.
SEBASTIAN	And so had mine.
VIOLA	And died that day when Viola from her birth
	Had numbered thirteen years.
SEBASTIAN	O that record[2] is lively in my soul!
	He finishèd indeed his mortal act[3]
	That day that made my sister thirteen years.
VIOLA	If nothing lets[4] to make us happy both,
	But this my masculine usurped attire[5],
	Do not embrace me, till each circumstance,
	Of place, time, fortune, do cohere and jump[6]
	That I am Viola, which to confirm
	I'll bring you to a captain in this town,
	Where lie my maiden weeds[7]; by whose gentle help
	I was preserved – to serve this noble count.
	All the occurrence of my fortune[8] since
	Hath been between this lady and this lord.
SEBASTIAN	[*To Olivia*] So comes it, lady, you have been mistook.
	But nature to her bias drew in that[9].
	You would have been contracted to a maid;
	Nor are you therein, by my life, deceived;
	You are betrothed both to a maid and man[10].
ORSINO	Be not amazed, right noble is his blood.
	If this be so – as yet the glass[11] seems true –
	I shall have share in this most happy wreck[12].
	[*To Viola*] Boy, thou hast said to me a thousand times
	Thou never shouldst love woman like to me[13].
VIOLA	And all those sayings will I overswear[14],
	And all those swearings keep as true in soul
	As doth that orbèd continent the fire[15]
	That severs day from night.
ORSINO	Give me thy hand.
	And let me see thee in thy woman's weeds.
VIOLA	The captain that did bring me first on shore
	Hath my maid's garments; he upon some action[16]
	Is now in durance[17], at Malvolio's suit[18],
	A gentleman and follower of my lady's.

230 · 235 · 240 · 245 · 250 · 255 · 260

Feste brings Malvolio's letter. It reports Malvolio's suffering and his indignation. Olivia orders Malvolio to be brought in. She proposes a joint wedding celebration for the two couples at her house.

 剧情简介：费斯特带来了马尔沃琉的信，信中反映了马尔沃琉的遭遇和他的愤怒。娥丽维娅下令将马尔沃琉带进来。她提议在她家同时为两对新人举行婚礼。

Characters 人物分析

Feste's revenge (in pairs)

In many productions, Feste takes great delight in reading out Malvolio's letter in a ridiculous voice. This can appear awkward, as the time for such fooling seems to have passed.

a Feste has not bothered to deliver Malvolio's letter as promptly as he could. It seems he is deliberately prolonging Malvolio's suffering and humiliation. Decide together what you feel this delay suggests about Feste.

b Feste uses a striking image to describe Malvolio – 'he holds Belzebub at the stave's end' – Malvolio is fighting to keep the devil at a distance (as if with a long staff or rod). With your partner, construct a tableau to show the image.

1 Reading the letter – three styles (in threes)

Olivia won't allow Feste to read Malvolio's letter, because he puts on a mad voice. So how does Fabian read it, and how would Malvolio speak what he's written? What does it tell us about Malvolio's state of mind?

• Prepare a reading (or a recording to accompany a media presentation) of lines 282–90 in three styles: as Feste, as Fabian and as Malvolio. Ask others in your class to decide which is the most appropriate interpretation, and why.

▼ 'I do but read madness'. What does this image suggest to you about how Feste feels about reading the letter and how the lovers might react to what they hear?

1 enlarge　释放
2 much distract　精神严重错乱
3 extracting frenzy　令人不得安宁的魔怔
4 Belzebub　魔王
5 stave's end　长棍的末端
6 gospels　福音书
7 skills not much　没多大关系
8 well edified　受到良好教育
9 *vox*　嗓音，声音（拉丁文）
10 right wits　实际智力
11 perpend　仔细听好
12 induced　劝说，诱使
13 semblance　外表，外貌
14 leave ... of　暂且不顾我这管家的身份
15 One ... on't　在同一天缔结良缘
16 at my proper cost　由我自己来承担费用

OLIVIA	He shall enlarge[1] him; fetch Malvolio hither.
	And yet, alas, now I remember me,
	They say, poor gentleman, he's much distract[2].

Enter CLOWN [FESTE], *with a letter, and* FABIAN

	A most extracting frenzy[3] of mine own	265
	From my remembrance clearly banished his.	
	How does he, sirrah?	
FESTE	Truly, madam, he holds Belzebub[4] at the stave's end[5] as well as	
	a man in his case may do; h'as here writ a letter to you; I should	
	have given't you today morning. But as a madman's epistles are no	270
	gospels[6], so it skills not much[7] when they are delivered.	
OLIVIA	Open't and read it.	
FESTE	Look then to be well edified[8] when the fool delivers the madman.	
	[*Reads madly*] 'By the Lord, madam –'	
OLIVIA	How now, art thou mad?	275
FESTE	No, madam, I do but read madness; and your ladyship will have	
	it as it ought to be, you must allow *vox*[9].	
OLIVIA	Prithee read i'thy right wits[10].	
FESTE	So I do, madonna; but to read his right wits is to read thus.	
	Therefore, perpend[11], my princess, and give ear.	280
OLIVIA	[*To Fabian*] Read it you, sirrah.	
FABIAN	[*Reads*] 'By the Lord, madam, you wrong me, and the world	
	shall know it. Though you have put me into darkness, and given	
	your drunken cousin rule over me, yet have I the benefit of my	
	senses as well as your ladyship. I have your own letter that induced[12]	285
	me to the semblance[13] I put on; with the which I doubt not but to	
	do myself much right, or you much shame. Think of me as you	
	please. I leave my duty a little unthought of[14] and speak out of my	
	injury.	
	The madly used Malvolio.'	290
OLIVIA	Did he write this?	
FESTE	Ay, madam.	
ORSINO	This savours not much of distraction.	
OLIVIA	See him delivered, Fabian; bring him hither.	

[*Exit Fabian*]

	My lord, so please you, these things further thought on,	295
	To think me as well a sister as a wife,	
	One day shall crown th'alliance on't[15], so please you,	
	Here at my house, and at my proper cost[16].	

Orsino proposes marriage to Viola. Malvolio shows Olivia the forged letter, describes what has happened to him, and demands an explanation. Olivia recognises that the letter is in Maria's handwriting.

剧情简介：奥悉诺向薇娥菈求婚。马尔沃琉给娥丽维娅看那封伪造的信，描述了他的经历，并要求得到解释。娥丽维娅认出信的笔迹是玛蕊娅的。

1 'You are she!' (in small groups)

In some productions, Olivia has looked away from the twins and now, at line 305, cannot tell which is Viola!

- This can be a very funny moment if played correctly. Have a go at performing it in a couple of different ways to gain the biggest laugh.

Themes 主题分析

Malvolio suffers a 'notorious wrong' (in pairs)

In performance, Malvolio often appears bedraggled and dirt-stained, his clothes in rags (破烂) and his cross-garters all unwound. In one production, he appeared in a strait-jacket (紧身衣).

a Think about how you would stage Malvolio's appearance and his manner of speaking. Try out different ways of entering and speaking lines 309–23. Speak very angrily; then in a very calm, dignified and reasoned style; and then as if you are close to tears. Finally, speak the lines as if you are utterly bewildered.

b Malvolio's line 'Tell me, why?' in line 323 is addressed to Olivia but should really be addressed to Sir Toby and friends. Together, write a short, one-line response to this blunt question from each of Sir Toby, Maria, Sir Andrew and Feste. They may have very different motives.

c Discuss the extent to which you want Malvolio to win the audience's sympathy for his mistreatment.

1	embrace	接受
2	quits	使自由
3	mettle	性情，本性
4	mistress	妻子
5	Notorious	不一般
6	peruse	读
7	Write from it	写出不一样的字迹
8	seal	（私人信件的）蜡封
9	in the modesty of honour	为了顾全名节
10	lights of favour	喜欢（我）的信号
11	lighter people	地位更低的人
12	geck and gull	笨蛋和傻瓜
13	invention	骗术
14	like the character	笔迹像
15	forms	行为举止
16	be content	安静，冷静

ORSINO Madam, I am most apt t'embrace[1] your offer.
[*To Viola*] Your master quits[2] you; and for your service done him,   300
So much against the mettle[3] of your sex,
So far beneath your soft and tender breeding,
And since you called me master for so long,
Here is my hand; you shall from this time be
Your master's mistress[4].

OLIVIA   Ah, sister, you are she!   305

Enter [FABIAN *with*] MALVOLIO

ORSINO Is this the madman?

OLIVIA   Ay, my lord, this same.
How now, Malvolio?

MALVOLIO   Madam, you have done me wrong,
Notorious[5] wrong.

OLIVIA   Have I, Malvolio? No.

MALVOLIO Lady, you have. Pray you, peruse[6] that letter.
You must not now deny it is your hand;   310
Write from it[7], if you can, in hand, or phrase,
Or say 'tis not your seal[8], not your invention.
You can say none of this. Well, grant it then,
And tell me, in the modesty of honour[9],
Why you have given me such clear lights of favour[10],   315
Bade me come smiling and cross-gartered to you,
To put on yellow stockings, and to frown
Upon Sir Toby, and the lighter people[11];
And acting this in an obedient hope,
Why have you suffered me to be imprisoned,   320
Kept in a dark house, visited by the priest,
And made the most notorious geck and gull[12],
That e'er invention[13] played on? Tell me, why?

OLIVIA Alas, Malvolio, this is not my writing,
Though I confess much like the character[14].   325
But, out of question, 'tis Maria's hand.
And now I do bethink me, it was she
First told me thou wast mad; then cam'st in smiling,
And in such forms[15] which here were presupposed
Upon thee in the letter. Prithee, be content[16];   330

Fabian reveals the plot against Malvolio and tells that Sir Toby has married Maria. Feste teases Malvolio, who leaves, swearing revenge. Orsino looks forward to his marriage to Viola.

剧情简介： 费边吐露了陷害马尔沃琉的密谋，并告诉大家托比爵士已经与玛蕊娅结婚。费斯特戏弄马尔沃琉，马尔沃琉离开，发誓要报复。奥悉诺盼望着与薇娥菈成婚。

Characters 人物分析

Malvolio's revenge

'I'll be revenged on the whole pack of you!' (line 355). Does Malvolio mean it – and does he get his revenge? Some people think that the line foresees the English Civil War, which took place forty years after *Twelfth Night* was written. The Puritans seized power, closed the theatres and attempted to end all frivolity (轻浮的行为) and merry-making.

a Try out different ways of delivering line 355: angrily, in tears, in a whisper and in any other way you think might work. Also decide how everyone present reacts – and how Malvolio leaves.

b Fabian is left to explain the actions of Sir Toby, Maria and Feste. In some productions, he is comically weasely (狡黠) and pathetic, in others he is reasonable. Try speaking lines 334–47 in a sympathetic way and then in a more self-serving and cowardly way. Which is most effective?

c Write a short story or poem called 'Malvolio's Revenge'.

Stagecraft 导演技巧

Creating a mood for (almost) the final moment

Everyone except Feste leaves the stage at line 365. Imagine you are directing the play. What atmosphere do you wish to create for the audience in these closing moments? A mood of harmony, with the characters pairing up happily as they leave? Or some other atmosphere?

- Write notes on how you would direct the characters to leave the stage to establish the mood you wish to create. Don't forget Antonio, who has been a silent watcher for so long.

▶ In this innovative 2008 production, a single actor played both Viola and Sebastian! What challenges and opportunities would such a choice provide a director?

1	practice 诡计，计谋
2	shrewdly 恶意地
3	grounds 动机
4	plaintiff 原告
5	brawl 争辩，争论
6	Taint 败坏，糟蹋
7	Upon … him 因为我们看不惯他那些顽固和失礼的地方
8	importance 强求
9	sportful malice 恶意的玩笑
10	followed 实行，完成
11	pluck on 引起
12	baffled 欺骗
13	interlude 幕间剧
14	whirligig 陀螺
15	most notoriously abused 受到极大的欺侮
16	entreat him to a peace 请他平静下来
17	convents 适合
18	combination 结合，联盟

This practice[1] hath most shrewdly[2] passed upon thee;
But when we know the grounds[3], and authors of it,
Thou shalt be both the plaintiff[4] and the judge
Of thine own cause.

FABIAN   Good madam, hear me speak,   335
And let no quarrel, nor no brawl[5] to come,
Taint[6] the condition of this present hour,
Which I have wondered at. In hope it shall not,
Most freely I confess, myself and Toby
Set this device against Malvolio here,
Upon some stubborn and uncourteous parts   340
We had conceived against him[7]. Maria writ
The letter, at Sir Toby's great importance[8],
In recompense whereof he hath married her.
How with a sportful malice[9] it was followed[10]
May rather pluck on[11] laughter than revenge,   345
If that the injuries be justly weighed,
That have on both sides passed.

OLIVIA   Alas, poor fool, how have they baffled[12] thee!

FESTE   Why, 'Some are born great, some achieve greatness, and some
have greatness thrown upon them.' I was one, sir, in this interlude[13],   350
one Sir Topas, sir – but that's all one. 'By the Lord, fool, I am not
mad.' But do you remember – 'Madam, why laugh you at such a
barren rascal, and you smile not, he's gagged'? And thus the
whirligig[14] of time brings in his revenges.

MALVOLIO   I'll be revenged on the whole pack of you!   [*Exit*]   355

OLIVIA   He hath been most notoriously abused[15].

ORSINO   Pursue him, and entreat him to a peace[16].
He hath not told us of the captain yet.

                                            [*Exit Fabian*]

When that is known, and golden time convents[17],
A solemn combination[18] shall be made   360
Of our dear souls. Meantime, sweet sister,
We will not part from hence. Cesario, come –
For so you shall be while you are a man,
But when in other habits you are seen,
Orsino's mistress, and his fancy's queen.   365

                          Exeunt [*all but Feste*]

Feste, alone on stage, sings about growing up, about being tolerated in childhood, rejected in adulthood, unsuccessful in marriage, and drunk in old age. But nothing really matters; the actors will always try to please.

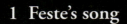

剧情简介： 费斯特一个人在台上唱歌，歌里提到成长、童年时得到的宽容、成人后的不被接受、婚姻的失败和老年时的醉酒。但没什么大不了的；演员总是会努力取悦观众。

1 Feste's song

Feste's haunting song closes the play. Learn the song and sing or speak it, individually or chorally, to bring out its mysterious quality.

2 A sombre ending

Directors often choose dark lighting and a sombre mood at the end of the play. Discuss why you think this mood is the tone with which so many directors want to leave the audience.

1 **foolish thing** 傻东西（指小孩）
2 **toy** 琐事，小事
3 **man's estate** 成年
4 **knaves** 品行不端的人
5 **swaggering** 趾高气扬
6 **came unto my beds** 变老
7 **tosspots** 酒徒，醉汉
8 **strive** 努力

(*Clown sings*)
When that I was and-a little tiny boy,
    With hey, ho, the wind and the rain,
A foolish thing[1] was but a toy[2],
    For the rain it raineth every day.

But when I came to man's estate[3],   370
    With hey, ho, the wind and the rain,
'Gainst knaves[4] and thieves men shut their gate,
    For the rain it raineth every day.

But when I came, alas, to wive,
    With hey, ho, the wind and the rain,   375
By swaggering[5] could I never thrive,
    For the rain it raineth every day.

But when I came unto my beds[6],
    With hey, ho, the wind and the rain,
With tosspots[7] still 'had drunken heads,   380
    For the rain it raineth every day.

A great while ago the world begun,
    With hey, ho, the wind and the rain,
But that's all one, our play is done,
    And we'll strive[8] to please you every day.   [*Exit*]   385

Looking back at the play 本剧回顾
Activities for groups or individuals

1 Styling (设计造型) the twins

Sebastian and Viola marvel that the other is alive. How closely should the actors playing Viola and Sebastian resemble each other? Does it matter if they are not 'identical'? Use this picture and the other images in this book showing different interpretations of Sebastian and Viola to help you compile an assignment on 'The twins in *Twelfth Night*'. It can include costume designs, notes and drawings of hairstyles and mannerisms the twins might share. A high-quality assignment will also feature an analysis of the dramatic effects caused by the separation and reunion of the twins. Make reference to key quotations illustrating their changing emotions of grief followed by initial hesitation and then joy!

2 *Twelfth Night* online

In the twenty-first century, the entire works of Shakespeare can be stored on a mobile phone. A production taking place in China can be viewed live over the Internet by a student in California or Berlin. Technology is breathing new life into Shakespeare's plays and making it ever easier to find out information and view performances.

- Work in a small group to design the content of a website or wiki for the play *Twelfth Night*. There should be different sections, perhaps based around the way the tasks in this book are organised ('Themes', 'Stagecraft' and so on). You may wish to use presentation software to include images or embed (插入) audio or video recordings of key sequences. The audience for the website should be people like you: students of the play seeking to extent their understanding and experience of this 400-year-old performance script using a very modern medium. Your teacher will advise you on how extensive they want the content to be.

3 Inspiring images of Illyria

This book is filled with images of productions of *Twelfth Night* from around the world.

- Select the five images from this book that you like best, and write a paragraph exploring and explaining what interests you about each one. What do you imagine was different or interesting about the production shown?

4 Making sense of the relationships

Using the character list on page 1 of this book as a starting point, design either a classroom display or a large presentation that shows the relationships and connections between the different characters. You should detail how the characters are linked, how they are attracted or repelled (排斥) by each other, and what they have in common or in contrast.

5 What *context*, friends, is this?

As you can see from the many different productions shown in this book, directors have chosen to set *Twelfth Night* in a number of different time periods and parts of the world. Some people have a preference for more traditional contexts (settings), such as the productions at Shakespeare's Globe in London, whereas others believe unusual or more contemporary contexts help bring a new beauty and perspective to the play.

- Write a short proposal to the artistic director of the national theatre of your country, outlining your suggestion for the context (setting and time period) of a new production. Give reasons linked to the play script for your suggestion.

6 The wedding video

The play ends with the promise of a wedding feast, and it is usual for speeches to be made at such events.

- Improvise or write wedding speeches for Olivia, Viola, Sebastian and Orsino. How will they explain what's happened to the guests? Who will they mention and thank? Will Malvolio or Antonio receive thanks or a mention? Record videos of these speeches.

7 Extended writing

You may well be asked to write an extended analysis of the play after you have read and (hopefully) watched it. Any of the following question titles are good starting points for extended analysis.

- **a** To what extent does the 'fun' that characters have in *Twelfth Night* lead to excess?
- **b** Explore the different types of love Shakespeare presents in *Twelfth Night*.
- **c** How do the differences between appearance and reality in *Twelfth Night* create both comedy and melancholy?
- **d** How far would you agree with the statement '*Twelfth Night* is a play that leaves a bitter taste in the mouth'?

Perspectives and themes 视角与主题

What is the play about?

Imagine that you can travel back in time to around 1600. You meet William Shakespeare a few minutes after he has finished writing *Twelfth Night*, just before he takes it into rehearsal with his company, The King's Men. You ask him, 'What is the play about?'

Perhaps Shakespeare would reply, 'Think about the title, *Twelfth Night*. You can take it as a story about the merry-making that happens for the twelve days after Christmas. Everything is about celebration, eating, drinking and enjoyment. But after *Twelfth Night* the carnival atmosphere ends, and it's back to the normal world.' You might disagree with this imagined response. One of the great challenges and mysteries of Shakespeare's work is that nobody really knows what he intended the audience to get from the play – and indeed if he had any specific intentions at all.

◆ **Write a short imagined script of a dialogue or interview between William Shakespeare and a time-travelling version of yourself. Ask him what the play was about, and perhaps why he thinks the play is still so popular more than four hundred years later. Try to include references to specific points or ideas in the play.**

Like most great artists, Shakespeare does not seem interested in explaining his work, but leaves it up to others. We can imagine him saying, 'Here it is. Read it, perform it, make of it what you will.' Indeed, *What You Will* is the subtitle of the play. Since *Twelfth Night* was first performed, plenty of people have accepted that invitation to interpret the play in their own way. The following pages outline some of those different readings. The variety of these interpretations shows that the play can be approached, explained and performed in many ways, all of which have a claim to being 'true'. In a sense,

what Shakespeare was thinking in 1600 matters less than what you think of it today. The play is still widely loved and performed all around the world in the twenty-first century.

You could think of *Twelfth Night* as simply the dramatisation of a fantastic story. A pair of twins are shipwrecked and land separately on the coast of Illyria. Each thinks the other has drowned. The sister, Viola, disguises herself as a boy, enters the service of a nobleman, Duke Orsino, and is sent by him to carry messages of love to the countess Olivia. A foolish knight, Sir Andrew Aguecheek, also hopes to win Olivia. But she takes no notice of Sir Andrew, rejects Orsino, and falls in love with the disguised Viola!

The result is all kinds of confusions, watched scornfully by the fool, Feste. In a parallel plot, Olivia's puritan steward Malvolio is tricked into thinking that she loves him. He is humiliated and mistreated for that delusion, mainly by Feste and Olivia's drunken uncle, Sir Toby Belch. Eventually all ends happily for most characters. Viola is reunited with her twin brother Sebastian, and their marriages to Orsino and Olivia are planned. But Sir Andrew Aguecheek gets a beating, and Malvolio ends the play angry and threatening revenge.

◆ **The two paragraphs above attempt to condense the plot of *Twelfth Night* into just a couple of hundred words. Imagine you only had a hundred words to convince a friend to come and see a great production of the play with you. How would you 'sell' the story to them in so few words?**

Genre （类型，体裁）

It is possible to classify *Twelfth Night* as one of several 'types', or **genres**, of play. Listed below are four different interpretations or perspectives from which you can read or analyse the play.

A joyous comedy

You could interpret *Twelfth Night* as a simple, straightforward type of **comedy** – that is, a very amusing and charming play, sunny and always enjoyable. *Twelfth Night* is filled with innocent laughter and preposterous (荒唐) situations, and it has a happy ending that restores harmony to the temporary confusion of Illyria. The critic Caroline Spurgeon described the play as a 'sophisticated and delicious comedy' that reflects an 'atmosphere of repartee (妙语连珠的谈话) and topical fun'. All the characters are likeable and funny, Sir Toby is a lovable rogue, and even Malvolio has his comic appeal, especially when he gets what he deserves at the play's end. In this view, the play is simply a delightful entertainment that must never be taken seriously.

A poignant (伤感), wistful (惆怅) comedy

Some take the view that *Twelfth Night* is a mournful and poignant play that is full of sentiment and wistfulness. The humour, apart from Sir Toby's coarseness, is witty and tender. There are many moving moments as Viola speaks her beautiful lines of love. She longs for a fulfilment that, until the end of the play, is beyond her grasp. A melancholic, nostalgic (怀旧) note is constantly struck by the many references to time ('The clock upbraids me with the waste of time'), and is also heard in the sound of the ever-changing sea that echoes through the play. Feste's songs are reminders that love, like life, will end ('Youth's a stuff will not endure'). The play is a plea for a quiet acceptance of the inevitable, and for finding solace (慰藉) in whatever temporary happiness comes our way.

A dark comedy

A different approach again would be to think of *Twelfth Night* as a dark comedy with troubling undertones (弦外之音). It seems light and amusing on the surface, but has dark and harsh depths. For example, the Polish critic Jan Kott described it as a 'very bitter comedy'. The 'outsiders' in the play are seen to suffer. Antonio is left sad and alone at the end. Malvolio leaves seeking revenge, not reconciliation. Orsino and Olivia are smug and self-centred, and learn little or nothing over the course of the play, and yet are permitted their hearts' shallow desires.

A political comedy

Others emphasise the political and historical messages or lessons in the play. Illyria is an oppressive society where no one at the top works, and this breeds self-indulgence in its idle aristocrats (贵族). The critic Elliot Krieger wrote that 'a ruling class ideology' operates within *Twelfth Night*. Sir Toby and his fellow conspirators are prompted by ill will towards Malvolio. The cruel baiting of Malvolio is little more than theatre as blood sport. Malvolio is a scapegoat (替罪羊), because Illyria needs him as someone to punish for the misdeeds of society. The play is a cruel satire (讽刺) that foreshadows Shakespeare's tragedies. It predicts the English Civil War, which will see the triumph of the Puritans and the extinguishing of theatre and merriment.

Combining perspectives

Most critical readings of *Twelfth Night* combine a number of the perspectives detailed above when analysing the play's meaning. As the images in this book demonstrate, directors and designers clearly try to emphasise these perspectives to a greater or lesser extent, depending upon their interpretation of the most important or dramatically interesting elements.

◆ Imagine that the friend mentioned in the activity on page 152 chooses not to come with you to see *Twelfth Night*. Write him or her a letter or an email describing your impressions of the play. Try to strongly adopt just one of the interpretations above, and emphasise the events and moments that led you to adopt that view of the play's meaning.

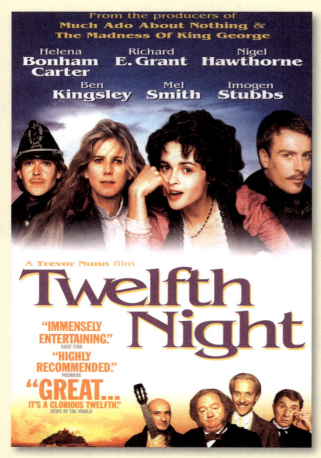

▲ This successful 1996 movie version of *Twelfth Night* demonstrated that the play's story, themes and characters can transfer well to modern media. Which elements or events in the play do you think could be explored in greater visual detail in film than on stage?

Themes

Love

Love, in its many forms, is an important theme throughout the play. The absence of love hangs heavy in the opening scenes, and love brings a happy ending for most of the characters at the end of the play. The very first line announces that love will be a central theme: 'If music be the food of love, play on'.

Twelfth Night presents a rich variety of types of love. Olivia and Orsino are the mourning lady and romantic hero of literary convention. Their self-centred love is transformed to genuine love by the constancy and integrity of Viola, who is the embodiment of true and faithful love. Even Sir Toby finds love of a sort with Maria. Sir Andrew and Malvolio learn that playing at love, or self-love, is not enough.

◆ Cut out a series of heart-shaped character cards. Give each major character a heart and write inside it how you think love affects them in the play. You could create a display of these, perhaps linking the different hearts using string to show how they are connected.

The modern idea of love is that individuals fall in romantic love and marry out of personal choice. Not everyone held that belief in Elizabethan England. Among the nobility and rich families, marriages were often arranged for the purpose of extending or maintaining wealth, land and power. Personal choice was less important. However, the economic reality of arranged marriages was often set aside in the stories and plays of the time. Instead, more dramatic notions of love came to the fore (占据重要位置).

Courtly love: Women were 'put on a pedestal' and worshipped from afar as unattainable goddesses (just as Orsino loves Olivia). Only by long devotion, trials and suffering could a man win his ideal woman, the 'fair, cruel maid' of literature. Such love was sexless and idealised. In reality, it often meant that aristocratic men like Orsino fell in love with the idea of love itself.

Romantic love: This was also idealised and non-sexual, but it included love at first sight, with marriage as its result. Viola, even though she is level-headed (头脑清醒) and clear-sighted, falls head over heels in love with the self-indulgent Orsino. Olivia is similarly entranced by her first sight of Viola disguised as Cesario.

Both these types of love produced the melancholy lover, the man who suffers for his love. Orsino fits this type as he sighs and fantasises about Olivia.

In Act 1 Scene 5, Olivia sets out the qualities that wealthy Elizabethans prized in men when she describes Viola/Cesario as having 'Five-fold blazon' (marks of being a gentleman).

◆ In the table below, the top row contains words that Olivia uses to describe Viola/Cesario's qualities. The bottom row lists more modern definitions of these words. However, the definitions do not correspond to the words directly above them. Connect each word in the top row to the correct modern definition in the bottom row. Number and rank how important you think these qualities should be in selecting a partner.

tongue	face	limbs	action	spirit
body	behaviour	speech	personality	looks

Although some critics point out that Viola and Olivia end the play subject to the usual hierarchy of marriage, most feminist critics argue that in *Twelfth Night* Shakespeare shows that love can potentially be a partnership of equals. Shakespeare saw that a woman's desires and capacity for feeling were on equal terms with a man's, not inferior at all.

◆ Design and write a Valentine's Day card from one character in the play to another. Make it anonymous and see if your classmates can guess which character the card is written by and destined for.

Appearance versus reality

Nothing is as it seems in *Twelfth Night*. A concern with the difference between appearance and reality runs throughout the play, creating a sustained sense of dramatic irony and giving the actors lots of opportunities for fun. The most notable examples are Viola's disguise as Cesario, and Malvolio's self-delusion that he is loved by Olivia.

Characters constantly mistake each other. Olivia falls for Viola/Cesario, thinking 'he' is a young man. Malvolio mistakes the forged letter as a true declaration of Olivia's love for him – his 'mistaking' is at first ludicrous (荒谬可笑) and funny, but then develops into cruel baiting and humiliation.

Viola and Sir Andrew are both tricked into thinking the other is a superb swordsman: a farcical (滑稽) duel is the outcome. Antonio defends Viola, thinking her to be Sebastian. He becomes bitter when Viola denies she knows him and does not return the money that Antonio lent to Sebastian. Orsino also turns against Viola/Cesario when he mistakenly thinks his faithful page Cesario has betrayed him and married Olivia.

Directors and designers use set, lighting, costumes and sound in a range of ways to emphasise the different themes and ideas explored in the play. What can you tell about this production from the lighting, furniture, costume and facial expressions of Olivia and Malvolio? What mood do you think the director is trying to create?

Feste, as a clown, can say things that those with a more conventional position in society prefer not to say. Many characters in the play try to hide their true feelings by keeping their private self and their public face separate.

◆ How honestly do you think the characters in this play express their feelings? Draw a balance beam diagram (see the example for Malvolio below) and write down the character's moments of honesty and dishonesty on each side. Include references/ quotations from particular points in the play. Which way would the balance tip if it were real?

| emotionally honest | emotionally dishonest |

Malvolio

Madness and melancholy

Madness, in different forms, runs through the play – and this too can be seen as a difficulty in discerning reality from appearance. Most obvious is the tormenting of Malvolio. Sir Toby treats Malvolio as if he has been driven mad by love, and locks him in a dark room. Feste, posing as Sir Topas, tries to convince Malvolio that he is indeed mad. Malvolio's ill treatment reflects the Elizabethan belief that the insane were possessed by devils, and should be confined in dark places (see p. 94).

◆ Identify three examples of behaviour in the play that appears outwardly to be mad (for example, Malvolio wearing bright yellow stockings all of a sudden). Write down each example in the centre of a circle. Draw a second circle around that first one, and in it write what the audience understands about the behaviour. Finally, add an outer circle with a short description of what you think Shakespeare's message might be. Is he simply trying to gain a laugh from the audience, or is there a deeper meaning?

Twelfth Night portrays the melancholy (which can seem a sort of madness) created by love and grief. Orsino, threatening to kill both Olivia and Viola in the final scene, is momentarily mentally unbalanced. Olivia has been told that Malvolio is 'tainted in's wits'. Passionately waiting for Viola/Cesario to arrive, Olivia exclaims 'I am as mad as he / If sad and merry madness equal be' (Act 3 Scene 4, lines 14–15). Olivia has lost a brother, while Viola and Sebastian both believe the other to be dead.

◆ Use a copy of the table below to explore the ways in which this intense melancholic sadness affects different characters.

Character (and point in the play)	Reason for sadness	How the sadness is overcome	Do you feel sorry for them?
Olivia in Act 1	The recent death of her brother	She falls in love with Viola/Cesario	A little, although she does seem rather too cold in her response to others in Act 1

Fun and excess

Twelfth Night revels in its own theatricality and sense of fun. Sir Toby, Sir Andrew, Fabian and Feste revel drunkenly and enjoy jokes and wordplay throughout. The emphasis on disguise in *Twelfth Night* means that the play is full of dramatic irony and amusing gender confusion! However, much of the 'fun' in the play is as a result of excess. Too much alcohol, too much mischief and too much deception create both humour and **pathos** (feelings of sympathy and pity).

◆ Create a top-ten list of the funniest moments in the play (with quotations). Decide upon a rank order, and explain why each moment is such fun.

◆ Create a list of five examples (with quotations) where the fun has either gone too far or is exposed as simply being excessive.

Time

A sense of time pervades (贯穿) the play. The shipwrecked Viola decides to go to Orsino's court, but leaves what may result to time: 'What else may hap, to time I will commit' (Act 1 Scene 2, line 60). Disguised as Cesario, she realises that Olivia has fallen in love with her, and exclaims, 'O time, thou must untangle this, not I' (Act 2 Scene 2, line 37).

Orsino reflects on the brevity of women's beauty, 'For women are as roses, whose fair flower, / Being once displayed, doth fall that very hour', and Viola agrees, 'To die, even when they to perfection grow!' (Act 2 Scene 4, lines 36–7, 39). Most famously, Feste taunts Malvolio at the play's end with 'And thus the whirligig of time brings in his revenges.'

◆ Draw out a clock face, placing Feste's quotation (above) in the centre. Next to each hour, write in or illustrate an example of how age and time is significant in the play.

Extended written responses

◆ Write extended answers to the following questions around the themes and ideas expressed in *Twelfth Night*. Use quotations from the play and, where possible, from critics to support your argument.

   a Explore the different ways in which *Twelfth Night* reveals the power and pain associated with falling in love.

   b To what extent does the drama in *Twelfth Night* stem from the fact that little is as it seems?

   c How far do you agree with the critic Ralph Berry that *Twelfth Night* is as much about 'real pain inflicted upon real people' as it is comedy?

   d *Twelfth Night* is a celebration of fun and a warning of the dangers of excess. Discuss.

   e Do you agree that *Twelfth Night* is an 'uneasy play about outsiders who lose'?

◀ Feste and Olivia in a 2004 production at the Albery Theatre.

Characters 人物分析

You can build up your understanding of characters by examining what they say, what they do and what other characters say about them. This is helpful for understanding lesser as well as major characters.

As you follow characters through the play:

- Select lines or phrases that you think are typical of them at different moments in the story.
- Collect examples of what other characters say about them.
- Note down examples of their actions – both major and seemingly less important.
- Carefully examine what some characters tell the audience directly when they are alone (soliloquies). Although these speeches appear to reveal the innermost thoughts of the speaker, they can be selective about what they disclose and can represent a one-sided version of events. The audience needs to be sceptical about the reliability of these soliloquies.
- Pay particular attention to how characters change and develop, and how Shakespeare shows us the different sides of their personalities.

◆ Make a display about one character, using your collected quotations and examples. Include illustrations and analytical comments.

◆ Use the examples to write an essay that explores how one character changes and develops through play, and analyses the effect this has on the audience.

◆ In threes or fours, devise essay questions on a chosen character or pair of characters. Examples might include:

- Why does Shakespeare include the character of Feste in the play?
- How does Shakespeare contrast characters in *Twelfth Night*? (Think about twins, types of lover, mistaken identities, parallel plots)
- Who does Shakespeare indicate is the lead character in the play, and how does he do this?

- In what ways might a director or the actor playing Malvolio show the tragedy as well as the comedy in his fall from grace?

Choose at least one question and produce an essay plan together. Present your plans succinctly (简要) to the rest of the class, using a maximum of five slides. Each slide needs to contain a key quotation for each section of the essay. Your talk should provide details and analysis.

Viola

Unlike the other characters, Viola does not seem to be in the grip of any illusion. Some critics think that Viola represents a contrast to other major characters who are deceived by appearances. Others have suggested that her dramatic function is to lead Olivia and Orsino out of their fantasies about love and help them realise what true love really is.

Virtually all interpretations of the play represent Viola as being truly in love. She is not self-seeking, but self-sacrificing. She speaks simply and directly about her love, in language that is sincere rather than affected. Her love for Orsino appears constant, deep and pure. Character descriptions of Viola often point out that she:

- remains true to Orsino throughout the play
- unquestioningly carries out Orsino's orders to woo Olivia
- speaks the most moving and sincere lines about love in the play
- tells Olivia what genuine love is really like
- is not interested in status, but in individuals
- is willing to die for love when Orsino threatens her
- ensures, through the example of her own genuine love, that Olivia and Orsino turn away from self-indulgent and self-deceiving love.

◆ Discuss the list above in pairs or small groups. Which of these observations do you agree with, and why? Rank them in order from 'totally agree' to 'totally disagree'. Are there differing opinions in your group? Why?

Shakespeare uses disguise as a plot device to suggest that Viola is a more complex character than she might appear at first sight. Forced to woo another woman on behalf of the man she loves, she is able to put into language the difficult subject of love, while mourning the loss of her brother and recovering from a shipwreck.

Some of Viola's actions seem to contradict positive descriptions of her. Audiences are often puzzled by just what she sees in Orsino, who some judge as self-centred, posturing and incapable of recognising true love. Viola's love for Orsino seems to make her blind to the less attractive side of his nature. Is she, in fact, deceived by appearances too?

Also, despite Viola's supposed clear-sightedness, in one episode of the play she is fooled into thinking that Sir Andrew Aguecheek is a formidable duellist ('a devil in private brawl')! However, her duping (受骗) here may be merely a device to fulfil the demands of the comic plot.

◆ As Viola, write a letter home to your best friend. Describe when you first fell in love with Orsino, explain what you find attractive about him, and talk about the long wait you had to endure before he noticed you and returned your love.

▼ Study this picture alongside the picture on page vi. Identify the scene where this moment takes place. In pairs, adopt the poses in the images. Then perform the scene, pausing after each line to thought-track (思路追踪) what Viola is thinking at this moment.

Orsino

Orsino has been described as 'Shakespeare's presentation of the melancholy lover', 'in love with the idea of love itself', and 'unable to distinguish between appearance and reality'.

◆ In pairs or small groups, discuss the images of Orsino in this book. Use your interpretation of these images, alongside your own knowledge of the play, to decide what the following quotations and statements suggest to the audience about Orsino and his love:

- 'Give me excess of it' (Act 1 Scene 1)
- 'Enough; no more' (Act 1 Scene 1)
- 'Love-thoughts lie rich' (Act 1 Scene 1)
- 'O spirit of love' (Act 1 Scene 1)
- 'sicken and so die' (Act 1 Scene 1)
- 'one selfsame king' (Act 1 Scene 1)
- 'my love, more noble than the world' (Act 2 Scene 4)
- 'such as I am, all true lovers are' (Act 2 Scene 4)
- 'as hungry as the sea' (Act 2 Scene 4)
- 'now heaven walks on earth' (Act 5 Scene 1)
- 'his fancy's queen' (Act 5 Scene 1)
- Orsino does not woo Olivia himself, but instead sends messengers.
- Orsino threatens to murder Viola/Cesario.
- Orsino switches his love abruptly from Olivia to Viola.

◆ Build up evidence for a character profile of Orsino by adding to this list of examples. Explore what each point reveals about his character.

Olivia

Olivia has vowed to shut herself away from the world for seven years in mourning for her dead brother, but she quickly breaks that vow when she meets Viola/Cesario.

Like Orsino, Olivia seems to confuse illusion with reality and mistake infatuation for love. Misled by outward appearances, her love proves similarly self-deceiving and sentimental.

◆ Consider the following statements about Olivia. In groups, discuss what these quotations and statements reveal about Olivia and how an audience might respond to her:

- 'Is't not well done?' (Act 1 Scene 5)
- 'Not too fast! Soft, soft!' (Act 1 Scene 5)
- 'Even so quickly may one catch the plague?' (Act 1 Scene 5)
- 'poor gentleman', 'A most extracting frenzy' (Act 5 Scene 1)
- Olivia constantly presses Viola/Cesario to visit her.
- Olivia marries Sebastian, thinking he is Cesario.
- In his portrayal of Olivia, Shakespeare balances her self-deceptions against her evident positive traits.
- Olivia is a capable mistress of her household, and possesses a wry (冷嘲式) humour.

◆ Build up evidence for a character profile of Olivia by adding to this list of examples. Explore what each point reveals about her character.

Feste

Fools were often employed in royal palaces and the great houses of noble families. Although they had the title of 'fool' (or jester or clown), they were much more intelligent than foolish ('a witty fool'). Their job was not simply to provide amusement, but to comment critically on contemporary behaviour. An 'allowed fool' was able to say what he thought. No punishment would follow, as Olivia explains: 'There is no slander in an allowed fool'.

▼ Consider the ways in which the characters of Olivia and Feste could be portrayed and cast. How do the Feste and Olivia in this image fulfil or disappoint your expectations? What comparisons and contrasts can you draw between this image and your own imagined portrayal of these characters?

Feste is an 'allowed fool', and an emblem and critic of the folly that runs through the play. He is employed by Olivia, and was a favourite of her father. He gets on well with Sir Toby, and is just as much at home at Duke Orsino's. Moving freely between Olivia's household and Orsino's palace, he links the love plot and the comic plots of the play. Only Malvolio dislikes him, and Feste takes revenge on the puritanical steward.

Feste delights in wordplay. He puns, riddles (打谜语), engages in repartee, invents mock-logical arguments and seizes any opportunity to create nonsense from words. His language demonstrates how meanings shift constantly in the topsy-turvy world of Illyria.

Malvolio

'O you are sick of self-love, Malvolio'.
Olivia's accusation sums up the traditional view of
Malvolio, which is that he:

- is highly critical of people he perceives as below him
- is disdainful towards Viola when returning the ring
- is intolerant of Sir Toby's merry-making
- has secret fantasies that Olivia loves him
- has a self-conceit that causes him to fall easily into the
  trap set for him
- does not realise how ridiculous he looks, smiling and
  cross-gartered
- cannot forgive, but thinks only of revenge.

Malvolio represents a puritanical disapproval of 'cakes and
ale' festivity. His fantasies, conceit and sense of superiority
cause him to be deceived by the forged letter. But in spite
of his arrogance, pomposity and lack of humour (and the
implications of his name, Malvolio = 'ill-wishing'), he is an
efficient and conscientious steward. His humiliating
treatment as a madman often makes modern audiences
feel uncomfortable.

◆ **In pairs, consider what you think of the view of
Malvolio expressed in the statements above. Does
his 'gulling' go too far, or does he get what he
deserves? Present your ideas to another pair, and
decide whether you are comfortable with the way
the play ends for Malvolio.**

Sir Toby Belch and Sir Andrew Aguecheek

Sir Toby Belch and Sir Andrew Aguecheek link the love plot
and the comic plots. They are recognisable characters in
dramatic tradition. Sir Toby represents the boastful, drunken
braggart. His name, Belch, suggests his earthy nature. His
behaviour displays the spirit of *Twelfth Night*: pleasure-
seeking revelling ('cakes and ale') and the rejection of
constraint (see notes on the festival of Twelfth Night on
pp. 172–3).

Sir Andrew is the traditional 'gull', a rich buffoon whose
foolishness ensures that he is easily fleeced (骗走) of his
money by Sir Toby. He has no chance of winning Olivia's
love, and is another character in the grip of illusion. He
thinks of himself as a lover, a scholar and a skilled duellist,
but each self-perception is comically exposed as a delusion.

Sir Toby is a bully, a cheat, a liar and a cruel practical joker.
He is also, like Malvolio, a hypocrite, because for all his
anti-authoritarian revelling he is acutely conscious of his
own social position as a relative of the high-status Olivia.
But he is also brave and witty, and his melancholy echoes
Orsino's. And Sir Andrew, for all his witlessness, has one
of the most endearing lines in the play, which suggests he
is yet another melancholy lover: 'I was adored once, too.'

'This is my lady's hand'. In this modern-dress production, Malvolio is deceived by the forged letter while Fabian, Sir Andrew and Sir Toby watch from the box hedge. (For other portrayals of this 'overhearing' scene, see pictures on pp. viii, 58, 62, 68 and 178.) This is a private moment for Malvolio, and a moment of delight for the others. What do we learn about each character from their reaction in this image?

The language of *Twelfth Night* 《第十二夜》的语言

Imagery

Twelfth Night is full of **imagery** – words or phrases that conjure up (使人想起) pictures or associations in the mind. When Maria says 'here comes the trout that must be caught with tickling' (Act 2 Scene 5, line 18–19), her image is of Malvolio, who can be trapped by flattery, just as a fish can be teased into being caught. Similarly, when Antonio says that his desire 'More sharp than filèd steel [a sword], did spur me forth', his image vividly suggests the piercing and painful nature of his feelings for Sebastian, which force Antonio to follow him.

Shakespeare's imagery stirs the audience's imagination, deepens the dramatic impact of particular moments or moods, provides insight into character and intensifies meaning and emotional force. Sir Toby paints a hilarious picture of Sir Andrew's cowardice: 'if he were opened and you find so much blood in his liver as will clog the foot of a flea [i.e. a very small amount], I'll eat the rest of th'anatomy [the entire skin and bones]' (Act 3 Scene 2, lines 48–9).

The Elizabethan world provides much of the play's imagery. For example, when Malvolio thinks he has truly captured Olivia's affection, he says, 'I have limed her'. The image is from the practice of trapping birds with sticky lime applied to tree branches. Elsewhere, animals and birds provide a rich source of images. Sir Andrew has 'dormouse valour', Fabian says Viola 'looks pale, as if a bear were at his heels', and Orsino angrily describes Viola as a 'dissembling cub'.

All Shakespeare's imagery uses metaphor, simile or personification (拟人). All of these are comparisons that in effect substitute one thing (the image) for another (the thing described).

A **simile** compares one thing to another using 'like' or 'as'. Sir Toby says that Sir Andrew's hair 'hangs like flax on a distaff' (a stick wrapped with fibres ready for spinning). Orsino recalls Antonio's face in the sea-battle: 'it was besmeared / As black as Vulcan' (the Roman god of fire, blacksmith to the gods).

A **metaphor** is also a comparison, suggesting that two dissimilar things are actually the same. When Viola speaks of 'that orbèd continent the fire / That severs day from night' it is an elaborate description of the sun. Elsewhere, Sir Toby's image of 'cakes and ale' is a striking metaphor for a whole world of celebration, festivity and hedonistic (享乐) enjoyment.

To put it another way, a metaphor borrows one word or phrase to express another. When, at the play's end, Feste says, 'And thus the whirligig of time brings in his revenges', his image is of a merry-go-round (旋转木马) or spinning top, and the 'wheel of Fortune', suggesting that time brings about the revenge on Malvolio that Feste has long wished for.

Personification turns all kinds of things into persons, giving them human feelings or attributes (属性). Viola personifies Patience in a vivid description of the effects of love that uses all three kinds of imagery:

> She never told her love,
> But let concealment like a worm i'th'bud
> Feed on her damask cheek. She pined in thought,
> And with a green and yellow melancholy
> She sat like Patience on a monument,
> Smiling at grief.
>
> Act 2 Scene 4, lines 106–11

Classical mythology contributes to the richness of the play's imagery. Elizabethans were more familiar with such references than most audience members today. In the play's first scene, Elizabethans would recognise that Orsino's image of being turned into a deer pursued by savage hounds comes from a story in Ovid's (奥维德) *Metamorphoses* (《变形记》). In this story, the hunter Actaeon saw the goddess Diana bathing and as punishment he was turned into a stag (雄鹿) and chased and killed by his own hunting dogs.

Similarly, Elizabethans, knowing that Jove is a god famous for his exploits in love, would find it appropriate that Malvolio thanks Jove for helping him (as he mistakenly believes) win the love of Olivia. In the same way, they would appreciate the humorous inappropriateness of Sir Toby's calling the diminutive (较小) Maria Penthesilea (queen of the female-warrior Amazons). In the production pictured below, you can see how small Maria usually appears on stage!

Many other images from Greek and Roman mythology occur in the play. You will find brief explanations of each at appropriate points in the script: Elysium (p. 4), Arion on the dolphin's back (p. 6), Diana (p. 18), Vulcan (p. 128), Jove (p. 24), Mercury (p. 22), Lucrece (p. 62) and Lethe (p. 112).

◆ Orsino's language in Act 1 Scene 1 contains a series of images that recur throughout the play: music, death, the sea, hunting, disease ('pestilence'), love and flowers. Choose one image, find as many uses of it in the play as you can, and work out a vivid and effective way of displaying your findings (e.g. in an illustrated spider diagram).

165

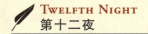

Antithesis （对偶）

Antithesis is the opposition of words or phrases. When Viola exclaims about Olivia, 'But if you were the devil, you are fair!', the word 'devil' stands in contrast to 'fair'. There is similar setting of word against word when Fabian, looking for forgiveness for the trick he and the others have played on Malvolio, hopes it 'May rather pluck on laughter than revenge' ('laughter' versus 'revenge').

Antithesis is one of Shakespeare's favourite language devices. He uses it extensively in all his plays. Why? Because antithesis powerfully expresses conflict through its use of opposites, and conflict is the essence of all drama. In *Twelfth Night*, conflict occurs in many forms: the formality of Orsino's elegant court versus the more relaxed household of Olivia; Malvolio's uptight puritanism versus Sir Toby's carefree revels; Olivia's resistance to Orsino's wooing; Viola's emotional struggle ('barful strife') as her love for Orsino clashes with her duty to act as his love messenger to Olivia.

Even more strikingly, throughout the play there are many conflicts of appearance versus reality (see p. 156): a girl mistaken for a boy, one twin for another, a forged letter for a true declaration of love. Nothing is quite what it seems in this play of mistaken identity. Viola's remark to the Captain 'that nature with a beauteous wall / Doth oft close in pollution', and her declaration to Olivia that 'I am not what I am', are just two antitheses that express the conflict between outward show and inward reality.

Antithesis intensifies the sense of conflict. In the 'duel' scene (Act 3 Scene 4) Viola, preferring peace to duelling, says she would 'rather go with sir priest than sir knight'. Antonio, mistaking Viola for Sebastian and feeling betrayed, vehemently exclaims, 'O how vile an idol proves this god!' Absurdly wooing Olivia, Malvolio dismisses Maria as unworthy of an answer: 'nightingales answer daws'.

Feste's deliberately confusing antitheses are reminders that the genre of *Twelfth Night* is comedy. Shakespeare therefore ensures that conflicts result in humour rather than, as in the histories and tragedies, in unhappiness and death, as when Sebastian declares Olivia 'betrothed both to a maid and man'.

◆ **Collect as many examples of antithesis or opposites as you can from *Twelfth Night* and write them in a list. Identify whether they contribute to humour, conflict or both in the play. Are there more antitheses connected to humour or to conflict? Why could this be? What might it suggest about Shakespeare's intentions? Write down your answers to these questions, using examples from the script to support your ideas. You might compare your list and ideas with a partner, or in a small group, to see whether interpretations differ.**

Verse and prose

About one-third of the play is in verse and two-thirds in prose. Theatrical convention was that prose was used by comic and low-status characters. High-status characters spoke verse. Comic scenes were written in prose (as were letters, such as the one Maria forges to trick Malvolio), but audiences expected verse to be spoken in serious scenes because verse was thought particularly suitable for lovers and for moments of high dramatic or emotional intensity.

Shakespeare used his judgement about which conventions he should follow in *Twelfth Night*, and it is obvious that he often broke with these conventions. Viola (high-status) switches frequently from verse to prose, and her first dialogue with Olivia (also high-status) is in prose. Sir Toby and Sir Andrew always use prose. They, too, are high-status characters, although their dramatic function is comic.

The verse of *Twelfth Night* is mainly **blank verse** – unrhymed verse written in **iambic pentameter** (抑扬格 五音步) . Iambic pentameter is a rhythm (韵律) or metre in which each line has five unstressed syllables (音节) (×) alternating with five stressed syllables (/):

×   /   ×   / × / ×   / × /
O time, thou must untangle this, not I

◆ Skim quickly through each scene in the play script. Make a list showing which scenes are mainly in verse, and which are mainly in prose. Suggest why this might be. Do you notice anything about the characters and situations where prose is being used?

◆ Find three or four examples of iambic pentameter in the play. What do you notice about the contexts in which this rhythm is used?

◆ Choose one short verse extract from the play (e.g. Act 3 Scene 1, lines 142–7) and one short extract written in prose (e.g. Act 3 Scene 4, lines 232–7). Note how the type of language used differs in these two extracts, and consider the effect on the audience that this is intended to have in each case:

a Is there a theme to the words used?

b Are they short/simple or long/complex words?

c How do the words appear on the page?

d How do the language and rhythm combine to emphasise the nature/purpose of the extract?

Write out the extracts on large pieces of paper and annotate with your answers to these questions. Add in any other ideas that you have about the language and rhythm.

Puns and wordplay

A **pun** is a play on words where the same sound has different meanings. This method of playing with words was very popular in Shakespeare's time. In the opening scene, Orsino hears the word 'hart' (male deer) but plays with it as if it were 'heart'. Sir Toby first appears juggling with 'exceptions', 'except' and 'excepted', then with 'confine'. Feste's first words pun on 'colours' (see p. 18), and he continues to play with words throughout *Twelfth Night*. Asked by Viola/Cesario, 'Dost thou live by thy tabor?' he replies, 'No, sir, I live by the church.' No wonder that Feste calls himself Olivia's 'corrupter of words'.

◆ Follow Feste through the play. Note examples from two or three scenes of what he says and how he puns or riddles with words. In a table or a short essay, compare the effect that this wordplay has on his onstage audience (the other characters), and on the theatre or movie audience. Consider whether these audience responses alter at different points or situations in the play.

◆ When Feste pretends to be a priest in Act 4 Scene 2, he uses 'educated' language to match. However, the phrases that he uses are simply intelligent-sounding nonsense. Read lines 11–14, 35 and 40 in pairs or small groups. Write out the nonsense phrases on paper and annotate them with comments that analyse:

• why we find things that we do not understand funny

• why we are impressed by people who use complicated language

• what this 'impressiveness' shows about both us and them

• whether puns are effective because we hear rather than see the words.

Songs

Orsino commands: 'If music be the food of love, play on', and a number of the scenes in the play are punctuated (不时打断) by songs. In Shakespeare's time, music often accompanied the action, and was played by musicians sitting above or at the side of the stage. Similarly, modern stage and movie adaptations will often add music to accentuate (突出) episodes in the drama.

However, in *Twelfth Night* Shakespeare chooses to include a professional musician, Feste, as one of the characters. Importantly, he incorporates songs into the script, so any director putting on the play has to consider how he or she will accommodate and stage these poems set to music.

The songs themselves seem not to bear any direct relation to the action that is taking place on stage, but instead present short tales and entertainment for the characters. Calls for song and music occur frequently in the play, and may reflect the festive name of *Twelfth Night*.

Shakespeare sometimes includes popular sayings and songs in his plays, and it may be that Feste's songs are there to provide an opportunity for audience participation – for example, when Sir Toby and the revellers wake up and upset Malvolio (Act 2 Scene 2).

◆ Read through all of Feste's songs, and make note of the context in which each takes place. The songs appear at:

- Act 2 Scene 3, lines 33–46 and 86–96
- Act 2 Scene 4, lines 49–64
- Act 4 Scene 2, lines 58–66 and 102–13
- Act 5 Scene 1, lines 366–85.

How you would want an audience to respond to Feste's songs? As a director, what steps would you take to achieve this audience reaction? Make notes in your Director's Journal.

◆ What do you think is the overall function of the songs in *Twelfth Night*? Write out one song on a piece of paper and annotate it with directions of how it should be performed to fulfil this purpose.

Illyria 伊利瑞亚

Shakespeare's Illyria is a fantasy land of make-believe (虚幻) and illusion. Such places exist under many names and in many cultures: Utopia, Far Far Away, Fairyland, Xanadu, Arcadia, the Land of Cockaigne, Shangri-La, New Atlantis, Dreamland. It is an enchanted world where happiness is truly possible: a fictitious world of romance, full of magical possibilities, thrilling and exotic (奇异), where the end result of dramatic excitement is joy and harmony.

▼ **Is Disney World a modern Illyria, where fantasy rules? Why do you think such places are so popular? What makes them so suitable as settings for storytelling and so appealing to an audience? Discuss and debate in groups.**

In other words, it's a state of mind rather than the real, historical Illyria, which was an area on the coast of present-day Albania and Croatia (see p. 34). It is a place that exists in the imagination, a realm in which characters are changed by experience. Shakespeare created similar worlds in his other comedies: the Forest of Arden (*As You Like It*), the wood outside Athens (*A Midsummer Night's Dream*), Belmont (*The Merchant of Venice*), Ephesus (*The Comedy of Errors*). In these exotic locations, confusions, errors and mistakes are made but happiness, reconciliation and marriage result.

Illyria is a capricious world of disguise and mistaken identity. Language itself is unreliable – words slip and slide into confusion. Even time itself is in question: Shakespeare can't quite decide whether Viola spends three months or three days with Orsino!

◆ **Can you think of other stories, movies or television programmes that rely upon similarly whimsical (离奇) settings? Do any of them share any qualities with *Twelfth Night*? Make a mind map of these fictional worlds, showing connections or similarities between them.**

Fantasy and everyday life rub shoulders in Illyria – a fairy-tale duke inhabits the same world as the earthy Sir Toby Belch, a very English drunkard. Everything is untrustworthy and larger than life. Common sense is mocked, and nothing is quite what it seems. Folly abounds – one of the chief characters, Feste, is called 'the fool'. The threat of madness is common (the word 'mad' occurs more times in *Twelfth Night* than in any other play by Shakespeare). Much madness is to do with love, but Malvolio is almost driven to real madness.

Illyria, for all its untrustworthiness, is a secure place. Brother finds sister; lovers will marry. Illusions are the way to find truth, and time will achieve a happy ending for most, but not all, of the characters. Some characters finish up with their heart's desire – or think they do.

The subtitle of the play, *What You Will*, was a common catchphrase (流行语) in Shakespeare's time. Perhaps it says to the audience: 'make of it what you like, it's make-believe, but don't take it too seriously, because nothing is of any consequence'.

◆ Make a display (a collage, photomontage [合成照片], computer presentation or other illustration) to show your imagined view of Illyria. Include quotations from the play.

Illyria: Shakespeare's England

Like all writers, Shakespeare reflected in his plays the world he knew. Illyria sounds like a far-away place – Orsino, Antonio and Malvolio are 'un-English' names (unlike Sir Toby, Sir Andrew and 'Mistress Mary'). But in so many ways *Twelfth Night* is full of the customs, sights and sounds of Elizabethan England.

Hunting and field sports: hounds, bird-bolts, beagle, stone-bow, staniel, cold scent, sowter, fox, haggard, feather, woodcock, gin, unmuzzled, whipstock.

Eating and drinking: buttery-bar, canary, sack, beef (thought to make Englishmen stupid), alehouse, tosspots, pickled herring.

Songs and dances: jig, galliard, coranto, caper, back-trick, sink-a-pace, catch, cantons, tabor, 'hold thy peace', 'Farewell dear heart'.

The countryside: squash, peascod, codling, turkey-cock, dormouse, grey capilet, oxen and wainropes, bawcock, chuck, biddy, sheriff's post, orchard, box-tree.

Familiar words or phrases: It's all one, Peg-a-Ramsey, cudgel, leman (sweetheart), cheveril glove, westward ho, the old Vice, asshead, coxcomb, knave, gull, what you will, coz, swabber, sneck up.

Clothes: gaskins, points, changeable taffeta, branched velvet gown, yellow stockings, cross-gartered.

Occupations: coziers, tinkers, weavers, stewards, spinsters (who spin flax on a distaff), knitters, grand jurymen, bumbaily, master crowner (coroner), parson, curate, Dick Surgeon, coistrill, groom.

Current affairs: Puritan, Brownist, yeoman of the wardrobe, Mistress Mall's picture, Lady of the Strachy, Dutchman's beard, the new map of the Indies, the sophy.

Places and customs: south suburbs, the Elephant, St Bennet, (the great bed of) Ware, parish top, inventories, tray-trip, cherry-pit, acqua-vitae, bear-baiting.

◆ Imagine you are a young, wealthy, Elizabethan gentleman. Write a short diary entry describing a weekend in Elizabethan England – with one day spent in Shakespeare's London and another on a trip to the nearby countryside. Use the words in the list above to give a powerful impression of the sights, sounds, activities and conversations of the time.

The attitudes and values explored in *Twelfth Night* are also a reflection of England in the 1600s. The 'Perspective and themes' section on page 152–57 has already explored attitudes to love and madness, but it is also worth reflecting upon what the play tells us about the way the average Elizabethan viewed drinkers, powerful women, figures of authority and religious leaders. Many of the laughs come at the expense of these 'types' of people. Do you think much has changed in the last four hundred years? Would Shakespeare laugh at modern comedy characters and see a resemblance to his own comic creations?

◆ Make a list of well-known comic creations or characters from recent years that you think bear a resemblance to a character from *Twelfth Night*. For example, is there a Disney character that reminds you of Sir Andrew? Explain why you see a connection or similarity between them.

'Merry' England

In many productions of *Twelfth Night* the actors wear the dress of Shakespeare's time. The play is set in Illyria, but Sir Toby in doublet (小双衣，流行于莎士比亚时代的男士紧身上衣，有的带短裙) and hose (紧腿裤，上部为**breeches** [短马裤]，下部为**stockings** [裤袜]) (fitted jacket and trousers, see image above) looks and behaves very much like an Elizabethan Englishman.

Shakespeare's audiences seem to have really enjoyed 'big' and expressive characters like Sir Toby and his friends. Characters such as Falstaff from *Henry IV, Parts 1 and 2* and Bottom from *A Midsummer Night's Dream* represent the fun-loving, drunken or vibrant personalities that may have been regularly found at the Globe Theatre or in the inns and taverns that Shakespeare and his actor friends would have frequented.

However, although all these characters are used to make the audience laugh, they are also all shown to be flawed. It seems that Shakespeare knew all too well that excess, greed and an overbearing (自负) personality could be a recipe for trouble as well as comedy!

◆ Use the picture above and the information on page 170 to compile an assignment (including illustrations and quotations) entitled: 'What do we learn about Elizabethan attitudes to fun, excess and authority in *Twelfth Night?*'

Twelfth Night
第十二夜

In Elizabethan times, the twelve days after Christmas, up to Twelfth Night on 6 January (Epiphany), were traditionally a period of holiday and festival. It was a time for celebration and revelry, sometimes known as the 'Feast of Fools'. All kinds of folly, pranks and deceptions were allowed in this period of high jinks (嬉闹), a topsy-turvy time of confusion and masquerades (化装舞会). A never-never land was created, remote from the everyday world. Normal behaviour and conventions could be suspended, and common sense and decorum were abandoned as people were released from their everyday inhibitions. Comedy and carnival, disguise and boisterous (喧闹) frivolity were the order of the day.

Authority was up-ended. For a short time, servants could order their masters about. Today, a relic of this tradition is the custom in the army for officers to serve Christmas dinner to the soldiers. In universities, private houses and the Inns of Court (the law schools in London), a 'Lord of Misrule' (often a servant) was chosen to become, for a short period, master of the household. He (never she) organised dances, masques and make-believe activities.

However, the major function of the twelve days was to remind the underdogs (弱势群体) where power really lay, and that the normal hierarchy would and must be obeyed after the short holiday. Twelfth Night itself marked the end of both the Christmas holiday and the holiday season. The next day it was back to the normality of hard work in the everyday world. The short time of pleasure was over. So 6 January was tinged with sadness, as the Christmas decorations were taken down and the festivities ended.

▼ Two masked men in a Mardi Gras (基督教忏悔星期二举行的狂欢节，在大斋节的前一天) parade through New Orleans, USA.

◆ Write about what might happen if a 'Lord of Misrule' was elected for a day in your school or college. What would you do if you were elected?

◆ Research modern periods of festivity such as the Notting Hill Carnival (诺丁希尔狂欢节), Mardi Gras festivals in New Orleans and Rio de Janeiro, and the Munich Oktoberfest (慕尼黑十月节). Present your findings to the class, showing how far you think each modern celebration is like the Feast of Fools of Elizabethan England.

◆ Using both the knowledge you have gained from this book and any additional information you can find through your own research, compile a 'top ten' list of recreational activities or 'good times' for Elizabethans. Present this list on a large sheet of paper, using as much illustration and decoration as possible. At the same time, compile the 'top ten' list for the present day (based on research or your personal opinions and ideas). To what extent have our ideas of a 'good time' changed over more than four hundred years?

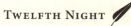

The image shown above is a section of a painting called *The Bean King* by Jacob Jordaens (1640s). The custom of appointing a Lord of Misrule from Christmas Day to Twelfth Night was widespread in Europe for many centuries. Its origins lay in the Saturnalia (农神节) of ancient Rome, a time when slaves and masters changed places and a mock king ruled a topsy-turvy world. At the universities of Oxford and Cambridge, this Lord of Misrule was known as 'King of the Kingdom of the Bean'. When the University of Cambridge unsuccessfully tried to suppress the Bean King and his revelry in 1646, 'some grave Governors mentioned the good use thereof, because thereby, in twelve days, they more discover the dispositions of Scholars than in twelve months before'.

◆ **What images in the painting above remind you of *Twelfth Night*? Discuss your ideas with a partner.**

Twelfth Night in performance 《第十二夜》的演出

First performances and origins

Sometime during 1600 and 1601 William Shakespeare, already a successful playwright, wrote *Twelfth Night*. The dates are certain for two reasons. First, because Maria's comment about 'the new map with the augmentation of the Indies' (Act 3 Scene 2, lines 62–3) refers to a map of India and the Far East printed in 1600. Second, because there is a record of a performance of the play at a Candlemas (圣烛节) (2 February) feast in 1602. John Manningham, a lawyer, wrote about a performance he saw at the Middle Temple, one of London's Inns of Court (see picture below). Part of his diary entry reads:

> *At our feast we had a play called 'Twelve Night, or What You Will' … A good practice in it to make the Steward believe his Lady widow was in love with him, by counterfeiting a letter as from his Lady in general terms, telling him what she liked best in him, and prescribing his gesture in smiling, his apparel, etc., and then when he came to practise making him believe they took him to be mad.*

In 2002, exactly four hundred years after John Manningham saw *Twelfth Night* in the Middle Temple, the Globe Theatre Company staged its own production there (see opposite). Discuss the challenges you imagine actors and directors face in performing the play in a space like this one.

Shakespeare's *The Comedy of Errors*, which also involves shipwrecked twins and mistaken identity.

Shakespeare probably took the idea of his play from an English adaptation of an Italian story, but he made significant alterations. In the original, the Sea Captain was a villain, Viola was imprisoned by the duke, and Olivia had a child by Sebastian. Shakespeare invented the Sir Toby sub-plot.

In creating Viola/Cesario, he drew on his earlier plays in which women dressed as men (Julia in *Two Gentlemen of Verona*, Portia in *The Merchant of Venice*, Rosalind in *As You Like It*).

◆ The image below shows the Middle Temple as it looks in the twenty-first century. It is likely that the production John Manningham saw in February 1602 would have been dark and possibly very cold, with candles for lighting and perhaps only strong ale to keep the audience warm! Imagine you were there and write a short description, similar to Manningham's, of the production.

Twelfth Night at the Globe Theatre

In Shakespeare's lifetime, *Twelfth Night* was performed at the Middle Temple and at the Globe Theatre, a round open-air theatre. The audience standing on the bare floor in front of the stage, the 'groundlings' (站票观众), got wet if it rained. Those in the galleries (who paid more), and the actors on stage, were under covered sections of the building and so were protected from the weather.

stood. Many of the productions are staged as Elizabethan and Jacobean (伊丽莎白一世和詹姆斯一世时期的) audiences probably saw them. In 2002, the Globe's production of *Twelfth Night* was staged in this way, and was performed in the Middle Temple for Candlemas (see p. 174). In 2012 the production was staged like this again, and this time moved to the Apollo Theatre, where attempts were made to recreate the atmosphere of the Middle Temple (see pictures on pp. 26, 76, 125 and 138).

▲ A modern audience at Shakespeare's Globe. The theatre was built using Elizabethan methods. The only modern feature is electric lights, which are used to allow plays to continue later into the afternoon as the days get shorter.

In Shakespeare's day, Viola, Olivia and Maria were played by boys. There were no elaborate sets on the bare stage of the Globe Theatre, but the actors dressed in attractive and expensive costumes, usually the fashionable dress of the times. Only a few props were used: a table, chairs, swords and tankards, and perhaps a box-tree behind which Sir Toby and the others hid to overhear Malvolio reading the letter.

A reconstruction of the Globe Theatre was rebuilt on London's Bankside and opened in 1996 as Shakespeare's Globe, close to the site on which the Globe Theatre first

◆ Some people have criticised the use of an all-male cast in the modern era. They argue that there are few enough good roles for women on the stage. Discuss or debate what you think about this with a partner or as a class.

◆ Imagine you are a fourteen-year-old boy in Shakespeare's company of actors. You've just been cast as Viola. Write a letter home to your parents, describing the part and your feelings at having been cast.

A growing reputation

Right from the play's first performance, Malvolio seized the imagination of audiences. In 1632, King Charles I wrote 'Malvolio' against the title of the play in the collection of Shakespeare's plays that he owned. In 1640, Leonard Digges praised Shakespeare in verses that included the following lines testifying to Malvolio's box-office appeal (票房价值):

lo in a trice
The Cockpit Galleries (廊台和楼座)*, Boxes, all are full*
To hear Malvolio, that cross-gartered Gull.

175

Perhaps Malvolio's revenge is that he has turned out to be the best-remembered character in the play! Also, the puritan attitudes of Malvolio may have seemed less amusing, and perhaps more disturbing, in the years following England's bloody civil war (1642–49).

In 1660, the diarist Samuel Pepys saw *Twelfth Night* three times. He thought it 'silly', and could not see the point of the title. The play fell from favour for almost eighty years after Pepys saw it, but other playwrights repeatedly drew on it as a source of ideas and language for their own plays.

▼ This image depicts the actor Mr Richard Yates playing Malvolio in the year 1776. The caption (说明文字) below the picture reads: 'Sweet lady, ha ha!' This is a slightly different version to the line used in Act 3 Scene 4 of this edition of the play.

Women on stage

We can't be sure exactly when the first female actors performed in *Twelfth Night*, but women were legally allowed to perform on London stages from 1660 onwards. As you can imagine, the presence of women in the cast would have changed some of the gender-based confusion that so much of the comedy is based around.

◆ How would the introduction of women to the London stage have changed the way that people viewed the play? Find examples of quotations where the audience interpretation might have changed if the lines were delivered by a woman instead of a man. Does it make the play less funny?

Eighteenth- and nineteenth-century productions

Eighteenth and nineteenth-century productions of *Twelfth Night* paid more attention to visual effect and 'realism', often featuring rich Elizabethan-style costumes, elaborate scene changes and large casts, all of which slowed the pace of performances considerably. Some productions even featured live horses! The dominant mood was of romantic happiness, with little emphasis on the darker elements of the play.

This was also an era in which the details of Shakespeare's plays were altered to suit the fashions of the time. For example, the poet Nahum Tate (1652–1715) famously rewrote a number of Shakespeare's tragedies, giving them happy endings! Similarly, in 1807, Thomas Bowdler (1754–1825) published a volume called *The Family Shakespeare* that quite extensively changed the scripts of the plays to edit out curses, sexual connotations or violence.

Throughout this period, many theatres were dominated by powerful 'actor-managers'. Men such as David Garrick (1717–79) and Henry Irving (1838–1905) were the 'stars' of the day, and audiences would flock to see their interpretations of key Shakespearean roles. These men would act as both star and director, and some accumulated huge wealth and fame.

◆ Research the famous actor-managers of the eighteenth and nineteenth centuries, David Garrick and Henry Irving. Suggest how you think they might have staged *Twelfth Night* and which parts they would have given themselves!

▲ This poster from 1820 gives details of a production at the famous Theatre Royal, on Drury Lane in London. It was essentially an opera version of *Twelfth Night*. What do you notice about the way 'Shakespeare' is spelled?

After its revival in 1741, *Twelfth Night* became increasingly popular. Many leading actors chose to play Malvolio. His 'darkened room' scene was played in a range of styles from tragedy to farce.

In the nineteenth century, it became fashionable to add musical scenes filled with spectacle and festivity – some productions were virtually operas. Sebastian, Olivia and Viola often sang, and Viola was sometimes played like a hearty and enthusiastic principal boy in a pantomime. The whole company would join in a song and dance at the play's end. One production included two shipwreck scenes, and opened with fishermen and peasants singing 'Come unto these yellow sands' from *The Tempest*. In another, Orsino and Viola married in Illyria's cathedral.

The modern era

Modern productions have tended to move away from such elaborate spectacle. The concern has been to explore the play's complex moods through close attention to language and characterisation. Old conventions have been reassessed: for example, in contrast with nineteenth-century productions, Olivia is now often played as a young woman, and Feste as a much older fool. There have been novel readings of the character Malvolio. One Malvolio left the stage apparently intent on suicide. Another gave his final words such evil undertones that it completely changed the comic mood. Yet another Malvolio bore a striking resemblance to Shakespeare.

Many modern productions stress the autumnal (渐衰), elegiac (sad, mournful) mood of the play (see p. 153). They suggest that fertility and romantic idyll (欢乐) will soon give way to decay and winter. There is a growing trend for modern productions to portray Illyria as a society undergoing change. So Illyria is set as a feudal, male-dominated society, exercising control through licensed foolery. But it is threatened by a more modern, efficient society, characterised by the 'new man', the self-made, humourless Malvolio. He is impatient with the old order, and intolerant of fun and festivity. Such productions tend to see the play as giving a forewarning (预警) of the struggles to come, in the English Civil War of 1642–49 and the closure of the theatres.

▼ In this 2012 production by the Royal Shakespeare Company, the eccentric appearances of Sir Toby and Sir Andrew (far left and far right) were in sharp and comic contrast to the dark, sombre, elegant look of the stage and the other characters.

▼ This is an image from a 2012 production by Propeller, showing an unusual approach to Act 2 Scene 5. Some of the actors are masked and in the background are three 'characters' not featured in the script. Discuss and suggest who you think these masked characters are, or what they represent. Why do you think the director has inserted such a detail in to the play, and why in particular in this scene?

Twelfth Night around the world

Shakespeare is the most performed playwright in the world. Productions of *Twelfth Night* can be found in most countries and have resonance (反响) or meaning in many cultures. Not only is the play performed internationally, but over the years directors have chosen to set the play in a number of different cultural contexts. Sometimes elements of the story are altered, sometimes contemporary language is added. Over the years, academics and playwrights have translated the play into hundreds of different languages.

The image on this page shows a production from 2009 by the famous Japanese director Ninagawa Yukio (蜷川幸雄). The traditional Japanese theatre style of kabuki was developing around the same time as Shakespeare was writing his plays, and this production sought to blend the two styles with added modern elements.

◆ Which characters can you identify in the image below? Do the characters' body language and costumes suggest which scene the image might show?

◆ Research kabuki (歌舞伎) theatre and discover its traditions and elements. You may be able to find a review of this production and write a report on what Ninagawa was trying to achieve.

Unusual or novel (新颖) approaches to staging *Twelfth Night*

Modern theatres allow directors to do extraordinary things on stage that Shakespeare could only have dreamed of doing. For example, recent productions have seen part of the stage turned into a swimming pool, an upturned grand piano dangled over the actors, and a North African village recreated as an imagining of Illyria!

Music is central to the play, and many productions use live music, just as Shakespeare would have done. Some productions, however, have the actors both performing and playing the instruments. Some use pop or dance music, sometimes with projected film images, to create a striking impact and a contemporary feel.

Some of the images of particularly original and creative productions may make you curious to know more. Others might baffle you and make you wonder what on earth the director was thinking!

◆ On pages 178–81 there are images of a range of innovative and novel productions from recent years. It is possible to read reviews for each of them online. Research one of these productions and write a short analysis of the approach the director took. Refer to the reviews the production received, and give your own opinion of the choices made in the staging of the production.

◆ If you have been able to see a production of *Twelfth Night* yourself, or if you have watched one of the movie versions or animated adaptations, write a short review aimed at someone yet to discover the delights of the play!

▼ In 2012, the Royal Shakespeare Company production featured a small swimming pool built into the stage, allowing Viola's rescue from the sea to be portrayed very literally.

This 2012 production of *Twelfth Night* by Faction Theatre took place on an entirely bare stage. In the scene where Feste, Sir Toby and Sir Andrew secretly watch Malvolio, they hide behind a box tree made of actors!

A 2005 open-air production in Regent's Park, London set the play on a remote tropical island – with a real parrot!

▲ A Hindi musical version of *Twelfth Night* was staged as part of the Globe to Globe festival in 2012 at Shakespeare's Globe. This festival celebrated the diversity of the ways in which Shakespeare's plays are interpreted and enjoyed all over the world.

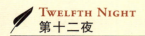
Writing about Shakespeare 笔论莎士比亚

The play as text

Shakespeare's plays have always been studied as literary works – as words on a page that need clarification, appreciation and discussion. When you write about the plays, you will be asked to compose short pieces and also longer, more reflective pieces like controlled assessments, examination scripts and coursework – often in the form of essays on themes and/or imagery, character studies, analyses of the structure of the play and on stagecraft. Imagery, stagecraft and character are dealt with elsewhere in this edition. Here, we concentrate on themes and structure. You might find it helpful to look at the 'Write about it' boxes on the left-hand pages throughout the play.

Themes

It is often tempting to say that the theme of a play is a single idea, like 'death' in *Hamlet*, or 'the supernatural' in *Macbeth*, or 'love' in *Romeo and Juliet*. The problem with such a simple approach is that you will miss the complexity of the plays. In *Romeo and Juliet*, for example, the play is about the relationship between love, family loyalty and constraint; it is also about the relationship of youth to age and experience; and the relationship between Romeo and Juliet is also played out against a background of enmity (敌意) between two families. Between each of these ideas or concepts there are tensions. The tensions are the main focus of attention for Shakespeare and the audience, and they also happen to be how drama operates – by the presentation of and resolution of tension.

Look back at the 'Themes' boxes throughout the play to see if any of the activities there have given rise to information that you could use as a starting-point for further writing about the themes of the specific play you are studying.

Structure

Most Shakespeare plays are in five acts, divided into scenes. These acts were not in the original scripts, but have been included in later editions to make the action more manageable, clearer and more like 'classical' structures. One way to get a sense of the structure of the whole play is to take a printed version (not this one!) and cut it up into scenes and acts, then display each scene and act, in sequence, on a wall, like this:

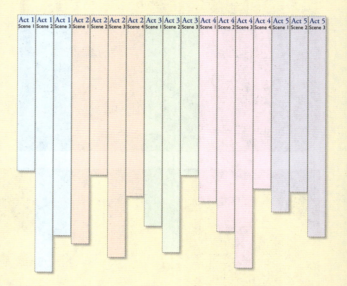

As you set out the whole play, you will be able to see the 'shape' of each act, the relative length of the scenes, and how the acts relate to each other (such as whether one of the acts is shorter, and why that might be). You can annotate the text with comments, observations and questions. You can use a highlighter pen to mark the recurrence of certain words, images or metaphors to see at a glance where and how frequently they appear. You can also follow a particular character's progress through the play.

Such an overview of the play gives you critical perspective: you will be able to see how the parts fit together, to stand back from the play and assess its shape, and to focus on particular parts within the context of the whole. Your writing will reflect a greater awareness of the overall context as a result.

The play as script

There are different, but related, categories when we think of the play as a script for performance. These include *stagecraft* (discussed elsewhere in this edition and throughout the left-hand pages), *lighting*, *focus* (who are we looking at? Where is the attention of the audience?), *music and sound*, *props and costumes*, *casting*, *make-up*, *pace and rhythm*, and other *spatial relationships* (e.g. how actors move across stage in relation to each other). If you are writing about stagecraft or performance, use the notes you have made as a result of the 'Stagecraft' boxes throughout this edition of the play, as well as any material you can gather about the plays in performance.

What are the key points of dispute?

Shakespeare is brilliant at capturing a number of key points of dispute in each of his plays. These are the dramatic moments where he concentrates the focus of the audience on difficult (sometimes universal) problems that the characters are facing or embodying.

First, identify these key points in the play you are studying. You can do this as a class by brainstorming what you think the key points are in small groups, then debating the long-list as a whole class, and then coming up with a short-list of what the class thinks are the most significant. (This is a good opportunity for speaking and listening work.) They are likely to be places in the play where the action or reflection is at its most intense, and which capture the complexity of themes, character, structure and performance.

Second, drill down (钻研) at one of the points of contention and tension. In other words, investigate the complexity of the problem that Shakespeare is exploring. What is at stake (成问题)? Why is it important? Is it a problem that can be resolved, or is it an insoluble one?

Key skills in writing about Shakespeare

Here are some suggestions to help you organise your notes and develop advanced writing skills when working on Shakespeare:

- Compose the title of your writing carefully to maximise your opportunities to be creative and critical about the play; or explore the key words in your title carefully. Decide which aspect of the play – or which combination of aspects – you are focusing on.
- Create a mind map of your ideas, making connections between them.
- If appropriate, arrange your ideas into a hierarchy that shows how some themes or features of the play are 'higher' than others and can incorporate other ideas.
- Sequence your ideas so that you have a plan for writing an essay, review, story – whichever genre you are using. You might like to think about whether to put your strongest points first, in the middle, or later.
- Collect key quotations (it might help to compile this list with a partner), which you can use as evidence to support your argument.
- Compose your first draft, embedding quotations in your text as you go along.
- Revise your draft in the light of your own critical reflections and/or those of others.

The following pages focus on writing about *Twelfth Night* in particular.

Writing about *Twelfth Night* 笔论《第十二夜》

Organising your thoughts

Many writing tasks on a Shakespeare play will ask you to simultaneously consider a variety of ideas and concepts. In this book, you will have seen that *Twelfth Night* has many themes and events. These can be difficult to recall or organise when you are asked to write something about them.

As a preparation for your writing, you might want to structure your thoughts and produce a visual web of events and key quotations or topics.

An effective way to do this is by creating a mind map like the example shown below.

◆ Begin by writing the key topic in the centre of a large piece of paper. Write your main Points

(P) along branches. Add sub-branches to these branches, on which you can add Evidence (E) such as quotations from the script to support your points, and Analysis (A) such as further explanation about possible audience reactions, Shakespeare's intentions and your personal response to the topics. Branches might be later used to organise the contents of paragraphs, using this Point-Evidence-Analysis (PEA) structure within an essay.

◆ Return to your mind map over time to see if you can develop your ideas and add in more detail. Experiment with drawing links between ideas or between other mind maps that you draw.

◆ Write an essay based on one or more of the mind maps that you create.

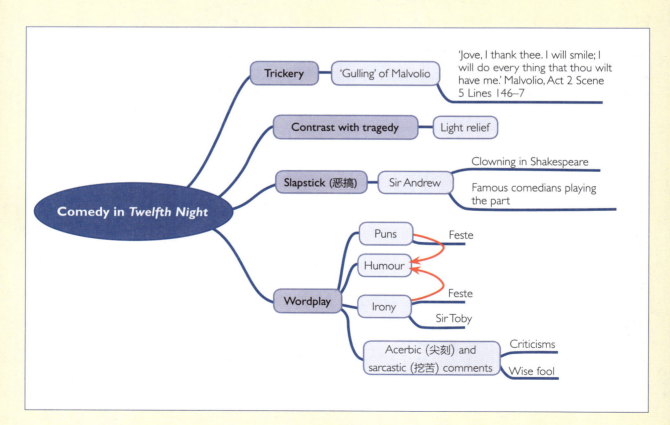

Generating your own writing titles

Planning to answer questions on general themes and past assessment questions can mean that you are not making new links and having original thoughts about the play. Sometimes questions can appear similar to what you have practised but a different focus, whether on a certain character or a less familiar theme, can actually make them difficult to answer. To be well prepared for the exam, it is essential for you to think of possible questions and plan answers to them.

◆ In pairs, collect as many past assessment questions as you can. You may wish to look on the Internet for examination board papers or questions aimed at different age groups.

◆ Look carefully at the wording of the questions, then generate your own versions of the questions by swapping the names of characters and topics or themes. Practise with the question below by substituting the underlined words with the words in the table below:

How important is <u>Viola</u> to <u>the development of the plot</u> in *Twelfth Night?*

Character	Event/theme
Orsino	comedy
Olivia	tragedy
Malvolio	wordplay
Sir Toby	theme of appearance and reality

Can you think of any other pairs of characters and events or themes that could be used to substitute the underlined words?

◆ Swap your list of generated questions with another pair, and use a mind map to produce a plan based on one of their questions. This will show how you can answer a question that you have not encountered before.

Empathic (共情) writing

It can be helpful to use creative writing to get under the skins of the characters in *Twelfth Night*, especially if you are performing the play or if your examination includes an empathetic element where you are asked to write as a character. Use the following tasks to imagine what it is like to be one of Illyrians that we have met in the play.

◆ Write a love poem or sonnet from Orsino to Olivia or from Viola to Orsino. What will they reveal about their feelings for the other? What will they reveal about themselves?

◆ Write the speech that Sebastian might make at his wedding reception about his new wife, Olivia. What would he say? What does he know about her?

◆ Malvolio disappears from the play promising revenge. Write a dialogue between Malvolio and another character (e.g. Feste, Olivia), revealing what has becomes of him and his plan for revenge.

An alternative view

In order for your answer on *Twelfth Night* to be of the highest standard, it is key to ensure that you consider alternative views and ways of seeing. The play is a comedy with tragic elements, so it creates varied interpretations and responses from different audience members.

◆ Using one of the questions that you generated in the activity above, produce a mind map plan. Then add in sub-branches that give alternative audience responses. Think of the responses of people in Shakespeare's time compared to those of people today, and how older and younger people or men and women might respond differently to certain themes or events. Can you think of other groups of people that may have alternative ways of seeing the performance (e.g. those in love or grieving)?

William Shakespeare 莎翁年表 1564–1616

1564	Born Stratford-upon-Avon, eldest son of John and Mary Shakespeare.
1582	Marries Anne Hathaway of Shottery, near Stratford.
1583	Daughter Susanna born.
1585	Twins, son and daughter Hamnet and Judith, born.
1592	First mention of Shakespeare in London. Robert Greene, another playwright, described Shakespeare as 'an upstart crow beautified with our feathers'. Greene seems to have been jealous of Shakespeare. He mocked Shakespeare's name, calling him 'the only Shake-scene in a country' (presumably because Shakespeare was writing successful plays).
1595	Becomes a shareholder in The Lord Chamberlain's Men, an acting company that became extremely popular.
1596	Son, Hamnet, dies aged eleven. Father, John, granted arms (acknowledged as a gentleman).
1597	Buys New Place, the grandest house in Stratford.
1598	Acts in Ben Jonson's *Every Man in His Humour*.
1599	Globe Theatre opens on Bankside. Performances in the open air.
1601	Father, John, dies.
1603	James I grants Shakespeare's company a royal patent: The Lord Chamberlain's Men become The King's Men and play about twelve performances each year at court.
1607	Daughter Susanna marries Dr John Hall.
1608	Mother, Mary, dies.
1609	The King's Men begin performing indoors at Blackfriars Theatre.
1610	Probably returns from London to live in Stratford.
1616	Daughter Judith marries Thomas Quiney. Dies. Buried in Holy Trinity Church, Stratford-upon-Avon.

The plays and poems

(no one knows exactly when he wrote each play)

1589–95	*The Two Gentlemen of Verona, The Taming of the Shrew, First, Second* and *Third Parts* of *King Henry VI, Titus Andronicus, King Richard III, The Comedy of Errors, Love's Labour's Lost, A Midsummer Night's Dream, Romeo and Juliet, King Richard II* (and the long poems *Venus and Adonis* and *The Rape of Lucrece*).
1596–99	*King John, The Merchant of Venice, First* and *Second Parts* of *King Henry IV, The Merry Wives of Windsor, Much Ado About Nothing, King Henry V, Julius Caesar* (and probably the Sonnets).
1600–05	*As You Like It, Hamlet,* **Twelfth Night**, *Troilus and Cressida, Measure for Measure, Othello, All's Well That Ends Well, Timon of Athens, King Lear.*
1606–11	*Macbeth, Antony and Cleopatra, Pericles, Coriolanus, The Winter's Tale, Cymbeline, The Tempest.*
1613	*King Henry VIII, The Two Noble Kinsmen* (both probably with John Fletcher).
1623	Shakespeare's plays published as a collection (now called the First Folio).

Acknowledgements 鸣谢

Cambridge University Press would like to acknowledge the contributions made to this work by Rex Gibson.

Picture Credits

p. iii: Tricycle Theatre 2008, © Donald Cooper/Photostage; p. v: Courtyard Theatre 2007, © Geraint Lewis; p. vi: Royal Shakespeare Theatre 2001, © Donald Cooper/Photostage; p. vii: Open Air Shakespeare Festival 2004, © Donald Cooper/Photostage; p. viii: Regent's Park Open Air Theatre 1999, © Donald Cooper/Photostage; p. ix: Royal Shakespeare Theatre 1994, © Donald Cooper/Photostage; p. x: Regent's Park Open Air Theatre 2005, © Geraint Lewis; p. xi top: New Diorama Theatre 2012, © Donald Cooper/Photostage; p. xi bottom: Young Vic 1998, © Donald Cooper/Photostage; p. xii top: Shakespeare's Globe 2002, © Donald Cooper/Photostage; p. xii bottom: Barbican Theatre 2009, © Geraint Lewis; p. 2: Royal Shakespeare Theatre 1994, © Donald Cooper/Photostage; p. 4: Royal Shakespeare Theatre 1994, © Donald Cooper/Photostage; p. 8: Chichester Festival Theatre 2007, © Donald Cooper/Photostage; p. 12: Royal Shakespeare Theatre 1994, © Donald Cooper/Photostage; p. 16: Royal Shakespeare Theatre 1994, © Donald Cooper/Photostage; p. 22: Donmar Warehouse 2002, © Donald Cooper/Photostage; p. 26: Shakespeare's Globe 2012, © Donald Cooper/Photostage; p. 28: Donmar Warehouse 2008, © Donald Cooper/Photostage; p. 35 top: Courtyard Theatre 2009, © Donald Cooper/Photostage; p. 35 bottom: Regent's Park Open Air Theatre 2008, © Francis Loney/ArenaPAL; p. 36: Royal Shakespeare Theatre 1994, © Donald Cooper/Photostage; p. 38: Chichester Festival Theatre 2007, © Geraint Lewis; p. 44 top: Chichester Festival Theatre 2007, © Geraint Lewis; p. 44 bottom: Royal Shakespeare Theatre 1994, © Donald Cooper/Photostage; p. 50: Royal Shakespeare Theatre 1994, © Donald Cooper/Photostage; p. 54: Donmar Warehouse 2002, © Donald Cooper/Photostage; p. 56: Donmar Warehouse 2008, © Geraint Lewis; p. 58: Albery Theatre 2004, © Donald Cooper/Photostage; p. 62 left: Chichester Festival Theatre 2007, © Donald Cooper/Photostage; p. 62 right: Riverside Studios 1987, © Donald Cooper/Photostage; p. 69 top: Donmar Warehouse 2002, © Donald Cooper/Photostage; p. 69 bottom: National Theatre 2011, © Geraint Lewis; p. 74: New Diorama Theatre 2012, © Donald Cooper/Photostage; p. 76: Shakespeare's Globe 2012, © Geraint Lewis; p. 78: Royal Shakespeare Theatre 2001, © Donald Cooper/Photostage; p. 80: Royal Shakespeare Theatre 1987, © Donald Cooper/Photostage; p. 84: Royal Shakespeare Theatre 1994, © Donald Cooper/Photostage; p. 88: Royal Shakespeare Theatre 2005, © Donald Cooper/Photostage; p. 90: Regent's Park Open Air Theatre 2008, © REX/ Alastair Muir; p. 96: Barbican Theatre 2009, © Geraint Lewis; p. 100: Novello Theatre 2005, © Donald Cooper/Photostage; p. 102: Regent's Park Open Air Theatre 2005, © Donald Cooper/Photostage; p. 109 top: Old Vic 2007, © Donald Cooper/Photostage; p. 109 bottom left: Albery Theatre 2004, © Donald Cooper/Photostage; p. 109 bottom right: Barbican Theatre 2009, © Donald Cooper/Photostage; p. 112: Young Vic 1998, © Donald Cooper/Photostage; p. 114: Royal Shakespeare Theatre 1997, © Donald Cooper/Photostage; p. 118: Nottingham Playhouse 1995, © Donald Cooper/Photostage; p. 122: Albery Theatre 2004, © Donald Cooper/Photostage; p. 125 top: Shakespeare's Globe 2012, © Geraint Lewis; p. 125 bottom: Renaissance Theatre 1988, © Donald Cooper/Photostage; p. 126: Royal Shakespeare Theatre 2005, © Donald Cooper/Photostage; p. 132: Young Vic 1998, © Donald Cooper/Photostage; p. 136: Tricycle Theatre 2008, © Donald Cooper/Photostage; p. 138: Shakespeare's Globe 2012, © Geraint Lewis; p. 140: Royal Shakespeare Theatre 2005, © Donald Cooper/Photostage; p. 142: Royal Shakespeare Theatre 2005, © Geraint Lewis; p. 144: Royal Shakespeare Theatre 1997, © Donald Cooper/Photostage; p. 146: Tricycle Theatre 2008, © Donald Cooper/Photostage; p. 148: Renaissance Theatre 2010, © Soeren Stache/dpa/Corbis; p. 150: Royal Shakespeare Theatre 1994, © Donald Cooper/Photostage; p. 154: 1996 poster for Twelfth

Produced for Cambridge University Press by
White-Thomson Publishing
+44 (0)843 208 7460
www.wtpub.co.uk

Project editor: Alice Harman
Designer: Clare Nicholas
Concept design: Jackie Hill